JADED HEART

THE DONNELLYS
BOOK FOUR

DOROTHY F. SHAW

PRAISE FOR DOROTHY F. SHAW

"*Unworthy Heart* reminded me of what I love about the romance genre."—The Book Tart

"*Unworthy Heart* by Dorothy F. Shaw made me think, made my heart happy, made me tear up and made me sigh in happiness. Shaw combines heat with heart almost flawlessly. I cannot wait for the follow-up books in this series."—Romance Novel News

"I fell in love with the series from book one…Grab your copy and buckle up for the ride. Dorothy Shaw doesn't do anything halfway."—Beyond the Valley of the Books on *Defensive Heart*

"Holy smokes, can Dorothy Shaw write a freaking awesome sex scene…"—Wicked Good Reads on *Defensive Heart*

"*Defensive Heart* by Dorothy F. Shaw is a good read which gives credence to the statement that opposites do attract."—Harlequin Junkie

"Even though there is plenty of sex in *Shattered Heart*, the author does not neglect the storyline at all – packing it full of romance, danger, trauma, healing, laughs, and the Donnelly family."—Crystal's Many Reviewers

"*Shattered Heart* is an emotional tear-jerker of a romance that had me reaching for the tissues on more than one occasion."—Romance Novel News

"Wow! What a sexy, steamy story that kept me reading from the first page."—Crystal's Many Reviewers on *Stripped Bounty*

"If you are into vanilla, forget this book! Characters larger than life and sex to die for. Dorothy F. Shaw painted a canvas that is both intriguing and close to hardcore."—Amazon Reviewer on *Stripped Bounty*

"Epic story! Rosie and Badger are amazing characters that pull you into the story. The sex is HOT, and the ending is perfect!"—Book Addicts PR on *Stripped Bounty*

"I was blown away by how easily the story was told by Dorothy F. Shaw"—CeeriJays Smexy HotReads on *A Few More Rules*

"*A Few More Rules* (a femdom novella) is a super-hot romance that sets the foundation well for a probable HEA between Rig and Beth. This story is a winner."—Romance Novel News

"WOW!!! This erotic, sensual short story will have you panting for more! These two beauties are more than fang bangers. The dark world of lust and sex will feed any appetite you desire."—Bookaholic and More Blog on *Playtime*

"I like books that grab my attention so much that I read a line and end up gasping or commenting out loud... and this one did just that - a few times! I'll definitely be reading it again."—Goodreads Reviewer on *Playtime*

"True to Dorothy Shaw's form, *Avoiding the Badge* is full of everything I love about her writing."—Amanda at Wicked Good Reads

"I liked the way the author brought about the truths that they had been keeping from each other, and I really enjoyed the steps that the two characters took in order to overcome the troubles in their path."—Amazon reviewer on *Avoiding the Badge*

"*Redeeming the Badge* is a second chance romance that is hot as Hades and with a backstory that will twist your heartstrings."—Amazon Reviewer

"This is a tale of love and heartache, dealing with some tough issues such as infertility, endometriosis, and miscarriage. It will tear at your heartstrings and make you believe in true love."—Amazon Reviewer on *Redeeming the Badge*

"Jeff and Tish are a good couple with incredible chemistry that makes you jealous. I can't recommend this series enough." —Amazon Reviewer on *Trusting the Badge*

"*Trusting the Badge* is a quick read for readers who enjoy a focus on relationship building, characters with tragic backstories, and some steamy moments." —Amazon Reviewer

"It was written in a way that I got very emotional reading it, most books don't make me cry. This one did."—Amazon reviewer on *Jaded Heart*

Jaded Heart

The Donnellys Book 4
© 2022 Dorothy F. Shaw

Even jaded hearts can be tempted into trying again.

When Angela Donnelly heads to Arizona for a family event, she meets older and hotter-than-hell, Garrett James.

Garrett runs a small concert venue on the outskirts of Phoenix…and that's about as close as he wants to come to the music biz. His hey-day in the late 90s, playing bass and singing with his band, Copper Seven, is long gone. Far from the limelight and willingly single, the only woman Garrett wants or needs in his life is his daughter.

That is until he meets the way too young for him, Angie. Long dark hair and long legs have always been his downfall and Garrett can't keep his eyes, or his hands off of her.

Angie might be young, but she's no fool. She knows a good thing when she's found one—Garrett is a once-in-a-lifetime good thing for her.

But Garrett can't seem to convince Angie that he's not her once-in-a-lifetime anything. As far as he's concerned, he's absolutely the wrong man for her with nothing to offer someone as promising as Angie.

Angie recognizes that Garrett has his heart fully guarded. But when he gives her everything she wants, except his heart, she knows this will be the fight of her life.

And Angie won't back down. Or give up.

DEDICATION

*This book is dedicated to the many still suffering alcoholics and/or addicts in the world. Please seek help from **any** 12-step fellowship in your area. You don't have to do this alone. There is help out there for you. My prayer is that you reach for it.*

To the families and friends please, please attend Al-Anon. The best way to help your loved one is to help yourself.

https://www.aa.org/
https://al-anon.org/

ACKNOWLEDGMENTS

A shout-out to my #1 beta reader: my beautiful cousin, Sherri Zak. Thank you so much. As always, your feedback is invaluable.

To one of my besties, author Sidda Lee Rain – for beta reading this sucker the first time around, oh so many years ago. It's changed a lot, so maybe you should check it out again? Also, you're still one of my most favorite people on the planet. Just saying.

To Daniel Badger for providing me with invaluable Bar/Concert Venue info. To my Night Writers sprinting group on FB. Once again, you kept my butt in the chair, which inevitably saved it!

To my awesome editor, Tera Cuskaden. Thank you for sticking with me for all these years! To David Faulkner for his generosity and his Fine Line Editing skills. To Kanaxa – my spectacular cover artist, thank you for making this cover gorgeous, but also for updating the rest of the Donnellys covers and making them even more gorgeous, too! You rock, chica! To Phill Webster! Thank you for gracing the cover of this book.

And finally, to my family, but mostly to my BWG (Boy With Glasses), aka my partner in crime, life and all married things. Thank you, babe, for always being willing to support this crazy dream of mine.

Quick note: Tarra Layne is an incredibly talented indie musi-

cian and singer, and Inept Hero is an incredibly talented indie metal/punk/rock band.
Please check out their work. #SupportIndie!
You can find them here:
https://www.facebook.com/TarraLayne
And here:
https://www.facebook.com/INEPTHERO

CONTENT/TRIGGER WARNING

This book contains a very broken hero and a very determined heroine. An age gap and a lot of angst.

Trigger Warning:

Jaded Heart goes into detail about what alcoholism and drug addiction can do to a person. It also touches on a past death as a result of an over-dose and the effect that has on family members.

Resources:

*To the many sick and suffering alcoholics and addicts in the world: please seek help from **any** 12-step fellowship in your area. And to their families and friends please, please attend Al-Anon. The best way to help your loved one is to help yourself.*

https://www.aa.org/
https://al-anon.org/

PLAYLIST

Ashley McBryde - *One Night Standards*
Gwen Stefani - *4 In The Morning*
Tarra Layne - *Heated*
Elle Henderson - *Hard Work*
Amy Winehouse - *Wake Up Alone*
Carley Pearce - *Day One*

"WHICH SIDE? WAIT, WAIT, WAIT." ANGELA DONNELLY SPUN around and stared up at the signs above the exit doors of Terminal Four at Phoenix Sky Harbor International Airport…sweating. To. Death. "Okay, yeah. I'm on the south side. Door number six."

"Perfect. I'm on my way."

Angie closed her eyes as the familiar dinging from the key entering the ignition came over the line, which was promptly followed by the distinct sound of the engine starting. *Really?* "*Ohhhmygahhhd, Celia.* You haven't even left yet, have you?"

"Sorry, *sorrysorrysorry.* I'll be there in fifteen. I swear."

"Seriously?" Angie dropped her purse on top of her suit-case. "Ugh. I'm already sweating my ass off. In fact, I can see it. It's melted on the sidewalk. And it's fucking gross."

"Ewwww. That *is* gross. And graphic. Okay…*loveyousorryloveyousorry*…be there in a few. Hanging up now so I can drive. Bye!"

"Fine, but don't get a spee—" Angie pulled the phone away from her ear and stared at the home screen. "Speeding ticket," she said to no one because her younger sister, Celia, had already hung up. "Okay then."

Angie pushed her long hair off her shoulders. She should go back inside and buy a water from the Starbucks she spotted while waiting for her bag. Ooh! Or maybe a Caramel Frappuccino. She frowned. She might appreciate the caramel yumminess, but her ass and thighs wouldn't. Oh well. She didn't much feel like lugging her suitcase back inside, anyway.

Pulling the hair tie off her wrist, Angie gathered up her hair and twisted it into a knot on top of her head. She cocked her hip to the side and fanned her face. Scrolling through her phone, she checked the weather app. Ninety-eight degrees out? Yeah, no.

Lugging her suitcase was exactly what she was going to do. Okay, maybe not lug since it was on wheels. But whatever. Who cared about semantics when a person was melting? Not her. That was for damn sure.

By the time she made it back outside to the curb—half-drunk water bottle stuffed in her purse and a tall Caramel Frappuccino in her hand—her phone was vibrating her ass cheek to the point of numbness. After dumping her purse back on top of the suitcase, she slipped the phone from her back pocket and answered.

"Hello?"

"Where are you? I'm circling. You went to the south side, right? Door six?"

"Mmhmm." Angie sipped from the straw. Whoops. She hadn't meant to take that long, but there was a line. "I didn't see you."

Her sister let out an exasperated-sounding sigh. "Coming around again."

"All right. I'm here. Waiting. Still sweating, by the way." She grinned, then took another sip and focused on the oncoming line of cars. "What color is your car again?"

Her sister laughed. "It's silver. And it's a truck, you goof."

"Oh, yeah. I forgot. Ooh! Is that you?" She raised her sweet, ice-cold beverage in the air. "I think I see you."

"Yes, that's me."

"Yay!" Angie took the phone from her ear and shoved it in her back pocket as her sister pulled her truck up to the curb.

Celia came around the front of the vehicle, grinning. "Starbucks? Really?"

"Well, can you blame me? It's hot out." Angie grinned and tried to look innocent. "I got thirsty."

"Poor baby." With a laugh, Celia gave Angie a quick hug before muscling Angie's suitcase off the ground.

Angie opened the passenger door. "It has wheels, you know."

"No shit, really? Get in before you melt, princess." Celia hefted the suitcase into the back seat of the truck with a grunt. "Good God, what's in this thing?"

"Oh, you know, everything." Angie shrugged before hopping inside the cab to the blessed AC, and then Celia slid behind the wheel. In the next minute, they were navigating out of the airport and heading for the freeway. Angie tilted the plastic cup in her sister's direction. "You want some?"

"I'm thinking you should just give it to me as payment." Celia took the drink and sipped from the straw. "Mmm. Especially because you didn't get me one. And while you weren't getting me one, I had to drive in circles waiting for you."

Angie laughed. "Fair enough. It's all yours. My ass doesn't need it anyway."

"This is why I opt for sugar-free." Celia grinned, sucked some more from the straw, and then set the drink in the cup holder. "Welcome to Phoenix in the spring. We're having a bit of a heat wave. But only a small one."

"A small one, huh? My body's in shock. It was seventy-five degrees when I left Burbank an hour and a half ago."

"It's the desert. Plus, climate change is real, sis. Pretty much anytime starting mid-May to mid-October is summer now." Celia turned up the volume on the radio.

Angie gazed out at the mountains in the distance and then

looked back at her sister. "Yeah, it's hot as hell, but it's a beautiful hell."

"That it is." Celia glanced over and smiled before focusing back on the road. "Glad you're here, Ang."

"Me too. A month-long vacation is just what I need. My dating moratorium is over, and I am *so* ready to hit the clubs and stretch my legs!"

"Clubs?" Celia groaned. "There goes my social life."

Angie frowned. "Ohhh, right. No worries. We can go to some gay clubs, too. You know I'm all down for that." She turned the AC dial up and adjusted the vent closest to her. "Aside from that, I'm confused. I thought you were dating someone."

"I was." Celia merged onto another freeway. "Past tense."

"That sucks. Sorry, honey." Angie reached over and squeezed her sister's forearm. "When did that happen?"

"A couple of weeks ago. No need to be sorry. It just wasn't working out."

"Yeah, I know how that goes. Still sorry, though." Angie swiped a stray hair away from her eye. "Maybe you should try a moratorium like me?"

"Uh, no, thank you." Celia visibly cringed, and Angie laughed. "I'm still surprised you followed through with a whole year."

"Shoot, you and me both." Angie looked back toward the mountains. She'd spent a year single, committed to a real deal, no relationship, no dating, no one-night stand, moratorium. Before making the commitment, there'd been a steady stream of guys in and out of her life. None of them were worth bringing home to the parents. There'd been a couple she liked, sure, but she'd never gotten attached to any of them.

Angie sighed and glanced over at Celia. "If you recall, it wasn't my idea. Cyn and her brilliant plans. Then along comes Shane, and boom, they're all happy ever after now."

"I do recall." Celia chuckled. "She tried and failed in the

best way, I suppose. But not you. I give you props. No way I could've followed through like you did."

"Honestly, it wasn't as hard as I thought it was going to be." Angie shrugged. "I'm glad I did it. I focused on work, reevaluated my goals, and set some new ones."

"New ones?"

"Yep. New ones." Angie grinned and played with the tendrils of hair hanging down at the base of her neck.

"Are you going to share or leave me in suspense?"

Angie laughed. "Time to put my degree to better use, little sister. My focus is still music, of course, so I'm shooting for Rolling Stone Magazine. I don't know if it'll happen, but I'm going to try."

"That's awesome!" Celia glanced at Angie, her smile big and bright. "I know you can do it, Ang. You just gotta put your mind to it."

"Aw, thanks, Celia. Don't get me wrong, I love writing indie music reviews for that small press in L.A. But…" Angie shrugged again. "I want more. But not until *after* this nice month-long vacation, though."

"You got this. It all starts right now." Celia grinned and turned the music up louder.

Angie tapped her thumb on the armrest to the beat of the song. "Country, huh? Who is this?"

"Yes, country. Ashley McBryde."

Angie grinned. "You never cease to amaze me."

"What's wrong with country?" Celia rolled her eyes. "Whatever."

"Nothing, just never took you for a country girl. Wait, is she singing about one-night stands?"

"She sure is." Her sister grinned.

Angie laughed, shaking her head. "Perfect."

She'd meant what she said; Angie really did need to stretch her legs, and she was glad to be back in Arizona. It'd been a few years since she'd been there. She missed her sister and her brother, Mark, but more than that, she needed a change of scenery.

Life was unfolding around her, moving forward, and she'd been standing still. Or at least that's what it felt like. Her younger brother Mark was graduating from ASU in a couple of weeks, and he'd go on to whatever it was he was planning to do with his life. Angie was excited for him.

Mark's graduation was the perfect opportunity to get out there and have fun...and do it with her brother and sister around her. They could be the three musketeers for a month.

Donnellys on the loose in Sin City...aka Tempe, Arizona. Perfect.

GARRETT JAMES STOOD on the loading dock at the back of the building he ran his small concert venue out of and signed the bill of lading for the delivery of booze that had just been unloaded.

He handed the clipboard back to the driver. "Thanks, man. Have a good day."

"You too, Garrett." After a brief handshake, the guy stepped away and made his way to his truck.

Garrett ducked inside and pulled down the steel garage door. For now, the building was quiet as a church, and he was alone. But not for long. The three bands he had lined up for the night weren't due to arrive for another five hours.

Once they got there, the building would turn into what could only be called "managed chaos" as they got set up, and his mixing engineer took them through their soundcheck. Truth be told, the real chaos would happen when patrons started arriving. But he loved it, every minute of it.

He'd have plenty of time to update the liquor inventory, catch up on paperwork, answer a couple emails, and then get ready to open. Perfect. Garrett took the back stairs up to his office two at a time and then settled behind his desk.

Two hours had come and gone before the sound of his cell ringing drew his attention. After picking up the phone, he swiped the screen and put it to his ear. "Who's this?"

"Knock it off, Dad. I'm totally running late. As usual, you didn't answer my text."

"What text?" Garrett leaned back in his seat and smothered a chuckle. He'd seen the text but hadn't replied yet.

"Ugh, give me a break. I know you saw it. Anyway, do you want something from Starbucks?"

"Ah, yes. Your daily caffeine run."

"You're one to talk. You live on coffee *and* chips. Makes no sense to me—hold on. Yeah, can I get two tall coffees—okay, I'm back."

"What's wrong with potato chips?"

"Uh, how about the fact that you're getting older and eating healthy is a tad important?" His daughter laughed.

"I don't know what you're talking about. I'm fine. Leave my diet alone."

"Someone has to pay attention to it. It's a well-known fact that married men live longer, you know? Honestly, with the hours you keep, I'll never understand how you aren't asleep at your desk the majority of the time." Chassidy laughed again. "So, before I pay, you want anything else?"

Garrett rolled his eyes. "Funny girl. You trying to set me up with someone, or did you mean something else besides coffee?"

His daughter barked a laugh. "I know better than that. Too many gold diggers out there. Ooh, they have those birthday cake pops you like so much. They look fresh, too. You want one? Two?"

"Sold! Bring me two." He shifted a stack of papers to the side for filing. "See? Who needs a wife when I can have cake!"

"Sick, sick man. Although, you're right. Cake is probably better than a gold-digging stepmother."

Garrett grinned and shook his head. "I'm so glad we agree."

"Well, I am a chip off the old block."

"Calling me old again, kid?"

"What's that?" His daughter laughed again. "You cut out. See you in twenty, Dad."

"Smartass." Garrett chuckled as he hit the "end call" button and set the cell back on his desk.

Glancing at the picture of Chassidy when she was five years old on the corner of his desk, he let out a breath and ran his fingers through his long hair.

She worked for him at the club for the last five years—handled all the bookings and was fantastic at it. All things considered, their relationship was rock solid, even though he drove her insane, and sometimes they fought—though that'd lessened significantly since she moved out of his house two years ago.

She was stubborn, just like he was, but Garrett couldn't say he was upset he'd passed that little trait onto her. Actually, except for his self-destructive ones, he'd passed a lot of good traits on to her. Considering he'd missed the majority of the first ten years of her life, that was saying something.

After one too many tragedies, Garrett finally hit rock bottom, cleaned himself up, and attempted to be a father for the first time in his life…and as far as he was concerned, Chassidy was all he needed to make a new beginning. It wasn't an easy road by any stretch, but they'd done okay.

He and his little girl. Chassidy was the only thing from his past he *didn't* regret.

The office line assigned to Chassidy rang. Instead of letting it go to her voicemail, he answered. "Copper Halo, bookings. How can I help you?"

"Hey, yeah, this is Josh Chasen. Manager for Gothic Princess? Is Chassidy available?"

Garrett looked over the lineup for the night. Gothic Princess was their opener. "Chassidy isn't available right now. Did you try her cell?"

"Yeah, but no answer. Hate to do this, but I need to pull the girls out of their spot tonight. Lead singer's got the stomach flu."

"Fuck sake, okay." Garrett sat back and let out a frustrated sigh. Damn musicians could be total flakes. Stomach flu likely translated to being too hungover to perform. He cringed at how jaded his thinking was, but honestly, back in his heyday, he'd used that same excuse a million times. It was the nature of the beast. "You got anyone that's any good you can refer?"

"Not off the top of my head. I'll ask around, though. Again, sorry. I feel real bad, man."

Garrett leaned forward and pinched the bridge of his nose. "Appreciate it. Thanks for letting us know. Take care of your girl."

Setting the receiver back in the cradle, Garrett grabbed his used coffee mug and headed into the bathroom to rinse it out. Filling a slot last minute could be easy, but often, the takers you got weren't very good. Sadly, just because a group of people got together that could sing or play instruments and called themselves a band didn't mean they actually could perform worth a damn. Likely, Chassidy had someone on the back burner she could call to fill the spot. He hoped.

Taking a deep breath, he reminded himself not to get too worked up. This was his life, a life he'd chosen. He owned his own business. Answered only to himself. But owning a business came with the good and the bad. In his case, it was music, musicians, people and lots of booze—though he didn't partake anymore.

Garrett took his seat again and leaned back in his chair.

Letting his head fall back, he closed his eyes and let his thoughts wander back to Chassidy.

Lately, she'd been dropping comments about him being single. He wasn't sure why. He preferred being single. Not that there wasn't the occasional hook-up or someone he casually dated. There were. It was just Chassidy wasn't exposed to them when she was young, and why should she have been?

Most women he met, even after all these years, proved to not be truly interested in him as a person, so why bother keeping them around?

As a single father, Garrett wasn't interested in disrupting the stable life he'd finally given his daughter. Her life had been far too unstable before she lost her mother, and then before he'd gotten cleaned up.

Memories broke through, and Garrett shuddered. He didn't like to think about his ex-wife, Amanda. Or her death. Or how he used to live, either. Really, any part of his life from that time.

It was ugly. He had been ugly, and as far as Garrett was concerned, that ugly needed to stay right where it was, in the past.

CHAPTER TWO

ANGIE closed the front passenger door to Celia's four-door pickup truck and looked at her brother Mark as he did the same with the back door. "We should've taken a Lyft here."

"Probably right. Worse case, we can take one home if Celia gets fucked up." Mark ran his fingers through the top of his dark brown hair. It'd grown longer since Angie had last seen it.

"I'm not gonna get fucked up. Told you both, I'm DD-ing. You're covered." Celia shoved her keys into her front pocket. "Let's go."

Angie and Celia caught up to Mark, and then Angie poked his arm. "What's this place again?"

"Copper Halo. Small concert venue. Indie bands and some old school—used to be famous—bands play here."

"Cool name, but, uh…you brought an Indie music reviewer, who happens to be on vacation, to a local concert venue? Perfect." Angie rolled her eyes. "Not."

"Who says you have to review anyone? Plus, I know the bouncer…so free entry!" Mark grinned over his shoulder.

Celia laughed. "Our brother is technically still a starving college student. No cover charge is damn important."

Mark shrugged a shoulder. "For another two weeks anyway. Now I gotta make what little money I have left last until the end of the month."

"Aw, don't worry, little brother. We'll cover you. Besides, you can pay us back when you start rolling in the dough at whatever job you land." Angie winked at him. "Lead the way. I seriously need a drink. And I'm starting to sweat."

"It's not even hot out!" Celia laughed, holding her arm out so the doorman could put a paper bracelet on her wrist.

"Oh, it's hot, baby. And so am I. So hot, you all can barely stand me." Giggling at her dorkiness, Angie pursed her lips and walked, more like strutted, past her sister and brother. She kicked in a little hip sway for the fun of it, too. It was time to get her party on.

Once inside, they made a beeline for the bar. The club was fairly large, with a decent-sized stage about fifty feet straight ahead of them, a dance floor right before it, and a long bar situated in an L shape along the walls to the right and back of the space. Highboy tables were scattered around. Along the left wall, situated at an angle to better see the stage, were several crescent-shaped booths with tables.

After glancing around the large area, Angie stepped to the bar and ordered three shots of Jameson and a beer each for herself and her brother.

The crowd was fairly thick, and the band playing was belting out a pretty decent punk tune. She raised her shot glass after her siblings lifted theirs from the bar. "To Mark's graduation! Congrats, little brother."

"Thanks!" Her brother smiled, lifting his chin.

"Sláinte." Celia nodded, her lips arched in a grin.

The three clinked their glasses together, knocked the bottoms on the bar top and tilted them back. Angie swallowed the golden liquid, relishing the burn as it coated her throat down to her stomach. She turned her glass upside down on the metal top of the bar and smiled as Celia and Mark did the same. "Best way to start a vacay!"

Mark picked up his beer. "Couldn't agree more."

"Let's check out the crowd gathered by the stage." Celia motioned over her shoulder.

Angie gazed over to the sea of people. "You mean the ones moshing?"

"I'm game." Mark laughed and walked in that direction.

"I'm not sure I'm game, but let's go anyway." Angie linked arms with her sister. "Lead the way."

The band was good, better than good, actually. Four young guys playing their asses off. The lead singer belted out the lyrics into the microphone as excitement vibrated from the crowd. Considering her job, the sight was one Angie was all too familiar with.

She never got sick of watching the different bands or solo acts, trying to find their way to the almighty record contract and make it big. Angie understood it. After all, she wanted to make it big, too. With her new goal of becoming a staff writer for Rolling Stone, for the first time in a long time, she felt like she wasn't standing still.

After a few more songs, Angie nudged Celia's hip and bent to her ear. "I need another drink. You want anything?"

"Water." Her sister turned in the direction of the booths behind them. "There's an open table. I'll grab it. Meet me there."

"Got it." Angie stepped away and weaved in and around the crowd toward the bar.

Seeing a clear spot on the far end along the back wall, she stepped up and waited for a bartender to come anywhere close to her. With her eyes locked on the blonde girl serving up drinks, she waited. And waited. And...tapped her nail on the metal top, impatience making itself known. *Okay then.*

Angie smoothed her hand along the cool, shiny surface

and then glanced down at the front panel. The bar was made entirely of metal, which she'd seen done before in other bars, but this one was different. It had copper plating along the front panel. Glancing around, she noticed there were several accents made from copper, too. The glass shelves holding the liquor bottles rested on frames made from copper pipes. The whole décor was really cool and worked well with the name of the club.

"What can I get you?"

Angie snapped her gaze forward to find the bartender had finally come over. "Sorry! Yeah, shot of Jameson, a bottle of 805, and a water."

The girl nodded and stepped away. Waiting again, Angie rested her forearms on the bar and glanced to her right, continuing around to the—she jerked her gaze back.

Whoa!

She blinked.

There was a *totally* hot, older guy sitting off to the side at the very end of the bar. Long dark hair, pulled up in—God help her—a man bun. He had a beard, but not too thick and a face made for modeling. Almond-shaped eyes—too far for her to tell what color.

Those eyes were locked on hers.

A shiver raced up her spine, and tingles broke out over every inch of her skin…and then her nipples got hard.

Holy shit! What's happening?

"Twelve fifty."

Once again, the bartender had to get her attention. However, this time, Angie didn't care. She only wanted to keep staring at him.

Who was he?

The gorgeous man lifted a coffee mug to his lips, his gaze locked on Angie's the whole time. She bit her bottom lip as her stomach warmed. Good Lord.

"Did you want to open a tab?"

Somehow, she managed to drag her gaze away from him. "Um, sure. Thanks." Angie pulled her credit card from her small clutch bag and handed it to the bartender. She tossed back the shot, flipped the glass over on the top of the bar, then gave him another look before grabbing the beer and water and turning away.

He was still looking at her as she made her way to the table Celia had found for them—Angie could feel his eyes.

Everywhere on her body.

The tingles were still in full effect, the warmth in her tummy spread all over her body, and she pulsed with arousal between her thighs.

Yes, Alex. I'll take "spontaneous orgasm with just one look" for a thousand, please? Jeezus chrispies.

Angie drew in a calming breath as she set the beer and water down on the table and slid into the booth.

Celia grabbed the plastic cup of water. "You okay?"

"Nope. Not. At. All." She fanned herself and looked over to his spot at the bar.

His focus was elsewhere. A feeling rose in her stomach and climbed up her throat…one that felt far too much like disappointment. Now, he was saying something to the bartender, but then he glanced back over toward Angie again.

Relief coated her insides like a warm blanket—what *is wrong with me?* Doing her best to brush off the unwanted emotions bombarding her nervous system, Angie drew in another deep breath, licked her lips and took a swig of beer.

Shit, another shot would probably help. But if she got up and went back over there, she might end up in his lap. Which was insane—absolutely something she would've done before her moratorium—but still insane.

Something was different about him. Angie wasn't sure what it was, but she knew, without a doubt, throwing herself at him was something women probably did all the time, and Angie sure as hell was *not* going to be like all the rest.

Huh, maybe her year moratorium had changed more within her than just her career goals. Interesting…

Fuck me! The night had been going fine—until he saw her.

The door was doing well, and patrons were still coming in. Chassidy had found a replacement band, and they were rocking it hard on the stage. Plus, the booze was flowing, which meant Garrett's till was getting filled.

But damn, what was it with him and chicks with dark hair and long legs? God knew he'd never understand it. The last brunette who'd caught his attention so fiercely was Chassidy's mother, Amanda. Sadly, that relationship sure as hell had crashed and burned in a blaze that looked nothing like glory.

Since his ex-wife, Garrett had steered clear of brunette women. As if they carried the black plague. Instead, he'd stuck to blondes or redheads. In a strictly non-relationship, one-night stand, or casual dating sort of way.

Unable to help himself, he glanced out at the crowd again, and yeah, there she was. The brunette—aka: black plague in flesh and blood with a beating heart and a warm body—was staring at him like she could see every part of his soul.

People said redheads were stealers of a man's soul. *Bulllll-shiiiit.* For him, it was dark hair accompanied by long legs— fucking hell. Those long, shapely legs. Legs so long they went all the way up and made an ass of themselves.

Garrett looked away as he smoothed his hand over his chin…and gave reeling himself in a try.

No go.

He picked up his coffee mug and swallowed the remains of the dark liquid—as dark as her hair.

When she'd turned and walked away from the bar, he thought he might get up and go to her. How he managed to stay in his seat was beyond him. The long length of her hair touched the small of her back, nearly to her ass. What a fine, full ass it was, too. Lots of willing flesh to grab and hold onto.

Still picturing it, Garrett groaned and took a swallow of the coffee. It had been an *impeccably* nice view. His cock had gotten a good look, too, because the fucker was ready to go several rounds.

He turned his focus to the bar. "Marlene, grab me a refill, please?"

Marlene Justice, his head bartender, nodded and then brought the pot of coffee he always had ready behind the bar. After topping him off, she went back to taking care of his customers. Garrett lifted the mug and blew over the hot liquid, and, what do you know, found her again.

Damn, she was young. Under thirty, he'd bet. Not that his dick seemed to mind. His smaller brain didn't care that Garrett was probably old enough to be her father. He cringed…yeah, there it was. Perfect way to throw a bucket of cold water on the flames.

With a sigh, he set the mug down and peered out over the crowd. For the rest of the night, he was *not* going to look her way. Too hot and too young equaled complication. Sure, he could take her upstairs and fuck her six ways to Sunday. Or take her back to his place—something he never did.

But then he'd have to put her in a cab home, all the while ignoring the plea in her eyes to spend the night. This one was so fucking pretty he was worried he might actually give in. Which was another hell no.

Been there.

Done that.

Got the divorce papers to show for it. Not doing it again.

Barely ten minutes passed, though it felt more like a hundred, and the next band was starting their set. Garrett scanned the crowd…and, without giving himself permission, spotted her instantly.

Dammit. So much for that.

Glancing at his watch, he stood and took a stroll to his office. The headliner, Inept Hero, would be out in thirty minutes, tops, and to kill some time, there was some invoicing he could handle. Leaving his spot at the bar wasn't his normal routine, but not looking her way was proving more difficult than he'd thought.

GARRETT KILLED the thirty minutes in his office, shuffling paperwork rather than completing it. He glanced at the clock and blew out a sigh. The headliner should've just started, which meant he had another hour to endure before closing time.

Stalling until he couldn't find anything else to "review," Garrett pulled himself up by his bootstraps, cursed himself a coward for avoiding a hot woman, and made his way back downstairs.

Hell, for all he knew, she might've already left.

As he passed the restrooms, the door to the ladies room swung open…and there she was.

Fuck me.

Against his better judgment, he stopped.

So did she.

They stood there for a long moment, taking each other in.

Jesus, she was pretty. Tall and curvy in all the right places. Her eyes were mesmerizing…but then her full lips arched into a small smile, and Garrett knew he was fucked.

She swiped her tongue over her bottom lip. "Hi."

One word. That was it.

That was all she said, and Garrett felt the single syllable arrow straight to his balls. "This isn't a good idea."

A look of confusion hit her face. "I'm sorry?"

Garrett took two steps toward her, wrapped an arm around her waist and bent his head to her ear. Christ, she smelled good. "This—" he squeezed her side, "—isn't a good idea."

"Hmm." She placed her hands on his shoulders. "It kinda feels like a good idea."

He ran his palm up her back to her neck, cupping the back of it, then walked them backward until her back hit the wall. A gasp came out of her, and her body went soft against him.

Garrett drew in a deep breath. Jesus Christ, her scent was making him dizzy, and she felt fucking fantastic pressed against him. Somehow, he managed to place his other hand on the wall above her head, thank God, because if he didn't, he was likely to touch other parts of her he shouldn't be touching. Like her full ass or her petite breasts or— *Fuck!*

He ran his nose along the edge of her ear. "Trust me when I tell you."

"But I don't even know you. Why should I trust you?" She smoothed her hands over his traps to the back of his neck, and every inch of his body came alive.

"I don't know you either. Guess that makes us even, right?"

She giggled. God, help him. The sound ripped through Garrett, and his dick thickened behind his zipper.

"Right. Even is good." She dropped one hand and slid it between them, finding his length behind the denim. "But I'll give you extra points if it convinces you that this—" she squeezed his engorged cock, "—is a *great* idea."

Jesus.

Fuck.

God.

Holy shit.

At that moment, he'd give anything to be inside her. Anywhere and in any way he could.

But that wasn't going to happen. He had to stop this now. "Based on what you got in your hand, it's obvious you've convinced him. But, sadly, I may take a little more effort." Garrett snaked his hand into her hair and gripped the strands close to her scalp tight. "I'm going to let you go. Then I'm going to walk away."

"But—"

Garrett didn't hesitate and stepped back. He couldn't. If he did, he was likely to take her by the hand, pull her upstairs to his office and bend her over the desk.

"Wait…"

Ignoring her, he kept moving down the long hall and out to the main area to his spot at the bar. Self-preservation was the game he was interested in. That was it. Because that little hot brunette he'd left in the hall was more than he could handle.

One touch. One kiss. One night wouldn't be enough.

Based on the lust pulsing through his system, Garrett was pretty certain he'd never get enough of her. Saving his ass was the only logical thing to do.

CHAPTER THREE

"Holy shit." In a complete daze, Angie stood in the hallway, right where he'd left her, with her back pressed to the concrete wall, drawing in breath after breath. More lust than she'd ever felt poured through her system, making her bones feel like rubber.

What the *hell* just happened?

Still dazed, she straightened her shirt and focused on trying to calm her racing heart. The scent of his cologne still lingered in her nose and on her hands. Holy God, his scent was like heaven, too.

Angie pressed her palms to her face, drawing more of him in before threading her fingers through her hair. She'd had her fair share of encounters with men, but not one of them had been as intense as what just went down.

And she didn't even know his name.

Unsure of what to do next, Angie slowly made her way down the corridor. She stopped at the mouth of the hall and glanced over at the bar. He was back in his spot, talking to one of the bouncers. She watched for a minute, debating if she should go over to him or not.

God, he was beautiful. In the hall, she'd gotten a good

look at his eyes; they were green with flecks of gold in them and utterly hypnotizing. When they'd stared at each other, she'd been held transfixed by his gaze.

His hair was a lighter brown than she'd originally thought. And he had a few strands of silver throughout, stemming mostly from his temples, but his beard was threaded with much more gray than his head.

It wasn't love at first sight. But it wasn't simple lust either. No, this was something deeper, something much more powerful. Time had stopped, and in that space between them was some sort of profound magnetic pull.

He looked at her as if she were already his.

It was crazy, but Angie felt connected to him in the depths of her soul, and that was before he'd even touched her. Maybe the man was right. Maybe getting near him was a bad idea. But that didn't seem to matter because every cell in her body had already come alive, and when he put his hands on her, it was too late. And she knew he felt it, too.

Someone bumped her shoulder from behind, and Angie grabbed the wall to steady herself.

"Shit. Sorry." A well-built, tattooed guy circled her elbow in his big palm. "You okay?"

"Yeah. All good." She smiled. "No worries."

"Let me make it up to you. Can I get you a drink?"

She glanced back over at her stranger at the bar. *Now,* he was watching. The same expression in his eyes as in the hall, but there was a harsher edge to it.

Hmm, not happy another guy's talking to me?

She looked back at the tattooed dude. "Actually? Yes. I'd love a shot."

"Done." With a bright smile, he released her arm and held his elbow out to her. "Allow me to escort you to the bar."

Angie smiled, linked her arm in his and walked with him. "I'm Angie, by the way."

"I'm Brad. Nice to bump into you." He winked. "What're you having?"

"Nice to be bumped into." She laughed. "Jameson, please?"

As Brad ordered, Angie glanced back over to the man who'd occupied her mind nearly the entire night. He was still watching her, and he didn't look happy. Too bad, so sad. Served him right for walking away from her.

Connection or not, as she'd decided earlier, Angie wasn't going to throw herself at him. Deep inside, she knew it was going to be damn hard to stay away, but that didn't mean she had to give in to it. Not yet, anyway.

"This one's on the boss."

Angie snapped her attention to the bartender as she slid the shots their way. Saying nothing, she picked up the small glass and looked at the bartender.

"Right on, Marlene. Where's he at?"

"His usual spot." Marlene, their bartender, tipped her head to her left before moving to another customer.

"Thanks, Garrett. Appreciate it, man," Brad yelled over the music and raised his shot in the air.

Angie followed his gaze. No fucking way. The man whose arms Angie had been in not three minutes before gave them both a curt nod and then sipped from his coffee mug. She leaned close to Brad. "Who's that?"

"Garrett James. He owns this place."

And now she had a name. "Cool." She tapped his glass with her own. "Thanks for the shot."

"Thank Garrett." He winked and tipped his glass back. "I'm thinking I still owe you one, though."

Angie knocked the edge of the glass on the bar before drinking it down. When she was done, she placed it upside down on the surface. "Nah, we're good."

"All right then. How 'bout I get your number?"

Resisting the urge to look over at Garrett, Angie focused

on Brad's face. He was definitely good-looking, though he wasn't really doing it for her. Which was strange because hello? Nice body. Nice face. Nice tattoos.

Perplexed, Angie tilted her head to the side. Normally, she'd be all over a guy that looked like Brad. But not this time. She shrugged. "I'm sorry. I'm seeing someone."

"Lucky guy, for sure." Brad smiled, took her hand and shook it. "Take care, Angie."

"You too, Brad. Thanks again." Angie watched as he walked off and got swallowed up inside the crowd. She didn't bother turning back around. She didn't have to.

Angie knew the "lucky guy" she'd claimed as her man was still watching her. Garrett had already rung every bell she possessed, and as a result, Brad hadn't stood a chance. Regardless of what Garrett had warned her off in the hall, Angie suspected he already knew where she stood and was exactly the reason why he'd bought them their drinks.

She'd gotten the message loud and in surround sound: He didn't much like another man by her side. Pfft. Bad idea, her ass.

Angie just had to figure out what the next move was.

<hr>

THE THROB STARTED behind Garrett's eyes the minute he saw her at the opening of the hall—with Brad's hands on her. A possessive rage had risen in his chest faster than he'd been able to process the unwanted and unexpected emotion.

He didn't like it—someone else touching her *or* his reaction to it. Or the goddamn sweet smile she'd given the guy.

Jesus Christ, he didn't even know the girl.

He rubbed his palm along the back of his neck and watched her as she made her way back to the table she'd been sitting at all night. Now, there was a guy in the booth along with the woman she'd been sitting with before.

When she sat opposite him rather than next to him, Garrett figured he wasn't much of a threat. Ugh… *For fuck's sake.*

Garrett rubbed his palms up and down the tops of his thighs as nervous energy pulsed through him in time with the hard beat of the music. Enough of this. He was losing his mental battle. He had to know.

Garrett shook his head at his stupidity and went for a stroll among the crowd. As he got closer to the stage, he finally found who he was looking for. Stopping near the backstage door, he jerked his chin at the dude, motioning him over. Holding out his hand, he gave the kid a brief shake. "How's it going, Brad?"

"Going good, man. Always good to see you. How you been?"

Garrett plastered a smile on his face. *Fab. I got a raging hard-on for a girl too young for me.* "I'm good. Real good. Hey, so that brunette you were with at the bar? She kinda looks familiar. What's her name?"

"Oh, yeah. I think she said, Angie. Yeah, Angie."

"Hmm. Doesn't sound familiar."

"Yeah, I've never seen her before, either. Gotta say, she's fine as hell, but she said she's got a man, so I had to let that go. Thanks for the shots, though."

"You're welcome." A man? What. The. Fuck. "Anyway, show's about to end, so I better get back up front. Thanks for coming out, man." Garrett gave him a fist bump and stepped away.

If she had a man, all his potential problems were solved. Then again, based on her roaming hands in the hallway, she sure wasn't acting like she had a man. Or maybe she didn't care.

If that was the case, Garrett could *easily* fuck her, but that wasn't the kind of man he was anymore. Back in the nineties, screwing someone else's woman wasn't a problem. He wouldn't even think twice, but those days were ancient history.

Garrett headed straight back to the bar, and how about that, managed to *not* look for Angie along the way. Consider the bullet dodged. The little field trip to find Brad had done the trick and successfully doused the flames. Again.

By the time he got up to the bar area, Marlene was pulling drawers from the registers. Garrett leaned his forearms on the edge and waited as patrons made their way to the exit doors. Another two hours to get the money sorted, and he'd be on his way home to his bed.

CHAPTER FOUR

ANGIE GLANCED UP AT THE PEOPLE HEADING PAST THEIR TABLE.
The band had finished, and she'd lost sight of Garrett right as
the last song had started. "Dammit, where is he?"

"Describe him again?" Celia stood.

Angie pulled her lipstick from her small bag. "He's got
light brown hair, and it's long and up in a man bun."

"A man bun? You're fucking kidding, right?" Mark picked
up his beer and downed the remains.

"Not kidding, totally fucking hot." Angie got up and
scanned the crowd again. "That guy, Brad said Garrett's the
owner."

Celia threw her arm over Angie's shoulders. "Maybe you
can leave a note for him with the bartender."

Angie scowled. "Hell no!"

"Okay then." Celia laughed and took a step away. "Why
not?"

"Because I bet he gets a ton of notes every night. I'm not
about to be one of his groupies." Angie put her hands on her
hips and circled in place. "We're going to have to come back
tomorrow night."

"And again, you're fucking kidding, right?" Mark set his empty bottle on the table.

"And again, totally. Fucking. Hot. My thighs are still on fire." Angie winked.

Mark scrunched up his face. "TMI, Ang. For reals."

Celia let out a laugh. "Let's go, freaks."

"Mmmgggrrruugghhh!" Angie took another glance around, frustration clinging to her neck like a spider monkey.

"Go easy, She-Wookie." Celia laughed and held her hand out to Angie. "We'll come back tomorrow. Promise."

"Okay, fine." Angie blew out another harsh breath, this time minus the Chewbacca sound effects, and grabbed Celia's hand.

Leaving before talking to him again felt like she was going against some primal instinct within her. As if she didn't grab this opportunity now, she might never get another chance. Which was crazy.

Seriously, considering Angie didn't know a damn thing about him—except his name and that he owned the venue—it shouldn't matter so much. But it did. On a fucking cellular level, kind of way.

Regardless, if she walked out of the building and never saw him again, then that was obviously how it was supposed to be. And there wasn't a damn thing she could do about it. Fate had its own timeline. Always did, and often it had nothing to do with what a person thought they wanted or needed.

Angie followed her sister and brother out of the venue, still scanning the crowd for him and silently praying that timing and fate were going to get their shit together for once. They had to.

Garrett had just finished loading the prepped cash register drawers into the safe when the venue phone rang. He glanced at the clock on the wall. Four a.m. Odd someone would be calling at that late—or early—hour. But with customers, one never knew.

It couldn't be someone who knew him personally because anyone that did, who might be having an emergency, would call his cell. Chassidy would call his cell…so he was reasonably sure it wasn't her.

He stared at the phone until it stopped ringing, hitting the automated voicemail. Garrett gathered up the deposit for the bank and headed for his office door—and the phone rang again. He looked back at the phone on his desk. Another customer at four a.m.? Not likely. "Fine. Let's see whose ass is on fire."

Garrett moved back to the desk. A glance at the caller ID display told him he didn't recognize the number, but he picked up the cordless receiver anyway. "Copper Halo."

There was a clearing of a throat, and then, "Garrett?"

All the wind left Garrett's lungs as her voice flowed through him, waking up his nerve endings as if someone had plugged him into an electric socket. Absent of all rational thought, he let himself fall into his desk chair. "Angie…"

"How did you—"

"Are you okay?"

"Yeah, I just…"

He sat there for a long minute, listening to her breathe, waiting for her to continue. When she didn't, he broke the silence. "I asked Brad what your name was."

"Mmm." She blew out a breath. "I looked for you at closing."

Damn, he knew… "I was in my office."

"I wanted to talk to you again."

Pulling his hair down from the bun, he sat back and ran his fingers through the length. "I told you this is a bad idea."

"And I don't agree."

She wasn't going to give up, and Garrett was no longer sure he wanted her to. Which was fucking stupid. He was a selfish bastard because she wasn't his to take, and though he was really trying to care, he just didn't. "Bet your man would agree with me."

"My man? But I don't—ohhh!" Her words bled into a breathy laugh.

The sound of her laughter rolled through him like a warm breeze, and Garrett wanted to hear it again. *Shit.* "You don't what?"

"I only told Brad that because he asked me for my number, and I didn't want to give it to him."

It shouldn't matter that she was a free agent, but relief blasted through him as if it did. *Shiiiit!* "Okay, so you don't have a man. It's still a bad idea, and it doesn't matter that you don't agree."

She let out a half-gasp/half-laugh. "It does matter."

He closed his eyes. God help him, she was killing him. "How old are you?"

"Now, *that*, that *does not* matter."

"Angie, answer the question."

She cleared her throat. "Fine. Garrett, I'm twenty-nine."

"Only two years older than my daughter. That makes me old enough to be your father."

"That's kinda kinky, no?"

He chuckled, couldn't help himself. "Of course, you went there."

"Well, yeah. Of course, I did. For the record, I'm down for a little bit of kinky, but please don't ask me to call you Daddy. That would be weird."

Garrett chuckled again, but this time stifled it. She was funny, and he didn't want her to be. Damn. "Cute. Why do I have a feeling you're not going to let this go?"

"Probably because I'm not. Listen, I just want to talk. Is that so bad?"

"It's four in the morning, and you want to talk, huh?"

"*Four in the Morning.* That's a fabulous Gwen Stefani song."

He could hear her smile through the line, and at that moment, he'd give anything to see it. "Yeah, it is. You realize most people are sleeping, and if not, they're doing other things at four in the morning, Angie."

"What sorts of things, Garrett?" Her voice had gone low and breathy as it had in the hallway when he had pinned her against the wall.

He ground his molars together. Now she was playing with him, and it was working. "Most people are either fighting or…"

"Or what?"

Garrett adjusted his rapidly growing erection in his pants. "Or they're fucking. Based on what you're showing me so far, you'd probably like to do both."

"That might be true."

Garrett groaned. "Okay, beautiful. As much as I'm enjoying this, I need to let you go."

"If you're enjoying this, how about you say goodbye rather than let me go?"

"Do you argue about everything?"

She laughed. "I'm not arguing."

"There you go again." Garrett stood as his lips split into a smile.

"Oh, man. Give me a break, will you?"

"Goodnight, Angie."

"See you tomorrow night, Garrett."

"What? Wait…" He listened a moment. "Angie?"

He pulled the receiver from his ear and stared at it before placing it back in its cradle. He could call her back, but what would be the point in that? Instead, he pulled the caller ID up on the phone and then programmed her number into his cell.

Not one of his brightest decisions, especially if he planned on nothing happening between them. He did it anyway, though. Fuck it. He shoved his phone into his pocket. Maybe she wouldn't show up tomorrow night, and that'd be the end of it.

But Garrett had a feeling, one he refused to examine fully, that even if she didn't show tomorrow night, he'd be seeing her again anyway. Because he'd be the one reaching out.

CHAPTER FIVE

"Thanks!" Angie closed the door to the Lyft and approached the entrance to the Copper Halo. Nervous tension bounced around her insides like a rubber Super Ball, and her hands were sweating.

She'd spent the night out with her sister and brother down on Mill Avenue in Tempe, and now, only a little buzzed, she was determined to see Garrett. Although she'd told him she'd see him tonight when they'd talked early that morning, there was no way to know if he was actually there.

But she wasn't going to let that stop her. It was nearly closing time, and she planned to hang out with him and talk while he did whatever it was club owners did after hours. Angie blew out a breath as she stepped in front of the doorman.

He smiled at her. "Show's about done. We'll be closing in the next thirty minutes."

She put on her best smile and tilted her head to the side. "Yeah, I'm here to grab a friend. Is it okay if I still come in? I'll pay the cover charge."

He shot her a wink. "Nah, with a smile like that, I'll give you a pass on the cover. Do need your ID, though."

"Aw, that's so sweet. Thank you!" Angie felt her smile grow to a genuine one as she pulled her ID out of her small purse and showed it to the bouncer.

"Cali, huh? Good to go. Hope you find your friend."

"Yep. Thanks again." Angie stepped past him and entered the club.

A thrash metal band was up on the stage, the sounds of the guitar and drums echoing through the large space, making her wish she'd brought a set of earplugs. In her job as a reviewer, hard metal wasn't a genre she often covered, likely because she didn't much care for the music. Hard rock and metal worked for her, but the scream-so-loud-you-can't-hear-anything-else kind of stuff? Not so much.

She glanced around the area by the bar, and when she didn't see Garrett, she moved to the opposite end from where he was sitting last night. Operation "He Called Me Beautiful" was officially underway.

Angie took a seat on the stool at the end of the bar and placed her small purse on the metal top. Nothing left to do except wait. And maybe have a drink or two. Angie ordered a Jameson and soda and kept her eyes peeled.

A few minutes after the band finished its last song and halfway through her drink, she checked the time on her phone. Almost two a.m. Damn, where was he? Angie supposed she could ask the bartender—the same one that was working last night—but she couldn't bring herself to do it.

The desire to be different still ran strong in her mind. She didn't want anyone to think she was just "some girl" sniffing around Garrett and his bar. She hoped he realized that she wasn't just some girl, too. Because she wasn't. Angie was different. And meeting him the way she had last night made her realize things had definitely changed for her in the past year.

She didn't want to go back to the way she was in the past. Not that how she was, was bad. But Angie knew things would be different going forward. And she was sure Garrett was going to be part of that different.

Angie's phone vibrated in her lap. Picking it up, she swiped the screen to read the text message from an unknown number.

+1 (480) 555-1111: head down the hallway, take a left at the end and head up the stairs. second door on the right.

Angie: Garrett?

+1 (480) 555-1111: thought we agreed u were going 2 call me daddy?

Angie laughed and saved his number into her phone with his own special label before replying with an LOL.

Daddy: come upstairs

Daddy: do not argue!

Angie: At least until I get up there, right?

Daddy: exactly

Angie: See you in a minute, Daddy. 😜

Daddy: lol ok yeah that's creepy

Angie paid her tab and then made her way down the hall and up the stairs—heart pounding in her ears with every step she climbed. When she reached the second door, it was closed, so she knocked.

The door swung open…and Angie lost her breath.

She braced a hand on the doorjamb and gazed up at him. He was taller than she'd realized the night before. Maybe just over six feet. His body was lean, not bodybuilder muscular, but definitely in shape.

His light brown hair was down, hanging to his shoulders. The few gray strands in it acted almost as highlights. His perfect lips, framed by his beard, were parted in a slight smile. His green eyes, as mesmerizing as they were the night before, roamed over her face and then down her body.

She felt them like a physical touch, and she had to suppress the moan that'd bubbled up in her throat.

"Hi." He leaned forward and kissed her cheek. "Good to see you."

"Good to see you, too." Angie smiled up at him as he straightened and stepped to the side for her to enter.

After closing the door, he moved around her, smoothing his hand along her lower back as he passed on his way to his desk and sat. "How long have you been downstairs?"

The view of his incredible ass wrapped in faded black denim she'd been treated to a second before he sat down played before her eyes.

To distract her one-track mind, Angie shifted her clutch to her other hand and glanced around his office. There was a bass guitar on a stand in the far corner. A small desk, with a laptop and phone on it, in the other. And a small powder room to the left. "Um, what time is it now?"

"Just after two." He moved some paperwork on the desk before leaning back in his chair. "Take a seat." He motioned to the couch on the far wall across from his desk.

"Okay. Sure." Now that she was with him, she had a sudden attack of no idea what to say. Angie moved to the sofa and sat. Hopefully, he'd do some talking, at least enough to settle the pack of wild bees buzzing around her stomach on high alert.

"How was your night?"

She crossed her legs, and his eyes followed the movement. Interesting. "My night was good. I was down on Mill with my brother and sister."

"Is that who you were with last night?"

"Yes. Celia and Mark."

"Older or younger?" He sat forward, resting his forearms on the desk.

The position caused the sleeves of his red T-shirt to stretch tight over his nicely defined biceps. Heat swirled in Angie's tummy, and she had to swallow a few times before answering. "They're both younger."

"Ah, you're the oldest. Makes sense."

She smoothed her palms down the sides of her thighs. And linked her hands on her knee. "Actually, no. There's ten of us."

His eyes went wide, darting from her legs back to her face. "For fuck's sake. *Ten?*"

Angie laughed, loving his reaction to both her body and words. "Yep, ten."

"Wow." He leaned back again and linked his hands behind his head, the effect making his biceps look even more tempting. "Where are you in the birth order?"

She smirked. "I'm lucky number seven."

"Seven has always been my favorite number." Garrett stared at her from his seat behind his desk.

Far too much furniture and floor space separated them, but that was a good thing. Safer that way. At least, that's what he kept telling himself. It was her perfectly shaped, long legs and the fact that she kept touching them—the short denim shorts she had on left all her smooth, creamy skin available for him to focus on.

The top she wore was nothing fancy, but the loose fabric clung perfectly to her petite breasts and hung off one shoulder. More tempting creamy skin that he could barely take his eyes off of.

"I'd say mine, too, but you might think I'm trying to suck

up." She pulled the length of her dark hair around one shoulder.

He raised a brow. "Are you?"

She tilted her head to the side. "The way you're looking at me right now tells me I don't need to."

"How do you think I'm looking at you, Angie?" Garrett shifted forward and tried to ignore the rising erection in his jeans.

"Like you want to know what it feels like to have my legs wrapped around your waist, Garrett."

Fucking hell! He barely suppressed the groan that'd risen in his throat. Their whole conversation had shifted gears faster than he anticipated. One minute they were talking about her family, and the next, they were having verbal foreplay, his dick now harder than a pile driver as the image of what she'd described branded itself on his brain.

She was right, he did want to know what it felt like to have her wrapped around him. But it wasn't only her legs. He also wanted to know what her lips tasted like and how they'd feel. He cleared his throat and forced himself to stay in his seat. "That what you came here for?"

"Yes and no."

"Told you, this is a bad idea."

She stood and walked to the front of his desk. So much for the safe distance between them.

"And I'm going to ignore that because I think it's a fantastic idea."

He focused on her eyes. "Seventh in the birth order pretty much ensured that you'd have to fight for what you want, huh?"

"Usually. Are you saying I'm going to have a fight on my hands?" She placed her palms on his desk and bent forward.

God help him, he wasn't going to be able to resist her much longer. She was baiting him, and he was ready to take a healthy bite. "One way or another, we're going to end up fighting."

She licked her lips. "As long as we can fuck, too."

Yeah, that did it. He was done for.

Garrett stood, snapped his arm out, caught her around the back of the neck and pulled her to him. He slammed his lips down on hers with such ferocious need he was afraid he might've hurt her. But she didn't pull away. Instead, she moaned and pushed her tongue into his mouth.

The taste of her swamped his senses, and his head spun. Garrett pulled away for a moment, pressing his forehead to hers. "*Fuck!*"

"Mmhmm. Exactly." Angie climbed onto the top of his desk.

Perfect. He needed her closer to him anyway. With his grip still tight on the back of her neck, he framed her jaw with the fingers of his free hand. He shook his head and let his gaze roam over her face. Jesus, her eyes. One brown, one hazel. "Fucking beautiful."

She blinked once as if taking in his compliment and then captured his lips again. She gave as good as he had, just as fierce, just as heated. Garrett let her, welcoming her hot tongue into his mouth. He tangled his own around hers, chasing, tasting, taking.

Oh, yeah, bad idea. Really fucking bad idea because now, Garrett didn't want to stop kissing her.

Heat swirled between them like some sort of ethereal energy, coaxing them higher. He nipped at her bottom lip before diving back into her mouth. She scraped her nails up his back before tangling her fingers in his hair. Garrett hooked her around the waist and fell back into his seat, taking her with him.

One moment bled into the next until they were both gasping and panting for breath. She was perched on his lap, straddling his hips and rubbing against him. Not a stitch of clothing had come off, yet he'd had his hands all over her body from her back to her fine, full ass and her breasts to her hair, and her thighs…her long, bare legs. He'd touched every part of those he could reach.

But beyond that, all they'd done was kiss. Garrett couldn't remember the last time he'd actually made out with a woman. It wasn't that he didn't want inside her lush body because he did. Badly. His cock strained against his fly, aching to come out. No doubt, he'd be inside of her soon enough.

But something about what was happening right at that moment seemed worth not missing, and Garrett was thoroughly enjoying every minute of whatever it was. Bad idea or not, the switch had been flipped. There was no going back now.

CHAPTER SIX

Angie had never been so turned on in her life. Never had a kiss felt so erotic. She was completely clothed, straddling Garrett's lap in his office, and all she was doing was kissing him.

She hadn't put her hands up his shirt or down his pants—though God, she wanted to. She might be rubbing against the thick ridge behind his zipper, but really, how could she not at least do that?

He was touching her everywhere, especially her bare legs. The feel of his calloused fingertips, as he caressed her thighs and sides of her calves, sent her body into freaking orbit. Once again, he moved his big palms to her ass, and Angie took advantage of his grip and rocked her pelvis forward.

Garrett groaned as he squeezed her butt cheeks and then ran his fingers down her legs again. She pulled from his lips with a gasp and stared down at him. "Holy wow! Don't stop."

"Wow, is right. Where the hell did you come from?" Gazing up at her, he brushed her hair away from her face.

Before she could answer, his mouth was on hers again. God, she hadn't been kissed like this since high school. His warm tongue had dominated her mouth with such intense passion she could barely think straight. Which was fine with her—

The sound of the door opening penetrated her haze of lust right as Garrett jerked away from her lips.

"Hey, Dad— Whoa!"

Angie froze, still on Garrett's lap, her back to the door. *Dad?* That's right, he'd mentioned a daughter last night on the phone, but Angie hadn't figured she'd be running into her at the bar. Let alone after two in the morning. *Shit.* Talk about awkward. She looked at Garrett and bit her bottom lip.

He glanced at Angie before peering around her. "Give me a minute, okay, Chassidy?"

"You got it. Sorry."

Once Angie heard the door close, she blew out the breath she was holding. "Shit."

"It's okay." Again, he smoothed her hair away from her face. "Probably a good thing we got interrupted."

"Speak for yourself. I was rather enjoying that. And this —" Angie smiled and rolled her hips.

He moaned and then sighed through his nose. "Yeah, I was enjoying that, too." He kissed her again, but this time didn't linger. "Better let me up."

With a whimper, she slid off his lap and straightened her shirt, then ran her fingers through her hair.

Garrett stood and adjusted himself in his jeans.

Good Lord... Angie stepped close to him and covered the bulge with her palm. "For the record, I want this."

He placed his hand over hers. "Yeah?"

"Mmhmm." She licked her lips. "Badly."

"Soon." He bent and kissed her one last time before stepping around her to the door.

Angie smoothed her fingers through her hair and straightened her shirt. She was about to meet his daughter. Wow... okay. Get it together. *Breathe, Angie.* Good grief, her lips were dry. She fished her lip balm from her pocket.

No big deal that she was sucking the girl's father's face off, right? Not at all. The big deal was more likely going to be how close in age they were. Speaking of, how close in age *were* they? Oh, yeah. That first night she'd talked to him on the phone, he'd said that Angie was two years older than his daughter. Awesome.

After glancing back at Angie one last time, Garrett swung the door open. "Come on in, honey."

"Thanks." The pretty girl with light brown hair made eye contact with Angie as soon as she crossed the threshold. "Hi, I'm Chassidy. Garrett's my dad."

Angie offered her palm. "Nice to meet you. I'm Angie. Sorry about the…that…you know." Embarrassment had a wave of heat spreading across Angie's chest, and she shrugged.

Glancing at Angie's outstretched hand, Chassidy ignored it and stepped past her, moving to the tall file cabinet against the wall. "Eh, no worries. It's not the first time I've caught my dad with a woman. Won't be the last."

Ouch… Okay, *that* wasn't very nice. The comment stung —in a way that Angie didn't expect it to. As in a jealousy kind of way. Angie looked to Garrett, who had an expression on his face she couldn't quite decipher.

He put his hands on his hips and frowned. "Hey, Chas, that wasn't cool."

"I better go." Angie stepped to him and placed a kiss on his cheek. "It was nice to meet you, Chassidy. Again, I'm really sorry."

"Wait a minute." Garrett pulled her back to him. "I'm not sorry."

Angie stiffened and looked up at him. "You know what I mean."

"Doesn't matter." He glanced at his daughter. "Chassidy, I'm going to walk Angie out, and then I'll be back so we can talk about whatever business couldn't wait until tomorrow."

"Go for it." Chassidy didn't bother turning around from the cabinet.

Shit, shit, and more shit. Obviously, Angie hadn't made a good first impression. Considering how close they were in age, she really couldn't blame the girl for being shocked. But then again, based on what Chassidy had said, this was something she'd often dealt with.

Not the first… Won't be the last.

Ugh, Angie's stomach rolled over on itself. Age differences aside, she *did not* want to be thought of as another notch in this man's belt. And it was obvious that's *exactly* what Chassidy thought Angie was.

Angie prayed that wasn't what Garrett thought she was as well because although she wasn't sure exactly how much she wanted, Angie knew she wanted to be much more than a damn notch in his belt.

Torn between replaying the awesome make-out session and how insecure she now felt due to the harsh reality of what his daughter had said, Angie stayed silent as Garrett led her down the stairs and out the main doors.

There was still bouncer staff cleaning up, and a couple bartenders at the bar. They'd likely have been interrupted anyway. She hadn't even thought about that.

Garrett turned to her when they got outside. "Where's your car?"

"I took a Lyft. I'll request one now."

"I can give you a ride home."

"No, that's okay. You need to get back upstairs." She smiled and ordered the car from her phone app. "See? It'll be here in four minutes."

He brushed a hair away from her cheek. "I'm sorry Chassidy acted like that. She's probably just being protective."

"That's a good thing. And she doesn't know me, I get it." She shrugged.

"Can I ask you a question?"

She stepped closer and wrapped her arms around his waist. "Anything."

"You ever hear of that band Copper Seven?"

"Yeah. They were really big in the late nineties. Good band. Why do you ask?"

"No reason. Just curious." He bent and placed a soft kiss on her lips.

Suddenly, the question didn't matter anymore. Her head fell back. "Mmm. I like those. Can I have another?"

He sighed. "You know if we start, we won't stop." He touched the end of her nose with his fingertip. "Besides, looks like your ride is pulling up now."

"Damn. You're right. Okay, wait…can I ask you a question now?"

"Better hurry."

"Scale of one to ten, ten being the best, how would you rate our kiss? Or my kiss, rather?" God, why was she asking him this?

He smirked. "Nine."

"Only a nine? Wow, tough crowd."

He rolled his eyes. "Okay, nine-point-five. No one's perfect."

Angie laughed and stepped back. "All right then." She opened the back door of the Lyft. "Text me later?"

"Sure." He slid his hands into his front pockets. "Night, Angie."

"Night, Garrett." She dropped into the passenger seat, closed the door and blew him a kiss. Angie watched over her shoulder as the driver pulled away from the curb.

Nine-point-five, huh? She shook her head and touched her fingers to her bruised lips. Jeezus chrispies, could she have sounded any more insecure? She never should've asked him that question. She rated his kiss a twenty. Hands down, the best kisser she'd ever kissed.

———

GARRETT MADE his way back inside the club, grabbed the cash drawers from the bartenders and then climbed the stairs to his office. To say he was annoyed was an understatement. He didn't appreciate Chassidy's reaction. At all.

Thing was, his daughter's behavior wasn't out of the norm. Sure, when Chassidy was a child, she never saw him with women. But once she was an adult, there were times—especially in the years since she'd started working with Garrett—where she'd run into him and a woman he'd been spending time with.

None of those relationships had been serious, and more than a few of them were younger than him. Truth be told, he never even considered them relationships. One- or two-night stands never were.

Those women weren't interested in the long term with him anyway, but even if they were, it always had more to do with his past career or his current one and the benefits his bank account offered.

Garrett had always known there was no future with any of those women, but Chassidy, purely on instinct, knew it, too. After the first one or two, she treated them all like they were disposable.

To say she was a bit protective of her father was an understatement. But Garrett saw her protectiveness as a good thing.

Except this time was different—not that he could say how yet. Garrett just knew in his gut that Angie was genuinely interested in him for reasons that had *nothing* to do with his former rockstar status, the club he owned, or his bank balance.

Hell, Angie didn't even know who he was in regard to Copper Seven.

She liked *him*.

Just plain old him.

He reached the top of the stairs and took the few steps down the hall to the office. However awesome it was that Angie seemed to be authentic, Garrett couldn't help but still be a little cautious. He'd be crazy not to be, but he'd have to see what happened, see how things played out.

Right now, he was going to find out what was up with Chassidy. Garrett opened the door and stepped inside.

His daughter was sitting at her small desk, her focus on the laptop screen. "Sorry to break up your party, Dad. I was in the area and needed to check on the final details of a booking for the beginning of next month."

He set the cash drawers down on the credenza. "Yeah, I hadn't expected you to walk in."

She glanced at him. "If you'd clear out the storage room next door, I could set up an office in there."

"Hey, come on. You moved out of my house. Now you want to move out of our shared office? Is this some sort of late-blooming adolescent rebellion?"

Chassidy smirked. "If only I were still an adolescent, that might count. But sadly, no. Anyway, that one was cute. Looks about my age, though. Are they getting younger?"

He moved to the safe, squatted down and opened it. "Very funny. You're still mouthy like you were when you were a teen. Her name is Angie, and yeah, definitely cute. Definitely young." With a sigh, he straightened. "You didn't have to be rude."

His daughter sat back from the laptop. "I wasn't rude."

"Come on, Chas, you were rude."

"Fine, I was rude." His daughter tipped her head to the side. "Look, I don't care how old she is. My concern has always been for you and your heart and what she's sniffing around for. I won't allow you to be used."

"Fair enough." Garrett leaned against the credenza and crossed his arms. "This one's different."

"Hmm." With a frown, Chassidy rubbed her shoulder. "Different, how?"

"Not sure yet. Not sure I'll even try and figure it out. But I can tell you this, she doesn't know who I am. So, we can check that concern off the list." Garrett grabbed the cash drawers and loaded them into the safe.

Chassidy laughed. "Be for real, Dad. Of course, she knows who you are."

Garrett went to his desk and sat. "I am being for real. She doesn't know."

"And how is it that you know this for sure? Enlighten me, please?" Sarcasm evident in her tone, Chassidy tipped her head to the side and stared at him.

"Curb the tone." He crossed his legs at the ankle and sighed. "I asked her if she'd heard of the band. She had, but recognition didn't dawn." He shrugged. "I'm betting she'll figure it out now, but until that point, until I asked, she didn't know who I was."

Chassidy snorted. "Anyone older than twenty-one knows who Copper Seven is, Dad. So, if she's not interested in you because of the band, then she's sniffing around because of the bar."

"That's the thing, Chas, my gut is telling me she's not sniffing at all. Besides, is it so hard to believe someone might be interested in your old man because they genuinely like him?"

Chassidy's expression turned soft. "Don't be silly. Of course, I can believe it. You're awesome. That girl would be lucky to have you, Dad. For the record, in case you've forgotten, I do want you to be happy and settled." She stood and moved to lean against his desk. "I just worry, you know that."

"I know you do. And I appreciate it." Garrett ran his fingers through his hair. "Look, it doesn't matter. I'm probably wrong, and whatever this is won't last long. You know me, I never let myself trust fully anyway. But, maybe if you see her again, you can be a little nicer?"

"You want me to be nice?" Chassidy rolled her eyes but then smiled. "I suppose. But only this once." She winked.

"Still want to move out of my office?"

"Hell, yes, I would love my own space. Then I can make out with guys in there all I want." She laughed and pushed away from his desk and resumed her seat at hers. "La la la… Back to work for me."

Garrett smirked. "Brat."

"Yep." She focused back on her laptop screen.

"Definitely not cleaning out the storage room for you now." He chuckled as he got to his feet. "I'm heading out. Don't stay too late, okay?"

"Not a problem. I'm almost done."

"Make sure Cody walks you to your car." He bent and kissed her cheek.

"Will do. Night, Dad."

"Night, honey." Garrett left the room and headed downstairs.

After stopping to remind his head bouncer, Cody Fox, to wait for Chassidy, he made his way to his car. On his drive, his thoughts stayed focused on Angie and how she felt in his arms.

He'd been surprised at the chemistry that erupted between them. She'd felt so *infuckingcredible* he could barely think straight. God, he hadn't wanted it to end either.

How long would it take for Angie to figure out who he was? An hour? Twenty-four hours? Garrett made the turn into his neighborhood. Would she call him when it finally dawned on her?

He ran his palm over his face and groaned. The sweet scent of her perfume still lingered on his hands, and the desire to text her rose like a tidal wave. He wanted more of her, which was exactly why he *didn't* send a text. Instead, he went to bed, her scent still deep in his lungs.

CHAPTER SEVEN

ANGIE SAT AT THE SMALL KITCHEN TABLE IN MARK AND Celia's apartment, enjoying a bowl of Fruity Pebbles. Her brother and sister were enjoying their own bowls. She glanced at Celia across the table. "Best cereal ever."

"Definitely," Mark said around a mouthful.

"'Specially at almost three-thirty in the morning after a night of drinking." Celia scooped up another spoonful and shoveled it in. When she was done chewing, she jerked her chin at Angie. "Tell us what happened with Garrett."

"Just leave out the X-rated parts." Mark grinned and sipped milk from the edge of the bowl.

Angie almost choked on her mouthful. After swallowing properly, she set her spoon in the bowl and raised her hand, palm up. "I'll do my best. No clothes came off. Does that help?"

"Bummer." Celia took another spoonful.

Angie sighed and swirled her spoon in her cereal. "Doesn't even matter though. We made out like a couple of high school teens. It was freaking awesome."

"Oooh! Was it a 'Cyn and Shane light your life on fire' kiss?"

Mark put his bowl in the sink. "Wait…a what?"

"Oh, jeez." Angie rolled her eyes. It'd been forever since their sister, Cyn, had shared about the "magic kiss" she'd had with Shane when they'd first gotten together. Angie and Celia had been by the pool at Cyn's house, and Angie had never forgotten the things Cyn had said about kissing Shane and how she'd never be the same again. He'd set the bar so high Cyn was sure she'd never find anyone else better.

Angie thought back to what she'd felt with Garrett. She wasn't sure if it was like what Cyn had experienced with Shane, but she was damn sure it'd been the best kiss of *her* life.

The kind of kiss a person never forgot.

The kind she for sure wanted again.

"Yoohoo, Ang?" Celia snapped her fingers.

Angie focused on her sister. "Hmm?"

"Yeah, okay." Celia pointed her spoon at her. "Judging by the dreamy, faraway look on your face, I'll take that as a yes."

Angie laughed and looked up at the ceiling. "Ugh…I dunno. Maybe it was?" She smiled and focused on her brother and sister again. "It was a twenty on a scale of one to ten, for sure."

"Damn." Celia sat back and let out a sigh. "Someday."

"I still have no idea what you two are talking about. But whatever. Sounds like you're gonna see him again." Mark stretched his arms over his head and yawned.

Celia stood and placed her bowl in the sink. "The deal is this, someday you're going to kiss a girl, and it's going to be so good she'll ruin kissing any other women for the rest of your life."

Mark frowned. "Pfft. That's crazy."

"According to Cyn, it's true. And after tonight, I might have to agree with her." Angie stood, and Celia took her bowl from her. "As far as seeing him again? I don't know. He said he'd text me tonight, but I haven't heard from him." She glanced at her phone.

"Eh, he probably got busy." Mark kissed her on her cheek. "I'm heading to bed before the sun comes up."

"Wait…hold a second. Who was that blonde Celia and I saw you with tonight?"

Mark stopped short. "What blonde?"

Celia narrowed her eyes are him. "Uh, the one with the incredible rack. She looked familiar. Is that the same blonde I've seen leaving the apartment at the witching hour?"

"Ooh, this sounds interesting." Angie grinned and glanced from Celia back to Mark. "Yeah, what she said."

"Just a friend." He shrugged, but the corner of his lip twitched.

"Hmm. If you say so, I mean, she *was* looking at you like you're the end-all be-all. Just saying." Angie looked down at her phone screen.

"Well, if he's had her in his room, playing with all her *assets*, then that's probably why she's looking at him like that." Grinning, Celia slid her hands into her front pockets. "Just a thought."

"Assets?" Mark shook his head, chuckling. "Whatever. Night, you two."

"Uh, huh. Night." Angie called after him and then glanced back to her phone. The urge to text Garrett was riding her hard.

Screw it. She pulled up his contact info and started to type a message.

"Don't do it."

Angie glanced up at her sister. "Why not?"

"Because you don't want to look desperate. Give the guy a chance to reach out."

"But…but…ugh." Angie clicked the phone off and let out a frustrated sigh. "Fine."

"Come on, let's just go to sleep. Bet you anything you'll hear from him tomorrow." Celia looped her arm in Angie's and moved them toward the bedroom.

"I hope so." Angie plugged her phone into the charging cable beside the bed and went to brush her teeth.

By the time she'd taken off her makeup and thrown on some pajamas, the brick wall of tired had come crashing down on her, but it hadn't done anything to dim the desire to text him. What if she just—

"Stop it and go to sleep, Angie."

"Shush. I'm checking Facebook." She typed in Copper Halo in the search bar, and when she found the page, started scrolling through the pics. "Hey, you know what's weird?"

"Hmmwhat?" Celia rolled over to face Angie.

"He asked me about that band Copper Seven right before I left. And I didn't think about it, but the name of his club is Copper Halo."

"So."

Angie looked at Celia. "Don't you think that's strange?"

"What? The club name or that he asked you about that band?"

"Yes."

Celia propped her head on her hand. "Ang, what the hell are you talking about?"

"Copper Halo. Copper Seven. The same names…sorta." Angie looked back at her phone screen. "And why would he ask me about the band?"

"Ummm…wild guess? He likes the band, maybe? The man owns a small concert venue." Celia laughed. "Go to sleep. You're not even thinking straight."

"I was tired, but now I'm wide the hell awake." Angie sat up. "I gotta see something."

"Okay, suit yourself." Celia plucked Angie in the arm. "I'm going to sleep. You see whatever you need to see, but do not, I repeat, do not text him."

"I won't. Jeez." Angie pulled the browser up on her mobile. "Don't think I won't get you back for the pluck when you least expect it, brat." She laughed.

With a snort, Celia rolled over and pulled the covers over her head. Angie typed Copper Seven into Google's search bar and found their Wiki page. She scanned the page, skimming through sections. *American rock band from 1992 to 1997…* Band members: *Chase Reynolds, vocals. Derrick Holmes, drums. Garrett James, bass— Whoa!* "No fucking way!"

Celia jumped and sat up. "What! Holy shit, you scared me. What is it?"

"Sorrysorrysorry! But *oh my God*, Celia. He… He's…he's!"

"He's what?"

"Look!" She shoved the phone in her sister's face.

"Jesus…" Celia took the device from her and focused on the screen. "Do you think it's him?"

Angie grabbed the phone back. "I don't know, but I'm going to find out. I mean, how many Garrett Jameses could there be in the world?"

"Wow. Okay, yeah. That's crazy."

Angie scrolled farther down on the page until she got to links to the band members names. Clicking, she found Garrett's Wiki page *and* his picture. She stared at the screen, at the picture of a much younger man.

A man who was most definitely the same man she'd made out with for nearly an hour!

"It's him, Celia." Angie stood. "Go to sleep. I'm going out to the living room for a bit. I need to figure out what to do with this."

"It's not that big a deal, is it? It's kind of a cool thing to have in common, you both being in the music industry. But, I mean, do you care?"

"Yes. But no. I mean, I like him. Probably more than I should. I need to think for a bit."

"All right. Don't stay up too late. And don't text him!" Celia laughed. "Love you."

"Good God, you're like a bulldog! I won't text him!" Angie laughed. "Love you, too, Celia."

Phone in hand, Angie made her way out to the living room. She knew the band, was familiar with their music. They'd been really good and had topped the charts and toured all over the world. But the band had ultimately self-destructed and broken up.

Garrett James was an extremely talented musician, but he was also one of the reasons why the band hadn't survived. Too much booze and drugs took a lot of bands down, and Copper Seven was no exception.

She'd meant what she said to Celia. She did like him. And it didn't matter that he'd been a famous rock star in a band. It was cool and all, but she wasn't some star-struck groupie or anything like that.

The only thing that mattered was if he still lived like he had during those glory days; that would be a big deal breaker for her.

After spending another hour reading anything she could find on him, including really disturbing information about his ex-wife, Amanda James and her untimely death due to overdose, Angie finally gave in to fatigue and got back in bed.

She didn't know what to think any more than she had when she'd first discovered who he was. However, there were two things she was certain of.

One, as she'd felt from the moment she laid eyes on him, Angie was not, under any circumstances, about to be one of his groupies. Two, she had her whole life ahead of her and a shiny, brand-new career goal. There was no way she'd get involved with someone who was all messed up on drugs or drank like a fish.

Her last thoughts before finally closing her eyes were that she was going to see him once she'd gotten enough sleep. Rather than drive herself insane wondering, she'd simply find out firsthand and go from there.

Garrett had woken that morning feeling restless, irritable and discontent. A constant hum of agitation and need crawled under his skin, making him jumpy, among other things.

His state of mind reminded him of days long ago when his sole focus had been getting his next fix or bottle of booze. Fortunately, he wasn't feeling those cravings, didn't want to pick up a drink or a drug. But he sure wanted something to make these feelings go away.

A nice long hike was probably what he needed before he had to be in the office to handle the day's business. After shooting a text to his closest friend, Freddie, to join him, Garrett headed out.

An hour or so later, he and Freddie sat atop Thompson Peak, located in the McDowell Mountains, looking out over the valley below, starting its day.

"Tell you what, no matter how many times we hike here, I'll never get tired of the view." Freddie took a swig of Gatorade from his Camelbak.

Garrett let out a grunt of agreement and leaned back. The hike had done the trick to clear his head, mostly. All he came up with, as much as he wanted to deny it, was Angie. She was the cause of his distress. Shit.

"You been quiet today."

"I'm always quiet." Garrett swiped the sweat from his forehead with the back of his hand.

Freddie chuckled. "Yeah, but not *this* quiet. What's up? Everything okay with Chassidy?"

"No. I mean, yeah. She's fine." Garrett blew out a harsh breath. His head was full of nothing but Angie, and he couldn't focus. Fuck's sake, he hadn't stopped thinking about her since they'd met two nights before. Her showing up again last night had been the last thing he needed and absolutely everything he'd wanted. "I met a woman."

"That's awesome. So why do you look like someone stole your puppy?"

"You know the typical for me: is she for real or just looking for a free ride?" Garrett shrugged and sat up, resting his elbows on his bent knees. "Problem is, I like her, and I'm hoping she's different from the others."

"I want that for you, man. I really do." Freddie nudged his shoulder into Garrett's. "What's she like?"

Garrett blew out another breath. What was she like? Shit, where did he start? Her curvy body? Her long legs? Her soft, perfect lips…all of that and more had been a temptation he hadn't been able to resist. But he wasn't about to share all those intimate details with Freddie. "What can I say? She's beautiful."

"They all are." Freddie chuckled. "What makes her different?"

Garrett shook his head. "She jokes and flirts like a pro. One minute it's all back-and-forth banter between us, and then in the next, it's a serious convo. Her confidence is amazing. She's totally sure of herself. The girl has seriously got my attention."

His friend grinned at him. "Sounds like all good stuff to me. Go for it. What do you have to lose?"

With another shake of his head, Garrett took a drink from his own Camelbak. He felt like he had everything to lose. With all the thinking he'd been doing, he'd yet to contact her. Which was shitty because he'd told her he'd text, and he hadn't.

Then again, he hadn't heard from her, either, so maybe all this brooding he was doing was pointless.

"I don't know, man. It's not like I've been looking for a relationship. Plus, I'm too old for her." Garrett ran his palm along the back of his neck. "What the hell does a young, beautiful woman like her want with a washed-up rock star who also happens to be a former drunk and drug addict?"

"Dunno." Freddie shrugged. "Have you asked her?"

"Nope."

With a chuckle, Freddie got to his feet and then held a hand down to Garrett. "Maybe you should start there."

"Smart ass." Garrett stared up at his friend. After a beat passed, he took Freddie's offered hand and got to his feet beside him.

Garrett couldn't shake the feeling that he knew in his gut she wasn't merely sniffing around because she was looking to score some free access to concerts and booze. It would be so much easier if that were the case. But that wasn't who she was.

He could tell by simply gazing in her eyes when she was perched on his lap that she was into him…just him: Garrett James. An older guy who happened to catch her eye at a bar.

Asking her seemed pointless. So, what the hell was he supposed to do now?

CHAPTER EIGHT

ANGIE SHUFFLED HER WAY TO THE KITCHEN, PRAYING THERE was fresh coffee and food. Considering it was almost one in the afternoon, she was beyond starving. The bowl of cereal she had the night before hadn't been enough to tie her over. "Mrrrpph."

Mark looked up from the paper he was reading at the kitchen table. "You look like hell."

"Love you, too. Coffee?" She pushed her hair over her shoulder.

"Fresh pot."

"Thank God." Angie poured herself a mugful and took a seat at the table. Caffeine first, then food. "Where's Celia?"

"Grocery store."

"Ah." She sipped the hot brew and glanced at her phone again. Not a single text had come from Garrett. She was frustrated, but there was no way she was going to send a message or, worse, call until she'd gotten some coffee in her.

After the first few sips, she realized she should wait just a little longer. She wasn't a morning person. At all. And anything she tried to say to him now would *not* come out the way she wanted it to.

She let out a sigh. "I need food."

"There's frozen waffles." Mark turned the newspaper over.

"That works."

After Angie ate her breakfast, she refilled her coffee and wandered to the bathroom. Desperation thrummed in her veins like a heavy rain. The urge to text him, call him, or show up at the club was starting to make her a little nutty. With her teeth clenched, she turned on the shower and pulled up one of her playlists on her phone before stepping under the spray.

With shampoo lathered in her hair, Angie danced in the shower to her friend, Tarra Layne's song "Heated." It was the perfect song to remind her that she was an independent woman who *did not* need a man. And being strung out on one, who she barely knew, was not gonna happen.

Angie leaned her head back under the spray, swaying her hips to the beat. She'd forgotten about this alternate version of the song Tarra had put out. It had a grungier electric guitar sound. Considering his background, Garrett would probably dig the song— *Dammit, do not think of him!*

With frustration plowing through her at her inability to get him off her mind, Angie finished up in the shower. With her hair in a towel, she decided to give it one more hour, and then she was going to text him. Screw it. One shot, and if he didn't reply, she'd put him out of her mind, never to be thought of again.

After all, a summer fling, or whatever this was between her and Garrett, wasn't exactly top of list for her. This month was supposed to be all about fun, not angst over some guy she'd just met. And really, if things did develop, in the long run, Garrett might be nothing more than a distraction from her new career goals. She didn't want that.

The door cracked open, and Celia poked her head in. "Hungry?"

"Nah—" Angie bent closer to the mirror and applied another coat of mascara. "I had waffles."

Celia opened the door the rest of the way and leaned a hip against the frame. "You hear from him?"

"Negative. I'm giving it one more hour, and then I'm texting him."

"Why don't you just call him?"

Angie looked over at her sister. "Honestly? I'm having a little internal war right now."

"Don't complicate it, Ang." Celia laughed. "Just call him. That's what I'd do."

"You're probably right." She applied some blush. "But, rejection is easier to take via text."

"He's not gonna reject you. He's probably just busy."

"Nobody is *that* busy, Celia." Zipping up her makeup bag, she shoved it into the cabinet. "Takes two fucking seconds to send a smiley face emoji."

"This is true."

"Yes, it is. So…he gets one hour, actually—" She glanced at the clock on her phone. "Less than that now."

"It's gonna be fine. You'll see."

"Well, aren't you little Miss Optimism?" Angie cocked one brow.

"Someone has to be, jeez." Her sister snorted. "I'll let you finish, little Miss Pessimism." Celia turned and left the bathroom.

Damn right, she was falling more on the negative, the glass is totally empty, side of the house. The guy said he would text and, what do ya know? No text. Not much positive could be gained from that. Whatever…

Angie piled her hair on top of her head in a bun and parked her ass on the couch. Even though she was on vacation, she had a couple of reviews she promised to do and planned to turn in by the end of the week. Instead of waiting, she decided to get them written and sent to her editor now. When she was halfway through the first, her phone dinged with a text message.

She sucked in a breath and peeked at it from the corner of her eye. It was clear it was from him, but the notification window showed only the first part of the message. Saved by the bell. Literally. Angie scooped up the phone and swiped the screen.

Daddy: hows ur day?

Angie stared at the screen, unsure of how to respond. Somehow, "Hey! So excited to hear from you. I've been obsessing about you nonstop since last night. How's your day been?" didn't quite seem like the appropriate thing to say.

"Is that him?" Celia plopped down on the sofa next to her. "Um…who the hell is 'Daddy'?"

Angie tucked her phone to her chest. "Rude!" She frowned but then laughed. "It's him. It's a little inside joke between us."

"You already have an inside joke?"

Angie couldn't stop the smile from forming on her lips. "Yes."

"Do I have to be a bridesmaid? I hate those dresses."

"Go away!" Angie shoved at her sister's shoulder. "You're a goof."

Celia burst out laughing. "I'm just saying. An inside joke? That's so cute, it's gross."

Angie laughed and glanced back at the screen. "I don't know what to say back. And how screwed up is it that I feel like I only now took my first deep breath of the day?"

"Yup, cute and gross." Celia leaned over and peered at the screen. "Oh wow, texts using old-fashioned text speak? Does the boy have a flip phone?"

"No, at least I don't think he has a flip phone." Angie laughed and then bit her bottom lip. "And that *boy* is not a boy at all. He's a grown man, so that's probably why."

"True. How old is he anyway?"

"Forty-six, according to his Wiki page, but I would prefer he confirms that himself." Angie groaned. "What do I say back?"

Mark strolled into the room and flopped down in the big chair in the corner. "Damn, forty-six? Dude barely made the rule for age difference."

"What rule?" she and Celia said in unison.

Mark pointed the remote at the TV and turned it on. "You know, divide by two and add seven."

Angie frowned. "Huh?"

"That's not a thing." Celia laughed.

"It's a thing. Trust me. Call any of our brothers and ask them." Mark found a basketball game to watch.

"Men are such pigs." Celia gaped at Mark and then turned her focus on Angie. "Is he serious?"

Angie shook her head, sure she looked just as aghast as her sister. "I don't know, but you know what? I don't want to know because, yeah, pigs."

Mark laughed. "Okay, delicate flowers. Don't hate the players. Hate the game."

"Oh my God, don't ever say that again." Angie laughed.

"Unbelievable." Celia rolled her eyes. "Okay, let's focus. Here's an idea: tell him your day has been awesome. Then, ask him how his day was. I know that's crazy. But try it."

"When did you get to be such a smart ass?"

Celia laughed and got to her feet. "I learned it from you."

Mark chuckled, shaking his head, but said nothing more.

"If that's the case, you better practice more." Angie snorted. "Okay, fine, I'm answering him."

"Thank the Lord." Celia strutted off. "I'm grabbing a shower."

"Mmhmm." Angie stared at the screen of her phone again. With a sigh, she started her reply, erased it, and started again. Then, once more, for good measure. Because nothing seemed right. Finally, she settled on a message.

> Angie: Hey you! Was wondering if I'd hear from you or not. My day has been a bit busy, but good. Yours?

She hit send and waited.

And waited.

And waited.

And waited…

"Oh, for fuck's sake!" She put her phone down and went back to her review.

"What's up?"

Angie looked up to see Mark staring at her. She sighed. "Nothing."

"Okay, if you say so." He smirked and turned his attention back to the game on TV.

Angie drew in a deep breath and focused on her laptop screen. The man was not only late in contacting her, he was also bad at replying in a timely manner. Which had Angie's frustration level spiking to epic proportions. Again. *Ugh.*

It didn't matter.

It shouldn't matter.

But dammit, it fucking mattered.

She managed to finish the reviews and email them off to her editor. As she was shutting down her laptop, her phone dinged again. She ignored it until she finished her task. He could wait for her…even if it was only three minutes.

God, boys were stupid. She knew this already. But apparently, grown-ass men were stupid, too.

His HIKE in the mountains and talk with Freddie had helped a little, but then he'd gotten to the bar, and all hell broke loose. Garrett had been more swamped than usual with a major supplier issue, a bathroom issue, inventory, clearing out old stock, and cleaning the bar from top to bottom. He also spent about two hours at Costco stocking up on the essentials and paper supplies.

He'd meant to text Angie earlier, but the day got away from him. Her reply to his message just now had been nice enough, but he had a feeling she was likely a little upset at not hearing from him sooner.

It wasn't personal. He'd been busy. He stared at her response for a moment or two, then set the phone down to grab himself a water from the fridge. Resuming his seat on the couch, he answered her, hoping to smooth any *sore* feelings she might have.

> Garrett: day was busy sorry 4 not texting sooner U have plans later?

Thirty seconds later, she replied. Garrett chuckled. Damn, she's quick.

> Angie: It's fine. No, no plans later. You have something in mind?

> Garrett: dinner? my place

> Angie: Sounds nice. What time and can I bring anything?

Bingo. Garrett smiled as he typed his reply.

> Garrett: 7 just bring me u

> Angie: Got it. BTW: Your punctuation is amazing.

> Garrett: My punctuation? Hmm. Come to dinner at 7 pm, and no, you don't need to bring anything. Satisfied?

> Angie: HAHA! Perfect. Is this where I say: yes, sir?

He chuckled, unable to stop the smile that curved his lips.

> Garrett: ur supposed to call me daddy, remember?

> Angie: Oh, damn. That's right. 😉 Need your address, please?

With the smile now permanently affixed to his face, Garrett sent her his address and then headed to the kitchen to plan their dinner.

After getting everything prepped and the chicken breast in the oven, he went upstairs to grab a shower. Garrett may not have been sure what to do this morning about this thing with her, but now he was going with his gut. It was better than ruminating over her for hours.

Plus, it wasn't like he could help himself; the woman was irresistible. Add to that the extreme chemistry between them, and this, in and of itself, was worth pursuing. If she turned out to be exactly what he feared, the short ride with her would be worth it, provided he kept a shield around his heart.

Shower done, Garrett eyed the button-downs hanging in his closet. He opted for casual instead, donning a pair of faded, clean jeans and T-shirt. Casual was who he was, how he was most comfortable. At the end of the day, even considering his former rock star fame, all the money—which had come and gone, and then come again—plus being the face of his venue, Garrett was just a T-shirt and jeans guy.

He added a squirt of cologne—because he wasn't a total slacker. After pulling his long hair back in a bun, Garrett called it good and made his way back down to the kitchen.

He checked on the chicken and then got the sides ready. Angie was due to arrive in the next twenty minutes, assuming she'd be on time. He grabbed a nice bottle of Sauvignon Blanc from the wine fridge for her, got it set up in an ice bucket on the counter and pulled the cork.

The table was set. The food was on its way out of the oven, and the smooth melodies of Etta James played in the background.

All he needed now was the girl.

In the next moment, Garrett heard a car door close out front. His heart skipped a beat, and he took a moment to compose himself, just a few deep breaths before he made his way to the door. When he got there, he peered out the side-light just as she reached the top of the stairs…and he lost his breath.

Fucking beautiful.

She wore a loose, champagne-colored blouse and a pair of skinny jeans that clung tightly to every inch of her long legs. Her long hair was pulled up on one side; the rest hung in a sleek length down around her shoulder and back.

That same attraction he'd felt for her the first night he saw her flowed through Garrett, and he swallowed as Angie turned around, presumably to take in the view.

Yeah, guarding his heart was paramount, but there was no way he was letting this go yet.

CHAPTER NINE

JEEZUS CHRISPIES, THE MAN HAD TO HAVE MONEY.

Angie got out of the Lyft and made her way up the sloping driveway and then climbed the decorative paver staircase toward a mammoth multi-level, Santa Barbara style house set into the foothills.

The drive had taken close to forty-five minutes, and although she knew she was still in Scottsdale, she was nowhere near the city proper.

When Angie reached the top landing, she circled around to check out the view. The sun was setting…and holy wow. The only thing more breathtaking than the house behind her was the blues and purples blending to pinks, with pale orange and red hues as the sun made its destination downward.

Southern California had pretty sunsets, but Arizona cornered the market on them, hands down. She glanced around. A whole lot of desert surrounded a handful of sizable homes, close enough so you could see them but not too close as to reach out and touch a neighbor. And off in the far, far distance were the lights of the surrounding cities, growing brighter as the sunlight diminished.

Angie heard the door open behind her and glanced over her shoulder with a smile. "Hi there."

"Whatcha doing?" Garrett crossed his arms and leaned against the frame of the door.

"Well—" Man, he looked good. Angie turned and walked toward him. "Not sure if you noticed, but you have this unbelievable view out your front door."

"I've noticed, yes." With a smirk, he glanced past her. "Where's your car?"

"Don't have one." She shrugged and shifted her small purse to her other hand.

His brow furrowed. "You don't have one?"

"Well, technically, I *have* one. But I'm only here for a month, so renting one would cost way too much."

"Wait…a month? Are you moving or something?"

"Oh shit, I just realized." Her eyes went wide. "I never— You don't—" she tilted her head to the side and sighed, "— Hmm. Sounds like we both have some things to share while you feed me."

"Is that so?" He clasped her hand and pulled her to him.

"Mmhmm." Angie leaned against his firm body.

With an arm wrapped around her waist, Garrett looked down at her, his expression heated. "Good to see you."

Angie gazed into his brilliant green eyes, and her stomach did a full somersault. At that, she amended her prior declaration. There was something more breathtaking than the Arizona sunset, and it was Garrett's green eyes. "Good to be seen, Daddy."

Angie barely contained her giggles when he let out a groan. "Okay, no. That's not going to work."

"Mmhmm, you sure about that?" She pressed her lips to his.

And in less than a second, everything around her disappeared and the chemistry between them took center stage. His tongue stroked over hers, and Angie's insides turned to molten lava, lust pooling hot and heavy in her limbs.

God Almighty, she could kiss this man forever.

Sadly, forever came too soon, and Garrett pulled away. "Mmm." He brushed his nose over hers. "You hungry?"

"Yes." She licked her lips, savoring the taste of him.

"Then let's get you fed." After giving her a brief squeeze, Garrett let go of her waist and took her by the hand into his house.

As he pulled her toward what she assumed was likely the kitchen, Angie looked around with wide eyes at his furnishings. The decor was a mix of rustic southwestern and Spanish styles. And it was unbelievably perfect.

Her parents weren't rich by any means, but they weren't poor either. Garrett's house, however, spoke to the money he had yet carried a warm, homey feel to it. Kind of like her parent's home. The money didn't impress her. On the contrary, it was the warmth that did it for her. "Nice little place you got here."

"Thanks. Not what you expected?"

"Didn't know what to expect, really." They entered an enormous kitchen with gorgeous dark wood cabinets and a large square island in the center. Angie stopped short and took in her surroundings. "Wow…my mother would *absolutely* die."

"Oh yeah? She like to cook or just the typical response to a big kitchen?" He smiled and moved to the stove.

"No. I mean, yeah. But she's a professional chef. Don't get me wrong, she's got one hell of a kitchen at home, but she'd die for that stove." She moved beside him. "She'd likely donate both kidneys for the fridge, too."

Garrett laughed as he pulled out a glass dish from the oven. "I probably should've asked." He glanced at her. "I hope you like chicken."

"Would kinda suck if I didn't, huh?" She raised both brows, and a grin tugged at her lips before she shot him a wink. "All good. Meat and poultry eater present and accounted for."

"Uh-huh. More like smart ass present and accounted for, too." He chuckled and set the pan on the stove before moving the food to a platter. "I will confess, I'm a little intimidated now that I know your mother's a chef. My chicken breast could suck."

Angie spotted the bottle of wine on the counter and moved to it. "I'm sure it won't suck. Mind if I grab some wine?"

"Yeah, shit. I appear to be failing at my host duties. Let me grab you a glass."

"I got it. Just point to the correct cabinet." Angie pursed her lips and held her arms out, motioning to the cabinets to her left and right.

"Third cabinet to the right of the sink." He smiled.

Angie found the glasses, pulled two down and then filled both half full. She held one out to him. "Here you go."

"Oh, no, thank you. I don't drink."

"What?" Angie put the glass she'd poured for him down. "But you own a bar."

"You are correct, yes." He pulled foil off a bowl of what looked like sweet potatoes.

She picked his glass back up and sipped from the edge. Guess she was drinking both. And now she knew the answer to the question she'd had last night. If he didn't drink, he likely didn't do drugs either.

But how the hell would she ask that question? *So, you do drugs still?* And if she was going to go there, why not also go with, *so, how were those glory days? Do you miss them?* Not really an eloquent way to go about that line of questioning. Maybe someday, if they became friends, she'd be able to interview him. Just definitely not right now. "You mind if I ask how come?"

With his back turned Garrett answered from the kitchen

table where he was setting the serving dishes. "Long story short, I had one too many that my body and mind didn't handle well when I was younger…so, let's just say I figured out I was allergic."

She tipped her head to the side. "Allergic?"

He faced her. "Yeah. Allergic." He came toward her and touched her arm as he passed. "How's the wine?"

Wow. Okay then. *Really?* "It's good. Great, actually. Thank you." She took a small sip as an awkward feeling crawled over her skin. Maybe she shouldn't drink in front of him? Wasn't that kind of rude or disrespectful? Then again, he was the one who put it out for her. Shit, what if he was just being polite? God, she had no idea. "Can I help you at all?"

"Nope." He stopped and pressed a kiss to her cheek on his way back to the table. "Pretty much got it all set."

Angie moved to the table. "Is this Etta James playing?"

"Yes. Surprised you recognized it."

"Stick around. I'm full of surprises." She set her glass on the table. "Speaking of surprises, this looks delish. And very fancy table setting, too. Did you do all of this yourself?"

"Delish and fancy?" He chuckled and motioned for her to sit. "Of course, I did all of this myself. Guess it'll be ditto on the surprises. I'm sure I've got plenty of my own for you, too."

"That sounds promising." After taking a seat, she folded the napkin on her lap and sat quietly as he took her plate and dished her meal onto it.

When he was done, he served himself and then sat in the seat to her left. She took another sip of her wine and, as they ate, made note of his smooth and easy but precise movements. From the way he set his napkin on his lap to the way he cut into his chicken breast and fed himself a bite, and the way he sipped from his water glass.

All of it done with manners that would make her mother beam from head to toe. Angie had to force herself to pay attention to her meal and not Garrett—and all his surprises.

His behavior was cute and so contrary to what she'd expected that now she had no idea what to expect.

But so far, she was sure enjoying the date—God, she hoped he considered this a date.

GARRETT FIGURED she'd ask him why he wasn't drinking. Although his first instinct, which has shocked the hell out of him, had been to tell her all about why he no longer drank or did drugs, instead, he gave her the standard response when people he didn't know well questioned him.

For whatever reason, and for the first time in years, he worried what someone might think of him—more specifically, what the stunning brunette, with purple highlights he hadn't noticed before now in her hair, thought of him.

"So, quid pro quo?"

He swallowed a mouthful of sweet potatoes before taking a drink of water. "Sounds like a plan."

She nodded. "Before we start, I have to ask. Is this bothering you?" She held up her glass of wine.

"The wine?" He raised his brows, and she nodded. "No. Not at all. Just because I can't drink doesn't mean you can't."

"Okay. Because that wouldn't be cool, you know? I mean —" she shifted in her seat, "—here you are sober, and it's not exactly fair. And if it were me, it would suck."

"I wouldn't go so far as to say 'sober'. I mean, yeah, I don't drink or do drugs anymore, but being sober is a whole other level." He let out a sigh. Apparently, he was going to get into it, after all.

Angie frowned. "How do you mean?"

"Well—" he shrugged. "—I'll just say, people who go to AA or whatever consider themselves to be in recovery and sober. But, people like me, who just stopped and don't go to meetings or whatever?" He shrugged again. "We're just people who don't use drugs or drink anymore."

He drew the line at getting into the politics of it. True, he didn't go to AA or any other 12-step recovery program, and people who did would say he was dry. Not in recovery, not sober, but dry.

To some, the differentiation was a really big deal. To Garrett, it wasn't. As far as he was concerned, as long as he wasn't using or drinking, he was good to go.

"I see." She blew out a breath, and then her beautiful eyes took on a soft expression. "Well, either way, it's really important to me that I don't ever make you uncomfortable."

Their gazes locked, and Garrett's heart damn near melted in his chest as warmth traveled through his body. Fast as he could, he shoved it aside. The tenderness she'd brought forth in him scared the ever-loving shit out of him, and there was no way he could allow that much feeling to take up residence within him. But he also couldn't let the thoughtfulness of her concern go ignored either. Dammit.

Garrett covered her hand with his palm. "It's all good. I promise. So, don't sweat it."

She let out a sigh. "Okay."

"Tell me about only being here for a month." He really did want to know about this. When she'd said it before, he'd been completely shocked. Angie only staying in town for a month changed things. In fact, it changed everything.

She smiled and sipped her wine. "Right. Well, I don't live here. I'm visiting Celia and Mark. He's graduating from ASU in two weeks. Whole family will be here for that. Then I'll stay another two weeks and head back home."

There it was. Garrett didn't have to worry if she was sniffing around or about his heart. He could just enjoy his time with her, have fun and then be done. He smiled. "Where's home?"

"Los Angeles. More specifically, South Pasadena." She

took a bite of her food, and once she swallowed, she continued. "Okay, my turn."

"Hit me." He wiped his mouth.

"I don't think you want me to do that. Seriously, I pack a mean right hook." She winked. "All right... How old are you?"

"Bad form!"

"It is not! It's totally fair." She giggled. "You asked me the other night, so now I'm asking you."

"Fair enough." He sipped his water. "I'm forty-six."

She raised a single brow. "You don't look a day over twenty-five."

"Smart ass. Told you, I'm old."

She sipped her wine and then grinned. "Mmhmm. Forty-six is not old. Your turn, Daddy."

Garrett smothered a laugh. "What's your favorite color?"

With a forkful of sweet potatoes on her way to her mouth, she paused. "Seriously? Of all the things you can ask, that's what you're going with?"

"What? It's a valid question." He chuckled.

"Well, honestly, I don't really have a favorite color. Favorites and me, we don't mix. I can never decide."

He tilted his head to the side, regarding her. "Interesting."

"It's weird, I know."

"Not at all." He loaded up his fork. "Your turn."

She sat back in her seat. "Okay, how about you tell me about Copper Seven?"

Shit. Garrett tensed, then cleared his throat and wiped his mouth with his napkin. "Wondered how long it would take you to figure it out. Or did you already know?"

"No. I didn't know. It hit me after you mentioned the band the other night. Though, considering...I should've realized it."

What did that mean? He leaned forward, resting his elbows on the table. "Considering?"

"Mm-Mm." She shook her head. "You still haven't answered my question."

"Right, right. Forgive me, ma'am." He smirked, reminding himself it was only a month; no point in pushing the matter. "Well, shit. There's a lot to tell. Anything specific you want to know?"

"Are you relieved it's over?"

"Wow, I've had plenty of people ask if I miss it, but no one has ever asked me if I don't." He swallowed some water. "It was fun, you know, for a while. But then it was crazy. Lots of partying. Too much partying. Then it wasn't fun anymore." Garrett placed his napkin on the table as the memories of his days with his former bandmates played behind his eyes.

It felt like forever since he'd seen or heard from the members of Copper Seven. Even longer since the days of sleeping—or passing out—in a tour bus and waking up—usually hung over—in a different city was a daily occurrence.

Of course, it wasn't all bad. He'd gotten to see and do some pretty spectacular things. But in the end, Garrett self-destructed, lost in a drug and alcohol-induced haze, and unfortunately, the rest of the members were spiraling out of control, too, so the band hadn't survived it. "I got tired, and I got sloppy."

He'd made it a point not to think about that time in his life. He didn't think about his ex-wife and her death either. Even if the band had survived all of their madness, he wouldn't ever want to go back, and thinking about it would get him nowhere but depressed…maybe even back in a bottle or a pile of drugs. He didn't need that.

"You earned yourself quite a reputation."

Pulled from his unplanned trip down memory lane, Garrett looked at her. Only a month or not, the doubts he had and what she might be after from him crept up his neck, making his skin itch. "I did, yes. But that guy? He's long gone. So, if that's who you're looking for, he doesn't live here anymore." Garrett stood. "In fact, he never lived here." Picking up his plate, he moved from the table and placed it on the counter next to the sink.

"Hey, whoa. What just happened?"

He heard her get up and come over to him. Instead of answering or looking at her, Garrett pressed his fists to the countertop and leaned toward the window, staring out into the darkness beyond.

Right then, he wasn't sure if he was truly annoyed with her or if the regret he'd tried to bury had come back to pay a visit, rearing its ugly head. He just knew his heart was racing, pounding in his ears.

"Listen, I'm not sure I understand what just happened, but I'm sorry if I said something wrong. I'm not looking for that guy. I don't even know that guy. Hell, I barely know you." She placed a hand on his upper back, and he flinched but forced himself to relax. "And for the record, it's you I'd like to get to know better."

Garrett looked over his shoulder at her. Sincerity infused her expression, and he saw the truth of her words in her eyes —her unique mismatched, brown and hazel eyes. "I'm not what you need, Angie."

"First, you bite my head off, and now you're going to tell me what I need?" She stepped to his side, leaned a hip against the counter and crossed her arms.

"Sorry for biting your head off." He turned to face her.

"Apology accepted. But tell me, Garrett, how is it you think you have the right to tell me what I need? Let's see… because you're older, so therefore, that makes you some sort of authority? Damn the patriarchy and their assumptions."

Garrett snorted. "Well, as I said, I am old enough to be your father."

She threw her head back and let out a harsh, clipped laugh. "You know, *that* particular dynamic keeps coming up. Makes me wonder what games might await me in the bedroom." She grinned, a devilish little glint in her eyes. "True, you may be old enough to be my father, but guess what, *Daddy*—"

His dick stirred behind his zipper at her use of the term. Garrett let out an exasperated sigh, but she continued right over him.

"—I already have a father, a good one, so that role's filled. And also, I don't have 'daddy' issues, so I guess that angle won't work either. So far, your reasoning holds no water."

Garrett raised his gaze to the ceiling and blew out a breath. "And she argues again."

"I save my fights for when I know I'm right."

He returned his focus to her, hooked an arm around her waist and pulled her to his body. Of course, her soft curves molded against him perfectly. "Yeah? I think you fight no matter what."

"No. Not no matter what, but as you already know, definitely for what I want." Angie ran a fingertip down the side of his neck. The light touch sent shivers down his spine.

"You've mentioned that." Garrett couldn't help the grin that formed. She had a fire burning in her eyes, one he could feel licking at his skin, and he wanted to play with the flames. "What you want and what you need are two different things, you know."

She stepped from his embrace, dropped her arms and glanced down her body. With slow, exaggerated movements, she ran her palms up her denim-clad hips to her waist, then up her torso, stopping right beneath her breasts before piercing him with another fiery gaze. "Seeing as though I'm a fully grown woman, I think I get to decide what I need and want."

Unable to hold back anymore, Garrett hooked an arm around her waist and pulled her body against his again, this time with a little more force. He wanted her there, maybe even needed her there. God, he didn't want to think about that. "And what is it you believe you want?"

She splayed her fingers over his chest. "You."

Garrett's thought processes had already gone haywire when he had her in his arms moments ago, but now, after witnessing her hands do what he'd been wanting to do since she'd arrived? No way he was waiting another minute.

He let his gaze roam over her features and then settle on her lips. Bastard that he was, there was no way Garrett would turn her away tonight—or any other night, even if he knew he had nothing more than his body to offer her for the next month.

Hopefully, Angie wouldn't want more than he was capable of giving because, in the end, when he denied her, it might just break them both. Granted, with all his past baggage, he was already broken. Angie, on the other hand, wasn't.

With a hard mental shove, he banished his conscience to a dark corner of his mind and…took her lips in a hard kiss.

CHAPTER TEN

Angie wasn't just being kissed. *She was being kissed.*

The intensity rolling off Garrett from the moment his lips pressed hard to hers was almost too much to take. But she wanted more…oh, so much more. It was unexpected and overwhelming and beautiful in the same way that a summer storm could be.

One moment he was looking at her, his expression almost blank, unreadable. And in the next, she was pressed against his body, and he was possessing her mouth as if he'd been starving for her forever.

After turning and backing her up against the counter, Garrett broke the frenzied kiss, panting as he stared down at her. "This what you want?"

"Mmhmm." She caught his bottom lip and sucked.

"I can't make you any promises."

"Not looking for promises." She ran her palm up the back of his neck and grinned. "I'll take an orgasm or two, though."

Once more, his lips tugged into a small grin. Small or not, she loved those little smiles she drew from him. It made her want to do anything she could just to see one. He smoothed a warm hand down her waist and around to her ass. "I want to touch you everywhere."

"Good because it's been a really long time since I've been touched."

"I'll have to remedy that. You try and keep up."

Angie raised both brows, and a giggle escaped. One minute, he's complaining about how young she is, and in the next breath, he's telling *her* to keep up? A little mental whiplash never hurt anyone, right? Alrighty then. "Show me what you got, Daddy."

Another grin and a low snort. "Jesus. You're gonna have to stop with that."

"*Ohhkaaay, fiiinnne.*" Angie tossed him an exaggerated eye roll. But the grin he gave her—her reward for the smart-ass comment—had every inch of her skin smoldering with desire.

Garrett took her hand and pulled her out of the kitchen, through the entryway, and upstairs.

This was it; no doubt they were going to have sex. And Angie had to admit she was a tad nervous. What would he be like? Gentle? Rough? Something in between? God, she didn't even care.

Call it completely cliché, but there was serious chemistry between them, so there was no way the sex would be bad. On the contrary, it would probably send her into some fourth dimension of sexual ecstasy.

With her mind racing a million miles an hour, anxious energy blasted through her. She licked her lips and drew in a deep breath.

The lights were off in his room, and Garrett led her to the bed, sat and pulled Angie between his parted legs. She had a fraction of a moment to take in the huge, uncovered windows across from them. The reflection of herself in the glass and the darkness beyond made her feel anonymous— And then he tugged her down to his lips again.

With a moan, she fell…

Angie let every part of herself fall into the amazing force of Garrett.

His taste, his feel, his scent—all of him filled her system, dousing her nervous energy and replacing it with undiluted, high-octane lust. With his tongue tangled around hers, he slid both hands beneath her loose blouse and cupped her breasts before grazing her nipples through the satin cups of her bra with his thumbs.

A lightning rod of lust struck her clit, and her stomach clenched at the erotic sensations vibrating through her. She jerked against him and gripped his shoulders. Garrett lay back on the mattress, and Angie followed, climbing onto the bed and straddling his hips. She broke the kiss and straightened to gaze down at him.

With his hands still up her loose top, he licked his lips. "Take this off for me."

The man didn't have to ask twice. Without hesitation, Angie pulled her top over her head and dropped it beside them on the bed. Then she unclasped her bra and removed it, too. The cool air in the room hardened her nipples further, and she ached for him to touch them again.

Garrett's eyes were wide as he gazed at her naked chest. "Beautiful."

The whispered word feathered over her skin as he slowly cupped her breasts like he'd done before. The heat of his big palms spread over every inch of her torso, drawing a shiver from her.

When he stroked his thumbs over her tight, bare nipples, Angie couldn't help the gasp that rushed out of her. His touch was light but not at all timid. The man knew what he was doing and how to do it.

"Sweet torture," she whispered as she bent forward and took his lips, shifting her pelvis to rub against the erection she felt through their jeans.

Garrett's hands landed on her ass, and he rolled his hips in response. Oh, God, how she wanted this, wanted him.

GARRETT PLANTED a heel in the mattress and rolled Angie to her back. Fuck's sake, she was on fire. So sexy, he thought he might spontaneously combust before he got them both naked. As he settled his body alongside hers, he gazed down at her in the dim light of his bedroom.

She pulled the tie from his hair and ran her fingers through the length. "Your hair is so soft."

"Ditto." He ran his fingers through her dark locks, then traced the arch of one of her brows with a fingertip, and then continued down her cheek and along her jawline. "I'm betting every part of you is soft." Moving down her slender neck, Garrett settled his palm on her breastbone, absorbing the feel of her heated skin.

When he grazed his knuckles over each hardened nipple, she arched and drew in a sharp breath. So responsive. So perfect. After sliding his palm down to her tight stomach, he bent his head and took one dark, peaked tip between his lips.

"Garrett..." The word was a raspy whisper carried on a gasp, and he felt her fingers tighten in his hair.

"Mmm." The little sting at his scalp sent a bolt of lust to his dick, which was already aching behind his zipper. The scent of her skin and the sweet taste of her nipple only served to drive him higher.

He wanted to take his time, make it last, but fucking hell, Angie was pushing all his buttons. Scary thing was, he had a feeling she had no idea the power she held.

Angie tugged at his shirt as he continued to suck her nipple. "I need this off you. Please, Garrett? I need to feel your skin."

He obliged her, releasing her breast long enough to tug his

shirt over his head. As he did that, she managed to get her jeans undone and shoved down her long, long legs. *Fuck me.*

"Jesus, those legs. I have no idea how you got those off so fast, but I'm grateful." She giggled, and Garrett felt it in his groin. He rose from the bed and turned to face her. "Lethal weapons."

"My legs?" She gazed up at him, raised one leg, and trailed the tips of her toes down his chest.

Garrett grabbed her foot and slid a hand down to her calf, massaging the muscle there. "Your legs *and* your hair."

"Hmm, never thought of them as weapons. But I suppose — Oh God, that feels good."

"Not as good as you feel to me." Garrett bent and pressed his lips to the inside of her knee as he ran both palms along the sides of her thighs. "I want to kiss and touch every inch of these." He slid his hands along the tops of her legs and then onto her inner thighs, opening her to him.

With two fingers, he stroked over the cloth covering her pussy. The fabric was damp, and a growl punched out of him before he could stop it. He needed to taste her. Garrett pulled the fabric aside, bent and dragged his tongue through her bare folds.

Angie's hips shot off the mattress, and her hands landed on his head, her fingers tangling in his hair again. "Oh fuck, yes! Fuck, Garrett!"

Jesus Christ, she was like heaven on his tongue. Garrett licked through her sweetness again before drawing her clit into his mouth. He needed this first. Then he needed inside her. Determination was the only thing forcing him to keep his pace slow. He wanted to make this last, but also call it self-preservation—when he got inside the heat of her, he might never be the same again.

Garrett pulled away only long enough to yank her panties off and then positioned between her legs again. "Fuck, you taste perfect, and I love that you're bare."

With his mouth back on her tight clit, Garrett circled the mouth of her cunt with two fingers. The sounds of her low moans had his cock jerking in the confines of his jeans. He slid his fingers inside, stroking her slick channel with a deliberate slowness.

He looked up at her and licked his lips, absolutely drunk on the taste and scent of her. "So tight. Sweet and tight."

"Garrett, please…I need you. Please?" She gripped his hair, pulling him toward her.

Once again, the sting shot a bolt of pleasure through him. The physical reaction shocked him. He didn't usually like his hair pulled. Plenty of women had tried over the years, and it was the fastest way to kill the moment for him.

Not this time.

Not this woman.

Angie's use of his hair to make her plea known dumped gas on the already blazing fire in his veins. Garrett rose over her and found her mouth. She licked and sucked at his lips as she undid his jeans, freeing his cock.

The warmth of her palm when she wrapped her slender fingers around his shaft and stroked his length almost had him coming all over her belly. "Angie…"

"Now. Need you inside me now." She kissed him again, shoving her tongue into his mouth and, at the same time, pulled him—literally by his dick—to her pussy.

"Fuck. Angie…" Already drowning in the sweet taste of her arousal, and now once more her mouth, the head of Garrett's cock met the slick lips of her cunt, and he pressed forward. *Oh, fuck, yesss. There she is.*

He should've stopped.

He should've put on a condom.

He knew that. Knew it was important.

But when her tight, wet heat enveloped the head of his prick, *he could not fucking stop.*

"Oh, yes. Baby—fuck, yes!" Angie tilted her hips forward,

meeting him pelvis to pelvis as he seated himself deep inside her.

Garrett dropped his face to her neck and drew in a strangled breath, trying for all it was worth to push back the orgasm which had immediately boiled to the surface.

So tight, so wet. So *fucking* hot.

She squeezed her thighs around him ever so slightly, and he bit down on her shoulder. Her sweet little cunt, her hot-as-hell body, the scent and taste of her skin…everything about her overwhelmed Garrett in a way that made every muscle in his body tighten with lust.

Angie shifted again and slid her hands down his spine to his ass, grabbed hold and rolled her hips. "Fuck me, Garrett."

"Have mercy on a man, Angela." Garrett gritted his teeth.

She giggled, and Garrett felt it arrow straight to his balls. Damn. After drawing in one more breath, Garrett started moving.

What began as slow and even thrusts quickly escalated to a fast and frantic rhythm. His orgasm tingled at the base of his spine, and his cock grew harder with each slide along the slick walls of her pussy.

Angie moaned, her warm breath ghosting over his ear and neck. Her hard nipples, another heavenly torment, glided against his sweat-slick chest.

Garrett groaned and ran a palm along her thigh to her ass. "Perfect…you are fucking perfect. Look at me. I want to watch your eyes when I'm inside you."

Angie did as he asked, her warm, dual-colored eyes focused on his, and he felt something shift inside him.

She rolled her hips, grinding her clit against his pelvis. Then dug her nails into his ass cheeks before dragging them up his back, making him even hotter for her. Garrett rose on a forearm and kept his gaze locked with hers. She cupped his cheek in her palm and bit down on her bottom lip as he pumped into her.

The sight of her teeth on her sweet flesh sent tingles racing down his spine and then straight to his dick. "Want to bite that for you."

"Do it." Angie pulled him down to her mouth, and he took what she offered and more.

Faster.

Deeper.

Hotter.

Fuck...*fuck!*

He was going to come.

INTENSE... God, this was so far beyond intense, Angie could barely think straight.

Garrett was between her parted legs, buried deep in her pussy, screwing her *ever-loving brains out*. About all she could do, besides pant, moan, gasp and whimper, was plant her heels in the mattress, move with him and go exactly where he was leading her.

Which clearly was orgasm heaven.

And his cock? God help her... When Angie wrapped her hand around that unbelievably rock-hard, perfect shaft, she'd let out a gasp that sounded a whole lot like she'd witnessed the second coming.

It was all she could do not to cry out in a resounding hallelujah! Followed by a thank you, baby Jesus! He was the perfect size. Average. Normal. As in not too big. Some women loved big cock, it was all they could talk about, but not Angie. She'd had enough of them to know that the old saying: anything more than a mouthful was a waste, was damn true.

Men may've been referring to breast size with the statement, but for Angie, it applied to penis size. Hands down, average, or even a little on the slightly less-than-average side, was always better.

Translation: Lots of sex and none of the soreness. Lots of blow jobs, with none of the gag reflex. Fucking perfect!

Aside from that, clearly, she'd lost her mind because he wasn't wearing a condom. She hadn't asked him to, never even mentioned it. And she *did not* have one fuck to give. His bare prick stroking her inner walls was the definition of divine. There was no way in hell she'd abide a barrier between them after this. Ever.

But more than all that, he'd made everything more intimate by insisting she keep her eyes on him. It made the pull she felt toward him so much more intense than it already was.

It was all too much, and she wanted to look away. She needed to. But she couldn't bring herself to, couldn't get enough of what was swirling between them.

Swept away in the storm of feelings, both emotional and physical, Angie raised her knees higher, which changed the angle of her pelvis and sent his shaft deeper. "Ba*ybby——nnggh-hohgodyess*!" She gripped his ass. "*Ohhh fuuuckkkk! Fuuuckkk!*"

Garrett let out a growl, dropped his head and bit into the side of her neck. She arched beneath him, completely at his mercy, as he slid one hand down to her hip and gripped her flesh hard.

Angie's clit throbbed, and her stomach tightened as the heat of her impending climax built higher. So close… Holy hell, his cock was stroking nerve endings she never knew existed, spawning tingles inside her she'd never felt before. God, yes, she was going to come—

"*Fuck!*" Abruptly, Garrett jerked away from her. "*Dammit!*"

The sudden loss of his body heat was profound, and a cool chill zipped over her, pebbling her skin with goosebumps. She tried to get her aroused head back online. "What's the matter? Are you okay?"

He was panting and covering his dick with his hand. "Yes. I just…holy shit. I…" He bent to the side, grabbed his T-shirt and placed it over his crotch.

"Did you…" She rose on her elbows.

"I did. Fuck. Yeah, but apparently—" He glanced down and pulled the wadded shirt away. "—Apparently, I'm still hard." Garrett climbed onto the bed, lay on his back beside her and then pulled her over him. "C'mere. We're not done."

"Oh, wow!" As Angie shifted into place astride his hips, one leg dragged over the very large wet spot he'd left on the bed when he came. Garrett pulled her down to his lips and slid the bulbous head inside her cunt. Her breath rushed out with a moan, and her head fell back as she slid down his hard cock. "Holy. Fuck."

"Yeah, no. I'm definitely *not* done with you." Garrett sat up, cupped one of her breasts in his palm and sucked the taut nipple between his lips.

Angie rocked her hips, grinding her clit against his pelvic bone as his length slid back and forth within her. She threaded her fingers through his hair, pulling him to her chest and pressed her lips to the side of his head.

When she came, it was going to be like an out-of-body experience.

Tension bloomed low in her belly, building and then uncurling to climb up her spine. They moved together, their pace increasing with each gasp and moan.

"Garrett…" she breathed and gripped the back of his hair.

"Ride it, baby. Come for me." Garrett looked up at her and then took her lips as he grabbed her ass cheeks and ground her against him, sliding her faster along his shaft.

Tingles raced along her skin, and sweat slid down her spine.

Faster.

Hotter.

Harder—

"Give it to me."

"Oh, God!" Angie's orgasm broke free. Endless waves of

pleasure flowed through her. Clit spasming, her cunt clenching down on his cock, over and over and over again. With her forehead planted on his shoulder, Angie squeezed her eyes closed and gasped for air as she rode the tremors echoing through her body.

A few minutes passed before her breathing returned to normal. But the buzzing in her head remained. Yeah, definitely an out-of-body experience. The haze from her orgasm made her feel a bit like she was floating.

Garrett stroked the back of her hair, then trailed his fingertips down her spine. "You okay?"

Angie raised her head and pressed a soft kiss to his neck. "Mmm. Perfect." She smiled. "But I don't think I can move."

He wrapped his arms around her waist. "That's okay, I don't want you to move."

She tipped her head back and gazed at him. "That was kinda incredible."

"Yeah. It was." One corner of his mouth twitched in a small grin, and he cupped her cheek in his palm.

Angie touched her mouth to his in a languid kiss. The sex was incredible—beyond incredible, actually.

He was amazing. They were amazing together.

Better than amazing.

Perfect.

The sex had been as close to perfect as she'd ever come. And the connection between them? She'd never felt anything like it before.

CHAPTER ELEVEN

After getting cleaned up and into his pajamas, Garrett crawled beneath the sheets and spooned up behind Angie. Her body was warm through the T-shirt he'd given her to wear as she settled back against him and let out a sigh. Her body jerked a little, and then her breathing deepened as she fell fully into sleep.

Still trying to process what'd gone down between them, he pressed his nose to the back of her hair and breathed her in. Yeah, sex had happened, but there was more to it than that.

First off, they hadn't used a condom, and he knew better than to do that. He knew he was clean, and Garrett hoped she was too, but in general, it was irresponsible. Christ, what if she wasn't on the pill? A baby at this stage of his life was out of the question.

Second, without that added layer of latex, he'd come way too fast. Way too fucking fast. Reason being, she felt way too good. All wet and warm, it was more than Garrett could handle.

But talk about losing your man-card. What a fucking chump. Jesus, Garrett had lost total control with her, and before he'd been able to get himself reeled back from the edge, his orgasm rushed to the surface like a bat out of hell. Thank you very much, Meatloaf.

Garrett had been straight-up mortified, at least until he realized his dick was still in the game—strange and out of the ordinary for him. But for whatever reason, the powers that be had smiled on him and returned his man-card, so he went with it.

Now he was curled up behind her, in his bed, darkness surrounding both of them, and he was…

One-hundred. Percent. Spooked.

Not from the lack of condom or the premature gunfire, and definitely not because the sex had been *really* fucking off the charts good. Nope, all that he could deal with.

It was what he felt swirling between them during the act that'd blown his mind and had him ready to run and hide. It was a chemistry he'd never shared with anyone, ever.

Kissing her, touching her, feeling her body move…all of it had drawn each moment into sharp focus.

Angie being the focal point.

Angie being everything.

It was the eye contact that'd done it. Christ, he'd asked her for it, too—though he had no idea what he was getting himself into because when their eyes locked, Garrett fell so deep into all of her, Angie's very soul, he was terrified he'd never be able to find his way out.

It scared him to think he might be that into her already. From a physical perspective, Angie checked all his boxes. But emotions took time. Building a connection took time. Pace, staying in sync, interests, lifestyle…these were all things that needed to be in place for a connection and emotions to grow.

There was no way that connection could have grown already.

But yet…

He liked her, for sure. No doubt. But it wasn't supposed to be like this. She was only going to be there for a month, for

Christ's sake. There wasn't supposed to be this kind of connection. Chemistry, sure. But connection? No way.

Panic sped through Garrett's veins. If he planned to continue this with her for the next month, guarding his heart was even more important than he thought. What swirled between them was relationship-level stuff, and he had no intention of going there with her—or anyone.

This was why, on the rare occasion when he did date, he kept things casual. No expectations. No deep commitment. Definitely no connection. Jesus, what the hell was he doing?

As thoughts bounced back and forth through Garrett's mind like a tennis match, he blew out a breath and tried to slow the train. He closed his eyes and focused on matching his breathing to hers…

After a couple of minutes, he opened his eyes. Unable to lie still, Garrett ran the flat of his hand down her arm to her hip. As much as the thought that this could turn into more scared him, the idea of *not* having *something* with Angie upset him, too.

Which was baffling. Maybe she'd be good with just doing the casual thing with him for the next month? Maybe she was one of those highly independent women who were more interested in growing her career and standing on her own two feet than she was in a full-blown boyfriend or, more, a husband or, God help him, kids.

Yes, all of that was possible. But not probable. Angie was young and smart. She had her whole life ahead of her. The last thing she needed was to get saddled with some old dude who wasn't willing to commit.

Fucking hell, why was he going there? She didn't even live in Arizona. Irritation settled at the base of his spine like an annoying itch, and Garrett let out an aggravated grunt. He needed to cool his damn jets.

Obsessing over something, anything, was the shortest road to insanity. Trying to "figure out" what to do when he should be enjoying what was in front of him, namely, the smart, witty, and incredibly hot woman in his bed, was also insanity.

Giving up, he pressed his nose to the back of her hair and, once again, breathed her in. He wasn't sure what shampoo she used, but he loved it. With a small moan, she shifted and snuggled her ass a little closer, pressing against his groin. Garrett spread his palm over her tummy and closed his eyes.

Damn. They fit.

CHAPTER TWELVE

ANGIE WOKE TO THE EARLY MORNING LIGHT SHINING THROUGH Garrett's unobstructed windows. The view was incredible, but holy shit, the sun was bright as hell. She glanced over her shoulder to find Garrett on his back beside her, still asleep.

She gazed at him a moment, in awe of how beautiful she found him and, at the same time, wrestling with the desire to scoot out of his bed and clean herself up before he woke. Lord knew she must look like a hot-mess: makeup all smeared, hair all tangled and oh-so-attractive. No thank you.

She rolled her eyes at her foolishness. There was no reason to let her mind wander down a rabbit hole of insecurity. This wasn't some young, shallow guy she was lying next to. Garrett was a grown man and likely knew by now that women didn't wake up all perfect and flawless.

Angie rotated to face him. Besides, his hair was going in all sorts of directions, too. She wasn't alone on the hot-mess express.

She placed her hand on his chest, feeling his heartbeat beneath her palm before she slid it down to his stomach. He stirred from her touch and exhaled through his nose before opening his eyes and peering over at her.

Angie smiled and kissed his cheek. "Morning."

"Mmm." He cupped the back of her head and cleared his throat. "You want coffee?"

She snuggled a little closer. "Yes, please."

"I'll go make some. Stay here." He pressed a kiss to the top of her head before rolling away and getting out of bed.

Angie pulled the blankets higher. "But you don't know how I like it."

He checked his phone, then set it back on the nightstand. "So, tell me how you like it?"

"Very light and very sweet. But it depends on what kind of cream you have." She smiled.

"Light and sweet, huh? Okay, I have half and half."

"Ah. Then definitely very sweet." She winked. "Some creams are sweeter than others."

"You can say that again." He leaned on the bed and pressed a soft kiss to her forehead. "Yours is damn sweet."

"Nice." Shaking her head, Angie giggled as Garrett shot her a grin before he made his way out of the room.

Not willing to lose her shot, she gave in to her urge and hopped from the bed, heading into his master bath. This was her chance to at least use the bathroom and maybe find some mouthwash, and she wasn't going to waste it.

After taking care of business in the toilet closet, she moved to the sink, washed her hands, and then ran her wet fingers through her knotted hair. She leaned close to the mirror. Jeezus chrispies, hot-mess was an understatement.

Did she always look this bad in the morning? And if so, how the hell had she not noticed before now? Angie ran her fingertips beneath her eyes, trying to remove some of the smeared mascara that had her giving raccoons a run for their money.

After doing the best she could with her eyes, she pulled open the vanity cabinet doors, locating the mouthwash. Three cheers for fresh breath!

As Angie finished up, a small smile arched her lips as memories of last night played through her mind. Every hot moment of sex had been incredible with him. Every damn moment. Heat spilled through her, settling low in her tummy.

Screw the day-old makeup and screw the hair, neither mattered.

Suddenly, all Angie wanted was to have sex with Garrett again. Maybe a few more times. He'd bring her coffee in bed. Which was incredibly sweet, and in return, she'd give him a good morning blowjob.

Because, really, what better way to show a man how grateful you were to him than a good, old-fashioned blowjob in the morning?

Aware of how fifties housewife that might seem to someone else, Angie had no fucks to give about what someone else might think. In her opinion, not being afraid to go after what she wanted was more "independent woman" than anything.

Besides, sucking cock was something Angie loved to do. As a result, they'd both get something out of her taking his dick down her throat. Equal rights for everyone involved. What the hell could be more independent woman than that? Not much.

Angie emerged from the bathroom feeling quite sure of herself with a fire, fueled by lust, smoldering in her belly. Right as she climbed onto his bed, Garrett walked into the room.

He set the small tray in his hands, with two coffee cups and two yogurts on it, down on the nightstand. "Brought you a yogurt, too." He handed her one of the coffee cups.

"I see that. Thank you." She settled on her knees and sipped the light caramel-colored liquid.

He opened one of the yogurts. "Did I make it right?"

"Mmhmm." She swallowed. "Perfect, actually."

He handed her the open yogurt along with a spoon—which was incredibly sweet—before moving to sit in the chair situated in the corner by the windows. Guess he wasn't joining her on the mattress. Hmm…

"Thanks." Angie set the coffee down on the table at her side of the bed and swirled the spoon in the yogurt. "What time is it?"

He sipped his coffee and set the cup down on the floor beside him. "A little after eight."

She groaned. "Too early. You always get up this early?" She spooned some yogurt into her mouth.

"No. Usually earlier."

"Earlier? I guess that's why you don't use curtains in here."

He raised an eyebrow, stirring his yogurt. "Why obstruct the view?" He spooned up a mouthful and swallowed. "The light doesn't bother me, and it's not like I have neighbors behind me."

She gazed out at the hillside that slowly rose into mountains. "Might be a few snakes or coyotes spying. I've heard they can be quite the peeping Toms."

He let out a chuckle before sipping his coffee. "It's all rumors."

"No, I'm serious. I read it the other day. There's been a ton of night vision binocular-wearing coyotes spotted all over the valley."

"Is that so?" This time, when he chuckled, it was almost a full laugh, but not quite.

"Mmhmm." She swallowed a spoonful of yogurt. The man either didn't find her as funny as Angie thought she was, or he was doing a damn good job of keeping a lid on his reactions to her.

No matter which, both sucked.

Angie frowned and took another sip of her coffee and just watched him as he sat quietly with his plaid pajama bottoms and T-shirt covering his lean body. After swallowing another mouthful of coffee, she stuck out her tongue at him and set the cup down beside the yogurt on the nightstand.

That got her another slight grin from him. Good enough. It was time to move to the next subject. Angie cleared her throat. "So, we didn't use a condom last night. Should I be worried about that?"

"I haven't had sex without a condom in over twenty years."

Angie's eyes went wide. "Seriously? Then why didn't you with me?"

"When the girl wants her cock, she wants her cock." He grinned and licked the yogurt off the back of his spoon.

"This is probably true." She laughed, liking his statement a little too much for her own good. Pushing the feeling aside, she continued. "Well, so you know, I'm on the pill, and I've been celibate for the last year, so we're good."

"A year? Wow. Care to share why?"

"Absolutely, but not right now." Clad in the T-shirt he'd given her last night, Angie slid off the bed and moved toward him. "Very sweet of you to bring me breakfast in bed, Garrett."

"You're welcome, Angie." He eyed her as she moved closer.

When she reached him, she placed her hands on his knees and bent forward, coming eye level with him. "Even though you made me sit alone while I ate, I figure I should show you exactly how grateful I am."

He smirked. "Far be it for me to turn away a demonstration of gratitude."

"Mmhmm. I thought you might feel that way." She rubbed her nose over his and then kissed him.

Garrett cupped her face in his palms as she went to her knees between his parted legs. Once again, his kiss sent her mind spinning. He kissed her with such passion, such intensity, Angie didn't think she'd ever get enough of his mouth on hers.

Sliding her hands down his chest, she was pleasantly surprised to find his cock already fully erect and tenting his pajama bottoms. Angie smiled against his lips and gripped the shaft through the thin fabric.

Garrett nipped her bottom lip. "What you got there?"

"Exactly what I was hoping for." Angie licked over where he'd bitten her and glanced down to where her hand held his shaft. She could feel the heat of him through the fabric, and her mouth watered at the prospect of that beautiful length gliding over her tongue.

"Mmm. What are you planning to do with it?"

She tugged the drawstring on his pants and pulled the waistline away from his body, revealing his solid shaft. "I'm going to suck it until you cum down my throat."

Garrett's whole body jerked, and he let out a low groan. "I think I like your version of gratitude." He leaned back and placed his hands behind his head.

"Just to clarify." She held his gaze and took his rock-hard prick in her palm. "I'm greedy. This is for both of us."

Garrett licked his lips and ran his fingers through her hair. "By all means, take what you want."

"So kind of you." Keeping her eyes on his, Angie bent forward and licked over the swollen head. The salty bead of arousal lingering at the tip coated her tongue, and she swallowed with a low moan before curling her tongue around the rim.

His dick bobbed a little as Garrett sucked in a harsh breath. Yes! This is exactly what she wanted. With everything he'd made her feel last night, she wanted to give him the same. Damn near every time he touched her, she'd gone breathless, boneless and utterly at his mercy.

Angie wanted him at her mercy, too.

Stroking once from root to tip, she ran her tongue around the edge again, then teased the slit at the tip with her tongue, tasting his pre-cum again. Moaning, she licked down and then back up the length.

With a deep groan, Garrett lightly gripped her hair at the back of her head. "Suck my cock, Angie."

Oh, hell fucking yes!

Angie closed her eyes and drew the bulbous crown between her lips and sucked. His fingers twitched at the back of her head, almost as if he wanted to grip the strands harder, maybe even pull her hair. Angie moaned. She wanted that. Hell, she wanted anything he was willing to give her.

Arousal pumped through her veins in time with her racing heart, the heavy beat arrowing straight to her clit, and she knew her panties were soaked. Reveling in the taste and scent of him, Angie took him deep into her mouth before rising back to the rim, swirling her tongue around the ridge of the head and then swallowing him to the back of her throat again.

God, he felt good, tasted good, too, and Angie moaned her appreciation with her lips pulled tight around his dick. She could do this all-fucking-day. And maybe she would.

CHAPTER THIRTEEN

Angie stepped out of the dressing room and spun in a small circle in front of Celia. "What do you think?"

"Wow! I freaking love that color on you!" Celia took a step closer. "The mint green really looks pretty against your skin."

Angie let out a giggle as she turned again and gazed in the mirror. "I'm kind of loving it, too." She glanced at Celia through the mirror. "Thanks for coming shopping with me. I know it's not your fav."

"Don't mention it." Celia crossed her arms. "To anyone. No, really. Anyone. I mean it." She stared at Angie, a serious expression on her face, before she finally smirked.

Angie laughed. "Whatever. Dork." She stepped back into the dressing room. "Only one more. I promise."

"Thank God. I'm starving."

Angie closed the curtain, took off the mint green pin-up style dress and hung it back on the hanger. "We just ate. Didn't we?" She checked her phone for a message from Garrett. Nothing as of yet, so she stepped into the yellow chiffon dress.

"Breakfast was four hours ago. If you can call one piece of

toast and coffee breakfast. My hangover is finally gone, and I need real food now. You need help in there?"

"Nah, I got it." Angie smoothed down the front of the flowy material before drawing the curtain back. "Mine's gone, too. It's been four hours?"

"Yes." Her sister frowned and tilted her head to the side. "So, that one's totally opposite of the other. But it's pretty, too. I like it." Celia nodded with a smile.

"Are you sure your hangover is gone?" Angie laughed. "You're not usually this…accommodating. Maybe it wasn't a hangover, and you're getting sick? We should see if you're coming down with something."

Celia shook her head and rolled her eyes. "Don't make me leave you here."

"Har, har. Okay, so you think this works for Mark's graduation?" Swaying her hips, she smiled at the way the soft material grazed her calves.

"Definitely. It'll be warm out, so that one'll be comfortable."

"Right." Angie nodded and looked down at the length. "You like the color?"

"Yes. It's all sunshiny and sweet creamy yellow."

"Sweet creamy?" Angie laughed. "Did that just come out of your mouth?"

"Shut up. I told you, I'm hungry!" Celia laughed, too. "Bag these two up, and let's go."

"But…but…shoes!"

"*Ohhhmyyygod, noooo!*" Celia flung her arms down to her sides and bent her body backward as if she was going to pass out. "Feed me *firrrrrst! I'm dyingggg!*"

"Holy shit, a little shopping, and you turn into a drama-queen diva!" Angie laughed. "Okay, okay. Food, then shoes."

"Thank you." Celia grinned, all sweet and innocent.

Angie rolled her eyes and moved back into the dressing room. Thinking about it, she was a bit hungry, too. She'd been so distracted with Garrett or the lack of hearing from him, and also trying to find the perfect dress just in case Garrett asked her out on a date, as well as another for her brother's graduation, she hadn't paid attention to the time.

Angie had woken that morning to what had become the norm from him, a GM—his version of Good Morning—text. She liked that he made that effort each day. It was thoughtful. And sweet.

Since she was sleeping when he'd sent the message, it was a couple of hours before she saw it, but when she did, she responded to him, asking what his plans were for the day.

He'd yet to reply.

And that was the issue she was having. He sucked at getting back to her.

Angie just wished he was consistent like he was with the GM texts the rest of the time, too. It'd been about a week since spending that first night with him, sleeping at his house, and although he texted her every morning, and she'd seen him most nights that week, there were often huge gaps of time in between communications from him.

It was annoying, to say the least, but worse, it had Angie constantly wondering if they were a thing or not a thing. Where this whole deal with him was going. Were they casual? Was it more? It sure felt like more.

Maybe this wasn't a bigger thing for him…

Angie pulled her shorts back on and slipped into her sandals. She'd hinted to Garrett a couple of times over the week that it would be fun if he'd come with her to her brother Mark's commencement ceremony or, at the very least, come to the after-party.

Garrett hadn't said much in response to her hints, and she wasn't sure if she was ready to just ask him outright.

Draping the dresses over her arm, she made her way to the register to pay. After setting the garments down on the counter, she checked her phone again.

Still nothing from him.

Angie let out a sigh and stuffed the phone into her back pocket. She knew Garrett was busy, such was the life of a business owner. But it only took two seconds to reply to a message or send a message at all.

Worse, Angie didn't want to bother him, so instead of just reaching out, she'd wait to hear from him. Last night, when she was out with Celia and Mark, she'd managed to resist contacting him until, of course, the booze took over, and then she'd drunk texted him a "*Whatcha up to, Daddy?*"

He hadn't replied to that particular message, but at least she got the GM text from him this morning, right? Ugh…sure.

The road to insanity was a long one, apparently because after only a week of seeing him—all while dealing with his communication constipation—Angie was steadily racking up the miles.

Annoyance pulsed through her as she paid the cashier and then headed out to find food with Celia. Honestly, the fact that she was already so strung out on the guy after only a week bugged the hell out of her. But at the same time, she knew it was because she'd connected with Garrett in a way she hadn't with anyone else before.

Like she told Celia when they were out last night, Garrett was different for her. It was only natural that she'd want to spend more time with him.

Blowing out a breath, she brushed a stray hair away from her eyes. If Garrett didn't text her by the time they were done with their mid-afternoon grazing session, she'd just have to give in and text him.

Maybe.

She frowned and checked her phone. Ugh! Still nothing. Jeezus chrispies, this was annoying.

CHAPTER FOURTEEN

GARRETT COULD NOT BELIEVE HIS FUCKING EARS! HE SAT BACK in his office chair and listened to the voicemail on his cell again a second time.

"Hello, Mr. James? This is Julia Martin. I'm Chase Reynolds' publicist. We're looking at an opportunity to be featured in Rolling Stone. They're doing a segment on popular rock bands from the nineties and two thousands, and Copper Seven fits their bill. We'd love it if you'd consider participating. If you could call me at two-oh-six—" Garrett stopped the message and put his phone down on his desk.

How the fuck did they get his cell number? No one had his goddamn cell number. No one that wasn't a personal friend, anyway. Garrett scrubbed his palms over his thin beard and scratched at his jawline.

Chase had been a friend, a good one, for a long time. But that was a lifetime ago. They weren't friends anymore. None of the guys were as far as he knew. When the band ended, they'd all gone their separate ways, and Garrett preferred it that way. That past life was dead and buried, and Garrett wasn't willing to dig it up.

With a resigned sigh, he stood, picked up his phone,

deleted the message and stuffed his cell in his pocket. There was no way in hell he was doing any interview. Ever.

CHAPTER FIFTEEN

GARRETT'S PHONE VIBRATED IN HIS POCKET RIGHT WHEN HE put the car in park. He'd meant to shut it off when he left his house and forgot. Knowing he had to keep himself focused, he ignored it.

He was too damn rattled over that call regarding the band and needed to get his head back on track before he talked to anyone. Blowing out a sigh, he stretched beside his car, loosening up his muscles before he headed out on his hike. Whoever was texting or calling could wait.

Once Garrett was finished with his hike, he headed to Costco and loaded up on some items for his house and the bar. By the time he got home, it was after six p.m. He plugged his phone in to charge and hopped in the shower.

Once done with that, he got dressed, pulled his hair up, and grabbed his cell from the nightstand. He and Angie were supposed to grab a quick bite before he had to head to the Halo for a few hours.

As he made his way down the stairs, he realized his phone was still off from when he'd gone on his hike. Shit, he never turned the thing back on. After the device booted up, he checked his messages.

Ah, shit. Lots of dings and alerts popped up, but the most important one was what he focused on. There was a text from Angie…from over three hours ago. Damn, that meant she'd texted him before he'd even shut his phone off before he went on his hike.

Angie was probably pissed at him. Not that he could blame her. He hit the little phone icon and listened as her cell rang in his ear a few times before she picked up.

"Hey."

"What're you up to?" Garrett stepped into the kitchen and pulled a bottle of water from the fridge.

"Nothing. Just sitting on the couch watching some TV. Was thinking about heading for a walk. You?"

He took a swig of the water. "Whatcha watching?"

"Reruns of *House* on Netflix."

"Good show."

"Yeah."

Garrett paused, wondering if she was going to say something else. Hmm. Maybe she wasn't upset after all. "Hey, so I just now saw your message. Sorry, I didn't reply sooner. I was busy."

"Yeah, that happens a lot."

Garrett frowned, feeling weary at the tone in her voice. "What? Me being busy? I guess…why do you say it like that?"

"Say it like what?"

Okay, yeah. He'd misread her. She was upset. "Look, Angie. I *am* sorry. Yes, I get busy. Not much I can do about that, though." She let out a sigh, and Garrett took a seat at the kitchen counter. "You going to stay mad at me all night?"

"I'm not mad. There's a difference between mad and disappointed, Garrett."

"There is. You're right." He rubbed his chin. "You still want to get a bite to eat before I go to the bar?"

"Okay, look. For the record, I know you're busy. And truly, I don't expect to hear from you every minute of the day, but a sign you're out there would be nice once in a while, you know?"

"Yes, I do—"

"But when you don't reply to my messages, on top of not hearing from you all day? It gets a little confusing."

Apparently, she wasn't done. "Angie—"

"And the last thing I want to deal with is being confused. Honestly, I have no idea what we're even doing, and I'm not saying I need a label or anything, but I could really do without the mixed signals crap."

Jesus, this woman liked to argue. Garrett smiled and shook his head. "I got it, babe."

"You got what?"

"I'm bad at texting. I get busy and forget. I get distracted. Sends mixed signals. I got it."

"Why do I feel like nothing I said penetrated, and why do I also feel like I nagged you?"

He chuckled. "If the shoe fits."

"Ugh. Whatever." She let out a small giggle.

"I take it you don't want to get dinner, then?"

"*Of course*, I want to get dinner! I even got ready, just in case you called. Which, by the way, annoys the shit out of me, but whatever. Where do you want me to meet you?"

God, she made him smile. "Tell you what, I'll come get you tonight."

"Mark was going to let me use his car, but okay. Come get me."

"All right. Leaving now. See you in a half hour."

"Garrett, it takes forty-five minutes to get to me."

"Never underestimate the skill of a racecar driver."

"But…you're not a racecar driver."

"How do you know? I could be." He laughed. He wasn't a racecar driver, but the back and forth was too much fun to resist. Plus, he knew it'd help lighten her mood.

She laughed. "Right. I'll make a note."

"See you in a bit, babe." Garrett disconnected and shoved his cell in his back pocket as he made his way out to his garage.

He much preferred the sound of her laughter over the tone of her temper. God, the woman was sensitive, for sure. Either that or she truly *was* always looking for a fight, which made him worry even more that he'd lost his mind for continuing this with her.

Garrett hit the button on the garage door opener and then slid behind the wheel of his Jaguar XJR. Lost mind or not, she was intriguing…which was why he was heading to pick her up.

Dinner with Angie would be a good distraction from the call about the band, which, even though Garrett had dismissed the idea, he couldn't stop thinking about.

CHAPTER SIXTEEN

Angie held Garrett's hand as he led her down a side alley to the destination he'd chosen for dinner.

The night air was warm, but the light breeze made it feel a lot like the climate in L.A. They were in Old Town Scottsdale, that much she knew, but where exactly, she had no idea.

Not that it mattered where they were. Angie would pretty much go anywhere Garrett wanted to take her. Both a good and bad thing, in her opinion anyway.

He'd been so damn charming when he picked her up from Celia and Mark's apartment, all doubts and frustration she had evaporated into thin air. The man had that effect on her.

"Here we are." Garrett turned toward her as he opened the door to the establishment.

Angie glanced up at the sign hanging above the entryway. "The Limestone Cafe, huh?"

"One of my favorite restaurants." He placed his hand on her lower back as she entered. The soft contact, something she felt down to her toes. "You're going to love it."

"I think I already love it." As she took everything in, Angie couldn't help but smile. "It's beautiful here, Garrett."

The restaurant was the perfect mix of rustic and elegant.

Open wood beams sectioned the dark, painted walls and white ceilings. The floors were a creamy, shiny marble, with prominent veining throughout. White linens draped over the edges of each table, and the twinkling candle at each centerpiece enhanced the glow from the sconces dotting the walls in the dining room.

He squeezed her hand and indicated they should follow the hostess. "Wait until you see the patio."

Excitement bounced through her, and when they stepped out onto the patio, Angie's eyes went wide. The man was not kidding.

Vines covered most of the three walls, as well as the teak, open-beam pergola enclosing the large space. Tall palm trees were situated in each corner, their fronds arching over the center, creating a natural canopy. On the far end was a mammoth stone gas fireplace, the low flames dancing around the ceramic logs in a hypnotic display. Multiple square and round, two-person tables, also draped in white linen, were situated throughout and various sconce and pendant lights hung from the walls and overhead from the pergola, creating a magical low-light ambiance.

"Wow…" Angie swallowed. Hell, the word "wow" didn't begin to cover it. The place was a thing of beauty.

He led her to one of the tables and her seat. Angie sat, and Garrett pushed her chair in. After he took his seat across from her, he removed the artistically posed napkin from its place in the water goblet and draped it over his lap.

Angie did the same. As a menu was placed down in front of each of them and their water glasses filled, she watched Garrett across the table, caught in utter awe of him.

She'd been to places like this in L.A. before, but she'd never been *brought* to a place like this on a date. No man, not a single one from her past, had *ever* given Angie this level of dreamy romance before.

Maybe it was because Garrett was older, but regardless,

she was enchanted by the entire gesture. Warmth spilled through her, pooling in her stomach. For God's sake, how could she not be in awe of him?

And yes, the man made a good living because, no doubt, this restaurant cost a mint, but the money he had, had nothing to do with how she was feeling.

No. Angie was overcome and overwhelmed, in the best possible way, because this gift had come directly from him.

From Garrett James.

Garrett James, the long-haired former rock star, turned small concert venue/bar owner. A long-haired former rock star who owned a home that was beyond gorgeous, but only because he'd put his stamp on it. Garrett James, the slightly rough around the edges man who had a side to him, she bet few got to see…a soft, refined side.

And he'd cast his spell on Angie.

Without a doubt, she knew she wanted more of him. But how exactly was that going to work? It was foolish to even think about a future with the man. She'd be going back to L.A. in three weeks. And lest she forget that she'd set a goal for herself, which she intended to see through once she was home.

Life was so unfair. It was just her luck to find what she felt was the perfect man, only to never really be able to have him. Angie let out a resigned sigh. No, life wasn't fucking fair.

The only thing to do was to make the most of the time she had with him. She needed to memorize all she could of him, especially this romantic side he was showing her. She'd need all of the memories to hold onto once life went back to normal.

He caught her gaze. "You okay?"

"As good as I can be." She glanced down and then up again. "But also, probably better than I have been in a while. If that makes any sense." Her lips curved in a nervous smile, and she adjusted her silverware. "Thank you for taking me here, Garrett."

"You're welcome." One corner of his mouth tugged into a small grin.

Electricity filled the space between them—a live connection that danced along Angie's skin, making her shiver. She cleared her throat, crossed her legs and picked up her menu. "What are you hungry for?"

"You."

Annnnd…cue the stomach drop.

Leave it to Garrett to say something she had no way to recover from. Which was probably part of some romantic, sweep her off her feet, plan he had. Either that or the man was just *that* fucking smooth.

His gaze was intent on hers, almost predatory. Animalistic. The expression in his eyes made her want to climb across the small table separating them and into his lap. Angie blew out a slow breath and stared at Garrett over the top of the menu. "I like it when you say things like that."

He rested his elbows on the table, clasped his hands together and leaned forward. "What else do you like?"

Angie set down the menu and then mimicked his pose. "I like it when you look at me like you are."

A quick smirk pursed his lips, but was gone just as fast. "How am I looking at you?"

Angie blew out another slow breath.

Oh yes, she wanted more of him. More of this sexual side, too.

Slowly, Angie swiped her tongue over her bottom lip and then dragged her top teeth over the damp flesh. Garrett's eyes tracked the movement. She tipped her head to the side. "You look at me like you want to lick every part of me and then fuck every part of me, too."

"Bingo."

Yeah, he wanted her just as much as she wanted him. Pure lust bolted down Angie's spine and struck between her legs, leaving her clit pulsing and her chest heaving in breathlessness. The man took her breath away. Angie crossed her legs, squeezing her thighs together and watched him.

He licked his lips.

Heat spread over her skin, and she had to fight the urge to fan herself.

And then, as if nothing out of the ordinary had happened or been said, he rested back in his seat and resumed looking at his menu. "So, I'm thinking we'll get the four-course. For the third, do you want the octopus or the branzino?"

Say what? Surprise at his abrupt change in demeanor blazed through her, mingling with the lust. With her head spinning, Angie glanced down at the menu and then back to him. "Um, what's branzino?"

"Fish."

"Ooh, yeah, no. No fish. I'll do the octopus."

"Perfect. I'll get the branzino, and we can share. For the fourth?"

She giggled, couldn't help herself. She was in no way a foodie. This may be out of Angie's league, but her mother would be loving it. Angie was for sure going to have to snap a few food pics to send to mom. "Definitely the spinach bolognese."

"Perfect. I'll get the duck." He set the menu down. "You know what kind of wine you'd like, or would you like me to order for you?"

"By all means. I trust you."

He gave her *that* look again, and Angie felt it deep in her stomach. Ooh, she was starting to think he liked taking control, and more so, her letting him take control. Good, because she liked it, too.

When the waiter came over, Garrett ordered her a glass of wine and then ordered their dinner. When her wine was delivered, Angie raised the glass. "Toast?"

Garrett picked up his water glass. "What would you like to toast to?"

"To trust." She smiled.

Garrett cleared his throat and then nodded. "To trust."

They clinked their glasses, and Angie took a sip. The flavors of cherry, as well as other fruits, coated her tongue, and she almost moaned.

"So, not many people can take a month off from a job. Are you independently wealthy or?" Garrett set his water glass down.

Angie laughed. "Good question." She took another sip of wine, wishing he hadn't asked about her job. This could go really, really badly, and she really, *really* wanted to have this night with him be anything but bad. Dammit. "This is wonderful, by the way. Excellent choice." He nodded, and she smiled before letting out a sigh. "Much as I would love to be, I'm not independently wealthy."

"Few are. Go on." He smoothed a hand down his jaw.

"Very true." She nodded. "Anyway, yes, I'm gainfully employed. No worries there."

Garrett leaned forward, resting his forearms on the table. "Good to know." He gave her a nod. "Are you going to tell me what you do?"

Maybe she could tell him just enough— "I'm a reviewer for a small online and print magazine in L.A. It affords me a lot of flexibility, hence a month off." She took another sip of wine.

"That sounds interesting. What do you review?"

Of course, he wanted to know. Why did God hate her so much? Nervous energy swamped Angie's system, and she swirled the red wine in her glass, trying for all it was worth to get control of herself. "What kind is this again?"

"It's a Pinot Noi—" He tilted his head to the side, a puzzled expression on his face. "Are you avoiding the question?"

"Maybe."

"Seriously?"

"Well, a little, yeah. I'm nervous."

"Why are you nervous?" He frowned. "What? You review porn or sex toys, or something other than mainstream items?"

"No, nothing like that." Now, who was the interesting one? Angie couldn't help but giggle at the fact that his mind went right to porn or sex toys. Jeezus chrispies, could this get any more uncomfortable? She gripped the cloth napkin in her sweaty hands. "Honestly, it's worse."

"Seriously?" He frowned before taking a sip of his water.

Okay, enough, Angie, spit it out. "Okay, okay. I'm an Indie music reviewer."

His eyes went wide. "Seriously?"

"You've said that word three times now." She took another sip of wine, hoping for some liquid courage and trying to drown the bouncing ball of nervous tension in her stomach. He was staring at her, not saying anything else…and this was exactly what she was worried about.

Dammit!

Angie placed her palms flat on the table. "Look, I get it, okay? Considering who you are, how this might look, and all? But, let me remind you, I didn't know who you were, Garrett, and you know that's the truth. And frankly, just because you own a small concert venue for mostly Indie bands does not factor because I was, I mean, *I am* on vacation. In my defense, this is one of those completely weird coincidences."

"I don't believe in coincidences, Angie."

"Really?" Caught off guard once again, she set her glass down. "Can you explain that, please?"

"Sure." Garrett shrugged. "Nothing happens in this world by mistake. You were meant to meet me. Not sure why yet, but your job and my past? No way I can believe that's an accident."

"Wait, Garrett." She leaned forward. "This is important. I didn't seek you out. I mean, not like that. Not *for* that. You know that, right?"

He reached across the table and covered her hand with his. "Of course, I know that. That's not what I'm saying. What I mean is, we were meant to meet, babe. You can call it a coincidence if *you* prefer. But how about we meet in the middle and call it fate?"

Babe...

Fate...

As she stared at him across the table, warmth spread through Angie once more, filling her heart, and she sighed. Didn't bother trying to hide it, either. Could she get up and climb into his lap right there? Would that be okay?

Fate...

God, she hoped meeting Garrett was fated. She hoped that same fate was going to lead them farther down the road together, somehow, some way. She needed to know more of him. She'd be a fool not to.

CHAPTER SEVENTEEN

"Stay by me." Garrett led Angie through Copper Halo's backstage entrance door and then directly up the back staircase.

He'd started the night intent on only taking her out for a small bite and then delivering her back home. They'd already spent a lot of time together that week, and although he enjoyed it, he had work to do, too.

Except…his plan went straight out the window the minute he'd laid his eyes on her as she walked to his car at the apartment complex.

Her makeup was flawless and light, and her long, dark hair hung straight down her shoulders and back. She wore a sage green, blousy satin halter top, and it looked like she wasn't wearing a bra because the top clung to her breasts in a way that made his mouth water. Tight dark blue jeans hugged her hips and ass, and on her pretty feet were a pair of high-heeled strappy sandals.

Garrett felt every bit of that outfit in his dick.

Which explained why, without any real thought and totally on a whim, he got lucky and got them into The Limestone Cafe for dinner, which had been amazing.

They talked, laughed and bantered—mostly because she argued over everything—and Garrett took any opportunity to tease her about that minor little habit of hers. The time with her had been good, better than good, actually. It'd been awesome.

They'd also flirted. Out of everything they'd talked about, hands down, the best part was the flirting. For fuck's sake, his dick had stayed semi-hard in his jeans nearly the entire time they were dining.

All Garrett could think about was how badly he wanted to be dining *on* her—any and every damn part of her.

Finding out about her job had been a surprise, but he rolled with it. There was a reason this woman was in his life. If he'd learned anything when he spent those ninety days in drug and alcohol treatment nearly nineteen years ago, it was that the universe had a plan.

Whether Garrett wanted to know what that plan was or not was debatable.

Now, instead of taking her back to her place and dropping her off, he was sneaking into his bar—hoping no one saw them—and up to his office so he could do all the naughty things he'd been fantasizing about doing since she approached his car, without being interrupted.

Reaching the top of the stairs, he stopped at the door and fished out his keys to unlock it. "The hallway's dark, so watch your step."

Angie pressed herself to his back and slipped her arms around his waist. "Will you break my fall if I trip?" She pressed her lips to his neck.

The warmth of her body and mouth on his skin sent a chill down Garrett's spine, kicking his desire into overdrive. He pushed the door open and took one step into the hall, ensuring she moved with him.

Once in the hallway, he closed and locked the door and then turned back to her. Garrett cupped her delicate face in his palms and pressed his lips to hers. Desperate to sate his need, he dove his tongue into her mouth, and Angie let out a sweet moan.

The sound of that moan vibrated down his spine, settling in his groin as his dick got impossibly harder. God dammit! He *could not* get enough of her. Like a couple of teenagers, they'd gone at it several times that week, making out—sometimes for hours. And that was in addition to the sex they'd had.

Garrett backed her against the wall and deepened the kiss. Kissing Angie had become something he craved, something he found he didn't want to stop doing.

The constant slow burn of chemistry between them erupted into an all-out inferno, and Garrett speared his fingers into her hair and tugged, tilting her head farther back. With one hand pressed to the wall above her head, he held himself over her and took from her mouth.

Releasing her soft hair, he explored her even softer skin beneath her satin top and then found her petite breast. *Oh, yeah, no bra.* Garrett rolled an erect nipple between thumb and forefinger, drawing another sweet moan from her. Then he tugged the hard point, and Angie pulled from his lips with a gasp.

It was nearly pitch black in the hall, save for the glowing "EXIT" sign above them, which cast a dark red glow over the space. Garrett stared at her shadowed features, knowing her eyes had likely glazed over with her own need.

It was a look he'd come to expect from her, as well as look forward to. He tugged the rigid flesh again. "You like that?"

"*Yesss.*"

The word came out in a breathy whisper that stroked over his skin, making his dick throb in time with his heartbeat. Garrett moved to the other nipple, pinched and tugged it, too. "More?"

"God, yes, please?" Angie slid a hand between them and

stroked his erection through his jeans. "I want this, too. Can I have it, please?"

Garrett felt the ask in his gut like a punch. The things this woman made his body feel… "Tell me what you want to do with it?"

"I want you in my mouth."

His cock jerked behind his zipper. Releasing her, he took a couple steps back and let his arms fall to his sides. "Take it then."

"Right here in the hallway?" She glanced down the dark walkway and then back to him. "What if someone sees us? By someone, I mean Chassidy."

He shook his head. "Chassidy's out of town for a few days with some friends."

A devious smile arched her lips, and then Angie was down on her knees in front of him before another moment passed. She pressed her mouth to the denim covering the hard ridge and blew out a hot breath. Garrett groaned and cupped the back of her head in his palm.

Tipping her head back, she gazed up at him, her face bathed in a red glow from the overhead sign. As she undid the button and pulled down the zipper of his jeans, he smoothed his thumb along her cheekbone and then threaded his fingers through her hair again.

"I love that you love my hair." She pushed his jeans over his hips and then tugged the waistband of his boxers down.

Before Garrett had a chance to respond, her mouth was on him.

Her hot tongue slid over the swollen head of his dick, and Garrett's head fell back. "Holy fuck, Angie!"

With her lips wrapped tight around the rim, she suckled and moaned, sending her pleasure straight through him. Garrett's skin went tight from head to toe, and his fingers twitched in the strands of her hair at the back of her head.

When she swallowed him deeper, he couldn't stop himself

from gripping the soft strands tightly, tugging…just a little. Not wanting to hurt her, he forced himself to ease up. The effort it took to maintain control with Angie, especially when she was giving him head, was mammoth.

Garrett rarely, if ever, lost control with a woman. Blowjobs and sex could be good. Hell, they could be mind-blowing, but none of those past experiences had ever come close to how things were with Angie.

He didn't know what to make of it, how to handle it. The realization wasn't new; it happened a lot when he was intimate with her, but each time it emerged to the surface, Garrett dug a hole and buried it again. He wasn't ready to deal with it. He just wanted to—

"You can pull my hair if you want." She circled his shaft in her palm and stroked him from base to tip. "I'd like it if you did."

Garrett gazed down at her. Again, before he had a chance to respond, she ran her tongue along the side of his shaft to the crown, then swallowed him to the back of her throat. Heat swamped his skin, and a shiver raced down his spine as his balls drew up tight between his parted thighs.

Jesus, he loved that she wanted him to be a little rougher, but he still wasn't sure he could let himself go too far. Testing his control, he gave the strands another tug, this time with only a bit more force.

Angie moaned around his dick, drawing him in and out, teasing the head with her teeth before swirling her tongue around the edge and then sucking in earnest… Garrett's head spun, and his orgasm crept up his shaft.

ANGIE CLOSED her eyes as Garrett's orgasm spurted into her mouth, coating her tongue and sliding down her throat.

God help her, she loved his taste. His scent. The way he

felt between her lips. But mostly, the way he responded to her touch.

Garrett James might be a locked box where deep emotions were concerned, but during sex, that locked box of his blew wide open. It made her want to get him naked any chance she got. So far, she'd been successful in that endeavor.

The sex was downright explosive, and it only got better each time they were together.

With a hiss, he drew back from her. "Goddamn, Angie."

She licked her lips and smiled up at him. The hallway was too dark to see his expression from her position on her knees, but it didn't matter. "I could do that all night long."

"Challenge accepted."

With a hand up from him, Angie got to her feet and swiped her thumb along her chin below her bottom lip. "Don't tempt me, I'm not kidding."

Pulling her to him, Garrett placed a soft kiss on the side of her neck and then gave her ass a gentle swat. "Trust me, I know you're serious."

A shiver raced down her spine, and she grinned. "I'm a serious girl who needs a serious fucking, too. You think you can handle that challenge?"

"Absolutely." He chuckled and pulled up his jeans before taking her hand in his and leading them down the long hall to his office. "When the girl wants her cock, she wants her cock."

"Damn straight." She smiled as she trailed behind him.

Her cock...

He'd said the same thing to her once before, the first time they'd had sex, actually. She'd liked it when he'd said it then, but now, hearing it again, she loved it. She wanted him to mean it, for his precious cock to be "hers" and only hers.

Because, in her mind, it already was. A dangerous line of thinking, but one she hadn't been able to stop her brain from heading toward.

After pulling his keys from his pocket, Garrett unlocked

the door and pushed it wide. He motioned for her to enter, and she stepped around him into his office. She moved to his desk and set her small purse down.

Angie heard the door close behind her, and a mere second or two later, Garrett was pressed against her back.

"What was that about a serious fucking?" He slid his hands around her waist to her stomach and then smoothed his palms up her torso to her breasts.

When he pinched and rolled her nipples, Angie gasped and let her head fall back on his shoulder. The sting of pain shot straight to her clit. Rubbing her ass against his already rising erection, she drew in a slow breath. The man had no issues with stamina, that was for sure.

"Unbutton your jeans and slide them down." His warm breath sent another bolt of sensation through her body, and then he nipped the side of her ear. "Now, Angie."

She couldn't suppress the moan that rippled out of her at the short command. Eager to do as he instructed, she undid her jeans and pushed them down her thighs. Each time they'd been together in the past week, he'd gotten a little more force-ful, his touch a little rougher.

Since that first night when they'd had an encounter in the bar hallway, she'd sensed a dominant side hiding within Garrett. And whenever he lost his control during sex with her, that dominant side emerged, even if only a little.

But he was always quick to reel it in. When he would spear his fingers into the hair at the base of her head, they would twitch on her scalp as if he wanted to tug, or if he was already tugging, maybe he wanted to tug harder.

She liked it. A lot. She wanted more of it.

Garrett took one hand from her breast and skated it down her body to between her legs. He slid two fingers between her aching folds, and she bucked against him, biting her bottom lip.

"So wet for me." His voice now a deep gravely tone as he toyed with her clit.

Angie couldn't even think about Garrett without getting wet. She moaned. "Always for you."

"I like that." Garrett moved his other hand away and freed himself from the confines of his jeans. "Need to feel that hot wetness dripping down my dick."

"I want that, too." Angie went to lean forward, but he stopped her.

"Stay like you are."

In the next moment, she felt his silky length slide between her barely parted thighs from behind. Grazing the mouth of her cunt, parting her folds and rubbing along her clit.

Angie placed her hand over his shaft, pressing it against her core as he slid back and forth. "Oh God, Garrett."

"So fucking hot." He gripped her hips and thrust forward again. "You want me inside you?"

"Yes." She slipped her hand lower and cupped his balls in her palm. Each time the bulbous head of his cock rubbed across her clit, a bolt of lust shot through her, making her knees weak. "Feels so good."

Garrett snaked a hand up her body to her neck and loosely cuffed her throat. "Want to make you come first."

Heat flooded Angie's limbs, and her cunt clenched in little spasms. A sound came out of her she'd never heard herself make before. Something between a moan, a whimper and a mewling kitten.

Angie turned her head to the side and found his mouth. Moving her palm to cover the underside of his cock again, Angie pressed him tighter against her folds.

Garrett rocked his pelvis, rubbing his length back and forth over her pussy. He built it, the sexual high between them and the lust-induced ball of tension in her tummy. Her impending orgasm fed off it. The tension inside her grew thicker, heavier as the juices from her cunt coated his shaft.

Her knees buckled, and he pulled from her mouth. "Come for me, Angie."

"Garrett!" With his cock pressed against her clit, she arched her back.

That was the last bit she needed, and Angie fell right over the edge, her body shuddering against his.

Her orgasm rolled through her like a tidal wave, and before she could take a breath, Garrett shifted, found the mouth of her cunt and pushed his cock inside her. The breath she'd meant to take in reversed, and she let out a loud moan.

"Fuck, yes! Holy shit, I feel your cunt clenching on me."

Shaking from head to toe, orgasm still echoing through her, Angie leaned forward and braced her palms on his desk. "Take it, hard!"

"Giving orders again?" Garrett's hands landed on her ass cheeks with a loud slap, and then with a growl, he grabbed her ass cheeks and rocketed into her. Fast and hard. His hips banged against her backside, and she rose on tiptoe, arching her back to give him more, to take him deeper.

"Yes!" Angie tossed her head back, knowing the ends of her hair would land along her lower back. "Harder, Garrett! Fuck me harder. I need all of you."

A deep groan came out of him, and a moment later, she felt his fingers tangle in her hair. He gripped the long length and yanked her head back. "Hard enough, or you want more?"

"More! Always more!" Oh, yeah. This was exactly what she wanted.

Finally, his control had slipped.

SOMETHING INSIDE GARRETT SHIFTED, peering out from beneath a rock it'd been hiding under. Fuck if he knew what to make of it.

While in the throes of complete ecstasy, he let his gaze travel from her gorgeous bare ass, up the length of her back, to her hair he had gripped in his palm. He was giving her what she wanted—fucking her hard and fast with her bent over his desk.

Thing was, he was getting exactly what he wanted, too—he just hadn't known he wanted it.

Further thought process wasn't possible because the gorgeous creature he was buried balls deep inside, as well as the orgasm, tingling at the base of his spine, was demanding his full attention.

He was going to come so hard his face might go numb. Then again, whenever he came with Angie, it was harder than he'd ever come in his life. So, correction: his face would definitely go numb. Hell, his whole body would.

"Garrett, oh God, yes! I'm gonna come again." She reached between her legs, and he knew she was rubbing her tight little clit.

"Give it to me." His cock jerked, and he slapped her ass hard. Holy shit! What the hell was he doing?

She groaned and pressed back against him.

Fuck it, she liked it, and he was going with it. No point in pulling back now. "Better take that pretty top off because I'm planning on coating your back."

"God, yes." In one swift movement, she pushed up, yanked her shirt over her head, tossed it aside and then bent over the desk again.

Garrett never broke stride—unable to was more like it.

Taking ahold of her hair again, he yanked her head back farther and pounded into her. Chills broke out all over his skin, and his orgasm crept up his cock. "Rub that little clit. Come for me, baby."

She moaned, whimpered, and took everything he gave her until he couldn't hold his climax back.

"Garrretttt!" Angie's tight cunt clenched around him as she orgasmed, and that was it for him, too.

Garrett pulled from her tight channel, palmed his cock and spurted his orgasm up her back. "Fuck yes!"

Wave after wave rose and crashed through him, and with each swell, hot semen spurted from him, painting her back and hair in too many hot, ropy lashes to count. Streams of his release reached the base of her neck.

With one hand still gripped tightly on her waist, trying to catch his breath and not pass out, Garrett stared through a wavy haze at what he'd produced, how he'd marked her.

Goddamn…

CHAPTER EIGHTEEN

"Celia, what time does the family descend today?" Walking from the bathroom, Angie pulled a hot roller from her hair.

"You say that like you're dreading their arrival." Celia snorted and closed the door to the dishwasher.

"Totally not. It's just…anyway. When do they get here?"

"Mom, Dad, and the rest of the L.A.-based clan are supposed to get in at two thirty. Jimmy and Sonja arrive closer to six, I think. I have to check. Oh, and Sarah is with them. And Liza gets in around—" Celia swiped the screen on her phone. "She gets here at nine-fifteen tonight."

"You're my hero. Can I be like you when I grow up?" Angie smirked and pulled another hot roller out. "How the hell do you keep all that straight?"

Celia shot her a sideways glance. "It's called a calendar, Ang. Ya know, the one on your smartphone? The one I know you use? Freak."

"You're right. But hey, you got it covered, so I didn't save any of it." With a shrug, Angie headed back to the bathroom, talking over her shoulder. "That leaves us three hours until the first show time. And, give me strength, all-day performances from there on."

Celia appeared in the doorway of the bathroom and leaned a hip against the frame. "Since when does family bother you?"

Angie shrugged again and then blew out a breath. "It doesn't. I'm just a little tense, I guess."

"About family?"

"No. About Garrett."

"Uh oh." Celia entered the space, dropped the lid on the toilet and took a seat. "What happened?"

"I invited him to the graduation and the after-party." Angie ran her fingers through the fresh curls, arranging them into some semblance of wild yet tame-looking order.

Angie had hinted enough over the past few days about the graduation and after-party, and it seemed Garrett wasn't catching on. And now she'd run out of time, family was arriving today, so last night, she'd straight up asked him directly. No more hinting.

"And?"

"I don't know if he's going to come. He hasn't given me a definitive answer. He's 'checking his calendar'." Angie shook her head.

"Okay, well, he does own a business, a pretty big one. So, if he can't come, at least he's got a good reason."

"Fine, but at least he could come to the after-party, you know?" Angie let out a resigned sigh and stared down at the countertop. Frustration beat through her in time with her pulse. "It was something I saw in his eyes and his tone of voice. I don't think he *wants* to come."

"Why would you think that?"

"I can't explain it. It's a feeling I have in my gut." She turned to face her sister. "It's too soon, huh? For him to meet the family? Maybe that's it. Do you think it's too soon?"

Celia tilted her head to the side. "I guess that depends on

where you think things are going with him. Honestly, I wouldn't have thought you'd want him to meet them. It's not like you have a future with him. You're going back home in two weeks, so why even go down that road?"

The question was a valid one, but more so, it was one Angie had been avoiding asking herself, especially after that romantic dinner and then when they were together in his office afterward…

Garrett was only supposed to be a fun fling while visiting Arizona, albeit an unplanned one, but fun nonetheless. However, things felt way deeper than just fun. At least for Angie, they had, and now she didn't know what to do.

A man was not on her agenda. *He* was not on her agenda. Yet somehow, he'd landed there. And at the top of the list, no less.

With a can of hairspray in her hand, Angie stared at her sister and tried really, *really* hard to ignore the truthful answer to Celia's question.

"Shit. You're falling for him, aren't you?"

Ding ding ding…we have a winner, folks, and she's sitting on the porcelain throne!

Angie turned away from her sister's penetrating gaze and sprayed a layer of hairspray over her curls. "I love how easy it is to do my hair in this state. That whole dry heat thing is awesome."

"Um, Angie?"

Oh God, she would rather be doing anything than having this conversation. She'd rather talk about nuns and priests or Vatican II than debate if she was or was not falling for Garrett James.

Adjusting a few renegade curls, she sprayed her hair again.

"Angie, the fact that you haven't answered me tells me that, yes, you are definitely falling for him."

"No. Stop it."

Celia laughed. "Okay, let me make sure I got this right.

Because honestly? I think it's kind of adorable and also a little funny."

"Har har har. Laugh it up." Angie pulled out her makeup bag and added a little more eyeliner.

"Uh, huh." Celia stood and moved beside Angie. "Let's review: you want him to come to our brother's graduation. And then you want him to hang out with all of our family at the after-party. All this, and you won't admit that you have feelings for him?" Celia tapped her bottom lip with the tip of her finger. "Yeah. That's a little thing we call denial."

Agitation itched along Angie's skin, and she glared at her sister through the reflection in the mirror. "I love you. But fuck off."

"Okay, yeah, I'm right. And I love you, too." Celia shifted closer, gave Angie a peck on the cheek and then left.

Yeah, no. Celia was wrong. Dead wrong. Angie wasn't falling for Garrett. She blew out a harsh breath.

Truth was, she'd already fallen…and in a big way.

But she wasn't ready to admit it to Celia or anyone else. Christ, Angie wasn't even willing to admit it to herself because this was not supposed to happen.

***

GARRETT STARED at the clock on the wall across from his desk. Angie had texted him a few times earlier in the day, but he'd yet to respond. Every time he heard his phone go off with a text chime, he'd checked to see who it was. Not all of them were from her, of course. But at least four were.

There was nothing from her that was lengthy, or that required a response. Just little kissy face emoticons or "thinking of you" notes. He kept meaning to reply, but then something else would happen—he'd get tied up, get distracted, or leave his phone somewhere, not realizing he'd left it—and before he knew it, several hours had passed by, and he hadn't responded at all. Not to one single message from her.

It was rude.

He was being rude.

He kept telling himself that when he had more than a minute to spare, he'd take the time to send her a heartfelt reply. Something meaningful. Or maybe even call her. Calling her would be best, but now he was wondering if he should reply at all.

The night before, she'd invited him to join her at her brother's graduation and then the after-party, and he'd immediately given the default answer, saying he needed to check his calendar, etcetera. It wasn't bullshit, he really did need to see if he was free, but honestly, he was a little freaked out about the whole idea.

Did she truly want him to meet her family? How could she?

Christ, maybe it was time to let this go, let her go— Problem was, he enjoyed the time they were spending together, and not just the sex. He wasn't quite ready for this— whatever it was with her—to be over.

Angie was sweet and fun. Funny and sassy, and he dug hanging out with her. A lot. He got off on their banter, too. She was smart, and she challenged him. There hadn't been a single moment yet where Garrett had gotten bored of her or wasn't interested in finding out more about her.

They'd only been seeing each other for two weeks, and although things were starting to look a lot like the start of a relationship, that didn't mean it *was* an actual relationship.

There was no way things were going to progress farther than where they were currently. He wouldn't let it. She was leaving in a couple of weeks. What would be the point? But he did like her. More than he'd expected he would.

That said, even if he wanted more—well, it didn't matter.

There wasn't going to be more.

End of story.

Honestly, it was a good thing she was leaving. Almost like he was getting a "get-out-of-relationship" free card, her impending departure allowed him to enjoy the time he had with her without any pressure of "more".

Plus, it was obvious the situation was working for her, too…so why on earth did she want him to meet her family? A better question was, why on earth was he toying with the idea of saying yes?

An ache began behind his eyes. Garrett squeezed them shut and rubbed them.

To add insult to injury, he'd gotten another call from Chase's publicist, Julia somebody, regarding the band interview. This was the third, or maybe it was the fourth, time she'd called. He'd lost track. Like the others before it, he'd let the call go to voicemail.

Garrett hadn't called the woman back after the first call last week, and he had no intention of calling the woman now —or ever. He was stressed out enough over the whole matter as it was; he didn't need to keep focusing on it.

Though it seemed, aside from his thoughts of Angie, the damn interview kept creeping in, taking up space in his head. As a result, his agitation level was on a steady rise.

Getting involved with the band again was too risky for him. The last thing he wanted was to be anywhere near the people he drank and drugged with. Talk about a trigger. It just…wasn't worth it.

His phone chimed again, pulling him from his thoughts. Letting out a harsh breath, Garrett picked up the device and swiped the screen.

Angie: Hey, everything okay?

Garrett stared at the message.
Reply or not?

Get in deeper or walk away?

Fuck!

He hit the call contact icon.

She answered before the second ring. "Hey."

"How's it going?" He leaned back in his chair.

"Going fine. You?"

"Busy day."

"Hmm. You get my messages?" Angie's tone was hesitant.

Garrett ran his fingers through his hair. "Yeah. Just had a lot going on. What'd you do all day?"

"Right, busy… Yeah, I've been busy, too. Welcoming family in all day."

Fucking hell, he hated when conversation was strained like this between them. It was disguised as small talk, but it was strained nonetheless. They hadn't even been on the phone more than five minutes, and the tension flowing through the cellular waves was so thick they'd probably short out one of the transmission towers.

It was his fault, though. He knew it wasn't right, leaving her dangling like he'd been doing, only to pull her back in once more. "How's that going?"

"Great. I'm heading out to grab my youngest sister from the airport soon."

"What time does she get in?"

"Nine. Listen, Garrett, can I ask you something?"

He rubbed the spot between his eyes, knowing the land of strained small talk was about to be left in the dust, and they were heading for straight up uncomfortableville. "Look, I know you want an answer regarding the graduation, but—"

"That's not what I was going to ask you."

"Oh. Okay, sorry I interrupted. Go on, please." Having no idea what she was about to ask, Garrett drew in a slow breath.

"I need to know what it is we're doing. I mean…I like you. I like spending time with you. I definitely like being in your bed. And I'm pretty sure you like me being there, too. But then, when I don't hear from you, it's really confusing."

He rubbed the back of his neck.

Cut her loose, walk away.

It was the right thing to do. Yet…he couldn't.

Garrett blew out a breath. "You're only here for two more weeks." He shrugged. "Why can't we just enjoy our remaining time together, just go with the flow?"

"Are you serious right now?" She let out a harsh, clipped laugh. "I *am* going with the flow, Garrett. But I can't *go with the flow* if you keep *shutting off the water!*"

Garrett jerked his head back as if she'd physically slapped him. Where the hell had her reaction come from? "Take it down a notch, Angie. I get that you're upset, but there's no reason to talk to me that way."

"Talk to you what way? For fuck's sake, Garrett, the mixed signals from you are enough to drive a sane woman off a cliff!" She blew out a harsh breath. "I'm just trying to understand where I stand with you."

"Look, I'm not interested in defining anything, but what I can tell you is I'm not seeing anyone else, and I don't intend to see anyone else while you're here. But I need things to stay casual. I can't do more than that, Angie. Christ, you don't even live here. Maybe the better question is, what is it that you're expecting?"

"I don't know what I'm expecting. I guess…just some consistency? I don't know. I'm not seeing anyone else, either. And by the by, I don't exactly live on the other side of the country, you know?"

"Then, we're good." They weren't good, not really, especially because of her last comment about living close. But it was all he had. Garrett would have to examine his choice of responses a little closer later.

Garrett paused, waiting for her to reply. When nothing came, he prompted her. "Angie, are we good?"

"I'm thinking."

Time to lighten the mood. "Do you want to meet me at the bar, and I can *help* you think?"

"Don't tease, Garrett. That's really not fair. I already told you I have to go pick up my sister." She let out a small groan. "Jerk."

A bit of relief slid through him, and he cracked a smile. "Well, can't blame a guy for trying, right?"

"I want you to come to the graduation and the party. I get it, okay? I know you're busy, so if you can't do both, then how about just the party? Please? It would mean a lot to me."

Okay, they weren't done. Christ. "I don't know, Angie."

"Why don't you know? Let me guess, meeting my family crosses your *casual line*?" Sarcasm dripped from each word she spoke.

The relief he'd felt mere seconds ago evaporated, agitation replacing it. "More like, I can't just drop everything and head to a party at the last minute. It's not a matter of *want*. It's a matter of *if*. And *if* I *can*, then I'll be there. If not, then you're going to have to find a way to get over it." He stood and stalked around his desk. Fucking hell, he didn't want to do this with her. "Casual means keeping expectations in check. No pressure. No commitments. Just going with the flow. Can you do that?"

"How in the hell—okay, fine. You got it. Casual it is. But apparently, in your world, it also means being monogamous, is that right?"

"Yes." Garrett couldn't believe he was even having this conversation—argument. He didn't need this complication. This shit with Angie, in addition to the Copper Seven interview BS, was more than he could handle.

"Thanks for letting me know. I mean, the rest of the free world has a different definition of 'casual' than you do, but hey, whatever, right?"

"You said you weren't seeing anyone else. What's the problem?" Garrett ground his molars together.

Angie let out a loud, frustrated-sounding groan and mumbled something he couldn't make out, then he heard her take a deep breath. "The problem is, you suck at communication, Garrett James. And I suck at reading minds. The other problem is, to me, 'casual' means I date a few people, as in more than one person. I may sleep with them, I may not. But, what I don't do is monogamous unless it's a committed relationship.

"And all you can tell me is to go with the flow. The flow, like I said already, you keep shutting off, but you want me to go with nonetheless. It doesn't exist, but go with it. And oh yeah, also, that you don't want to be with anyone else, and to be monogamous with me. Well, I don't know about the land of Garrett, but to the rest of the free world, that's a fucking relationship, buddy!"

"Enough, Angie!" His tone was harsher than it should've been, but he'd had about all he could take of her outburst, and there was no point in continuing. "This conversation obviously isn't going anywhere but in circles. I'm going to go, and I'll call you tomorrow."

"Whatever."

She hung up before he had a chance to say another word —which totally chapped his ass in ways he hadn't expected. Shock and frustration beat through his veins in time with his thudding heart. He moved to the edge of his desk and pressed his fists to the hardwood. Was she fucking out of her mind?

Yeah, totally out of her damn mind.

Except, no. Not exactly.

Fuck!

No. No, this was not happening.

Garrett was *not* going to deal with this level of drama. He'd had a long day, way too much shit on his mind, and it wasn't even close to being over yet.

Agitation made his skin itch, and Garrett blew out a harsh breath in an attempt to shake it off. Too bad it wasn't working. God, had she really said "whatever" to him? Jesus Christ, he felt like he'd just had an argument with his daughter. *Oh, fucking hell!*

He sat his ass back in his desk chair. That wasn't a line of thinking he needed to entertain. Angie was young, yes, but the last thing he wanted to do was think of her in the same context as his daughter.

That said, he'd be homicidal if some guy was treating his daughter the way he was treating Angie.

Fuck.

She was right. He was one hundred percent sending mixed signals.

Problem was, he wasn't sure how to stop what had begun between them. He knew he wanted her; that was obvious. But he also knew he needed to keep boundaries in place, boundaries around his heart. Giving in and giving Angie more of himself was too risky. But pushing her away felt like shit.

Talk about the epitome of confusion.

CHAPTER NINETEEN

"Hey, Mark!" Angie stopped short as she came out of Celia's bedroom and was face to face with her brother.

"Oh, hey, Angie." Mark stepped the rest of the way out of his room into the hallway—with the blonde from two weeks ago in tow. He held out his arm, indicating Angie to go ahead of him.

Angie paused and raised a brow, tipping her head to the side. "Who's your friend?"

Mark rolled his eyes and stepped to the side. "Sabby, this is my sister, Angie." He motioned between them.

"Hi Sabby!" Angie smiled. "I remember seeing you out a couple of weeks ago, right? In a bar on Mill…can't recall the name of it, though."

Sabby nodded and smiled back. "Yeah. Handsome Sam's, I think. It's good to meet y—"

"Where you off to?" Mark shoved his hands in his front pockets.

Wow, did he just cut the poor girl off like that? How rude. Angie gave him her best WTF face and then turned her attention to Sabby. "Good to meet you, too, Sabby." Angie focused on Mark again and tried not to poke him in the arm. "Anyway, I'm heading to the airport to pick up Liza. Celia's on her way back from the store now."

Angie turned and walked down the hall to the living room. She grabbed her purse and pulled out her lip gloss. Her brother followed but headed to the door of the apartment, Sabby right behind him in silence.

He stopped before opening it and looked back at Angie. "Cool. Yeah, I was at the hotel earlier with Mom and Dad for dinner. Are you dropping off Liza and coming back here?"

Was he trying to see if he was going to get alone time at the apartment? Maybe so…but why had he been so rude to Sabby? Angie glanced at him. "Nah, thinking we're going to grab Sara, and the four of us are going to head out for some fun. Let all the married people hang out together. The single ones need some of their own time."

He raised both brows. "Are you officially single again?"

"I don't know what the hell I am. Let's just leave it at that." Angie let out a sigh. "You two want to meet up with us?"

"Ah, no. Sabby has something she's doing later." He glanced at the blonde, then back to Angie. "I'll text you later and let you know if I'm heading your way." Mark opened the door and stepped out.

"Okay. Sounds good." Angie swore she saw Sabby's lips part as if she was about to say something else, but as soon as Mark looked at her, she closed her mouth. What the hell? Weird and— *Oh my God, Sabby's* just *a booty-call!* Duh, Angie hadn't even thought about that.

Apparently, from how Mark was acting, this girl was the kind of fuck-buddy a person didn't tell anyone about. Especially their family. Damn, was her brother ashamed or something? That would suck in lots of different ways. Based on what she and Celia saw the other night, Angie had really hoped Mark had a special thing happening—more than just a sex thing, anyway. What a bummer.

Angie pasted on a smile and did her best to sound easygoing, even though things felt awkward as hell. "Bye, Sabby! It was good meeting you."

Sabby glanced back and gave a small smile as she tucked a lock of blonde hair behind an ear. "Same to you."

Jeez, the girl looked…sad. Really sad. Like heartbroken, sad.

Actually, she kind of looked like Angie felt.

Then again, Mark *was* kind of being a bit of a dick to the girl. Worse, maybe Sabby wanted more with Mark than the typical fuck-buddy relationship? Yuck. Angie had been there and done that. Had been on both sides of that coin. But only the receiving side was the one that sucked.

Thank God that wasn't the situation with Garrett—then again, it kind of was. Shit. Dread climbed up Angie's throat and lodged itself there like a boulder. She swallowed the lump down and blew out a slow breath. She was *not* just Garrett's fuck-buddy.

At least, she better not be.

God…

Was she?

Sadness filled Angie's heart, and she plopped down on the couch, defeat wrapping around her like a wet blanket. Keeping things "casual" and "fuck-buddy" were entirely two different things, right? Casual might mean something different to Angie than it meant to Garrett, but it didn't mean she was merely the regular booty-call bed partner.

A person didn't take their "Netflix and chill" hookup to dinner, or better yet, cook them dinner. They also didn't do sleepovers.

Angie ran her fingers through her hair and pulled herself back from the brink of what-the-fuck-is-going-on-ville. She and Garrett were dating. Angie may not be his girlfriend, officially, but they were having a relationship regardless. And as far as Angie was concerned, things had progressed way past casual after the first week, but whatever. That was his problem to work out.

She had no intention of seeing anyone else, had no desire to, either. But she sure as hell wasn't going to tell him that. If he wasn't willing to make a solid commitment to her, then he didn't need to know that she'd already committed herself to him.

Besides, she was still pissed at him for the way he'd shut her down on the phone earlier. If he wanted her to be exclusive to him, it was up to him to make that happen. If not? Then she guessed this little tryst they were having wouldn't last much longer than her time in Arizona.

She'd have no choice but to put an end to it and move on.

God…

God!

Angie dropped her face in her hands.

Why did the idea of putting an end to things with Garrett make her want to throw up?

CHAPTER TWENTY

"I like him a lot, but I can't read him." Angie tipped the bottle of beer to her lips. Mark's graduation was awesome, and now the after-party was in full effect.

Her older sister, Cynthia, the sibling Angie was closest to, rocked her hips side to side and rubbed her growing baby bump. "What does that mean exactly?"

"It means he's sending mixed signals." Maiya, Angie's sister-in-law, held little Joanie up against her shoulder and patted the baby's bottom. "Hate that crap."

"Exactly, and it's making me effing crazy. He said he wants to keep things casual, no labels." Rolling her eyes, she set the beer down on the table. "Damn, she's gotten so big. Gimme." Angie made grabby hands, and Maiya turned her three-month-old baby girl over to her auntie.

"You just saw her two weeks ago." Maiya laughed as she brushed her hands down the front of her shirt.

"I know. That's a long time, and she's gotten huge." Angie nuzzled the baby's soft neck. Lord, Maiya and Ryan's precious baby girl made her all soft and gooey inside. She absolutely couldn't wait for Cyn and Shane's baby to be born.

"All right, so he's sending mixed signals. Screw it. Maybe

you should let him go. No point in sticking around for some guy, who by the way, at his age, doesn't know a good thing when he sees it." Cyn placed her hands on her lower back and arched a bit. "Freaking back is killing me. Is this normal, Maiya?"

Maiya shrugged. "Getting closer to the third trimester, chica. So yeah, hate to break it to you. It'll probably get worse."

Angie rubbed her newest niece's back in slow circles. "That's the thing, Cyn. You're totally right. We even had a fight last night when we talked on the phone. I should move on, and normally I would—especially because he pisses me off so fast my head spins. You know me, I don't tolerate this kind of sh—stuff from anyone. But with him, it's like *all I do* is tolerate it. Something's different about this guy for me."

"Uh oh." Maiya raised both brows.

Cyn smiled at Maiya. "Uh oh is right. You thinking what I'm thinking?"

Angie glanced between them. "No. No, 'uh oh.' Tell me what the hel—heck you're both thinking?"

"Oh yeah, darn right." Maiya snorted.

Cyn giggled. "Celia will confirm."

"Anytime you two want to stop talking in code would be fantastic." Angie huffed and shifted the baby to her other shoulder.

"Not code." Maiya winked with a big smile plastered across her beautiful face. "You've fallen for him. As in hook, line and sinker, fallen for him."

Angie rolled her eyes. "Tell me something I don't know. No need for Celia to confirm that. And, duh, that's exactly why I haven't dumped him yet. When I'm with him, or God, if I even just think about him, my entire body lights up. It's not love…yet, but it's a whole lot of like."

Cyn glanced around. "Okay, I need a freaking seat."

Maiya dragged a chair over. "Here, Momma. Sit." She

focused on Angie again. "Yep, I remember how that felt. Your brother still makes me feel that way."

"But at least my brother was clear about what he wanted." Angie frowned.

"Not at the beginning, he wasn't. I mean, he came around a lot faster than I did, but still. At first, I had no clue what he was doing with me. He didn't either."

Cyn stretched her legs out and crossed them at the ankle. "It makes sense. I mean, it's only been what? Five minutes? Give him a chance to realize what he has."

"A second ago, you told me to dump him." Angie patted her niece's diapered bottom.

Cyn linked her hands under her belly. "Yes, and that's definitely one way to get him to realize what he has."

"Sadly, sometimes that's true." Maiya crossed her arms.

She loved her sisters—and that included her sisters-in-law, too. But damn, they were all hopeless romantics. Angie recalled sitting in Maiya's formal living room, plotting a trip to send Cyn to Texas to win Shane back. Now, it was Angie's turn in the relationship hot seat.

Her sisters would likely come up with some grand scheme for Angie to execute. Thing was, she didn't want to have to do any of that with Garrett. Not that what they'd done to help Cyn and Shane along was bad, or even that it hadn't worked —it had, or Cyn wouldn't be happily married and a little over six months pregnant right now.

Point was, Angie wanted her relationship—whether or not he wanted to admit it was a relationship—to happen because it was meant to. And she wanted it to happen because he wanted it to happen, too.

Relationships were complicated and took work, but at the same time, things needed to grow organically. Not poked, prodded, or pushed along. Not manipulated at all. Just…naturally.

So far, things with Garrett were off balance. She was

having feelings for him far faster than was sane. And clearly, he wasn't feeling the same, but then again, when they were together—naked—it was really clear to her he felt *something*.

Definitely something more than just that his dick was wet. She could see it in his face. The way he touched her. How his breathing quickened when she touched his body. The sex was off the charts, yes, but in his eyes, Angie could see so much.

She desperately wanted to see that same look *outside* of the bedroom when their clothes were *on*.

And for fuck's sake, she wanted him to call her. To text her. To just…communicate with her, like every other normal person on the planet did with each other.

Angie wanted Garrett to open up to her the way she was unable to stop herself from opening up to him. And so far, that didn't seem like it was ever going to happen.

He was the one that needed to go with the damn flow. She was flowing just fine. As far as the long-distance thing went, and her job goals? Well, if she wanted him bad enough, she'd have to find a way to make all of that work. Question was, was he willing to do the same?

With a frown, Angie nuzzled the baby's neck and drew in a deep breath, letting Joanie's sweet scent calm her. "I don't want to play any games. If I leave him, I'll do it because I am done and ready to. Even though he didn't show up tonight, which pisses me off and hurts my feelings, I'm not done with him yet. I should be, but I'm not."

Maiya touched Angie's arm. "You do what's right for you, Ang. We got your back no matter what, chica."

Cyn nodded. "Definitely."

Angie kissed the top of the baby's head. "Thanks, you guys."

God, she loved her sisters.

GARRETT PULLED into the parking lot of the hotel where Angie's brother's graduation party was being held and parked his car. But that was about fifteen minutes ago. He drummed his fingers on his steering wheel, peering out the passenger window, trying to decide if he should go in or not.

The ringing of his cell startled him, and he jumped and grabbed for the device sitting in the cup holder. Garrett swiped the screen. "What's up, honey?"

"Hi Dad. Just figured I'd check on you."

"Oh, yeah? Why's that?" Garrett tipped his head back and closed his eyes.

"Because when you left the bar, you looked like you were heading to a funeral instead of a party."

Garrett let out a sharp laugh. "That bad, huh?"

"Yes, that bad. What's the deal?"

"I don't know, Chas. I'm not sure what I want to do." He glanced toward the entrance.

"Dad, seriously, you like this girl. She likes you. You finally moved me out of your office so you could have privacy with her. Why are you overthinking this?"

"I didn't need privacy, you did." Garrett frowned. He was totally full of it. He hadn't wanted a repeat performance of Chassidy busting in on him with Angie again. "I'm not over-thinking, I just..."

"Oh, my God. Yes, you are. One hundred percent."

Garrett rubbed the back of his neck and let out a sigh. "Chassidy—".

"Dad..." She let out an exasperated groan. "Just get out of the car already. You're wasting time."

With discontent pulsing hot in his veins, Garrett bristled at his daughter's harsh tone.

Freaking kids grow up and think they can talk to their parents any way they want...

But she's right, dammit.

Garrett sighed. "You don't have to take that tone with me."

"Fair enough, but someone needs to kick you in the ass." She laughed.

Garrett shook his head and couldn't help but laugh, too. "More like, I shouldn't have answered the phone."

"Well, you did. So…sorry, not sorry." Chassidy giggled.

He let a moment pass and thought about Angie, thought about how she made him feel. Yes, he liked her. He liked her a lot. "You know, not for anything, but when did you get so pushy?"

"I'm exactly how you raised me to be. This is your doing."

"Yeah, yeah. Likely story." Garrett smiled. "Love you, honey."

"Love you, too, Dad. Now, please go have fun."

After saying goodbye, Garrett disconnected the call and stared at the entrance to the hotel once more. It was late, maybe even too late. Though he hoped not.

He opened the car door and angled out of the Jag. When he started across the parking lot, he spotted Angie emerging from the exit, a bunch of bags in her arms, and a whole shit ton of people, kids included, around her.

The temptation to get back in his vehicle before she noticed him raced through Garrett like a lit fuse on a stick of dynamite. He froze, unsure if he should even bother now… until his daughter's words came back to him. *You're wasting time.*

He didn't want to waste any time. More importantly, he didn't want to waste Angie's time. Garrett let out a short but sharp whistle to get her attention. "Angie!"

She jerked to a halt, her head moving slowly in his direction. He knew the minute she spotted him because even at the distance he was from her, Garrett could see her smile. So pretty and bright as the damn sun.

The woman took his breath away.

Nervous anticipation spilled through him, and his stomach

got tight, but he moved toward her despite his nerves twitching under his skin. After she handed some of the bags she was holding over to another woman, she turned toward him but stayed where she was and waited.

The journey across the blacktop felt a lot longer than it should have, but he used it to his advantage and drank in the sight of her the whole way.

God, she was beautiful.

Her dark hair was down and straight, cascading over each shoulder and down her back. She wore a yellow dress that stopped just above her knees—the flowing layers of it clinging to her curvy frame. At the end of her long, long legs, on her pretty feet, were a pair of stiletto strappy sandals.

Jesus, every inch of his skin got tight and molten heat pumped through his veins. Angie lit up every single one of his senses.

A good portion of the people that she'd exited with had kept moving, and only a few women remained by her side. Garrett steeled his nerves, swallowed down the glue that had locked his jaw in place, and greeted her. "Hi."

The expression in Angie's eyes was soft. "You came."

"I did." He glanced at the other women before returning his focus back to Angie. "Late, but I made it."

She shrugged one shoulder. "Better late than never."

"Hi, I'm Maiya." The redheaded tattooed woman to Angie's right stuck out her hand. "I'm Angie's sister-in-law."

"Oh, sorry. Yes, Garrett, this is Maiya." Angie raised a hand toward Maiya and then the other woman. "And this is Cynthia, my sister. And you already know Celia."

Garrett shook Maiya and Cynthia's hands. "Nice to meet you." He looked to Celia. "Actually, I don't think Celia and I have been formally introduced. But I've heard a lot about you." He shook Celia's hand, too. "It's nice to finally meet you, Celia."

"Don't believe a word she tells you. But then again, I've

heard a lot about you, too. So maybe that applies to both of us." Celia laughed. "Glad you showed. Not sure I would've heard the end of it if you hadn't."

"Celia, really?" Angie dropped her head in her palm.

Garrett smirked. "Is that so?"

All the women with Angie laughed, but Angie rolled her eyes. "Okay, enough of that, thank you very much. All of you, shoo, please? Give us a minute?"

"It's really good to meet you, Garrett. We'll have to find some time to visit before we all go back to L.A." Maiya smiled and hooked an arm around Celia's shoulder.

Garrett hadn't known what to expect, but he hadn't imagined a tribe of women surrounding Angie. It was a good thing, a great thing, actually. He smiled. "Definitely. There's a local band playing tonight at the Halo, my club. Not sure if Angie told you, I own a small concert venue. You're all welcome to come down and have a drink or two. On me, of course."

"Well, considering my ankles are the size of my calves right now, I may have to pass, but thank you for the invite." Her sister, Cynthia, smiled, and that's when Garrett realized the woman was pregnant—very pregnant.

Jesus, he was distracted. He nodded. "Of course. Completely understandable. Another time, then."

"Hmm—" Her sister-in-law, Maiya, looked over her shoulder. "Wonder if one of the nieces would babysit. Ryan and I could use a little adult time."

"Aw, dammit! That makes me want to go now." Cyn frowned. "Let me go find Shane and see what he wants to do."

As both sisters went in search of their men, Celia tagging along with them, Garrett focused on Angie and caught her gaze. He wasn't sure if he was reading her expression right, but it looked a whole lot like she was happy he'd shown. Maybe even happy he'd invited some of her family to the bar. At least, he hoped that was it.

For some reason, she also looked a little sad, and that confused him. He ran his palm down the warm skin of her shoulder. "You okay?"

Angie stepped close, wrapped an arm around his middle, and pressed her face to his neck. "You showed."

He rubbed her back. "Yeah, babe. I did."

"Thank you." She pressed a tender kiss to his neck.

The soft scent of her perfume wove into his lungs, making his skin tingle, and her warm body felt like heaven against him. She stayed close, her face pressed to his neck, and Garrett didn't want the moment to end. To think, he'd almost missed this.

All the reservations constantly plaguing him about their situation melted away, at least enough, so the only thing that mattered right then was the woman he held in his arms.

Him making it to the party meant more to her than he realized. He should've gotten how important it was to her, but knowing it now made the decision to show up the best one he'd made so far.

Garrett squeezed her side. "No need to thank me, Angela."

Her nose still pressed to his neck, she drew in a deep breath. "I love how your skin smells."

Desire tingled low in Garrett's stomach. "I'm pretty fond of yours, too." He slid his hand to rest above the curve of her ass. "Fond of quite a few things of yours, actually."

She moaned before tilting her head back to gaze up at him. "Might have to sneak upstairs when we're at the bar."

"Temptress." He slipped his palm lower and patted her ass.

She bit her bottom lip. "Tease. Do that a little harder, and we won't make it to the bar."

"I take it that means you're not mad at me anymore?"

She rolled her eyes. "You know, Garrett James, you do piss me off. A lot. And really, it's because I get disappointed. I don't know how to read you, and that's really, *really* annoying. And I'm not too sure of this whole 'casual' business either. But no, I'm not mad anymore. Though, a good round of hate sex might be necessary to get any residual frustration out of my system."

He raised both brows. "Hate sex?"

"Yeah. You know…you pull my hair. I bite you. You pull my hair harder. Then I scratch my nails down your back. Then maybe I pull *your* hair." She pursed her lips, then raised a brow. "Then you fuck me so hard neither of us can see straight."

He narrowed his gaze and studied her. Six sentences out of her sexy mouth, and his dick had gone rock hard at the vision she painted in his mind. Why the hell he was responding with such virility to the marathon round of near-violent sex she'd described, he had no idea. But he was.

Once more, Angie stirred something inside him no one else ever had, and he had a feeling whatever it was she'd woken in him wasn't going dormant again as long as he was with her. Bottom line, the joke she'd made before was no joke at all. They weren't going to make it to the bar.

CHAPTER TWENTY-ONE

"You're totally staring at my ass right now, aren't you?" Angie glanced over her shoulder at Garrett.

He crossed his arms, and the corner of his mouth quirked in a grin. "Damn right, I am. That little skirt and those thigh-high socks? Best outfit for bowling. Ever."

She rolled her eyes. "Had I known this is what we were doing tonight, I'd have worn something different."

"My evil plan worked." He winked. "Go ahead, throw the ball. I want to see what color panties you have on."

"Yes, Daddy." She winked before focusing on the bowling lane ahead of her. She heard the low chuckle come out of him as she lined up her shot. Angie was quite sure that when she threw the ball down the lane and, as a result, was bent forward, Garrett was going to get a clear view of her simple white panties.

He'd said they were going to hit a few bars in town, a good way for him to keep social in the industry. They were supposed to be down on Mill Avenue, but instead, they were at a kick-ass neon bowling alley taking advantage of rock-n-bowl night.

The lights were dim, the black lights were in full effect,

and her white panties were going to be all aglow. He wanted a show, so a show is what he was gonna get.

After a moment to focus on the highlighted pins, Angie took a few steps forward and stopped right before the foul line. With her feet spread wide, she swung the ball between her parted legs and then released it down the lane—a perfect execution of the kiddie throw because the ball was always too heavy for small children.

But for her, the choice of throw enabled her to flash her panties for Garrett.

"Sweet Jesus."

Angie straightened and watched her ball roll down the lane and…hit the center pin just right, knocking all the pins down.

"*Yay!*" Grinning from ear to ear and clapping her hands, she spun around and faced her opponent.

Garrett's eyes were locked on her, his lips drawn into a small smirk. "Nice throw."

She raised a single brow and strutted to him. "You're not the only one with evil plans."

As she went to pass him, he snagged her arm and pulled her against him. With one hand, he framed her jaw, and the other he placed on her ass, his long fingers tickling the curve where her buttock met thigh, just below the hem of the skirt. "Cotton panties?"

"Mmhmm." Her eyes flicked to his lips, then back to his eyes as a tremor of arousal zipped through her. "Hundred percent."

Garrett traced the seam of the panties on one ass cheek. "Can't believe you got a strike."

"Sucks for you, I know." She grinned. "Nine more frames to go."

He traced his thumb over her bottom lip. "I don't think I'll survive nine more frames."

"No?" Angie raised her brows in mock shock. "Why's that?"

He bent and nipped her bottom lip. "Because my cock is so hard for you right now, I'm tempted to drag you out of here and fuck you in the parking lot."

Heat blazed through Angie, and her clit throbbed, but she let out a blasé sigh and played it cool. She wasn't going to let him off that easy. "Are you trying to get out of bowling? You're not worried I'll beat you, are you? I mean, really, I'm not that good."

"Oh, you're very, *very* good, Angela." He let out a soft chuckle and pulled her tighter against him.

The press of his hard length into her lower belly was her undoing. Angie's panties got wet, and she drew in a slow breath. After letting it out, regaining some control of her lust, she went on. "You know, you're kind of cheating."

A frown creased his brow. "Cheating?"

Angie ran her palm up his chest. "Yep, cheating."

"How do you figure?"

"You're trying to distract me."

"Nope. Never." He blinked as if he hadn't a care in the world and once more traced her panty line.

Rising on tiptoe, she brushed her lips over his ear. "My white cotton panties are nice and wet. And my clit is throbbing. I'm so hot for you right now, I bet I'd come before you even got your entire cock sunk deep inside my pussy."

Garrett stiffened and cleared his throat. Then cleared it again. "Temptress."

"Takes one to know one." She giggled, then smoothed her palm down to the top button of his jeans. "Think you can throw the ball with a hard-on?"

"What do I get if I can?"

Angie nipped his earlobe. "Anything you want."

"Done." He took a step back and then moved around her.

The abrupt loss of his body heat sent a shiver racing down Angie's back.

Damn, the man was scary good at flipping some internal switch and turning off all emotion. Or at least appeared like he'd turned it off anyway. She smoothed her hands down her waist, then the front of her skirt, and focused on catching her breath.

Her family had all headed back home after Mark's graduation party a few days ago. Though Ryan and Maiya, kids in tow, and Jimmy and Sonja, with Sonja's daughter, had gone off to explore the Grand Canyon.

Garrett hadn't had time to hang out with much of her family the few days they were there. He was too busy. Angie had been super bummed about it, but she understood or tried to understand anyway. Not like she didn't know how his life was.

But maybe in a few days, when her brothers and their spouses came back down to the valley, they could all hang out before they had to get back to their respective homes. Maybe grab dinner at Garrett's house or something?

She was hopeful, though she knew she shouldn't be.

Hope was turning out to be her Achilles heel, so was timing, for that matter. Would things ever line up for her and Garrett? She hoped it—*ugh! There I go again!*

Mr. Calm, Cool, and Collected scooped up a bowling ball, lined up his shot and released it. Angie focused on him. The man was totally unaffected, as if nothing had happened between them. How in the hell did he do that?

Angie had never seen anyone shut off their emotions as fast as Garrett could and with such complete precision. One minute, he was all over her, and the next, it was like her presence didn't register on his radar. At all. She may as well be invisible.

So baffling. And unnerving, to say the least.

She blinked as the ball struck the pins, and all ten fell, scattering on the end of the lane. *Unbelievable!*

"Your turn." Garrett clapped his hands together as he walked back to her, a serious look on his face.

Angie smiled, shaking her head. "I think I need a drink."

———

"Upstairs now. Take off all your clothes." Amazed they'd made it back to his place without him pulling off the road and burying his face beneath that little skirt of hers, Garrett closed the front door to his house and locked it. After flipping off the exterior light, he faced Angie. "Leave the socks on."

"Ooh, Daddy." The tone in her voice was laced with lust, her gaze gone soft, but there was a hint of laughter dancing in her mismatched eyes. "So bossy."

The Daddy label, although it had started as a joke between them, did things to his body he'd never admit. Although he'd never been one for kink or dominance, he was well aware of the many variations out there. The real Daddy/baby kink was more extreme than what he and Angie were toying with. Their version being more on the vanilla side of that particular world.

In the past, this kind of kink would've never appealed to him. Garrett would argue it didn't appeal to him now. Except it did with Angie. Everything with her appealed to him. From the moment he'd laid eyes on her, she fired every one of his engines.

Garrett cleared his throat, reaching for some small thread of sanity to try and calm his burning desire for her. Far too often, he found himself battling for control over his mental and physical reactions to her.

He crossed his arms. "Considering I *am* a boss to a lot of people, I suppose it's not a far stretch to be bossy when necessary."

God, everything was different with Angie. Every damn thing—he'd be a fool to admit to her, or anyone else for that matter, how much it scared the ever-loving shit out of him. That little thought was between him and the universe. No way he was ready to deal with his feelings for her yet. At least not until she was gone.

Standing at the foot of the staircase, Angie crossed her arms and jutted out her chin. "What if I don't do as I'm told?"

Fuck it. He moved to her, all too willing to play her game. "Then you'll have to get a spanking. Bad girls always get a spanking."

Her eyes went wide. "Garret James! You wouldn't even put me in time-out first? You'd go straight for spanking?"

Circling her tiny waist in his arms, he pulled her close and gazed down at her. "Something tells me a time-out really won't do the trick." He bent to her ear and ran the tip of his nose along the petite shell. Fuck, she smelled good. "I'm betting you'd rather have your fine ass spanked until it's pink and stinging."

The little whimper she let out arrowed straight to his dick, making it throb behind his zipper. Jesus, she made him ache for her. Did the woman have any idea how she affected him? Probably not—

Bold as usual, Angie raked her short nails up his torso. "Maybe I would." She threaded her fingers into his hair. "Maybe I'd even misbehave just to see how far you'd let me go before you punish me." She pressed her petite breasts against him and slid her other hand between them to grip his length. "Then again, something tells me you like the idea of me misbehaving."

Garrett chuckled as lust barreled through him like a freight train. Okay, so maybe she did know how she affected him. Still, Garrett couldn't let her get the upper hand. He'd already swatted her fine ass once or twice when they'd had sex before, but what he had in mind now was going to be way more than that.

Nuzzling her neck, taking in more of her sent, he ran one hand along the small of her back, raised his other hand, and — *SMACK!*

With a startled yelp, Angie jerked her head back. "Ohhhh-myyygod!" With her gorgeous eyes wide and bright, she pressed her lips together.

"Still want to misbehave?"

Giggling, Angie nodded. Without another word, she turned and ran up the stairs.

Garrett watched as she disappeared into his bedroom. With a shake of his head, and after adjusting his erect cock, he took a quick detour into the kitchen, procured two water bottles, and then headed up the stairs to join her.

Spanking was definitely on the agenda.

CHAPTER TWENTY-TWO

Angie lay on her stomach on the bed, wearing only her thigh-high socks and white panties. Nervous energy, mingled with heady anticipation, had her skin tingling from head to toe. As she stared out the big bedroom window to the darkness beyond, her stomach was in a knot, and her heart beat so hard, she could hear it in her ears.

Since the fabric of her skirt covered the area he'd connected his palm with, the one slap to her ass cheek he'd delivered hardly stung. But the shock of it had been intense and pleasurable.

Now, there was nothing but her thin panties to protect her skin from the sting his hand could deliver. At the thought, a little moan escaped.

Angie was no stranger to bed play, though nothing too intense. And spanking had been something she'd enjoyed. However, the idea of having Garrett spank her was somehow hotter than any of her other experiences in the past with the act.

The bedroom door opened, and a shiver ran down her spine. Angie stayed silent, listening to him move around the room, and then watched his dim reflection in the darkened glass of the window as he undressed at the foot of the bed.

The outline of his naked body and his rock-hard erection sent a heady quiver through her. God, she loved his cock.

A small smile curved her lips. Crossing her feet at the ankle, she bent her legs in the air. "I was a good girl and did what I was told. Mostly…"

"Too bad your defiance cancels out the compliance." The bed dipped slightly with his weight as he climbed onto the foot of it. "Guess that means you're getting a spanking."

Another shiver raced down Angie's spine, this time radiating outward, raising goose bumps along every inch of flesh. Her pussy was already wet, had been since downstairs, but the anticipation boiling in her blood kicked her arousal into overdrive, making her stomach tighten as her clit pulsed. "If I promise to be good going forward, will you go easy on me?"

"With the way you argue? Not a chance." He smoothed his palm down the center of her back to the swell of her buttocks. "But if I do decide to go easy, it'll only be because you earned it."

Angie was well aware of how full her ass was. She embraced it completely. The thought of Garrett spanking it, making the flesh jiggle, might freak some women out, but not Angie.

She'd learned early on men loved that shit. They loved watching a full ass shake and ripple. They didn't care about cellulite on an ass or thighs, either. More for them to grab onto—one guy had informed her years ago. "What is it you want me to do to earn it?"

"For now, just hold still." His voice had gone so low and gravelly it sent another blast of heady lust right through her.

Garrett smoothed his palm over one cotton-covered buttock, then the other, and Angie bit her bottom lip.

All at once, she wished she hadn't kept the panties on. But maybe he'd tear them off, or at least jerk them down her thighs—another round of shivers raced down her spine at the thought, and she almost groaned.

The urge to touch him filled her mind, but she didn't dare. The game was too fun, too intense. And she was dying to know how far he'd go with it. Each time they had sex, his control slipped a little more. This was yet another step toward that side Garrett tried so hard to conceal within himself.

Again, as he'd done in the bowling alley, he traced the arch of the seam of her panties along the bottom of her ass cheeks. His touch was feather-light, and although she'd been anticipating he might be rougher with her than in the past, the softness was even more titillating.

"Spread your legs."

Angie did as she was directed, and then she felt the tip of his finger trail down along the cleft of her bottom to her core. He pressed his fingertips against the covered mouth of her cunt before continuing to her clit, tracing light little circles over the throbbing bud.

A moan bubbled out of her, and she arched her hips, seeking more from him. He was teasing her, driving her higher.

"You've soaked through your panties, Angela."

God, she was going to spontaneously combust! "Yes."

"Hmm." The bed dipped, and she felt him position himself between her spread legs. "We should probably get these off you."

"Yes, please." Panting, mouth gone dry, Angie licked her lips.

Once again, she felt only his fingertip as he traced the seams that ran between her thighs, deliberately avoiding the center of her wet panties. Then she felt his breath on her lower back before he pressed his lips to each dimple above the curve of her bottom.

"Better yet, because you *love* to challenge me and left this pretty white cotton on—" he drew little circles over her clit

again. "—I'm going to make you keep them on a little longer."
He pressed a soft kiss to the waistband of her panties.

Heat blazed through Angie, and her whole body shivered.
God, she needed mo—

Garrett gripped an ass cheek hard in each hand, slipped
his thumbs beneath the fabric, and traced along the edges of
her labia.

Oh, wow!

Wow!

Teasing. Stroking. Playing with her.

Fucking bassists and their long fingers! God bless them!

"Garrett." His name came out on a moan, and she shifted
her hips, desperate for more contact.

SMACK! "Stay still."

Fuck, yesssss! Fire raced from her ass cheek to her clit, and a
guttural moan came out of her.

He smoothed his hand over where he'd connected with
cotton and skin. And then, before Angie had a moment to
recover from the sting of the first slap, he spanked her again.
And again. Alternating sides. Gripping each cheek before
smoothing his palms over the heated flesh to soothe it.

The combination of the duller sting from where her
panties covered her skin and the sharper one, where he
connected with bare flesh, had Angie writhing on the bed,
arching to meet his strikes, moaning as lust coated every inch
of her insides like hot syrup and her clit throbbed to the point
of pain.

Garrett rose behind her and then yanked her hips up. "On
your knees, ass in the air, chest on the mattress."

"Oh, my God, yes!" She gripped the blanket in her palms.

He pressed his hard length against her covered cunt and
thrust his pelvis forward, barely catching the edge of her clit
and tormenting the mouth of her pussy. Angie panted as her
head spun, her entire body thrown into a maelstrom of physical sensations fueled by pure lust.

And then he jerked her panties down over her ass.

GARRETT'S AROUSAL had flooded his system, overwhelming his senses and body to the point that pre-cum was dripping in long, thin streams from the tip of his throbbing hard cock.

Angie had an ass *any* man would go insane for—God knew he'd lost all logic and reason over the sheer perfection of it. Truth was, she had *a lot* of things a man would lose their mind over, and if the lucky bastard wasn't careful, his heart, too.

For Garrett, it was looking like he was the bastard on deck, but whether or not he was lucky was questionable. The risk was far too great with her.

Shaking off his way too emotional thoughts, Garrett focused back on the task at hand.

With a palm to her lower back, Garrett urged her to lie flat on the bed again and then straddled her legs, ensuring she wouldn't be able to move. After scooting back a bit, he pressed a soft kiss to each pinkened butt cheek.

With the backs of his fingers, he smoothed his knuckles across the warm skin of her backside. Fucking hell, she was pure temptation. "You have an *incredible* ass, Angie."

With glazed eyes trained on him, she let out a soft sigh, but then a grin curved the corners of her sweet mouth. "Thank you, Daddy."

Garrett chuckled. The woman must want to be spanked. Which worked for him because he wanted to spank her. That made the situation pretty fucking perfect in his book.

He glanced down at her face, then back to her round ass. Once more, he smoothed his palm over the now cooling skin. It was time to make it burn hot again. "Defiant little brat."

Without wasting another second, he raised his hand and slapped it down on one full butt cheek. As a low groan came out of Angie, he smoothed the tender spot with his palm and watched a shudder run through her body.

He wasn't done with her…not by a long shot.

Raising his hand again, Garrett smacked a mound of flesh, this time connecting with the other side, and then followed up with several more swats, alternating side to side of her delectable ass.

The full, round flesh jiggled with each slap, making his cock jerk and throb as pre-cum ran down his shaft to his sac.

Angie moaned, whimpered, and begged for more. Even though he'd positioned himself over her thighs to limit her movement, she still tried her damnedest to angle her ass higher to meet his palm as it came down and connected with her skin.

For God's sake, it was one of the hottest sexual moments of his entire life. As long as Garrett lived, he'd never forget it.

When he could take no more himself—and her ass was a beautiful and bright shade of pink—Garrett smoothed his palm over the hot skin and then gripped the soft flesh. Then he spread her ass cheeks, exposing her tight little hole. "I want you here."

"God, yes! Take me there, please?"

Jesus, could she get any more perfect? "Soon."

Captivated, Garrett continued to massage and grip her bottom. His dick was about to explode, his balls pulled up tight, and every inch of his skin was hyper-sensitive. Yes, for sure, he wanted inside her ass, but not yet. Not tonight.

Instead, he pulled her hips up higher, bent forward, and slid his shaft between her voluptuous ass cheeks. Thrusting forward and back, there was no way in hell he would last long. Angie arched deeper, rocking in time with his strokes.

Garrett's orgasm tingled from the base of his spine to his balls. Unable to hold back any longer, he thrust forward once more, and as his climax barreled up his shaft, he pulled back and spurt hot ropey lashes of his creamy semen all over her ass and her lower and upper back.

His orgasm was endless, and even though the head of his cock was almost too sensitive to touch, he was still hard as steel—because that was the effect she *always* had on his body. Needing more of her, Garrett angled his dick between her thighs, found the entrance to her tight cunt, and thrust deep inside her saturated core. "Fuck yes!"

Angie reached back and clawed at his thighs. "Garrett, baby, yes!"

"So fucking tight. So fucking wet." Garrett pressed his hands to her semen-covered lower back to support his weight. Sweat coated his chest and stomach, and he sucked in harsh, deep breaths as he drove into her sweet pussy. Goddamn, he'd gone as mindless as she was. "My cum is all over your back and ass, baby. I like it there, want it there." He thrust harder. "Rub your tight clit for me. Now I want your orgasm coating my dick."

Angie slid a hand beneath her body, and when she let out a moan so high pitched, it was nearly a scream, he assumed she found her target. Since he'd already orgasmed, he could focus on pleasing her completely.

He wanted her to come, ached to feel her tight channel clench around him. Needed to hear how rough her cries got as her body went over the edge. And then, once she'd settled from her climax, he'd work her up for another.

"Garrett!" She clawed at the sheets with her free hand.

"Yeah, baby girl! That's it, give it all to me." Garrett drove deep, then stilled. Her cunt clenched around his prick. Rapid little spasms squeezed his shaft, and he let out a groan. "Milk my cock, Angie."

"Ohhhgahhh! Mmmohhhgodohgodohgod!" She jerked her pelvis in short thrusts, riding the wave of her orgasm as high-pitched moans mingled with her gasps for breath.

As each aftershock hit her body, her core clenched around

him, and Garrett ground his molars, biting back a growl. When she'd finally caught her breath and her body had gone lax beneath him, he slid from her tight channel.

Garrett bent and pressed a kiss to her jawline. "Don't move. I'll be right back."

Angie nodded, and Garrett retrieved a warm, wet washcloth and cleaned up her back and ass. Tossing it aside, he stared down at the beauty that lay before him. Her ass was still pink, and he could make out faint handprints, too.

In awe, he ran the tip of one finger over the light marks.

She'd wanted that from him.

He'd wanted to give it to her.

After a moment, she opened her eyes and gazed at him. Garrett's chest got tight, and a lump formed in his throat. Damn, he was a total goner.

In less than three weeks, a connection had formed between them—one unlike anything he'd ever had with anyone before her. They clicked in ways he couldn't ignore, even if he wanted to.

Fuck's sake, what was he going to do? This wasn't supposed to happen.

After clearing his throat and doing his best to put the brakes on the emotional runaway train in his head, he bent close to her ear. "Roll over, baby girl. I need my mouth on you before I fuck you again."

When Angie turned her head to look at him, he pressed his lips to hers, and when he pulled away, she did as he asked. Not capable of dealing with all the overwhelming emotion ping-ponging around his brain, he decided to do the only thing he could handle at the moment.

Garrett climbed onto the foot of the bed, settled between her long, spread legs, and went to heaven with her on his tongue.

CHAPTER TWENTY-THREE

"The décor in this place is amazing." Sonja, Angie's brother Jimmy's girlfriend, smiled as she smoothed the back of her pinned-up hair, but then turned her attention to her daughter. "Casey, put your napkin on your lap, honey."

"Mom, please don't…" Casey looked up at everyone, her cheeks blazing red before she dropped her eyes to her lap.

Jimmy leaned close to Casey. "Pfft. Mom, please don't? What-*everrrr.* Come on, kid? You know how this works. Expecting your mom to not ask you to use your manners is like expecting her to not breathe." Jimmy winked at Sonja, and she stuck her tongue out at him. "See? I just got her to stick out her tongue—*in a public place*! I think you can handle the napkin, Case."

"Okay, fine." Casey grinned. "As long as you make her do that again. At least three more times."

"These two—" Sonja rolled her eyes and shook her head. "Two peas in a pod, I swear." She let out a loud and long sigh before sipping her mimosa.

Ryan laughed. "That does not surprise me in the slightest."

"Me either." Maiya laughed as she put baby Joanie up against her shoulder, patting her back.

"Don't swear. You never swear." Jimmy grinned as he leaned close to Sonja and pressed a kiss to her cheek. "Just remember, we're *your* peas in a pod, mo chroí."

Sonja cupped his cheek in her palm. "I love you, too, baby."

Angie smiled as she let her gaze travel around the table. Ryan and Maiya, and Jimmy and Sonja. And each of their kids had made it back from the Grand Canyon safely, and they had all met up for brunch before flying back to their respective homes the next day.

In the last three weeks, Angie had missed Ryan and Maiya and their kids a ton. Jesus, she loved those kids. But she'd *really* missed Jimmy. He and Sonja lived in Manhattan, and Angie had been saying she wanted to go visit them but had yet to make it out there.

Angie liked Sonja a lot. And although the woman was conservative and was also the polar opposite of the type of women Jimmy had been with before, she turned out to be perfect for him. Plus, her daughter Casey was a sweetheart.

From the stories Angie had heard, the girl had been quite a handful when she was younger. At the age of seventeen, no one would've expected Casey to turn into the kid she'd become. Although she still looked like that rebel fifteen-year-old she was when Jimmy entered her life—with her bright purple hair, her black, cat-eye winged eyeliner that gave most makeup models a run for their money, and her piercings that were definitely interesting, she was so much more than all of that.

The girl was a straight-A honor roll student, looking at colleges to attend after she graduated. Casey was also an artist who had gotten damn good at industrial art, thanks to Jimmy and had thankfully given up the whole rebel against mom act.

She was the perfect example of why a person shouldn't judge a book by its cover.

Yeah, Angie needed to get out to New York sometime soon. She glanced over at Garrett. Would he consider coming with her? God, that'd be amazing. Hell, the idea of having him all to herself on a non-stop flight to JFK sounded like heaven to Angie.

Garrett must've noticed her staring and bent close to whisper in her ear. "You okay?"

"Yeah. Just… daydreaming a little." Angie smiled.

He found her hand under the table and linked his finger with hers. "You can tell me about it later."

"So, Garrett, have you always owned a bar?" Maiya set Joanie down in the infant car seat situated in the chair beside her.

Garrett squeezed Angie's hand under the table. "It's been my gig for the past fifteen years."

Ryan leaned back and hooked an arm around Maiya's shoulders. "The place is great. Must be a lot of work, though."

"It is. But I guess it's like any other line of work. You get out of it what you put into it." Garrett sipped his coffee.

"Ditto. True for my artwork, too." Jimmy leaned forward, resting on his forearms. "The pieces I feel less attached to tend to not sell as fast."

Garrett let go of Angie's hand. "Art? What kind?"

"Industrial mostly. Basically, I weld shit I see in my head, and lucky for me, people want to buy it." Jimmy shrugged. "I'm not sure I'll ever understand it, but I'm damn grateful for it."

"Honey, luck has nothing to do with it. Your talent is a gift. The fact that you're humble and not arrogant about it is also something rare." Sonja covered Jimmy's hand on the table with her own and looked at Garrett. "He's amazing, Garrett.

Truly. You should check out his website sometime. You might find something you'd like for your bar."

"Sonja, come on, babe. The guy doesn't need t—"

"For sure. I'd be happy to take a look. I'm betting you've got something that would fit right into my decor. Or maybe I'll commission a piece." With a smile, he glanced at Angie. "You're a writer. James is an artist. Does everyone in your family have talent?"

"I wanted to be, but writing reviews hardly constitutes being a writer." Angie shrugged.

"You used to write short stories when you were a kid, Ang. Don't pretend you don't love writing." Ryan set his coffee cup down.

"I'm not. I've even set some new work goals recently. Oh, look! Here comes the food." Angie cut a glare at Ryan, praying he'd shut up. She could feel the heat from embarrassment rising in her cheeks. Those stories were ridiculous kid ramblings, nothing serious. Certainly nothing worth reading.

"New goals?" Garrett took a sip of his coffee.

"Yes." She looked at Garrett. She hadn't told him anything about her Rolling Stone aspirations yet, not that she had any reason not to share. He hadn't had any problem with her being a music reviewer; he likely wouldn't have one with her reaching for higher ground.

"There were poems, too, Ry. Don't forget the poems." Jimmy sat back as his omelet was set down in front of him.

Angie blew out a breath. God help her. "Are you two done yet?"

Her brothers laughed. As Jimmy cut into his omelet, he glanced back at her. "You know better than that. We're never done."

"Short stories and poems, huh? Plus, a new work goal? Interesting." Garrett smoothed his palm over her thigh. "You planning on sharing that with me?"

"Of course." Angie's Belgian waffle with fruit and

whipped cream on top was set in front of her. "Ooh, this looks so delicious, doesn't it? And *I am* starving."

"Mmhmm." Garrett squeezed her thigh, then pulled his hand away when the waiter set the breakfast burrito he'd ordered in front of him. "You can tell me later."

"So, what did you do before you owned the bar?" Maiya looked over as she cut up her son Jacob's pancakes for him.

Anxiety crawled along Angie's skin, and she closed her eyes, searching for some unknown well of calm within her. Would Garrett answer Maiya's question directly? He rarely talked about Copper Seven. As in never.

Jesus, leave it to Maiya to dig into his past. As if she had some sort of sixth sense, Maiya just *always* knew things. Her sister-in-law called it her "gut instinct." If it wasn't that, then Angie had no clue why Maiya was asking.

Unless—maybe Celia had said something? She was the only one who knew about Garrett's past life, and she could have told Cyn and Maiya. *Dammit.* Angie grabbed her mimosa and took a long drink.

Jeezus chrispies, Garrett was probably going to be pissed.

GARRETT STARED at Angie's sister-in-law, wondering where her questions about his past came from. These days, the only people who asked things like that about his past were usually looking for a story.

But Maiya wasn't an undercover reporter, and she wasn't seeking him in any sort of sexual or romantic way, so…the woman was just being friendly, making conversation, and Garrett was being paranoid.

"You writing a book, Maiya? Or, wait, you're from the Census Bureau, huh?" James chuckled and cut into his omelet.

"Yes, totally writing a book. And surprise, you're the main

character, Jimmy!" Maiya winked at her brother-in-law. "Whatever, pea in a pod." She laughed. "Eat your omelet. I was just curious."

Garrett used the momentary distraction and filled his mouth with some of his breakfast burrito. Talk about paranoia. He needed to chill out. Maiya's question was merely coming more from a place of wanting to get to know him— and likely trying to figure out if he was worth a damn for Angie.

Plus, he was a lot older than Angie. It wasn't like her family was blind. They were well aware of their age gap.

He sipped his coffee. "No worries, James, Maiya, really. It's all good. Before I owned the bar, I used to be in a band. But that was a long time ago."

"Oh, now that's fun! I used to know a lot of bands back in my wild single days." Maiya glanced at Ryan, a small smile on her lips. "Such a hard industry to make it in. But I bet you made some awesome memories trying."

Angie coughed and wiped her mouth with the napkin.

Garrett had to stifle a laugh. Apparently, Angie hadn't told her family about who he was or his past. Once more, it was obvious his gut instinct was dead on with her. Her interest in Garrett was pure, like he'd always thought. He smoothed his palm down Angie's thigh. "I would agree that the music biz is not an easy one. Definitely hard to make a living. It was fun, for sure, though. Lots of memories, too. But I much prefer the steady income of the bar."

"I hear that." Ryan nodded and bit into his food. "Especially when you have kids."

Jacob sipped the last of his drink. "Daddy, can I have more milk, please?"

"Sure, little man. Hang tight." Ryan ran his palm over his son's head before waving down a server.

"Do you have any kids, Garrett?" Maiya slipped the pacifier back into Joanie's mouth.

Jimmy leaned toward his sister-in-law. "Maiya, give the guy a break, will you? He's barely gotten a bite of his breakfast."

"What? I'm just making conversation." Maiya frowned and stuck her tongue out at James.

Angie dropped her head into her palm and let out a groan. Garrett almost spit out his coffee at the look Maiya was giving James. Ryan was stifling a laugh and keeping his focus on getting his son, Jacob, more milk. Sonja sat, calm as a cucumber, as she smoothed the palm of her hand up the back of her pulled-up hair.

Wow, so this was Angie's family…well, at least some of her family. Banter at the dinner—or, in this case, brunch—table. Organized chaos: kids asking for things, a baby sleeping…no, wait, crying. Yup, crying. Maiya scooped the infant up from the carrier. The server came and brought a fresh cup of milk for Jacob.

"How fortunate you and Angie have music in common." Sonja raised her mimosa glass to her lips. "I know with James, finding things we both liked wasn't easy."

James leaned forward on his forearms. "Not so much that it wasn't easy. We had plenty in common. It was more that Sonja kept insisting we had nothing in common because of our age difference."

Sonja rolled her eyes and sipped from her champagne flute. Casey started giggling.

And the plot thickened…

"See? I told you age wasn't a thing." Angie gave him a side-eye glance before cutting into her waffle.

"Age is only a thing if you make it a thing. Right, mo chroí?" James leaned over and whispered something to Sonja. She giggled and swatted him away.

Ignoring Angie's comment, Garrett cleared his throat and then wiped his mouth with his napkin. "I have a daughter. Chassidy."

"Aw, precious! How old?" Maiya positioned the baby at her chest to breastfeed her.

"She's twenty-seven. My pride and joy, truly. She's my booking agent at the Halo." As to not be rude, Garrett averted his eyes. However, it wasn't like there was anything to see.

Maiya was discreet, managing to do so without putting a tent over her and the baby so a mother could take care of their child. He could only imagine how annoying and difficult those things were to use.

Why people got so up in arms over women breastfeeding their babies in public, he'd never understand. God knew most of this shit he saw on the news daily was more cause for concern than a mother feeding her baby in public in the most natural way possible.

Garrett hadn't been around much when Amanda was breastfeeding Chassidy, but he knew she likely handled it in the same way Maiya was now. Angie would probably handle it the same when she had babies of her own, too.

Maiya glanced down at the baby and adjusted her. "That's awesome. I assume you've met her, Angie?"

Angie looked up from her waffle and wiped her mouth. "Uh, yeah. I met her briefly. But we haven't had a lot of time to get to know each other." She sipped her mimosa. "I'd like to, though."

"You should. For sure, chica." Maiya smiled.

A pang of guilt hit Garrett in the stomach, and he signaled the waitress for more coffee. Nothing like a little family time to highlight all the shit you weren't paying attention to. He really should encourage Chassidy to talk to Angie…or something. Except, Angie was leaving in a week. Jesus, this was complicated.

Garrett sat back and glanced around the table. Still, orga-nized chaos reigned. Another server brought a small bowl of fruit to Jacob and then delivered a refill of orange soda to

Casey. Ryan pressed a kiss to Maiya's forehead, then tended to Jacob.

James was younger than Sonja, and obviously, things worked between them. As serious as that woman appeared to be, James had a smile coming from her lips simply by looking at her. Sonja's daughter seemed good with them being together because she smiled every time her mother did.

Maiya and Ryan appeared to be opposites as well—at least judging from the way they dressed so differently from one another, yet totally in love—with two gorgeous kids. From the outside, everyone looked happy, amazing, content...not perfect, but normal for sure.

The thought made Garrett shake his head. Being a musician who made it big, then an addict/alcoholic who crashed and burned, there had never been anything normal about Garrett or his life.

CHAPTER TWENTY-FOUR

Sitting behind his desk in his office at the Halo, Garrett glanced at Angie. She was sitting across from him on the sofa, her laptop balanced on her legs, working, or rather, setting up her schedule for when she went home at the end of next week.

He was supposed to be working, too, but his eyes were starting to cross from trying to reconcile paid invoices from unpaid ones. Looking at Angie was much more preferable. He leaned back in his chair and stretched his arms over his head.

She glanced up and caught him staring. Her soft lips arched in an even softer smile. "Yes?"

Garrett dropped his arms and leaned forward. "Tell me about the job goals you mentioned this morning at brunch with your family."

Her eyes flashed, and she tilted her head to the side. A series of emotions played over her face, ones he couldn't decipher. The hairs on the back of Garrett's neck prickled, and he let out a slow breath. What was she thinking about?

After what felt like too long, she finally spoke. "Well, let's see. At some point in the last year, I decided I wanted to grow my career."

"You just decided? Out of the blue?" Garrett raised both brows.

"Yeah, pretty much."

"Hmm." He was sure there had to be more to this. "Doesn't seem like you."

"Why do you say that?" She gave him a half laugh.

"Because, yes, you're determined, but you're much more complex than that."

She raised her brows. "You think I'm complex?"

"I know you are. So spill, what prompted the desire for change?"

"Okay, fine. You want to know, I'll tell you." She drew in a deep breath and let it out, her chest rising and falling with the action. "It's silly and a little embarrassing, so promise, no laughing."

He nodded. "I promise."

"M'kay. My sister, Cyn, the pregnant one…"

"Yes, I recall."

"Well, before she was all happily ever after married and preggers, she decided she wanted to be single for a year. She asked me to do it with her. So, I did. Then she backed out. But I didn't. It wasn't like I had anything else going on, so why not, right?" She shrugged. "Anyway, during that time, I stayed focused on me. My apartment, my life, my career, you get the point. Hence, deciding I wanted more out of my career, to be better."

"Now *that* sounds like you." He leaned back again, linking his hands across his tummy. "So, are you looking to write books? Journalism? What?"

She drew in another deep breath. "I want to write for Rolling Stone. Be a staff writer. I'll start with reviews if I have to, but I want the real stuff—not that reviews aren't real, but you know what I mean." She waved a hand back and forth in front of her. "But I want to be a writer. Maybe it's not with

Rolling Stone. Maybe it's with some other publication? But I would prefer to stay with music."

Suspicion crept up the back of Garrett's neck, tightening the muscles. He tipped his head to the side, stretching. So, she wanted Rolling Stone, so what? It made sense, considering what she did for a living. It was a logical step.

Besides, it wasn't as if he'd shared that he'd been getting calls about interviewing with the magazine. Angie had no clue, so there was no reason for him to wonder…yet he did.

He swallowed and glanced at his computer screen, then back to her. He needed to get a grip. Angie's goal to work for them had nothing to do with him. It was just a weird coincidence. It had to be. Though, he didn't believe in coincidences. One way to find out.

"When did you apply with them?"

"Oh, I haven't yet." She shrugged. "I planned to do that after I got back home."

See? Her goals had nothing to do with him. Garrett let out a slow breath, his shoulders relaxing as relief spread through him. "Why music?"

Angie smiled, and her eyes lit up. "I love music. Always have. My mother said I wouldn't go to sleep without music playing when I was a baby." She shrugged. "I guess it's always been a thing for me."

"It's always been a thing for me, too." Warmth filled Garrett's chest, and he smiled as he studied her. The way she talked with her hands. Her mannerisms. The way her mouth moved when she spoke. How she brushed a stray strand of hair out of her eyes. Three weeks, and he was still captivated by her.

"Who would've thought?" She winked. "So yeah, that's it. My goal. Not sure if it'll happen, but I've got as good a shot as anyone, I suppose." She shrugged again before returning her focus to her laptop screen. "But we'll see."

"Angela Donnelly, as tenacious as you are? No doubt in my mind, it'll happen."

Her eyes met his again, but instead of commenting, she just smiled. But her eyes, her eyes were soft and sweet, and he knew she felt his words how he'd meant them: sincerely.

It wasn't lost on him that the one place she dreamed of working was the one place he was being asked to interview with. Again, Garrett didn't believe in coincidences. Was this a sign from the universe that he was supposed to do the interview? Was he supposed to use it as a way to help Angie? Or was he supposed to just leave all of it to fate?

Garrett looked back at his computer monitors. He couldn't be sure what to do. But he didn't have to know. Things had a way of working out exactly how they were supposed to. For now, all he had to do was enjoy this last week with her.

CHAPTER TWENTY-FIVE

Angie sat across from Chassidy at Garrett's dining room table. Neither Garrett nor Angie had expected his daughter to join them for dinner, but when Chassidy showed up at the front door, Garrett hadn't turned her away.

Who was Angie to question it? It was his house and his daughter. The man could do what he wanted. If she was ever going to "go with the flow," now was the time.

Besides, considering Angie was falling for the man, getting to know his daughter was probably a good idea. That didn't mean she wasn't a ball of nerves sitting there trying for all it was worth to eat the dinner he'd made as well as make conversation.

This was the first time she and Chassidy had seen each other since Chassidy walked in on Angie and Garrett making out in his office three weeks ago.

"Food, okay?" Garrett glanced over at Angie.

She chewed and swallowed the mouthful of spaghetti she'd just stuffed in and then wiped her mouth. "Food's delicious, thank you."

"His spaghetti and meatballs are my favorite." Chassidy smiled as she twirled her fork in her plate of spaghetti.

Garrett smiled, too. "Lucky for you, it's what I had planned for tonight."

"No denying that," Chassidy said around a mouthful of food.

Angie grinned at Garrett's daughter. Talking with a mouthful of food was something that often happened at Angie's parents' house, too. It was an innocuous thing, but it made Angie relax a little, and the tension in her shoulders eased.

"I see your table manners still need some work, though." Garrett laughed.

"Mmhmm." Chassidy shrugged as she chewed, and then glanced at Angie and raised both brows.

Angie giggled and forked up a mouthful. Yeah, hopefully, this was going to go okay. And yes, they were close enough in age to be sisters, which, as Garrett had said when they first met, he was old enough to be Angie's father, but that just didn't factor for her.

He was older, so what? Sonya was older than Jimmy— only eleven years, but still.

Garrett's cell rang from the kitchen counter.

Angie looked over her shoulder and then back at him. "You want me to grab your phone for you?"

"Nope." He took a piece of garlic bread from the serving basket. "Let it go to voicemail."

Okay then. Angie looked at Chassidy, and Chassidy gave a slight shrug of one shoulder and took a sip of her wine.

The phone stopped ringing, but then, not two seconds later, started again. With a sigh, Garrett glanced over toward the telephone. "Shit."

"Grab it, Dad. Could be something important with the bar." Chassidy cut into a meatball.

Garrett took a sip of his water. "Whatever it is, it can wait until we're done with dinner."

Angie tried to ignore the ringing, but seriously, why not just get it? "Babe, it's okay, really."

The telephone stopped once more, and he grinned. "You're right. It's absolutely okay. Now, eat."

And then the phone started ringing again…

Chassidy scooted her chair back and stood. "For God's sake. I'll—"

"No. Stop. I'll get it." Garrett got up, dropped his cloth napkin on the table and stalked to the counter. After picking up the phone, he glanced at the screen and then walked out the back door before he even had it to his ear.

Chassidy sat back down. "I swear to God, the man has a personal vendetta against technology and communication."

Angie laughed. "God, I wasn't going to say anything, but you are so right."

"Yeah, well, you'd think a man like him wouldn't be so communication challenged, especially considering he runs the venue like a tight ship and was once a huge rockstar, but he is. Let me guess, his responses to texts or calls are sporadic, at best, am I right?"

"Ohhhhmyyygoddd, yes!" Shaking her head, Angie sat back and then took a long swallow of her wine. "Saying it's frustrating doesn't do it justice. And he says it's no big deal, but yeah, it's a big deal, and it makes me more than a little pissy."

"Believe me when I tell you, I know. I don't get pissy; I get furious at him about it." Chassidy rolled her eyes.

Relaxing further, Angie took another sip of wine and then smiled. "I can't tell you how relieved it makes me feel to know this." She cleared her throat. "I mean not that you get angry at your father, but that he has this same problem with everyone. Makes it feel like maybe it's not a big deal after all. Even though it feels that way, at least now, I know it's not personal. Thank you for that." Angie raised her glass, and they clinked them together in salute, or solidarity, maybe. It was a good start, regardless.

Chassidy nodded. "Happy to help."

Angie glanced at her wine glass, then back to Chassidy. "I'm glad we're finally getting to spend a little time together."

A sincere smile arched Chassidy's lips. "Me too. I probably should've dropped in sooner. I've been wanting to apologize to you for how I treated you the first time we met."

Holy awkward. "Oh, that? No, no. Oh, my God. Not at all. Think nothing of it. I mean, I get it. Your dad and I were in a rather precarious position." Angie raised both brows and let out a nervous laugh. "God knows what that must've looked like to you. Seriously, if I walked in on my parents like that—" *Jesus, what am I saying?* "Not that I'm saying I'm your mom or anything. Or that we're your parents…Fuck. Sorry! Oh, God. Okay, I'm an idiot. Ignore me, please? I'm going to shut up now and eat my dinner."

By the time Angie finished her diarrhea-of-the-mouth, which turned into a nightmare of what-the-fuck, Chassidy was damn near doubled over laughing.

Unsure whether to think the girl was laughing at the idea of Angie being her mom or at the fact that she was babbling like a fool, Angie blinked and glanced over her shoulder, praying Garrett would be back soon to rescue her.

Chassidy finally got the laughs under control, pushed her thick hair away from her face and fanned herself. "Angie, please do not take this wrong, but that was the funniest shit I've heard in a long time."

Awesome! Heat spread through Angie as if she was sitting on top of a hot stove fueled by natural embarrassment. "Funny because I'm a moron or because the idea of me being your mom is funny?" Chassidy burst out laughing once again. Angie groaned. "Oh, hell. I'm doing it again."

"No, no—" Chassidy waved her hands, still giggling. "Neither. Honestly, it was funny because I've tripped over my words like that too many times before, as well. I only hope I look as cute as you do when I do it."

Letting out a relieved breath, Angie closed her eyes and dropped her head in her palm. Apparently, she'd become the comic relief for Sunday dinner. Better that than her first thought, which was that she'd unintentionally offended Garrett's daughter in the worst way.

Angie couldn't ever be the girl's mother—primarily because they were only two years apart in age, but still. Even if Garrett married Angie and she officially became Chassidy's stepmother, she'd never really be her *mother*—step or otherwise.

Wait, what?

Good God, even inside her head, Angie had a one-way ticket to Stupidville. And sadly, the thought of Garrett marrying her, even entering her mind, was the first stop along the journey to that whacked-out little town where delusional people like her could buy their very own straitjacket.

Wanting nothing more than to crawl under the table, she downed the rest of her wine in one gulp and reached for the bottle. Maybe if she got drunk, she'd stop saying stupid shit. Or maybe she'd say something else asinine, but at least she'd be too shitfaced to care.

"Seriously, I knew what you meant, and no, you didn't offend me. At all. So please don't worry." Chassidy took a sip of her wine. "Honestly, I can see why my dad likes you."

In an instant, Angie's eyes went wide, and her insides turned to marshmallow. "You think your dad likes me?"

Chassidy jerked her head back and frowned. "Of course he likes you." She shook her head. "Why would you think he didn't?"

Angie sighed. "He's just…hard to read, is all."

"Trust me, Angie. If he didn't like you, you wouldn't be in this house right now. The man one-hundred percent likes you."

Angie placed her hand on her chest. "God, Chassidy, that means so much to me." She leaned forward. "I really want to make him happy."

Chassidy smiled, her pretty green eyes twinkling. "Then just keep doing what you're doing, lady. Whatever it is, it's working." She held up a hand and then laughed. "Just spare me any of the more sordid details, 'kay?"

Angie laughed. "Deal."

GOD DAMMIT, impromptu or not, the last thing he wanted to do was interrupt his dinner with his daughter and Angie. Taking some stupid call could wait, except apparently, it couldn't.

Grabbing the phone from the counter, he stepped out his back door, swiped the screen and pressed the phone to his ear. "This is Garrett."

"Well, fuck me! Hearing your voice makes it feel like I just saw you yesterday."

Chase Reynolds' voice came through the line as all of Garrett's breath left him, and a bolt of nervous anxiety shot down his spine. Two sentences from the guy and every damn memory came flooding back like a tsunami.

Garrett flopped down into one of the patio chairs. "It definitely wasn't yesterday, Chase. Regardless, I guess it's good to hear your voice, too."

"You guess?" Chase Reynolds...former lead singer for Copper Seven and former best friend of Garrett James, laughed. "How the fuck're you doin', man?"

Garrett shook his head, unsure how to answer the question. So much had changed. Yet...somehow, hearing Chase's voice, they felt the same.

They'd done too much partying together and shared everything, including women. Though Garrett hadn't shared

Amanda. That was the only woman who'd been off limits. But the same was true for Chase's wife at the time, too. Though, as far as Garrett knew, Chase had been married at least three more times since then.

Garrett leaned back in the patio chair and blew out a breath. If memory served, they'd been neck-and-neck on the drinking and drugging self-destruction highway. Garrett had crashed and burned hard, and Chase hadn't been far behind him. Actually, all the members had been struggling.

Though he and Chase had both gotten cleaned up, Chase had continued with his music career…and Garrett hadn't. He had no idea about the rest of the guys.

Garrett sighed. "Pretty damn good, Chase. How about you?"

"That's awesome to hear, man. Just fuckin' awesome. You still own that bar?"

How the hell did Chase know about his bar? Garrett frowned. "Yeah. Small concert venue. It's going well."

"Nice. Yeah, I heard you'd gotten into that business a few years back. Would love to come check it out sometime. How's Chassidy?"

"She's fabulous. Twenty-seven and beautiful. I'm blessed." Garrett ran his fingers through his hair.

"Fuck, twenty-seven? Jesus, we're old." Chase laughed.

Another dose of anxiety filled Garrett's veins. His skin itched from head to toe, his hands were sweating, and he thought he might vomit up everything he'd eaten thus far. "Look, as much as I love this reunion catch-up, I'm in the middle of dinner, so I'd appreciate it if you got to the point of your call."

"It's all good, man. Not trying to waste your time. I called for a reason, sure, but it's hard not to catch up, too. Even a little, ya know? It's been years, man."

"Yeah, I get it." Garrett blew out a breath. He didn't want to come off like an asshole, and he knew that's exactly how he was coming off. He drew in another breath. "I got the calls from your publicist. Since you're calling, I'm figuring you're aware I hadn't called her back."

"Good to know you at least got the calls."

"I did, yeah. And sorry for not getting back to her. But honestly, Chase? I'm not interested. It sounds like a great thing for you, though, not sure about the rest of the guys, but that's not my life anymore."

"I told her you wouldn't be interested. But you know these publicists, they don't stop. Next thing I know, she's got me calling you direct."

Garrett rolled his eyes. "So, you're fucking her, huh?"

Chase busted up laughing. "You know me too well."

"Some things never change."

"You're right. Some things never change, but listen, some things do. You changed. No more partying and a successful businessman. You doing meetings?"

Garrett frowned. "Nah, not since I got out of rehab. What about you?"

"Yeah, I'm all good. I mix it up, hitting AA meetings two, three times a week, and once in a while, I hit an NA meeting. Hard when I'm traveling, but I got a kick-ass sponsor, and I make it work. But, hell, look at you, man, you landed on your feet. Meetings or not, you're still clean. That means a lot. You should be proud. Whatever you're doing is working, so keep doing it."

Garrett wasn't sure if the praise Chase was dishing out pleased him or pissed him off. Garrett didn't need anyone to tell him he should be proud. Pride was the last fucking thing he needed. He also didn't need anyone telling him what to do. Or how to do it.

Sure, 12-step recovery people would say that because he didn't go to meetings, he was dry and not actually in recovery. So what? As long as he didn't use or drink again, that counted for something. AA meetings didn't work for him. Never really had. They especially didn't work with his schedule. Back then, he was busy being a father and starting the business. Now, he was busier than ever, keeping that business going and being a boyfrien— *Fucking hell, really?*

Okay, enough of this shit show.

Garrett hung his head forward and rubbed the back of his neck. "I appreciate that, Chase. Really."

"Look, I'll let you go, but do me a favor, yeah? Just think about it…the interview. It's a great opportunity for all of us. Who knows, if it goes well, maybe we can do a few reunion gigs. Get the magic back. No pressure, though. But listen, at least let's hook up next time you're out in L.A., okay? It'd be fucking awesome to see you."

There it was.

Chase was seeking some sort of reunion.

"Sure. I'll think about it." It was a lie. Garrett didn't want to be part of any article, no matter how big the magazine was. He sure as hell wasn't interested in a reunion, no fucking way. His gut twisted in a knot of fear. He was never going back to the band or that life.

"Sweet. I'll give you a shout in a few weeks. Later, man."

"Yeah. Later—" Chase disconnected before Garrett even finished saying his goodbye. Typical frontman, typical Chase Reynolds.

The guy was a dick to a lot of people—a total arrogant asshole. But to Garrett, he was different. Always had been. They'd been best friends and started the band together. They'd stayed tight and in lockstep as they made their climb… partying the whole way.

He stood and ran his fingers through his hair and over his scalp. When Garrett's ex-wife had OD'd and died, he'd lost all hope of controlling his drinking and drug use. Yeah, he and Amanda had been divorced for a couple of years at that time, but that didn't mean Garrett didn't still feel for the woman.

A part of him would always love Amanda. She was the mother of his child, for Christ's sake.

Garrett hadn't been able to forgive himself for getting her hooked on the drugs, to begin with, and as a result, became a tornado of guilt and self-destruction. Garrett was just gone, emotionally, but also physically and as a result, the pause button got pushed on Copper Seven.

Unfortunately, it'd taken Garrett a couple more years before he was ready to get cleaned up. His poor daughter had suffered during that horrible time, though Amanda's parents had taken good care of her. Thank God.

It wasn't until after Garrett had gotten out of rehab that the band officially broke up. They'd tried to get him to come back, but at that time, Chase and the rest of the guys were still partying, and Garrett just…he was done. He couldn't do it. If memory served, Chase finally went to rehab right after the group parted ways for good.

Garrett blew out a harsh sigh, trying to clear all the memories flooding his brain. Yeah, he was glad to know his old friend was still sober and doing well. Chase was right; some things *did* change, but Garrett's guilt and regret hadn't.

It was still just as thick as it'd been all those years ago.

CHAPTER TWENTY-SIX

"Seems like you and Chassidy hit it off pretty good."
Garrett stretched an arm along the back of the couch and
propped his ankle on his knee.

"We did. We talked a little when you were outside on that
call."

"About?" He took a drink of his coffee.

A smile arched Angie's sweet lips as she pulled her long
hair over one shoulder. "You, of course." She took a drink of
the coffee he'd made her. "Kidding." She raised a brow.
"Sort of."

He let out a chuckle. "I bet."

With a devilish smirk, she rolled her eyes. "Don't worry, we
only talked about you a little bit. I gotta say, I like her. A lot,
actually. She's smart and funny and strong. The best kind of
person to have in your corner. You should be proud."

Warmth filled Garrett's chest at the kind words Angie
spoke about Chassidy. He didn't feel he deserved any of the
credit for how awesome Chassidy was, though. Amanda
couldn't have the credit either. Considering how fucked up
they both were, it was a miracle Chassidy turned out as
normal as she had. "I am proud. She's amazing. And yeah, I

know, I'm her father, and all fathers should feel their kids are amazing, but Chassidy really is. Considering the shitty start she had in life, thanks to her mother and me, she really could've ended up being an emotional mess or worse."

Angie shifted her feet under her on the couch and then played with the ends of her hair hanging over one shoulder. "You never talk about your ex."

Garrett frowned and cocked his head to the side. The question had caught him off guard. "Amanda? There's not much to talk about."

Angie's brows rose. "Is there another ex-wife I'm not aware of?" He shook his head, and she laughed. "Of course, Amanda. From what I read online, there's a lot to talk about."

With his coffee mug in his hands, he stared into the dark liquid. She was poking at his past, at things Garrett didn't like to delve into.

The urge to tell her everything nearly overwhelmed him, but he held back. Angie was leaving soon. Why on earth would he get into all the deep and ugly parts of his past? But he also knew if he didn't give her something, even a high-level answer, she'd push, and they'd end up arguing.

Considering he had less than a week with her before she went back home, the last thing he wanted was to lose time to an argument. He glanced up at her.

"Wow, you look like I kicked your dog or something, babe. If you don't want to share with me, then don't. It's okay. I just thought…" With a frown, she looked away from him and mumbled something he couldn't hear.

Chris-sakes, the disappointment mingled with frustration in her expression, hit him straight in the gut with a solid, one-two punch.

Garrett let out a resigned sigh and took another swallow of his coffee. "Relax, please. I don't have the energy to fight with you tonight." He set his mug on the coffee table. "Yes, of course, there's a story there, Angie. I don't talk about it a lot because it's ugly. Really ugly. But if you want to know, I'll tell you. Or better yet, ask me whatever you want, and I'll answer. Then you might get whatever you're looking for."

She narrowed her gaze as she sipped her coffee and then set the mug on the end table. "Garrett, I just want to learn more about you. That's all. I'm not *looking* for anything in particular. And I'm especially not trying to upset you."

He glanced up at the ceiling and blew out a breath. "I give the woman what she wants, and she still argues?"

Angie rolled her eyes at him and did her best to hide the smile, trying to arch her lips.

He chuckled, couldn't help it. "Go ahead, please? Ask me anything."

She drew in an exaggerated breath. "Okay, fine. You two were actually married, right?"

"Yeah, of course." His head jerked back, and he raised both brows. "Wait. That wasn't on my Wiki page? I'm gonna have to update that fucker."

Angie burst out laughing. "It was, but you know how that stuff isn't always accurate. And to be honest, I wasn't focused on that. I was more intent on reading about the band. But feel free to rip the site a new ass."

"I will. Damn, haters." He winked at her. "Anyway, yes, we were officially married."

"For how long?"

Garrett thought for a moment. "Seven years, I think?"

"You think?"

He chuckled again. "Yeah, babe. It's been a long time since that all went down. I'd have to look up the dates if you need to know for sure."

"No. It's fine. Go on, please?"

"Did you ask another question?" The annoyed look she shot him pretty much told him to stop toying with her. "Relax, babe. I'm teasing. But honestly, you were the one asking questions."

"Okay, fine. Why did it end?"

"There it is." He leaned forward and rested his elbows on his knees. "It ended because I was a sloppy mess, and unfortunately, Amanda was, too. When we were like that, we were completely toxic for each other. An endless cycle of hurting each other. It needed to end, and I had to go."

"Were you still in love with her when it ended?"

He jerked his gaze back to her. Why would she want— "Why does that matter now?"

"It doesn't, I was just curious."

"To be honest, I was relieved it was over." Unease crept through his system, and needing to move so he didn't crawl out of his skin, he stood, mug in hand, but paused. "You want more coffee?"

Angie stared up at him for what felt like forever before finally answering. "Sure."

Drawing in a relieved breath, Garrett took her mug and headed into the kitchen. He needed to get a grip on why talking about Amanda, or his past in general, with Angie set him on edge.

Sad part was he'd decided to tell her about tonight's phone call with Chase and the interview, but instead, they were talking about everything else. The woman had no clue what was going on with him, and at this point, why bother telling her? Their time was coming to an end.

Besides, letting her in on his dilemma served no purpose. It wasn't like he was going to do the interview.

Garrett knew too well what was coming next in their conversation. She was going to want to know more about his drinking and drugging days. He grabbed the cream from the refrigerator and added some to her fresh coffee.

He hated talking about that part of his life. It was embarrassing. To say he felt shame about all the damage he'd done was putting it mildly. At times, he felt smothered by all the guilt and regret he carried.

Garrett thought back to the first time he'd had Angie over for dinner. It felt like forever ago, yet it had only been three weeks. He'd given her a little more than the standard "allergy" answer regarding why he wasn't drinking wine with her, but he hadn't gone much deeper.

He'd wanted to tell her more, but ignored the foreign urge, pushing it aside. So much had happened between them since. At this point, there was no denying that if she asked him again, he'd tell her everything. The instinct to be open and honest with her, to bare all of himself, beat inside him like a drum.

But the question remained: should he embrace the urge or bury it? Again, she was leaving soon…why let his guard down now? Garrett turned, leaned against the counter and stared down at his feet.

For the past three weeks, there had been several occasions Garrett had let his guard down, nearly opening his heart and giving Angie more of himself, and each time, he'd shoved the urge away.

Opening up had never been part of his plan. Now he was trying to find some way to deal with his feelings and get them under control. But he was no closer to doing that, or worse, how he was going to handle their inevitable ending.

Like the day he met her, Garrett still felt—knew in his bones—that he could trust her. She wasn't after anything more than just him. Not the rockstar and not the bar owner. Just him. Angie was genuine, and that went a long, long way.

An ache started behind his eyes. Garrett shook his head and pinched the bridge of his nose. God, he never should've started this with her. Should've just ignored her advances and let it go. The thought of losing what she had become to him was just too fucking tragic to handle.

So here they were. She was ready to go back home, and Garrett was in deep…deeper than he'd ever thought possible.

GARRETT ENTERED the room with their fresh coffees, and Angie set her cell phone down on the coffee table. "Was wondering if you got lost in there."

"I was making sure it was perfect for you."

"Aw, that's sweet. I definitely don't expect perfection." She took the warm mug from him and set it on the table beside her phone. "Though I one hundred percent appreciate your effort." She smiled. "Thank you."

He took a seat on the other end of the couch, the same spot he was in before while they were talking. Her phone dinged three times, the text alerts coming in rapid-fire one after another. Clearly, someone was intent on reaching her. Garrett nodded toward the device. "Hot date?"

"Absolutely." She raised her palm in the air and shrugged. "I mean, I don't know if you've noticed, but there's a line of men around the corner. I'm in high demand."

"I have noticed, yes." With a slight smirk, he propped his ankle on his knee and took a sip of his coffee.

Angie was damn sure he hadn't noticed anything. Especially since guys were most definitely *not* banging down her door. Even if they were, they didn't stand a chance. She wasn't interested in anyone but the man before her.

Angie picked up the phone and read the messages. After sending a brief response, she set the device down on the end table. Picking up her mug, she refocused on Garrett and took a sip of her coffee. "If you must know, it was Mark. He's heading out with friends, wanted to know what you and I were up to."

"Got it."

Angie tilted her head to the side, regarding him, once again trying to read his mood and his frame of mind. His expression was a little more open at the moment, more obvious. As in, he was draped in tension.

It clung to him like a wet blanket from the moment he returned from getting them fresh coffee. True, there'd been some minor tension when they were discussing his ex-wife, but now it was flooding the room.

Angie crossed her legs. "I told him we were talking, having a quiet night in."

"You can go meet them if you want."

"Are you saying you want to go meet them together?"

"No. Not tonight. I'm kind of tired, but you can go if you want." He drank from his mug. "You should go."

Seriously?

She had only a few days left in Arizona. Yes, she loved her brother, but she wasn't going to give up the time with Garrett. She'd see her brother when he moved back home in the next couple of weeks.

Angie frowned as a bubble of hurt feelings filled her stomach, lodging a lump in her throat. "Garrett, no. Jesus, I don't want to go. Not unless you come with me. But honestly, even if you did, I'd rather stay here and talk."

"Okay, hon." He raised his hands in the air like he was surrendering. "It's fine."

Angie frowned again. Why was she always so damn sensitive and trigger-happy when it came to him? Forever getting her feelings hurt or offended and upset at any little thing he said. As if everything he said was meant as a personal attack on her.

Angie knew better than to believe that everything in the world was about her. It wasn't. But jeezus chrispies, she never knew what he meant or how he intended to mean it. She blew out a breath and shifted in her seat, uncrossing and re-crossing her legs.

It was certainly *possible* he was just trying to be nice, giving her an out in case she'd rather spend time with her brother. But the tension…the tension rolling off of him was telling her something entirely different.

And Angie had a feeling she knew what the cause was. "Can I ask you more about the drinking and drug use?"

Garrett tugged the tie free from his hair and ran his fingers over his scalp through the long length. "Sure."

She smirked. "Sure is such a non-committal answer. If you don't want to talk about it, it's okay. Just say so."

"No, it's fine. We can talk about it. How's this? Yes, Angie, ask me what you wish?" He picked up his mug. "Better?"

"Yes, Daddy. Much." That got a chuckle out of him and a small smile. Unable to help herself, Angie smiled back. "Okay, how about you start at the beginning? What happened?"

He let out a sharp chuckle. "Sounds like you're interviewing me. You sure you're not working for Rolling Stone magazine already?"

"Shit, don't I wish?" Angie rolled her eyes. Screw it, she stood and relocated next to him on the couch. "That would be really fucking cool, though, huh? One hell of an achievement to be hired without an application." She let out a little laugh and then laid her hand on her thigh, palm up, and after a moment, Garrett threaded his fingers with hers. "No, this is me being interested in you. So, tell me, please?"

He let out a deep sigh and squeezed her hand. "It's been over seventeen years since I've had a drop of alcohol or a drug in my body."

"Wow! That's a long time."

"Yeah, I guess it is. There's not much to tell about those days." He shrugged. "They're a blur, really. The stuff I did… the places I ended up. Not attractive, Angie. It was a dark time in my life, as it is with any addict/alcoholic. Aside from that, the significant parts you already know. I lost my wife—and then, not long after, she overdosed. I lost the first ten years of my daughter's life and…well, as far as the band goes, I can't say I lost them. More like I gave them up." He glanced down into his coffee mug. "The worst part of all of it was that Chassidy's life, the first ten years, was not good or safe until I got cleaned up."

He'd told her a lot without really saying much. So typical of Garrett to keep it short and straight to the point. She'd take it. She'd take whatever he'd give her. "Is that why you stopped, because of Chassidy?"

"Nope." He took a drink of coffee.

That answer shocked her. She shifted her body to face him. "Really?"

"Told you, it was dark and ugly. I had lost everything I loved. Chassidy was suffering, and it still wasn't enough to get me to stop." Garrett let his head fall back to rest on the back of the couch.

"Then…what was enough?"

"I couldn't stop. One day, December fifth, I woke up, and I wanted to stop, and I couldn't."

"Right—"

"When you can't stop, and you want to, you go get loaded. Plain and simple. Fuck the drugs, the booze was the go-to. Always. Except, the more I drank that day, the more sober I got. It was fucking miserable. Never mind, confusing." He let out a chuckle. "Nothing like the routine of burying all the shame and guilt in a bottle and having that bottle—my constant companion—the one thing that always made it better, fail me. Fuck, I felt so betrayed."

"Wow, that's…scary."

"Tell me about it. I was fucking terrified. So, I checked myself into rehab in Orange County." He rubbed his eyes. "My body and brain were so fucking pickled, detoxing nearly killed me. Fucking DTs. Look up Delirium Tremens sometime. It's some crazy stuff." He sighed. "Thought I was losing my mind, or that I was dying or both. As it turned out, both had already happened, really. I was a walking dead man, and I was definitely out of my mind. But what I learned there was that, at the heart of it, I was sick. Spiritually, mentally, and physically sick."

Once again, Angie was in awe of him. A deluge of feelings and emotions hit her heart and mind, making her skin feel tight. Good lord, she felt so much for him. More than he'd ever know. More than she could ever tell him. She stroked the back of his hand with her thumb and swallowed the lump that'd risen in her throat. "And you've managed to stay away from it ever since?"

"Yeah." He looked over at her. "I can't say it was easy in the beginning, but it's gotten easier over the years."

She smiled. "Addiction is baffling. You'd said before it was like an allergy, right?"

"Well, it is, actually. Something else I learned in rehab. They made us study the Big Book of Alcoholics Anonymous and attend meetings. Someone who AA considered a saint, Dr. Silkworth—a prominent doctor in the nineteen-thirties who specialized in treating alcoholics—taught that once an alcoholic starts drinking, they can't continue drinking without something they call a phenomenon of craving beginning. It's like an instant thing that happens, too. He believed, and I can't say I disagree, that the phenomenon of craving is a manifestation of an allergy. Which is what makes people like me different than you and other normal social drinkers."

"That's some amazing but scary stuff."

"Yeah, I know. It's hard to imagine for someone who can have one glass of wine and call it good. For me? Why have a glass when you can have a whole bottle? Hell, why stop at one bottle? Why not a whole case?" He laughed.

"God, I can't imagine drinking an entire bottle of wine myself. The peeing would be endless!" Angie laughed, and he chuckled, too. When their laughter subsided, Angie thought back to that first night they'd had dinner together at his house. "With all that stuff you learned, I would think you'd want to go to meetings. How come you don't?"

"It's not really for me. They made us go when I was in rehab. When I got out, I went a few times but didn't stick with it. Between Chassidy and the bar, it was hard to keep up." He shrugged. "I never really felt like they helped me. Doesn't matter. I'm doing just fine on my own." He winked at her.

God, she hoped he was. Angie bent and pressed a soft kiss to his lips. "Yeah, you are."

"Mmm. Even better now." Garrett ran his fingers through her hair and down the length.

Angie felt hope spring up inside her chest like a tall, bright sunflower. It was foolish to let it grow, to feed it. But she couldn't help herself. He'd given her so much tonight, much more than he had before. And she'd cherish it forever, cherish him, too…if he'd let her.

CHAPTER TWENTY-SEVEN

A few nights later, Angie rolled over in bed and curled against Garrett's warm body. She couldn't sleep, couldn't shut her mind down long enough to fall into a nice, deep slumber. She was leaving in two days. Less than that now because it was four in the morning.

Of course, Garrett was having no issues sleeping and was snoring rather loudly, which wasn't helping her situation, either. She rolled over again, this time a little harder than usual—careful to not be so careful. With her back to Garrett's, she scooted closer, bumping him, not deliberately, of course. *Okay, maybe a little deliberately.*

His breath caught mid-snore. With a sleepy groan, he rolled over and spooned up behind her. Hmm, this could be a good option. Middle of the night sex, anyone? Angie reached back, found Garrett's pajama-covered hip, and ran her palm down his thigh. As she stroked his leg, she pressed her ass against his groin and rocked her hips ever so slightly.

And…nothing.

Not even a change in breathing pattern, for God's sake.

Defeat coated Angie's insides. Sighing, she pulled the

covers back and, this time, moved carefully so as to not wake him and got out of bed.

He'd worked all day and then had a show that night. He was running all over the damn place at the Halo because a couple security guys called out sick, and then one of the bartenders didn't show. Needless to say, he was busy. More than usual.

First stop was the kitchen, where she grabbed a water bottle from the fridge. The second stop was the couch. Angie wrapped a blanket around herself, clicked on the way too big flat-screen TV, and found Netflix.

Grey's Anatomy would do the trick since there were a ton of seasons and episodes to watch—a perfect alternative to her own life drama.

Two episodes later, Angie hit the small powder room downstairs to pee, then went for another water bottle from the kitchen. As she made her way back through the dark house, following the glow from the TV, she rounded the corner and walked right into Garrett's chest.

The water bottle slipped from her hand, and she belted out a scream.

"Shit!" He gripped her upper arms, steadying her. "Damn, Angie, breathe."

"Sorry! *Sorrysorry*." She pressed her palm to her chest. "You scared the crap out of me."

"What are you doing up?" He rubbed his hands up and down her arms.

She let out a sigh. "I couldn't sleep."

"Why's that?"

She glanced down at the floor, spotted the rogue water bottle and stepped out of his embrace. "A lot on my mind, I guess."

Garrett looked into the family room. "*Grey's Anatomy?*"

"It's a distraction." She shrugged and moved past him back to the couch.

After she'd wrapped the blanket back around her, Garrett settled next to her, but then he shut the TV off. "Okay, how about we talk about what's on your mind instead?"

Suspicion and surprise slithered through Angie's mind as she regarded him. This from the man who never talked about anything? "Hang on. *You* want to talk?"

"Why do you say it like that?" He clasped her hand in his.

"Like what?" *Shit, that sounded really defensive.* "Sorry, I'm just a little caught off guard. You're not usually one to talk about things with me. Except for the other night when we talked about stuff." *Not doing much better here, Ang.* "I mean, ugh. Sorry, ignore me. I'm happy to talk about it."

He probably thought she was losing it. Which, who could blame him? She was feeling pretty crazy—sounding it, too.

Garrett squeezed her hand.

Taking the hint, Angie drew in a deep breath and prayed anything that came out of her mouth next wasn't going to sound desperate or weak or stupid. "I'm going home in a day."

"I know."

"You're okay with me leaving?"

He stared at her in the dim light of the room and squeezed her hand again. "No, I'm not okay with it, but it is what it is."

Angie frowned and looked down at their joined hands. "I'm not okay with it. At all."

"But you have to go, hon."

Drawing on every ounce of courage, she looked up at him and decided to let it fly. "When I go, what does it mean for us?"

"What do you want it to mean?"

God, where did she begin? Didn't the man have any idea how much she wanted him? How much she wanted *them*? Jesus, did Garrett James have any idea about anything where Angie was concerned?

GARRETT WATCHED AS ABOUT thirty different emotions passed over Angie's face. The woman would suck at poker. He knew what she wanted from him without her saying another word.

This was it—the moment where he needed to do the right thing by her. Garrett needed to let her go. Deep down, there was no denying anymore that he'd developed feelings for her, but that didn't mean he needed to act on them.

He and Angie were in two entirely different places in their lives, so why keep going? What was the point? Also, he knew from his time touring with the band that distance was hell on a relationship.

Garrett looked down at their linked hands and touched the tips of her fingers with his free hand. Fucking hell, the thought of letting her go made his chest ache and put a hole the size of the Grand Canyon in his gut.

How was he supposed to end this?

"I guess…" She drew in a shaky breath and looked down at their hands as he played with her fingers. "I guess I don't want it to mean we're over."

"Angie—" The words lodged in his throat. The ones that explained all the reasons they should go their separate ways. He cleared his throat. "Babe, you have your whole future ahead of you, and you have your goal for your career. Rolling Stone, remember?"

Her head jerked up. "Of course, I remember. But what the hell does that have to do with us?"

Dammit, the last thing he wanted to do was argue with her, so instead of letting her fists-swinging tone get a rise out of him, he paused, allowing himself a chance to take a breath before attempting to explain things. "What I mean is, you have so much ahead of you, good things. Great things. I don't have anything anymore. I've lived my life already. It was crazy, and great, and horrible, and now that part is over, and my life…it's exactly how I want it."

"Jesus, Garrett, you talk like you've got one foot in the grave."

"No, that's not what I mean." Christ, this felt all wrong, but regardless, he knew it was the right thing to do. "I can't give you what you need, Angie."

"You know, when I met you, you also told me you couldn't give me what I needed. And now you're saying it again. What exactly do you *believe* I need, Garrett?"

"Someone younger. Someone you'll marry, have kids with."

Angie jerked her hand from his. "Are you fucking kidding me?"

"Not one bit." With his heart pounding in his ears, he resisted the urge to get up and pace. She was going to fight him on this until he was ready to pull his hair out.

Judging by the thoughts he'd had about the whole situation between them and the feelings he'd developed for her, he'd end up giving in for sure. Garret would let her win primarily because he didn't want to give her up any more than she wanted him to give her up.

But he couldn't let that happen. Somehow, he had to find a way to stay strong.

"None of that matters. And I don't want someone younger. I want you!" She stood. "Jesus, Garrett, don't you get that? Or is it that you don't feel the same way I do?" Even though she was yelling, the tears were thick in her voice. She stormed away from him but paused at the bottom of the stairs. With her back still turned, she added, "I don't get it. With everything amazing that's happened between us, why don't you want me and us?"

Garrett bolted off the couch to go after her. When he caught up, she was in his closet, tossing her things into her bag. Irritation blazed through his veins. "I never fucking said I didn't want you!"

"Yeah, well, you never said you *did* either."

"Angie, stop." He gripped her by her upper arm and turned her to face him. "Stop, please. I don't want to fight."

She brushed the tears away from her cheek. "Why are you doing this?"

Garrett caressed the side of her soft hair, then swiped the tears from her other cheek. "Baby, I'm trying to do the right thing by you."

She sniffled. "The right thing is never seeing me again? Is that what you think?"

Garrett's heart shattered into a million pieces. Fuck, he didn't know what he thought anymore. This was only supposed to be a month!

Even still, he wanted to pull her into his arms and never let her go. Garrett wanted her in his bed every night. On his couch watching TV with him, eating dinner at his dinner table…he wanted so many things, but it wouldn't be like that. Long distance never was.

In the end, he'd get hurt, but worse, she'd get hurt, too. He couldn't have that. He'd hurt and let down enough people in his life. The thought of adding Angie to that list was more than he could handle. He had to make her understand.

Garrett glanced away and then back to her eyes. "No, not seeing you again is not what I want. But it's more complicated than that." He took her by the hand and led her out of his closet to the bed. "I think we need to try to sleep. Talking like this, in this state of mind, isn't a good idea, babe."

She yanked her hand away. "That's the whole reason why I was downstairs. I can't sleep, Garrett." She crossed her arms. "Explain it to me. Please? Do it, and then I'll go."

God, she was stubborn. Garrett placed his hands on her hips. "Come on, Angie. I promise I'll explain it in the morning."

Glancing over her shoulder, she motioned with one hand to his bedroom windows. "Looks like morning to me."

He let out an exasperated sigh. She wasn't going to stop, not until she got something from him. "Okay, fine. First off, long distance is complicated, but that's the least of it. Pace, staying in sync, interests, future desires…it all factors. Sure, you say now that you don't want someone younger, but you can't tell me you don't want to get married someday? Have kids? That requires someone younger, Angie. You need to think about the long term because I'm forty-six. Having kids at this age would be—" He shook his head, overwhelmed with just the idea of raising a child at his age. "I couldn't do it. And I can't say marriage was ever on my list of things to try again, either."

"That's quite a list." She crossed her arms.

"I've given this a ton of thought."

"You know what would be good, Garrett? Maybe if you tried sharing these things with me *when* you're thinking of them. That would be great."

Christ, she was relentless with her mouth. Frustration surged through him. He let her go and then balled his hands into fists. "I can't share everything with you in real time, Angie. I'm not wired that way."

The answer was out of his mouth before he'd had a chance to stop it. The excuse was such a bullshit one. He was ashamed the minute he'd given it. Garrett sighed through his nose. "Look, I'm sorry, okay? I get it. You're right. I should've talked to you about it."

She stood frozen, arms crossed and still sniffling. "This doesn't have to be so complicated."

"That doesn't change the fact that it still is." Garrett lay back on the bed. "Please come lay down with me." A few heartbeats later, he felt the bed dip as Angie climbed beside him. He turned on his side to face her. "Tell me what it is you want."

"I don't want to go, Garrett. I have to, obviously, but why does that mean we can't still see each other?"

"As I said, long distance is complicated, babe. Frankly, it sucks. Believe me, I know."

"Yeah, it's complicated. And I'm sure it sucked for you with Amanda when you were on tour. But that's not what's happening now. And it's not like I live across the country. I'm only six hours away by car and a little over an hour by plane. It could work, Garrett. We could make it work. We could stay in sync and stay at the same pace."

He ran a fingertip along her jawline. God, she was beautiful and soft and sweet…and he was totally gone for her. "You think you can handle the distance? Think about it. You get upset with me now because of how busy I am, and you're right here. What happens when you're in L.A., and I'm too busy to call or text?"

"I don't know. To be honest, I guess I keep hoping you'll get better at that." She cracked a small smile.

He rolled his eyes. "What if I don't?"

"Then I guess I'll have to accept that you suck at communication, and I'll find a way to make it work. I'll call Chassidy." She smirked.

"Fabulous. Leave Chassidy out of this."

"Okay, fine. Now, what did you mean by interests, lifestyle and future wants? So far, we have the same interests. At least, I thought we did."

Garrett drew in another breath. He wasn't sure this mattered as much as he'd tried to say it had before. He sighed. "We do, for the most part. But who knows, we could turn out to like completely different kinds of foods or political parties."

She rolled her eyes and swatted his arm. "Whatever. That's ridiculous."

"It's true." He leaned forward and pressed a soft kiss to her lips.

"Really? Okay, tell me. Are you against a woman's right to choose?"

"Not at all. Your body, your choice." He raised both brows. "If I was, would that be a deal breaker?"

She laughed. "Absolutely."

"Maybe I should change my answer, then." He chuckled.

Angie swatted his arm again. "Too late!"

He laughed again, but then he sobered. "What about kids, Angie? What about marriage?"

Her brows pulled together in a frown. "I don't know, Garrett. I mean, yeah, if I'm being honest, I always figured someday I'd have kids, but not right now. Right now, I'm focused on my career. And you, I'm focused on you. If I don't ever have kids, then so be it." She shrugged. "As far as marriage goes, again, maybe someday, but in the long run, it's just a piece of paper."

Garrett stared at her, afraid she was just saying what she thought he wanted to hear, sacrificing what she truly wanted and needed to stay with him. Eventually, she'd resent him for a choice she made for him. There was no way around that. If they continued, this could be the thing that led to their demise.

Garrett swallowed as a feeling he couldn't describe settled in his gut. Frustration? Defeat? Resignation? Sadness? Maybe all of them. He traced her jawline with his fingertip. God, he couldn't do it, couldn't end things with her. He was weak and selfish, and in the end, they'd both suffer for it…all because he didn't want to let Angie go.

She must've seen something in his expression because her face went soft. "Aside from all that marriage and kid stuff, regular differences don't matter. I mean, really, God forbid two people have different tastes. Call me crazy, but shouldn't that be the case? We do exist outside of one another. It would be weird if we had every single thing in common. It would be boring. Never mind annoying to othe—"

Jesus, she was great at distracting him, making him forget why he should be ending things. Garrett threaded his fingers into the back of her hair, gripped and pulled her to his lips. Enough with the talking for one night…or morning.

Angie moaned, and he swallowed it as he stroked over her tongue with his. Garrett rolled her to her back and moved between her parted thighs.

"GARRETT, OH, GOD!" One minute they were talking, the next Angie was on her back…

He'd gotten her panties down her thighs, pushed her T-shirt up and slid his cock deep inside her.

Panting, Angie raised her knees high and crossed her ankles over his back.

Now she was mindless, lost in the scent, taste and feel of him. Their conversation wasn't over, not a chance, but for now, for this moment, Garrett was hers. She was his. And they were going to keep seeing each other. Thank God.

Relief blazed through Angie, and she licked along the side of his neck to his ear. "Am I your girl?"

Rising on a forearm, Garrett gazed down at her. With his free hand, he cuffed her neck before sliding his palm down her sternum to one breast. He massaged the flesh, then tugged at her nipple. "Yes."

Angie rolled her hips. "What about your good girl? Am I your good girl?"

Nodding, he bent and sucked the nipple he was toying with into his mouth.

"Say it, Daddy. Say, I'm your good girl."

Garrett let out a deep groan and bit her nipple, tugging it hard with his teeth. Angie gasped as her orgasm started to rise. He moved his hand down her side to her hip and raised her thigh higher. Thrusting his pelvis forward, he drove into her, grinding against her clit. "Ask me again."

Fuck, she was going to come. "Am I your good girl, Daddy?"

"Yeah, you fucking are." Garrett slapped the back of her thigh, connecting with the lower side of her ass cheek.

The sting from the slap radiated outward and sent a bolt of heat straight to her clit. Angie cried out and dug her nails into his upper back. "More!"

He slapped her ass again and then rose up, resting his weight on both hands. "Can't get enough of you, Angie. Sweet cunt, sweet and hot mouth, sweet body. All of you."

Gazing up at him, Angie knew she was where she was supposed to be. It wouldn't be easy, the travel back and forth, the communication, but it didn't matter. None of that crap mattered. What mattered was what they had between them right then. She cupped his cheek in her palm. "You're mine."

He took her mouth in a hard kiss as her body exploded, her orgasm rolling through her in waves so strong her entire body shook from head to toe.

CHAPTER TWENTY-EIGHT

ANGIE HIT SEND ON THE TEXT TO GARRETT AND THEN WALKED up the metal boarding ramp to the Southwest aircraft. Boarding the plane for what she hoped would be the first of many flights from Bob Hope Airport in Burbank to Sky Harbor Airport in Phoenix.

It'd been a little over three weeks since she'd gone back home to L.A. Twenty-one days since she'd seen Garrett. Too many minutes to count without the feel of him and the scent of him. And every single bit of it had sucked.

To say Angie was excited, desperate even, to see him would be an understatement. Her body vibrated with giddiness as if every inch of her was yearning for him. God, she hoped he was as excited as she was.

After getting everything stowed, she killed time checking her email and then scrolling Instagram while the other passengers boarded. Garrett likely wouldn't respond to her text, but that didn't mean she wasn't holding out hope that he would. She always did.

No matter how many times she tried to tell herself not to

expect a reply or a call, Angie would end up disappointed anyway. She had no one to blame but herself, though.

Just like she thought several weeks ago, early in their casual (his definition, not hers) relationship, hope was absolutely her Achilles heel—expectation, the arrow that took her down every damn time.

You'd think after three weeks of doing the long-distance thing, she'd learn to let that crap go, to not expect him to be any different than how he was. The man was busy; he was running a concert venue for shit's sake.

And the truth was, he *had* gotten a little better at responding to her. Sometimes, he'd respond or call, but usually not both. And then, on rare occasions, he would do both, lighting up her phone in Technicolor Majesty. God, she loved that. And it always took her by surprise, sending shock and excitement barreling through her. She just wished he'd be a little more consistent with it.

Good or bad, Angie knew in her heart and soul Garrett was where she was supposed to be. And the fact remained, she'd fallen ass over teakettle for an amazing man who had a hard time communicating because he was busy running a business and also because he just sucked at it overall. Chassidy had confirmed that.

And shit happened, right? There were worse things a person had to deal with in relationships. So, it didn't matter. The heart wanted what it wanted. Hers wanted Garrett...the communication-constrained, amazing, sexy, exciting, gorgeous Garrett.

Intent on making this whole deal work, as the plane backed away from the gate, Angie booked her next flight to Phoenix. So what if she hadn't yet taken off on this first flight? They were about to, so scheduling in advance made perfectly good sense.

They hadn't discussed it yet, but Angie had settled on every other week visits if she could manage it financially. And maybe he'd help with the cost. Hopefully, he'd agree with her plan, too.

It was a good balance. Giving them time together, as well as time apart. After all, she still had a life in Los Angeles to live. She had friends and her job, though she could do her job anywhere, sort of. The writing part of it, anyway. When she was home, she needed to be attending indie concerts, whether they be in a coffee house, a public house, or a small concert venue. An every-other-week schedule allowed her to balance all that.

And if her dream to write for Rolling Stone came to fruition, she'd…well, she'd have to cross that bridge when or if she got to it. She still hadn't applied with them. Why she was putting it off, she wasn't sure.

Angie finished booking the next flight and then turned off her phone. Garrett's schedule was jam-packed running the Halo, but maybe he'd come out to see her occasionally, too. She hoped anyway…

There was that word again—hope. Such a slippery slope that four-letter word tended to be. Angie cringed and stared out the small oval window as the plane taxied down the runway. Taking a weekend off from the bar here and there had to be possible, right?

Angie hoped he was willing to do it. Dammit, there was that word again.

The plane left the ground, engines screaming as Angie, once again, told herself that everything would work out the way it was supposed to. Challenges or not, nothing worth having ever came easy. And although he was definitely not easy, Angie believed Garrett was worth having.

Once landed, Angie made her way to baggage claim and then out to the pickup curb. Right on time, too, as Celia was just pulling up.

Angie had planned to take a Lyft to her sister's apartment, but Celia insisted on coming to get her. After tossing her suitcase in the truck's backseat, she hopped into the front seat.

Angie leaned over and gave Celia a peck on the cheek. "Thanks for grabbing me. You didn't have to."

Celia snorted as she pulled away from the curb. "I know I didn't. But I'm awesome, so you're welcome."

Angie chuckled. "You really *are* awesome. Speaking of awesome, I was thinking…"

"Uh oh." Celia glanced at her, then back to the road.

"Hey! Be nice." Angie playfully pushed her sister's shoulder. "So, since Mark went back to Mom and Dad's, I was thinking, maybe I can take his room for a little while?"

Celia nodded. "Yeah, that's fine. At least until I find a paying roommate. Honestly, I'm not even sure I want a roommate again, so that kind of works out."

"Not a bad idea. As long as you can swing rent on your own, no point in a roomie. Unless it's me, of course, because I'm totes a great roommate." Angie gave her a cheesy grin.

"I could get a smaller apartment, too. But I hate moving. Plus, it's pretty much summer, so that's a big hell no on moving in the heat. Definitely not right now."

Angie looked over at her sister. "If I could pay you some rent, I would. But I can at least buy groceries and help with the electric bill, stuff like that."

"All good. I'm straight on rent. If you want to help in other ways, I won't tell you no, especially if you're eating my food. Plus, Mark didn't even try to sell his bed or dresser; he just left it for me to deal with, so you'll have that to use."

Angie wrinkled her nose. "Ooh, but…how clean is that mattress?"

Celia laughed. "It's actually oddly clean. Believe it or not, and Mom would be so proud, he used a mattress cover and changed his sheets regularly."

"Huh. Must've been all those booty calls with infamous Sabby."

Celia laughed and shook her head. "Oh, God. Don't remind me."

"I gotta say, I'm so curious about that girl. Maybe we should call him and ask him about it."

"Yeah, I bet he'd love that." Celia laughed. "Seriously, doesn't matter what we do. A Donnelly can go off to college, move out of state, move back home, get married or…whatever, but we never escape one or all of us butting into each other's business."

Angie laughed, too. "Well, we're a big family. That's the way it goes. He needs to suck it up and be glad it's us bugging him. Instead, he could be dealing with Katie."

Celia snorted. "Or Mary Claire."

"Right? Good God. She's just… I love her, but no. Something's missing in her life." They both laughed, and Angie moved her hair over one shoulder. "Okay, yeah, so maybe we shouldn't ask him."

"Probably not." Celia exited the freeway. "When do you see Garrett?"

Angie glanced back at her phone—still no text from the man. "I think tonight? But I haven't heard from him yet."

"Okay, well, did you want me to take you home or over to the bar?"

"Yes, but no. I'd rather get to your place and unpack first. I'll try to call him afterward." Angie blew out a breath and dropped her phone in her purse.

"Okie doke then. My place it is."

Angie sat quietly the rest of the drive. Once they were at the apartment, Angie took full advantage of the empty closet and dresser, unpacking all her stuff, and then got the bed made. After she was done, she grabbed a snack from the kitchen and shot Garrett another text.

It was nearly eleven p.m. on a Thursday night, and she knew he was working, yes. But he also knew she was coming into town. So, the least he could do was take a hot second and reply to her damn text.

God, this man.

———

GARRETT PULLED his phone from his pocket when it vibrated. Checking the preview on the notification, he swiped the screen and read the message.

> Angie: Hey, haven't heard from you, so I'm figuring you're busy. Do you want me to come down to the bar?

Yeah, he'd been busy. But that wasn't new. This was the third text she'd sent so far that night. He hadn't had a chance to respond to any of them yet, and every time he attempted, someone else came up to him needing something.

Although the tone of her text didn't seem it, she was likely annoyed at him but hadn't lost *complete* patience yet. Now the night was wrapping up, and finally having a moment to himself, he pulled out his phone to reply.

Garrett knew if he waited any longer to answer her, she would go from annoyed to full-on pissed-off mode. Though it wasn't like he could blame her. Anyone would be pissed at not hearing back from someone.

Though seriously, Garrett hoped she wasn't mad because he was in no mood for a fight.

> Garrett: welcome back! If you want 🙂

It was nearly midnight, and it would be closer to twelve-thirty by the time she arrived. He'd close the bar down and get them out of there. Even though he was exhausted and wanted nothing more than to go home and sleep, Garrett *was* looking forward to seeing her, kissing her, touching her—

In an instant, his dick thickened behind his zipper. Yeah, he was definitely looking forward to seeing her. A groan escaped, and he glanced around. Thanks to the loud music from the band on stage, no one standing near him heard.

A little after midnight, the band finished their final song, and Garrett headed to his perch at the bar and assumed his position. Security staff worked to herd the crowd out the exit doors, and the bartenders cleaned up, getting the coolers and bottles of booze restocked for the following night's work.

Once the crowd was out, he'd pull the cash drawers from the two registers and head up to the office. As the last few patrons lingered, Angie came strolling in the main entry doors. Garrett's breath lodged in his chest, as it always did when he caught the first glimpse of her.

All legs and long dark hair…fucking sexy as hell.

Just inside the entryway, she stopped and spoke to his head bouncer, Cody. Her smile was sweet as she laughed at something Cody said. She rose on tiptoe, laid her hand on Cody's shoulder and gave the guy a peck on the cheek.

A spike of jealousy drove through Garrett's gut so deep he gritted his teeth.

What in the fuck!

The motherfucker better *never* think about touching Angie. Like ever.

The swift rise of such a dark and powerful emotion shocked Garrett. He gripped the side of the metal bar top. The last thing he needed was to get up and knock the ever-loving shit out of his head bouncer.

Garrett blew out a harsh breath and ran his fingers over his scalp, through his hair. So much for keeping things casual. Shit. Where the hell this alpha-male possessive bullshit was coming from, he wasn't sure, but the desire to drag her upstairs, bend her over his desk, fuck her till she screamed his name before marking her body with his cum, seemed like a stellar idea.

For fuck's sake, she should know better than to tease him in this way. Assuming she had any idea how she was affecting him like this— *What the hell am I thinking?*

Shame and embarrassment filled Garrett's veins like quicksand. How arrogant to think that her talking to Cody, who also knew she was with Garrett, as in "with" him, immediately meant she was purposely fucking with him?

Hello, jealous asshole. Nice to meetcha! Good Christ, what in the holy hell was wrong with his brain function?

Before Garrett could sort out and examine each of those ridiculous thoughts, Cody pointed toward him at the bar. With a nod, Angie followed where Cody pointed and spotted Garrett.

Their gazes locked, and he wanted to drown in her eyes— her amazing, mismatched eyes.

Fuck me.

As she strolled to him, her nice round hips swaying side to side, his cock went rock hard. Garrett's inner caveman roared like an animal about to pounce on its prey, and tingles spread over every inch of his skin. He drew in a deep breath, trying to get a leash on his desire.

When she reached him, she tucked a long lock of hair behind an ear and gave him one of her soft and sweet smiles. "Hi there."

Losing the battle of getting himself under control, Garrett gave in and let his eyes roam over her face, down her body, and then back again to meet her gaze. "Good to see you."

"It's good to be seen. I missed you."

"Missed me, huh?" He stood and opened his arms for a hug.

Angie moved into his embrace and spoke against his neck. "Yes, I missed you."

Jesus, she felt good against him.

As much as he tried to ignore his feelings, he'd missed her, too. But instead of telling her how he felt or even telling her how perfect and beautiful she looked, he wimped out and pressed a kiss to the top of her head. Yes, he trusted her, but being *so* vulnerable with her was still just too hard. "Was just about to take the drawers upstairs. You want to hang down here or come up with me?"

She tilted her head back to make eye contact. "I want to come up with you, of course."

"Works for me." He stepped back from her.

She tugged at his T-shirt. "Hey, how about a kiss?"

"If you insist." He let a small smile curve his lips as he bent toward her and gave her a quick peck.

When he straightened and stepped away, the expression on her face told him she wasn't happy with the chaste kiss he'd given her. That was okay. She'd get over it. What Angie didn't know was if he gave her any more than that quick little kiss, he'd end up leaving the cash drawers downstairs and dragging her upstairs and having his way with her.

Especially because now that she was in front of him, and he'd also had his little "reaction" to her interaction with Cody, he was amped up in a way he'd never felt before. He supposed this was another opportunity where he could clue her in on his realization, but feeling and looking like a desperate asshole didn't make rank on his to-do list, so he left it unsaid.

Shaking off the insecurities and emotions and ignoring his hard-on, Garrett moved behind the bar to the first register. Work had to be done first. At the very least, the money had to be brought upstairs. If he didn't get the drawers counted and balanced because he was busy fucking his girl, then he'd just have to do it in the morning.

His girl…

Shit.

Yeah, Garrett had missed her. Maybe too much.

CHAPTER TWENTY-NINE

Angie giggled as Garrett nuzzled her neck while hooking the clasp of her necklace for her. "You better stop. This is *very* distracting."

The man was killing her, slowly, with his lips and tongue and hands and cock.

"Is it?" He pressed his hips against her ass. "I can't help it."

"As much as I love this, I'm hungry, so you must feed me. Then you can fuck me. *Again*."

Garrett smoothed a hand down her side and around her stomach, pulling her back to his chest. "What if I only put the tip in?"

Angie burst out laughing. "You had the tip in. And then the whole thing in——" She groaned, and her belly got tight recalling how she'd ridden him on his bed. And how hard she'd come. "And I loved all of it, every delicious inch." She arched, grinding her ass against his obvious erection.

In one swift movement, he pulled away from her and smacked her on the ass. Hard!

"Ouch!" Doing her best to tamp down her grin, she glared

over her shoulder at him as she rubbed her stinging butt cheek. "What the hell was that for?"

"A promise of what you're gonna get later." He grinned, and Angie's stomach somersaulted. Jeezus chrispies, he was beautiful. "Come on, we're going to be late for our reservation."

Angie rolled her eyes. "FYI, I'm not the one making us late…plus you're a tease, you know?"

"Sure do." He strolled to the bathroom door. "Meet you downstairs. You got five minutes."

"You're bossy, too!"

"Sure am," he called from somewhere in his bedroom.

Looking back at the mirror, Angie couldn't help the smile that arched her lips. This was her second trip in for the weekend.

They'd had an awesome night last night when she'd gotten into town and an even more awesome day today. With any luck, they'd have an awesome evening before he needed to head down to the Halo. And after he was done there, they'd have an awesome night in his bed.

With a dreamy, if not totally cliché, sigh, Angie applied a light coat of lip gloss, sprayed her hair one last time and then headed downstairs to meet Garrett.

<hr>

"WHERE ARE WE GOING AGAIN?"

With one hand on the wheel, Garrett slid his other along her thigh. "There's a new restaurant and wine bar in Chandler I've been hearing about. Figured we'd check it out."

"A wine bar? Honey, you don't drink."

He could see her staring at him from the corner of his eye, and his heart warmed with appreciation, knowing that his not being able to imbibe alcohol was something she was considerate of. Her concern wasn't necessary, but still, the woman had no idea how much it meant to him that she cared. "Right, but you do."

"Yeah, I do, but I don't *have* to." She placed her hand on top of his. "I mean, seriously, you have to spend every night in a bar as it is, we don't have to go out to one in your off time. I want you to be comfortable."

This time, Garrett couldn't stop the smile that spread across his lips. "It's not a big deal for me. The reason I can work around it, go to places that serve it, and also have it in my home is it doesn't bother me. I'm not tempted. In fact, it's the exact opposite." He raised their now linked hands to his lips and kissed her knuckles. "Plus, the fact that you or other normal people I've met over the years that don't *have* to have a drink or can have just one, or worse, can actually *not* finish a drink…still fascinates the shit out of me, so, it's all good."

"You know, I don't know if I'll ever grasp this fully."

He glanced at her, then back to the road. "What part?"

She shrugged. "Let's say I had to give up chocolate but had to be around it every day, I would lose my damn mind. One hundred percent."

"I guess the question would be, was the chocolate killing you? The reason you lost a job, a dream, or your family?"

"That's one way to look at it, I suppose, but I'm not sure that's possible where chocolate is concerned. I mean, it's candy, not cocaine."

"To some people, candy is cocaine." He let go of her hand to make a left through an intersection.

"Okay, yeah, true. Then I guess maybe? I don't know. Like I said, I don't think I'll ever fully grasp it. I get that you can't and shouldn't ever drink again. I just don't get why it doesn't bother you."

He glanced at her again. "Does it bother you?"

"What? The fact that you can't drink or do drugs?" She frowned. Her expression almost one of confusion that he'd asked.

"Yeah."

"Hell no, it doesn't bother me. That's silly. That's like asking me if it would bother me if you could never have sugar because you were a diabetic. It's part of you. I accept all parts of you."

Again, warmth filled Garrett's chest, spreading outward to coat his limbs with a specific feeling. One he hadn't expected to feel. At a loss for words, he reached over and took her hand again.

From the corner of his eye, he could see that she was staring at him, and he was willing to bet she was waiting for some kind of reply. At the next red light, Garrett leaned toward her and took her face in his hands. "I find you amazing, Angela Donnelly."

Her eyes went wide, but then her expression softened. Without giving her a chance to respond, he kissed her. After only a few seconds, the car behind them beeped its horn, and Garrett broke the sweet kiss and settled back in his seat.

Pressing his foot down on the accelerator, he drove through the intersection. Any minute now, she'd say something. It was how she was wired, and although at times it drove him to fucking distraction, he was also coming to find it was merely something that was part of her—something he could accept, too.

"Why?"

There it was.

Garrett had to suppress a chuckle. "Why what?"

"What about me do you find amazing?"

He shook his head, a slight smile arching his lips, as he pulled into the parking lot near the restaurant. "You just are. The things you say and think. Your outlook on life and people. The way you see things, it's rare."

She tilted her head side to side. "Wow, thank you. But, I guess, blame my parents? Two old hippies from the sixties tend to be pretty open and accepting of all things."

He pulled into a parking spot and shut down the engine. "Are you all like this?"

"Hmm…yeah, pretty much. Though my two oldest sisters, Katie and Mary Claire, are definitely not as laid back."

He angled out of the car, and so did she. When he came around the back, she slid her hand into his, and they walked toward the restaurant. "Where are they in the birth order?"

"Lucky numbers one and two." She let out a laugh. "Third is my brother, Joey. Joseph Jr."

He held the door open for her, and once she walked inside, he followed. "Did I meet them?"

"They were here but had already left the party by the time you got there. At the bar later that night, and then a few days later at brunch, you met Ryan, Cyn and Jimmy, and their spouses, Maiya, Shane and Sonja."

"Cyn is the pregnant one, right?"

"Yes. Oh my God, and *so* excited about that baby coming." Her eyes sparkled as she smiled.

The hostess seated them, and after they both got settled, he helped Angie pick a glass of wine. She hadn't talked a whole lot about her family, and he had to admit, the whole big family thing was fascinating.

He wanted to know more about it, more about her, just… more. The glow in her eyes when she mentioned her sister having a baby was a jab in his side, though. She'd said before that she didn't want kids right now, and possibly never, but Garrett knew in his bones that'd change. Her excitement was evidence of that.

Yet still, selfish as it was, he wasn't ready for this to end between them, so he let it go, like he had when they'd first discussed it.

He watched as she looked over the menu, her expression filled with curiosity, wonder, and excitement, as if everything she did was for the first time, and it was all new and fresh and filled with fun.

She was intoxicating, heady and hard to resist. Angie drew him in over and over again, keeping his attention without even trying. To think, he'd almost missed this, nearly given her up. Thank God he hadn't.

For now, he was all in with her, for as long as she'd have him anyway. "What kind of wine do you want tonight, babe?"

Angie gave him her soft smile. "You pick."

CHAPTER THIRTY

Angie shut her laptop down as the plane started to make its descent. She'd written three reviews between the time she waited to board at the gate in Burbank and later on the plane during the flight. She had two more to write when she got to Celia's, or…wait, was she going straight to the Halo tonight?

Angie frowned and slid the computer into the soft protective sleeve. She sent him a text asking him, but hadn't heard back yet, though she could have a text waiting for her when she turned her phone back on. He *was* getting better at responding, after all.

They'd been "together" around four months, and things had been going great between them for the most part. Of course, whenever Garrett did slack off, and she got on his case about his inconsistent communication or his consistent changing of plans, his answer was always the same: "Can't you just go with the flow?"

Sure.

Awesome.

Great.

Angie was happy to go with the flow. That was if there

actually was a flow to go with. Sometimes, she had no clue where the flow was anymore. And Angie considered herself to be a pretty laid-back chick. At least she used to be. Garrett managed to make that laid-back side of her look like a control freak on speed.

Honestly, she suspected *no one* could ever be as casual as he expected them to be. And she had another feeling, "go with the flow" was merely his way of ensuring things stayed as casual as he wanted them to be.

Casual…now that was funny. He refused to call what was between them a relationship. As far as Angie was concerned, she was in a "situationship"…she chuckled and closed her eyes.

God knew enough red flags were waving that she should step away, but the problem was, every time she was with the man, all those red flags *magically* turned green, and she was hooked all over again.

The plane landed—a little harder than usual, and Angie gripped the end of the armrest to keep herself steady in her seat. As the aircraft settled into a slow taxi to their gate, she turned on her phone.

Ding! Ding! Dingdingding!

A series of text message alerts came in, along with emails. The plane parked at the gate, and *everyone* in the cabin stood at the same time. She'd have to wait to check once she got off the plane. The late evening flight was only half full, so it wasn't like it would take long for everyone to get off.

Alone in her row, she stepped out into the aisle and pulled her carry-on down from the overhead. After stuffing her PC into it, she made her way off the plane. Next stop, baggage claim. Maybe she'd pee first.

As she navigated the long corridor of Terminal 4, she checked her messages. Lo and behold, there was one from Garrett! Relief blasted through Angie, blanketing her insides with calm, and she drew in a deep breath—as if she hadn't been breathing *at all* until right at that moment.

It never ceased to amaze her that a simple text from him inspired such a profound physical and emotional reaction in her body. From the start, this was how she'd responded to him, physically and emotionally.

Swiping the screen, she read his response to her earlier inquiry.

> Daddy: if u want you can come here but I'm pretty busy tonight so I won't be able 2 give u a lot of attention

Doubt crawled up the back of Angie's neck like a spider, and a boulder the size of a mountain settled in the pit of her stomach. This was the kind of crap that made her worry. Did he even want her there? Did he care one way or another?

And… "give her a lot of attention"? Where the hell had that come from? What, did he think she was too needy or some such bullshit now? *Oh, for Christ's sake!*

She stepped to the side of the corridor and replied.

> Angie: Just landed. Are you sure you want me there?

Before she could tuck the phone into her back pocket, it dinged with a reply. Wow, he was two for two so far tonight. Amazing. But damn, if she wasn't losing count of her emotional whiplash score. Angie swiped the screen.

> Daddy: Yes

She rolled her eyes. The man of many words over here…

> Angie: Okay, I'll see you soon.

God, she was tired. Not like she could claim jet lag, but maybe jet worn applied? This was maybe her seventh—no eighth flight to Phoenix. Every other week, like clockwork, she'd been flying in. Honestly, it was all becoming one big, blurred routine.

And sadly, Garrett had yet to come to L.A.

It was starting to wear her out and down, and how she hadn't gotten sick yet from all the air travel was a mystery. But she hadn't, and here she was, yanking her purple, twenty-four-inch hard-side spinner off the turnstile.

For the love of all things holy, her bag was heavy, but the exhaustion filling Angie's limbs like freshly poured cement felt heavier.

This traveling shit was seriously getting old.

Once she got her bags situated, Angie headed toward the exit to call for a Lyft. When she looked up to ensure she didn't mow anyone over, Garrett was standing in front of her—a small bouquet in his hand.

Holeeeey shit!

Hello, red flag looking a whole lot like bright green!

"Oh, my God, what are you doing here?" And this was what he did, the reason why she hadn't broken things off with him. He'd be an uncommunicative jerk, totally insensitive to her needs, wants, schedule, life…you name it. And then the SOB would do something on a whim, sweeping her clean off her feet, and she'd fall madly in love with him all over again.

"Figured I'd come pick up my girl. That okay with you?"

His girl?

Oh, wow.

Wow…

Yep, green flag!

As she stared at him, every square inch of Angie's body melted, and she sighed.

He'd come to get her. With flowers, no less. Damn, she was so screwed.

Angie couldn't stop the smile from forming, but she did manage to stop the tears that threatened to make an appearance. "Of course, that's okay with me."

"Good. Trade me." He handed her the small bouquet and took her suitcase.

"Okay." Angie dipped her head and drew in the aroma of the flowers. "They're so sweet." She moved to him, tiptoed up and kissed him. Before she pulled away, she rubbed the tip of her nose over his. "Thank you, honey."

He gave her one of his small smiles. "You're welcome, babe."

Flowers could be considered cliché to some, but Angie didn't give a crap. She wasn't even a woman who cared about getting flowers from a man. But that didn't matter either.

Garrett James had bought her flowers! It was awesome, wonderful, and sweet, and meant so much. God, it meant the world!

GARRETT PAID the parking fee for the airport garage and then got on the freeway. The look on Angie's face when she saw him was priceless. He could tell by her text replies that she'd been annoyed, but unbeknownst to her operation, "get out of the bar and pick her up" had already been in the works, so all was well in the world now.

Except now she was being really quiet as they drove. Rather than happy surprise, the look on her face when she'd seen him at the airport had been one of complete shock, like he never did nice things for her, and that just wasn't true.

Yes, he was busy a lot, and because of that, he couldn't always call or text when she wanted him to or pick her up from the airport, much less surprise her.

But that didn't mean he had no feelings or that he didn't have any feelings *for her*. Garrett had a lot of feelings for her.

Deep ones. More than he'd wanted or was supposed to have and more than he could ever admit to her.

Regardless, telling her how he felt would only make things harder for them in the long run. They'd already blown past casual, but that didn't mean he'd allow things to go full-steam ahead, either. He needed to keep one foot on the brake pedal.

Glancing her way, he laid his palm on her thigh. "You okay, babe?"

"Yeah. Just tired. Wait, wasn't that our exit—" She pointed out the window as they passed the off-ramp. "Okay… where we going?"

"Home." He focused on the road.

"Don't you have to go back to the bar?"

"Nope. I'm taking the rest of the night off."

She sat up straight and faced him. "Really?"

"Yep, really." He squeezed her thigh. "Are you hungry?"

"A little." She smiled and settled back in her seat.

He turned his palm up, and she threaded her fingers with his. "Good."

The drive wasn't long, and once Garrett got her suitcase up to his bedroom, he left her to get her things situated and went back down to the kitchen to get a snack ready for them.

He pulled out a series of cheeses, fruit preserves, hummus, olives and crackers. He also grabbed a bottle of red wine for her. By the time Angie came downstairs, Garrett had everything set up on a tray on the coffee table in the family room, and he was kicked back on the couch, scrolling through Netflix for movie options.

Her steps slowed as she got closer. "Wow, what's all this?"

"A snack."

With a crooked smile on her adorable face, she sat beside him. "No, I'm sorry. This isn't a snack, honey—"

"What're you talking about?" He chuckled.

"Cheetos or popcorn with a soda is a snack. This is a banquet of amazingness."

"Tomayyto, tomahhto." He spread some brie and preserves on a cracker, then handed it to her.

"Killing me, Mr. James." She took the offered cracker and bit into it.

He handed her the glass of wine. "Hope not, Miss Donnelly. Just intending to feed you."

"Be careful." She looked at the dark fluid in the glass and then back at him. "You keep this kind of Romancelandia stuff up, and I might just get used to it."

He barked a laugh. "Romancelandia?"

She swirled the wine in the glass and grinned. "Yep. Like you're trying to sweep me off my feet or something."

"Do you want me to sweep you off your feet?" He bent toward her.

She lowered the glass and leaned closer to him. "I'd love that."

Her scent filled his lungs, and he soaked it up. She was sweet and soft, and, God, he was glad he'd decided to pick her up and take the night off. Garrett brushed his nose over hers. "How about we start the feet sweeping with a movie?"

She giggled, and Garrett felt it through his whole body. He pressed a soft kiss to her lips and then pulled back just enough to run his fingers through the long length of hair hanging over her shoulder. "Is that a yes, you'd like to watch a movie with me? I'd like to watch one with you."

"Yes, I'd love to watch a movie with you, honey."

"Good." He moved back from her. "What do you want to watch?"

"No clue. What have you found so far?" She shifted closer to him on the couch and then sipped her wine. "Ooh! This is really yummy. What is it?"

"It's a Malbec. And not too much. There are some comedies, dramas, horror."

"No horror." She spread some hummus on a cracker. "Any chick flicks?"

"Um." He sipped his water.

Angie laughed. "Oh, come on. Don't be *that* guy."

"What guy is that?" He popped an olive in his mouth.

"The guy who can't watch romance."

"Who said that? We can watch a chick flick if you want. It's a win/win for me."

She sipped her wine. "How so?"

"You'll get all cuddly, and then when I take you upstairs, we'll have awesome sex." He set up another cracker and handed it to her. "Pick what you want to watch. Then we'll both be happy." He grinned.

She took the cracker, but instead of eating it, she regarded him with both brows raised. "You saying we don't have awesome sex now?"

"Pfft. I would never say that. We have better than awesome sex." Garrett spread some cheese and preserves on a cracker for himself and then popped it in his mouth.

"Damn straight, we do." She ate the cracker. "Best sex of our lives."

"Maybe."

"Uh, uh, no. Garrett James, you admit it right now!" Laughing, she rose up and straddled his lap.

"Admi—well, hello there." Garrett grinned. He loved this kind of banter and teasing with her. He ran his palms up her thighs to her ass and cleared his throat. "Admit what?"

Angie bent and brushed her lips over his. "Admit that we have the best sex of your life."

"Wait a minute, you said, 'our' lives? How did this get turned around on me?" Gazing up at her, he took a moment to soak in her beauty. Fucking hell, she was gorgeous. All he wanted to do was be near her...

God damn, where was that brake pedal he was so hell-bent on having underfoot?

"Daddy, you know exactly what I meant." She ran her fingers through his hair at the base of his scalp.

He had it down tonight; unlike the man bun he often wore it in when he was working or pretty much doing anything outside of bedtime. Angie loved it both ways, but she really loved running her fingers through the length and even pulling it when they were having sex.

Garrett tilted his head back and nipped her chin. "Maybe you should be clearer."

"Mmhmm. How's this for clear?" Tipping her head down, she pressed her mouth to his, but he took over from there.

As he ravaged her lips and tongue, Angie could feel his cock growing hard. The stiff length pressed into her inner thigh. Rising, she tugged at his jeans, and when she got them undone, she reached in and palmed the hot length.

Garrett pushed her shirt up and found her breasts, pinching both nipples through her bra.

Angie let out a gasp. "What about the movie?"

"Fuck the movie." Garrett tugged down the bra cups and sucked one stiff peak into his mouth, and continued to tug and roll the other between his fingertips.

Fire blazed through Angie's veins. She'd never get over how fast her body responded to his touch. Christ, even a simple look from him would cause her nipples to get hard. They'd been at each other no more than five minutes, and so far, there'd been only kissing and fondling, but her panties were already soaked.

With great reluctance, Angie let go of his cock, and pulled her top off. The bra was the next article of clothing to go. As she stood to shed her jeans and panties, Garrett pulled his shirt off.

She raked her gaze down over his smooth lean chest, down his abs, and the thin trail of hair to where, because of the open fly of his jeans, his straining cock lay against his abdomen. "You know I want that in my mouth."

"Why's that?" With lust swimming in his gaze, he raised his arms and linked his hands behind his head. The pose made his torso look even more delectable.

She licked her lips and went to her knees between his parted legs. "Because you taste so fucking good."

Garrett took his length in hand and stroked from base to tip. "Oh, yeah? Why else?"

"Because it's mine." Good God, she could watch him jack himself all day long, but right then, she wanted in on the action. Angie bent and licked over the head, catching the bead of pre-cum that had gathered at the tip.

"Fuck, yes, it is." Garrett rolled his hips.

Again, she licked over the crown, and he moved his fist up and down the shaft, and then she sucked the swollen head into her mouth. Garrett continued to stroke, and on the down motion, Angie chased his hand with her mouth, sucking his prick to the back of her throat before coming back up to the head.

Garrett arched and gripped her hair in his other hand, halting her movement. "Need inside your cunt."

Looking up at him, she gave the crown one last suck before she released him and climbed up to straddle his lap once more. As Angie positioned him at the mouth of her cunt and then slid down his length, inch by inch, she locked her gaze with his. "Say it, honey. Tell me."

His hands were on her ass, and he squeezed her full cheeks. "My cunt. My ass. All of it, mine."

"Yes, baby. Always." Angie rolled her hips, grinding her clit against him as his shaft slid in and out of her channel. She cupped her breasts, pinching her nipples. "What about these? Are these yours, too?"

"Fuck yes." Garrett leaned forward and pressed his face to her sternum before he licked his way to one breast and then bit the tight bud. "Every perfect inch of you."

Every perfect inch of me…

Hearing him say these things filled Angie's heart to the brink of overflow. Did she wish he said more things like this when they weren't naked? Of course. What woman wouldn't?

Angie knew he meant the things he said—even in the throes of an orgasm. But for whatever reason, during sex was when he chose to lavish her with flattering words, as if he was saving them up. Or maybe it was just easier for him when they were intimate like this, or…maybe when they were like this, he couldn't help himself. Either way, she'd take it.

As was the case with most everything with Garrett, Angie would take what he was willing to give her. She wanted more, always more, but sometimes, if she let go of all expectation or longing, what he gave her was enough.

Rocking her pelvis back and forth, Angie's orgasm built, spreading like warm honey through her body and filling her limbs. "Garrett, oh, God!"

He slapped her ass with both hands. "Come on my cock, baby. Let me feel your beautiful, tight cunt grip me."

Garrett slid his fingers between her ass cheeks and stroked over her asshole, and Angie's climax hit like an earthquake. She bucked against him, riding the high as wave after wave rolled through her.

"That's my good girl."

Still moving her hips back and forth, her pace slower now, Angie collapsed against him. "Love when you say that."

"Oh, yeah? Why's that?" Garrett stroked the tips of his fingers along her spine.

"Because it's hot as hell—" Angie rose off him, turned around, and straddled him reverse cowgirl style. When she slid his hard cock deep, she glanced over her shoulder and couldn't help but grin. "Also, because we both know I'm not always a good girl. Sometimes I'm bad, too."

"Fuck yes, Angie. Oh, God, I love it like this."

A thrill went through her from head to toe. "I know."

As she moved, rocking her hips, Garrett moaned, groaned

and even growled a few times. He had a firm grip on her ass cheeks, and Angie loved every single second of it. Leaning forward just a bit and balancing herself on his thighs, she let him fuck into her cunt, knowing at any moment, he was going to come.

With a slight shift, he pulled free of her cunt, but slid his cock between her legs. "*Unnghhhyes!*"

Angie leaned back and held his shaft up against her labia. The first spurts of his orgasm shot up her stomach, nearly reaching her breasts. With a moan, she cradled his dick against her clit, rocking her hips and stroking his shaft with her pussy lips and hand.

"Fuck, Angie! Yes! Oh, God, yes!"

Hot spurts of semen coated her stomach and fingers. As always, he came a ton for her, producing more ejaculate than any man she'd ever known before. That was all hers and only hers. No one else would ever draw that out of him. And Angie freaking loved it.

Even after he was spent, Garrett held onto her hips. His breathing heavy, his cock twitching ever so often against her palm. Angie stayed quiet, letting the moment stretch between them.

After a while, he broke the silence. "Angie?"

"Yeah, honey?"

"Hands down, best sex of my life, baby."

With a soft smile, Angie rose off of him, turned and re-straddled him so she was facing him. She smoothed her hands over his cheekbones, then traced the line of his straight nose.

She dipped her head and pressed her mouth to his in a soft kiss. Pulling back, she took in his features, his expression… the softness in his eyes.

And her heart melted. *God, I love you…* "Mine too, honey."

CHAPTER THIRTY-ONE

Garrett stood on the curb at Burbank airport, waiting for Angie to pick him up, wondering what *in the hell* he was doing in Los Angeles again. Technically, he knew. It was to see Angie, but he wasn't happy about having to be there to do it.

Still, he couldn't recall the last time he'd been in L.A.; frankly, he didn't want to. Yes, the weather was great, but aside from that, there wasn't much else good about it. In his opinion, anyway.

Except, of course, that Angie lived here. But that was beside the point. Unfortunately, L.A. held nothing but bad memories for him.

Regardless, he needed to get over it because it was her birthday weekend, and Garrett had promised her that he'd come. They'd been dating for the last 6 months, and she'd been doing all the traveling, so it was about time he got his ass out here and shared some of that burden.

Just so happened her birthday was the kick in the ass he needed, so here he was. At least for one trip, anyway.

A red BMW three-series pulled up to the curb in front of him, and he watched as the passenger window went down.

The driver, a gorgeous brunette he knew all too well, leaned over the center console. "You looking for a ride, hot stuff?"

Garrett bent forward, peering into the interior of the vehicle at her. "Hot stuff, huh? Cute. Pop the trunk." She did, and Garrett tossed his bag inside. After closing the deck lid, he slid into the passenger seat.

Angie had a smile on her face so big it was damn near contagious. Almost enough to lighten his mood. Almost. He let out a sigh and forced himself to smile because, yes, he was a grumpy asshole, but he wasn't *trying* to be a dick, too.

She frowned. "Everything okay?"

"Yeah. Just tired." Hoping she'd take the hint, he looked over his shoulder to see if the way was clear to pull out. "Nice car, hon."

Smile gone, she rolled her eyes. "Whatever. You hate BMWs." She leaned toward him, gave him a quick kiss and then pulled out into the minimal airport traffic.

"Put on your belt or—"

The seatbelt alarm started binging. Garrett glanced at her as he put on his seatbelt.

"Yeah, that. Thanks." She stopped at a red light. Both hands on the wheel, staring straight ahead, lips drawn in a line.

Great, not even five minutes, and he'd managed to upset her. He needed to get them back on track before they argued over nothing. And he didn't mean the fun kind of banter back and forth about the BMW. "I do not hate them."

"Uh, huh. You told me, and I quote: 'BMW drivers are all assholes.'" She gave him the side eye.

He put his hand on her thigh. "Exactly. I hate their drivers, not the cars themselves."

She let out a gasp but then laughed. "You're such a jerk."

"Maybe so. But to be fair, I didn't know you had a BMW. It's kind of like entrapment."

"Entrap—what?" She laughed. "Again, whatever with a

capital W. And like I'd tell you I owned a Beemer after your little comment? Not gonna happen, dude."

"I've progressed from a jerk to a dude?" He leaned toward her, drew her hair away from her neck and ran his nose along her ear. "I'll take it."

She shivered. "Cheater."

Garrett snaked out his tongue and licked at her earlobe. "From dude to cheater? Not sure that's an improvement. Why cheater?"

"Okay, fine, how about tease?"

He smoothed his palm up her thigh and slipped it between her legs. "I don't think I'm teasing."

Angie let out a little moan. "Jeezus chrispies, you smell so good."

"Mmm. So do you."

After stopping for another red light, she turned her face to his, and he kissed her properly. She did smell good, and she tasted good, too.

He pulled away before the cars behind them started honking. "It's good to see you."

Her expression softened. "It's good to be seen."

The car behind them honked anyway, and she jumped and then refocused on the road.

Garrett let out a short laugh. "All good, hon."

"Ya know, not all Beemer drivers are assholes. I'm not an asshole. My brother isn't either." She reached for his hand.

"Bimmer." He grinned but did it staring out of the passenger window.

"And now you sound like Ryan."

"Smart guy. Knows his cars."

"Are you insinuating that I don't know cars?"

"Not at all. By the way, who's Ryan?"

Angie changed lanes. "You're kidding me, right? My brother. The other *Bimmer* owner in the family. He's also a Porsche guy."

"Then I definitely like him."

"Good to know." She laughed. "By the way, honey, you met him and had drinks with him, or rather, he drank, you had coffee at the Halo when my family was there. Then you had brunch with him and other members of my family about a week later. Any of this ring a bell?"

"Oh, right! Ryan. The one with the baby. I knew that." He squeezed her thigh, and she let out a little squeal. "Pay attention to the road. I remember your family. But cut me some slack, there are a lot of them."

"Fine. And I'm just saying right now, if I have an accident, I'm going to let the cop know it was the snob Jag owner sitting in my passenger seat's fault."

Before he could stop himself, he laughed. Out loud and from his gut.

"Oh my God, did you just laugh? Like, really laugh? And at something I said?" She glanced at him, her eyes wide as saucers. "I can't believe it. I'm totally shocked!"

He shook his head. "Whatever."

"And now you're talking like me? You think I'm funny, *and* you're using my lines? What's gotten into you, Garrett James? Are you feeling feverish?" She tried to put her palm on his forehead.

Garrett swatted her hand away…laughing. Again. Wow, what the hell was going on with him? Not sure what else to say, he leaned over and kissed her cheek. "Stop. I've always thought you were funny."

It was true. He did find her funny. Angie was funnier than she even realized, and there were many times she had him chuckling, but sadly, like his daughter and the few friends he hung with *kindly* pointed out many times, he rarely let out a full laugh.

He'd come to the conclusion that big, loud laughs weren't his style. That was okay. Garrett was serious and reserved, too focused on life and things that needed to be done, and he needed to stay that way.

It was the way he'd kept himself straight and gotten his life back on track. Why change what worked? That said, pulling a full belly laugh out of him was a rare thing and…Angie had done it.

If Garrett thought about it, he'd have to admit she pulled a lot of things out of him that others had failed to do. No matter how much he wanted to deny it, she was exactly what he had always needed in his life. There were too many examples he wasn't able to ignore.

But even with that small admission to himself, Garrett was still giving the old denial train a run for its money. He just wasn't ready to believe this could last. The odds were just not in their favor.

ANGIE PULLED into her apartment complex and parked in her assigned spot. She was still drunk on gallons of excitement over the fact that Garrett had laughed at her—or with her. Either way, the sound had been so full of life and happiness, Angie felt it from the top of her head straight down to her toes.

But then, for whatever reason, Garrett had gone deep in thought the last part of their drive, and based on the look he had on his face, he'd only now realized she'd parked the car.

She hit the trunk button. "Ready to see my little shoebox?"

"Definitely. I love shoeboxes. Very comfy and easy maintenance." He smiled as he got out of the car and then grabbed his bag from the open trunk. "It's quiet. What city are we in again?"

She closed the deck lid and strolled past him. "I'm always

amazed at the things I tell you that you don't pay attention to. South Pasadena."

"That's right. Damn. For the record, it's not that I don't pay attention. I do. I just forget. I'm old, remember? He followed close behind her as she navigated through the walkway, bisecting two buildings and then up one flight of stairs to her unit.

"Likely story, Daddy." She stuck the key into the lock and opened the way for them. "The 'I'm old' thing is getting, well, old. No, uh, pun intended." She laughed, stepped into her apartment and waved him through.

He set his bag down and glanced around her living room, dining area and kitchen. "Fab shoebox."

"Thanks!" She hung her purse on the closet door handle in the entryway. "It's quaint. And quiet, like you said. No one above me or beside me. Another bonus, considering the location, the rent is reasonable."

"How long have you lived here?"

"Five years." Nervous energy bounced through Angie like a rubber superball. Garrett was in L.A.! In her apartment! And now she didn't know what the hell to do with him.

Needing someplace to focus her energy, she opted for the kitchen. The only thing to do when she got in there was open the fridge. She'd wanted to get him to L.A. for the last five of their six months together.

They'd finally hit slow season for the bigger shows at the Halo, so lo and behold, here he was. But what now? She spoke without looking away from the inside of the fridge. "You want something to drink?"

Garrett slid his hands over her hips and then around her waist. Angie jumped, straightening. His lips were right next to her ear. "Water's fine, hon."

She stood in place a moment, her back to his chest, and took in the feel of him. With a sigh, Angie let her head fall back against his shoulder. "I can't believe you're really here."

"Why not? I told you I'd come." He smoothed his hands up her torso.

"I know, but until you got on that plane, I didn't think it would happen." Angie felt him stiffen, and she cringed, knowing her answer hit a nerve. Damn her inability to shut her mouth and just enjoy the moment. "Sorry, that came out wrong."

"It's fine. Let it go. I'm here, and that's what counts."

She closed her eyes and blew out a relieved breath. She didn't want to fight with him. When he'd first gotten in her car, he was moody as hell, and she had to work really hard to not take it personally. But then both their moods lightened up, thank God. The banter in the car was nothing more than their typical playful exchange…which, if she wasn't careful, could lead to a stupid argument, but luckily, that hadn't been the case on the ride.

Regardless, she wanted to make the most of his first trip, not waste it arguing. "I'm really glad you're here, honey."

"Me too." He kissed her cheek. "How about a tour?"

"Of my shoebox? Well, I don't know. I mean, are you sure you're up for it? It's really easy to get lost in here. We might not find our way back to the main part."

He chuckled. "We should take provisions then?"

"That can be arranged." She turned in his embrace and circled his neck in her arms. "Drinks and snacks are a must."

"On it." Before letting her go, he pressed a kiss to her forehead. "You grab the needed hydration products. Where do I find the snacks?"

Angie pointed to the cabinet to the right of the stove. He nodded and moved the two feet it took to be in front of it. After he opened the cupboard door, she shook her head and laughed. "What took you so long?"

"Long walk." He winked and pulled down a container of almonds and another with peanut butter-filled pretzels. "These work for you?"

"Seeing as they're in my cabinet and I bought them, they definitely work for me." The refrigerator door was still open, cooling off the kitchen and wasting energy, so she reached in and grabbed two water bottles and closed it up. "Anything else? Should we start a pot of coffee? It could be morning by the time we find our way back."

"We can wait on the coffee, but for the record, I'm liking the idea of how long this 'tour' of yours is going to take. Should I also take my bag with me?"

She grinned. "You should absolutely take your bag with you."

"Yes, ma'am." He gave her a salute before stepping out of the kitchen. Angie followed. With their snacks cradled in one arm, he grabbed the leather duffel bag with his free hand. "Lead the way, my trusty tour guide."

"You got it." Unable to stop herself from giggling, she moved the twelve feet or so it took to be in the center of her living room. "As you can see, this is the living area, complete with a forty-inch flat-screen television and gas fireplace situated in the corner. It makes for cozy viewing during the winter months." A few more feet to the end of the room. "Here we have the functional sliding glass door, and beyond…one moment." She set the water bottles down and slid open the door. "Beyond, we have a modest yet semi-spacious patio. Complete with two chairs for lounging and decorative twinkling lights…because I'm *very* fancy."

"Quite fancy, yes." He nodded, a serious expression in his eyes, as he stepped out onto the deck. "I'd forgotten how much greener L.A. is compared to home. The trees are nice."

"I quite enjoy them." She leaned against the metal doorframe. "Are you ready for more, or do you need a rest?"

Garrett laughed again, and Angie felt it wrap around her like a warm blanket. Holy cow, giddiness was pumping through her veins like a kid on Christmas morning. Hearing him laugh had been such an unexpected boon, one she knew she'd never get enough of.

Angie had tried on countless occasions to get the man to laugh, but he never did. She had no idea why he kept giving her this gift tonight, but she wasn't about to ask him. It didn't matter why. What mattered was that Garrett was in her apartment.

Her apartment, for the sake of all things holy!

And he was smiling *and* laughing…for her.

For *her!*

CHAPTER THIRTY-TWO

"DON'T NEED A REST YET, THOUGH *I* AM GETTING A LITTLE fatigued. However, I shall persevere." Garrett watched the light in Angie's eyes come alive as she giggled.

Damn, she was beyond beautiful when her smile reached her eyes like it was right then. He wasn't sure what he'd done to inspire it, but hopefully, she'd clue him in so he could do it again.

"Well then, please follow me, sir. I have *sooo* much more to show you."

Garrett moved past her, and she slid the door closed, locking it.

"Brace yourself. This will be the best part yet. A true adventure." She reached her arm out to her side, indicating the hallway before moving in that direction. "The hall of memories awaits us."

God, the silliness was coming more and more easily with her tonight. He had to admit it felt good to goof off. Because yeah, not that he wanted to admit it to his daughter or friends, but maybe he did need to laugh more.

This playing around with Angie brought out a side of Garrett he'd managed to forget or bury—he shook his head.

Yet another sign that he was right where he was supposed to be. Just…*fuck!* He needed to—

"Garrett?"

He jerked his head up. "Yeah, babe?"

"You okay?"

"A few months ago, I got a call regarding Copper Seven."

"You did?" Her brow furrowed in a pronounced frown.

He had no idea he was going to tell her. One minute, he was trying to figure out how to keep things at their current pace, and the next, he was opening up and sharing… He sighed. "They want me to do an interview."

"They do? That's awesome!" She grabbed his shoulders, practically bouncing in front of him. "When do they want you? You must be so excited. Wait…are you going to do it? I know that's not your life anymore, but oh, honey—" she clapped her hands together "—that would be so awesome for you. I mean, it's a great marketing opportunity for the club, right?"

Good Lord, the woman could talk when she wanted to. She'd barely even take a breath, never mind let the other person get a word in edgewise. Garrett chuckled, and after setting down his bag and the snacks he'd been carrying, framed her waist with his hands and pulled her against him.

When he was sure she had come to a stopping point, he grinned and attempted to answer her questions. "I don't know if I'm going to do it. I don't know when it is because I haven't gotten all the details. To be honest, I'm not excited. I don't want to do it, but Chase won't stop bugging me and wants an answer sooner rather than later. And, let's see, yes, the club." He winked. "It could help the venue, yes. Or it could hurt it."

"Chase Reynolds?"

"The one and only."

"Wow, he was pretty wild back in the day, too. How's he doing now?"

"He's fucking his publicist, so I'm guessing he's doing fine."

Angie blurted a laugh. "There are worse things, I'm sure. So, why don't you want to do it?"

Garrett cursed himself for opening this can of worms, but it was too late now. He'd backed himself into a corner, and now he needed to give her something. But could he really go into the deep reasons of why he didn't want to do the interview?

He was at a crossroads, and he knew it.

Damn…

Every time he even briefly considered what this interview and possible reunion could mean for the band, anxiety and fear filled his entire body. Garrett was terrified that if he opened the door to that old world, he'd end up using and drinking again.

He gazed down at Angie, her eyes alight with excitement and hope for him. She was everything he wanted and everything he didn't deserve.

Nope, no way he could share all that with her. Garrett's stomach twisted into a knot, and he took the coward's route. "As you said, it's not my life anymore. Between the bar and Chassidy—"

"And me?"

"Yes, and you, too." He gave her a small smile. "I don't know if I want to invite all that shit back into my world."

"I get it, I do." She leaned forward and kissed him, slow and sweet. Teasing him with the tip of her hot tongue. Garrett moaned and pulled her tighter against him.

"Mmm." Angie moved from his lips and framed his face with her palms. "Whatever you decide, I support you. You know that, right?"

He rubbed his nose over hers as the pressure in his chest started to ease. "Yeah."

"Good." She smiled and dropped her hands to his shoulders. "You want to see the rest of my shoebox, now?"

"Depends." He nipped her bottom lip. "Is there a bed in your shoebox?"

"Mmhmm." She slid her palms down his arms.

"Perfect." Garrett took her lips in another kiss. Equal parts relief and frustration flowed through him. He was glad he'd told her, but not glad that he'd not gone all the way and shared how he was really feeling.

Why did he always make things so hard between them? He had his shot to let her in, really let her in, and instead, he chickened out. God, he was pathetic.

Plus, he neglected to tell her the interview was with Rolling Stone. As far as he knew, she still hadn't applied with them, but the idea she might be able to use him where that was concerned plagued him. It was better, safer for both of them if she didn't know.

Angie moaned, pulling him from his thoughts, and he swallowed it, deepening the kiss.

Fuck it, it didn't matter. What mattered was that he had her in his arms, and like always, the sparks were flying between them.

Besides, what could be more important than burying himself inside her…while in the great state of California, no less? Hmm. Maybe Los Angeles wasn't so bad anymore…

ANGIE BROKE the kiss and took Garrett by the hand, pulling him the rest of the way down the hall to her bedroom. When they got to her dim room, she let go of his hand and moved to the side of the bed. "Do you want the light on?"

From the entrance to her bedroom, Garrett glanced at the window, then back to her. "No." He took a single step toward her. "What I do want is for you to take all your clothes off and then lay back on the bed, arms over your head."

Angie's insides went molten hot with arousal. A flush rose up her neck so fast she thought she might pass out. All she could do was nod…and follow his direction.

Without breaking his gaze, she pulled her shirt over her head but left her bra. Taking a deep breath, she skimmed her hands down her torso to her hips, then around the waistline of her pants. Garrett tracked her movement, his eyes laser-focused on her waist.

A small smile arched her lips, and she unbuttoned her jeans, then pushed them down and off each leg. Standing with only her underwear and bra on, she hesitated, needing more from him: something, anything to encourage her further.

Searching his expression and body language, Angie saw what she needed. His breaths were faster than normal, his eyes roaming from her toes all the way up her body…and then he licked his lips.

"The rest." His voice was deep, gravelly, the words coming out almost in a growl. "Not going to tell you again."

At his command, Angie's stomach jumped, and her clit pulsed with arousal. Moisture coated her panties, and it was all she could do to push the material off and then remove her bra. Her mouth gone dry, she climbed up on the bed, laid down in the middle and raised her hands above her head.

Garrett walked the three steps to the foot of the bed and stared down at her. They were both breathing heavily, but aside from that, the silence in the room was deafening. The sexual tension was enough to drive her out of her mind.

Angie swallowed past her dry throat. "Garrett…"

"Don't move until I tell you." Garrett grabbed her by one ankle and slid her down the bed. "Spread those long legs for me."

Once again, Angie did what he asked. He leaned forward, smoothing his hands up her inner legs from ankle to thigh, and then he knelt on the floor, resting his body on his forearms between her spread legs.

With the tip of his finger, he traced a line along the crease where her thigh met her core and then did the same to the other side.

Sweet and horrible torture. "Garrett…"

"Shhh."

Angie bit her bottom lip. God, he was killing her. She didn't dare move—then again, if she did, she might end up with a spanking. Although—

"Love this bare pussy." He said the words so low she barely heard him. "Love how slick it is for me and how tight, too." Garrett dragged two fingers down her center, then up again, only to spread them enough to squeeze her swollen clit between them.

"God!" Angie hissed and thrust her hips up.

Garrett pressed the palm of his free hand down on her lower abdomen, holding her to the mattress. "No, no moving. You understand me, baby girl?"

Angie nodded, her body practically vibrating with need.

"Use your words. I asked you a question. Do you understand me, baby girl?"

"Yes." She nodded.

"Yes, what?"

Oh, God! Was he… "Yes, Daddy."

"Yeah. Fuck yeah, that's what I wanted to hear." Garrett bent his head, and with her clit still pinched between his fingers, he tongued the sensitive nub. Lapping and sucking at it, all while stroking it between his two fingers.

With multiple sensations assaulting her at the same time, Angie tried to arch her back and then tried to roll her hips, aching for more of his mouth, but he held her still. She wasn't able to reach for him either, at least not without disobeying his direction to keep her arms above her, so instead, she gripped the pillow under her head and held on, letting him attack her clit and pussy exactly how he wanted.

This was heaven, and it was torture. And she loved every second of it. But dammit, she needed more. "Garrett, please…"

Letting her go, he slid his hands beneath her ass and raised her off the bed. "Please, what?" Before she could answer, he pressed his hot tongue inside the mouth of her pussy, then dragged it up to her clit.

Angie gasped, desperate to close her eyes and give in to the sexual bliss he was leading her to, but instead, she forced herself to watch him. He was being so intense, and something told her she needed to stay with him, stay connected.

With his eyes locked on hers, he continued his assault, alternating from fucking her with his tongue and then licking and sucking her clit. Taking her high only to bring her back down again. It was incredible, it was wonderful, and it was fucking torture.

Angie was mindless, moaning and crying out, unable to form words anymore. Until finally, he sucked her tight clit into his mouth, hard and then harder…and Angie exploded.

Her orgasm rushed so fast to the surface she barely had time to register it. Garrett let go of her ass and wrapped his arms around her thighs, holding her tight to his face as he continued to suck, and her cunt spasmed in orgasm until her whole body was shaking.

Angie thrashed her head side to side on the pillow, crying and moaning his name. Only God knows what she said; she was that far gone, but Garrett wasn't done, oh no. He was far from done.

Jerking away from her, he stood, ripped open his jeans and then drove his cock balls deep inside her. In the next moment, he had his lips on hers, shoving his tongue deep inside her mouth.

With a moan, she licked and sucked his lips, tasting herself on him.

He broke from her lips and snaked his hands down her back to her ass, tilting her hips up and pulling her pelvis hard against his as he thrust up into her. "Hold on to me, baby girl."

Again, she did as she was told, wrapping her arms and legs around him. The feel of his cock head each time he drew out of her and back in, the way her taut nipples rubbed against his shirt, and the way the edges of his open jeans dug into the back of her thighs, drove her higher and higher.

Garrett fucked her hard, and then harder, showing her no mercy…until they both exploded, splintering apart in each other's arms. He spurted his release inside her, and Angie's cunt clenched around his girth, spasming in climax, milking him of every drop.

God, this man. He was killing her.

I love you…

Angie squeezed her eyes closed, willing back the tears. Whatever he needed, she wanted to give him—after all, she was taking every bit of what he was giving her. Nothing in the world mattered more than what was happening between them. Nothing mattered more than this moment between them.

Garrett pressed his forehead to hers, both gasping and out of breath. No words were spoken. Nothing needed to be said. At least not out loud.

I love you…

At that moment, Angie knew she was never, ever letting him go.

CHAPTER THIRTY-THREE

"Did I tell you how excited I am that you're here with me?" Angie reached across the center console and covered Garrett's hand with her palm.

His lips curved into a slight grin. "You did. More than a few times now."

"Well, I'm making sure you know it." She squeezed his hand. "Besides, it was really freaking cool tooling around Hollywood with you today. I gotta say, getting us in at the last minute for brunch at that Mediterranean restaurant? You're pretty damn smooth, Mr. James."

"What can I say? I still got it." He grinned. "The rockstar card still works in L.A. I guess."

Angie turned onto the freeway, heading toward her parent's home. "Ooh, and so humble, too." She laughed. "No, really, you knew what you were doing going all smooth-talking, rockstar to the hostess. Though considering her age, I was surprised she recognized you."

"She didn't." Garrett laughed. "The owner recognized me."

Angie let out a gasp. "You totally cheated!"

"Not technically. But can you blame me?" Garrett laughed again, the sound making Angie's body tingle with desire. "You think some early twenty-something-year-old child could recognize me?"

She shrugged. "Anything's possible. Back to what I was saying—" She smoothed her hand down his thigh. "Watching you in action, your voice all low and sexy… Mmm, every time I think about it, I get horny."

"Angela, we're on the way to your parent's house to have a birthday party for you, and you go and tell me that you're horny?" He shook his head. "That's going to earn you a spanking later."

"Yippee!" Angie laughed and accelerated past a car going too slow. "Is that my birthday present?"

"No." He leaned over and kissed her cheek. "Now, focus on the road before you kill us."

"Whatever. I'm an awesome driver."

"Uh-huh."

"Pfft." Angie turned up the song streaming to her radio via her iTunes playlist on her phone.

It was Elle Henderson's "Hard Work," and it was *the* perfect song for her and Garrett. Being with him was the definition of hard work, but she wouldn't trade it for the world. She smiled. "This is totally your song, baby."

"Mine, huh?" He turned the song up a little louder.

Angie sang along with the lyrics, grinning as she navigated the traffic. Cloud-nine was a nice place to be. She had Garrett in L.A., which was amazing. She got to spend the day with him in her world. And now they were heading to her parent's house for a birthday dinner that would be to die for—all for her.

No doubt, she was flying high for sure.

"I'm thinking this song goes both ways."

Angie glanced at him. "You're seriously saying that to

me?" She frowned, but...okay, he might have a point. "Alright, fine. Maybe. *Mayyyybee* it applies."

"Ain't no maybe about it. It's only fair. Especially since you're making me listen to all this girly chick music."

Angie's mouth dropped open, and she gasped. Okay, maybe he had a point about that, too. "Tonight, you get to hear my good friend, Tarra Layne, sing. She's not girly. She's bluesy-country rock. Anyway, she's badass, so don't worry your pretty little head."

"My pretty head?" Garrett leaned over and pinched her side. "Funny girl. You must want a spanking later."

"Don't know what you mean, Daddy." She grinned and made the turn into her parent's neighborhood. "Okay, serious moment. You ready for this?"

"An awesome dinner made by your mother? What's not to be ready for?"

Angie rolled her eyes. "I meant the large dose of Donnelly you're going to get. Plus, meeting my parents."

"Bah. Bring them on." He stretched his arms out in front of him, laced his fingers, and cracked his knuckles. "Parents don't scare me. Plus, I'm old enough to be your father. I was born ready."

She pulled into the driveway and put the car in park. "You're *hilarious*."

"So are you." He smiled as he opened his door and then got out of the car.

Angie got out as well, and after coming around the front end, she took his hand. "Come on, Mr. Smooth-Talking Rockstar."

Right as they started up the walk to the front door, Garrett swatted her ass, and Angie let out a yelp.

Despite what a great time they were having together, Angie was feeling some serious anxiety about Garrett finally meeting her parents and most of her family. Nervous energy was boomeranging around her stomach, and the quick slap to her ass actually distracted her enough to take the edge off. A beer would shave a little more off her anxiety, too. God, she hoped there was beer. Or maybe wine…

Ugh. She shouldn't be worried, but she was. No doubt her family would love him. But what if Garrett didn't like them back?

Though her family was awesome, they could be a lot to take. And Katie and Mary Claire would probably grill him more than Maiya had back in Phoenix. Angie swallowed a lump that formed in her throat.

Oh, God, her sisters were going to make him crazy. He was older than her oldest sibling, for God's sake! It was bad enough that Garrett had had an issue with their age gap; Angie didn't need her sisters making a thing of it, too.

Angie should've given them a stern warning. Why hadn't she thought to do that? Yeah, right, as if that'd work—

Garrett stopped them. "You're all of a sudden quiet. What's up?"

"Nothing, just…" She swallowed and blew out a breath. "I'm just nervous for you to meet everyone. I hope you like them, is all."

He cocked his head to the side. "You hope *I* like them? Shouldn't you be worried that they might not like me?"

"Don't be silly. They're going to love you." She shook her head. "Everyone loves you." Angie climbed the few steps onto the portico, then opened the front door.

"Everyone does not love me."

"Yes, honey. They do." She stepped inside, and Garrett followed.

He wrapped his long fingers around her upper arm and pressed his lips close to her ear. "Do me a favor, hmm?"

"Of course," she whispered.

"Stop arguing for at least ten minutes." He chuckled, then kissed her cheek. "Lead the way."

"Ugh, you're lucky I like you. And I'm not arguing!" Laughing, Angie took off her jacket, tossed it on the sofa in the formal living room and then continued toward the kitchen. "Not trying to argue, anyway." She waved her hands at him. "Shush. Enough." She laughed. "Hey, Mom, we're here!"

Angie's mother appeared in the kitchen doorway, dish-towel in her hands. "I thought I heard the door. Happy birthday, my beautiful girl!"

Angie stepped into her mother's embrace. "Thank you, Mommy." She turned, arm around her mother's waist. "Mom, this is Garrett."

As was her mother's way, Roseanne's bright smile made its appearance as she reached her hand out. "So nice to finally meet you, Garrett."

Garrett shook Angie's mother's hand. "It's wonderful to meet you as well, Mrs. Donnelly. I've heard so much about you."

"Likewise. And please, call me Roseanne." Her mother glanced between Angie and Garrett. "Dinner's almost ready. Everyone is all over the place, as usual. They're all waiting to meet the mysterious Garrett. Although Maiya and Cyn have been rubbing it in Katie's and Mary's faces that they already got to meet him."

Angie laughed. "I bet that's been fun to watch."

With a laugh, her mother turned and headed back into the kitchen. "I plead the fifth." Roseanne glanced over her shoulder when she got to the stove and then waved the towel at them. "Go on, we've got about twenty more minutes before we eat. Then I can't wait to hear all about how your visit's going."

And that was that. Mom gave Garrett the usual mom treatment, and Garrett had been his typical polite self. But Mom was the easy one. Dad was easy, too. It was Katie and Mary who were the guard dogs of the family.

Angie looked at Garrett. "You ready?"

"Told you already." He winked.

"Oh, right, you were born ready." Angie laughed, took his hand and led him to the back family room.

Family time was always a good time. Most of the time, anyway.

"ATTENTION, everyone: The birthday girl and her beau have arrived!" With a big grin on her face, Maiya's announcement was loud enough to penetrate the chaos in the room, including the noise of the football game on the TV.

Angie wanted to turn right around and escape with Garrett in tow. But no, she couldn't do that because he'd already stepped past her and went right over to Maiya.

He bent over and kissed Maiya on the cheek. "Good to see you again, Maiya." Then he turned to Ryan. "Ryan, awesome to see you, too."

"Right on, man. Glad you made it across the desert." Ryan got to his feet from his spot on the floor where he was playing with Joanie and shook Garrett's hand, clapping him on the back.

Angie stood, feet frozen to the carpet, as Ryan introduced Garrett to everyone in the room. She wasn't sure what to do or say. A pack of wild bees had taken up residence in her head, buzzing so loud she could barely hear herself think. Her stomach had gone tight. And to make things even worse, as usual, when she was a nervous wreck, her hands were sweating. How special.

"He's really good-looking." Her oldest sister, Katie, bumped Angie's shoulder. "By the way, happy birthday, sweetie."

"Hi, Katie. Thanks." Angie smiled and hugged her sister. "You think so?"

"Uh, yeah." Katie grinned and popped her brows. "Silver fox, anyone?"

A laugh burst out of Angie. She covered her mouth, and as everyone in the room looked her way, she bent close to Katie. "Not so much silver in him, though. But yeah, that's applicable. Honestly, Jerry has more silver than Garrett does."

"*Rrrawwwr*, I know. The man still curls my toes." Katie giggled.

Angie looked at her sister, wondering who the hell she was. "Did that just come out of your mouth?"

Her sister smiled. "Hell yeah, it did. Twenty-four years and counting, and I'm still in love with my husband. Sue me."

Angie couldn't stop the smile that now pasted itself to her face. Leave it to Katie to be the distraction she needed. So typical of Katie, since she was the oldest and most responsible of all of them, plus she tended to take on the mom role.

But to go down the "my husband is hot as hell" road wasn't one Katie often went down with her, or anyone really. Katie was always the serious one. Moody, grumpy, stern. Critical of most all of them, too.

Angie took in her sister. "You're still pretty hot, too, Katie. And by the way, I think it's cool you're still so attracted to your husband and still in mad love with him. I hope he returns that favor."

Katie raised a brow, and a smirk curved her lips. "Believe me, he does."

"Okay, TMI. You can stop now."

The *other* mom in the family, Mary Claire, came over. "What are you two giggling about?"

"Oh, nothing." Katie crossed her arms.

"You know, I could use a laugh, too, Katie. You don't have to be so…mean." Mary frowned.

"You could use something, that's for damn sure, Mary." Katie moved her hands to her hips. "Why don't you try wishing our baby sister a happy birthday? Start there, maybe?"

"I would love a drink. How about we get a couple of those?" Angie smiled. The last thing she wanted was to get in the middle of a spat between Katie and Mary. Not a fun place to be. It could get ugly.

"A drink sounds great." Katie turned around and headed for the kitchen.

Mary scowled. "Ugh, she's such a bitch."

"No fighting tonight, please?"

"Who's fighting? I'm not fighting." Her sister scowled. "I only came over to say happy birthday to you." Mary threw her hands up in the air. "God, I give up."

Angie watched, dumbfounded, as Mary Claire walked away. Damn, something was going on with her sister because, if Angie wasn't mistaken, Mary's eyes had filled with tears. Mary had been extra sensitive since before Cyn and Shane had gotten married, and now it seemed it was getting worse. Yeah, something was up—shit, Angie hoped everything between Mary and Camden was okay.

On emotion overload, as Angie turned to get herself a drink, she spotted Garrett heading her way. She stopped and smiled. "Hi there. Did you meet everyone?"

"I did. Well…not everyone because Celia and Mark aren't here." He glanced around. "Right? I didn't miss them, did I?" He chuckled.

Angie laughed. "There's going to be a test later."

"Shit. I hate tests." He winked. "I should start a cheat sheet."

"You should. Actually, several Donnellys are missing. We'll go over that later, though." She tiptoed up and gave him a quick peck on the lips. "Can I get you something to drink?"

"Coffee or water would be good."

"You got it. Have a seat, and apparently—" She motioned to the television. "We're watching the game."

Joey Jr., Angie's oldest brother, came over. "Hey, happy birthday, Angie." He pressed a kiss to her cheek. "Can I get you two a beer?"

"Thank you! And yes, I'll have a beer, but Garrett will have a water. Unless there's coffee."

"Coffee or water?" Joey cocked his head. "We got plenty of beer, man. You sure?"

Panic rose inside Angie, flooding her system as she glanced between Garrett and Joey. "No, he—"

"Nah. I'm all good, really." Garrett raised his hand. "I'm allergic to alcohol, so no beer for me."

"No shit? Wow, that's gotta suck. All right." He clapped Garrett on his shoulder. "Water or coffee coming up. Beer for the birthday girl. Birthday shots later!" He smiled and stepped away.

Angie moved close to Garrett and lowered her voice. "Babe, I wasn't going to—"

"I know, hon. It's okay." He took her hand and squeezed it. "Automatic response for me. Just…habit, that's all."

"Aunnie Anwie, birday!" Her two-and-a-half-year-old niece, Madi, wrapped her arms around Angie's legs.

"Thank you, Madi." Angie bent and picked her up. "Did you grow since I last saw you? I think you did."

Madi giggled, scrunching up her face before patting her tummy. "No… Mommy's lelly goo!"

"Wait, what?" Angie's eyes went wide, and she glanced at Garrett, then back to Madi. "Momma's lelly what?" Angie practically ran to Stephanie, who was sitting on the love seat. "Um, Steph, so, little miss Madison said your lelly goo? Should I assume she's saying your belly grew, and I'm going to also assume she doesn't mean you're getting fat!"

"Holy shi—cow. You're pregnant, and you didn't tell us?" Maiya grabbed Joanie before she crawled underneath the end table.

"I…well…crud." Stephanie sucked her lips between her

teeth. But then, with a laugh, she rolled her eyes and looked at her daughter. "Madi, your secret-keeping skills need work."

Cyn started laughing as she shifted Shane Jr. in her arms. "Called it." She glanced at her husband and poked him with her toe. "Did I not call that?"

Shane smiled from his spot on the floor, not taking his eyes from the game on television. "You totally called it, girl."

"Love you." She laughed. "Don't get too comfortable down there. Your son just dropped a load in his diaper."

Madi started crying. "I *fordoooooot.*"

Angie cupped the little girl's head in her palm. "Aw, it's okay, sweet girl. You got excited, is all."

"Double crud on a stick. Did not think she'd get my meaning. Sometimes, I think she's smarter than all of us." Stephanie stood, and Angie passed Madi to her. "Don't cry, Dolly. Mommy's sorry, it's not your fault. I was teasing." She kissed Madi's cheek and then glanced around the room at everyone. "We only found out a couple of weeks ago, and I didn't think it was fair to announce at Angie's birthday party."

"That's sweet." Angie hugged her, squishing Madi between them. "But that news is an awesome birthday present! How far along?"

"About ten weeks now. So, just barely. Almost too soon to tell anyone. Except, jeez—" Steph shifted Madi on her hip and placed a hand on her barely-there mommy tummy, pressing her loose shirt tight against it. "Look at this. It's like my uterus exploded or some madness. I'm not even kidding. Stretch pants for days. Already."

Madi spotted Joey as he entered the room. She held her arms out, tears still visible on her little cheeks. "Daddy!"

"What happened? Did you miss Daddy that much?" He chuckled and handed Angie her beer and a bottle of water to Garrett. "My mother's got about sixteen different kinds of K-Cups in the kitchen. Figured I'd let you figure that insanity out and get you a water in the meantime."

"Works for me." Garrett smiled and took the water from her brother.

After taking Madi from Steph's arms, Joey took his spot on the floor next to Shane and sat Madi on his lap. "What I miss?"

Stephanie shrugged. "Cat's out of the bag, hon."

"Congrats, old man." Shane chuckled and took a sip of his beer.

"Thanks, and who you calling old?" He slugged Shane in the arm and then blew Steph a kiss. "All good, babe."

"You heard me. 'Scuse me, I got a diaper to change." Shane laughed and got to his feet. He scooped Shane Jr. up from Cyn's lap, kissed her cheek and made his way out of the room, snuggling the baby and mumbling something about how stinky he was.

Sweetest thing in the world watching that big hunk of a man cuddle a baby. Angie couldn't help but smile.

Maiya shifted closer to Cyn, making room for Angie on the couch. Angie took the spot as Stephanie settled back onto the loveseat. Garrett sat on the floor near Joey and Jerry, Katie's husband.

Angie took a sip of her beer and then another. Organized chaos, sort of. But at least there wasn't any Katie or Mary drama. Well, very little, anyway.

Her brother-in-law, Cam, Mary's husband, wandered in through the French doors from the backyard with his two boys, Camden Jr and Steven, in tow. Jacob, Ryan's oldest, was with them, too.

Angie shifted, tucking one leg beneath her, and waved. "Hey, Cam. Hey, boys."

"Hi, Aunt Angie. Happy birthday!" All three boys echoed each other as they ran to her.

They each hugged her and then, like a little wolf pack, headed out of the room, Angie assumed to play upstairs, which was likely where her nieces were. She'd know soon enough if the boys started annoying the girls.

"Good to see you, Ang. Happy birthday." Cam bent and kissed her cheek, then found a spot on the floor with the other guys.

"Hey, Cam, this is Garrett." Angie pointed her beer at Cam. "Garrett, this is my sister Mary's husband. Their two boys just headed upstairs with Ryan's son."

"Nice to meet you." Garrett reached out his hand, and Cam shook it.

"You're the infamous Garrett. Man, Mary hasn't stopped talking about the older guy Angie's been dating. I swear that woman has an opinion about everything." He shook his head. "Never a dull moment."

Angie frowned at Cam's statement regarding her sister. What he said and the tone he used had no love in it, no innocent humor, either. But it was sure laced with what sounded like a whole lot of resentment. Not good.

And right on cue, as if she'd heard through walls, Mary stepped into the family room and stopped in front of her husband. "I'm surprised to know you were even listening, Camden."

Shit, that tone wasn't much better. Really, not good. At all. Sadness bled into Angie's heart. She looked at Garrett and shook her head. He gave her a slight nod, his expression soft, and she took it to mean he understood, and she shouldn't let it get to her. At least, that's what she needed it to mean.

Life wasn't perfect. Families weren't either, and that included hers.

"On that note, I think I'm tired." Cam got to his feet. "Angie, enjoy your birthday dinner. Garrett, nice to meet you. Maybe we can bullshit another time." He nodded and gave everyone else in the room a salute. "Later, peeps."

"Seriously, Cam? You can't just leave." Mary followed him

out of the room. Her voice trailed off as they got farther away from the family room.

The sadness Angie was already feeling doubled, spilling over into her limbs. Whatever was going on with Cam and Mary was none of her business, but she did hope they'd work through it.

She hated that they were so obviously having problems. They had kids. A life together. They were a family, and they loved each other. They had to work through it.

God, she hoped.

———

"...HAPPY BIRTHDAY, DEAR *ANGIEEEEE*—" Garrett sang along, staring at the brood of people and kids, all singing to Angie, and knew that every single one of them loved her— "Happy birthday to *youuuuuu!*"

With a huge smile, Angie held her hair back in one hand, bent forward and blew out her candles. Three of the youngest kids helped her blow. Everyone clapped and cheered. Garrett crossed his arms and took it all in. Amazing...really amazing.

Her family was really cool. Not perfect, not without fault —that was obvious from the sulking and grumpy mood Angie's sister, Mary, was in since her husband Cam had left early. But even with that, they were, dare he say, normal?

Then again, normal was relative. Either way, with only one sibling, a sister he barely heard from, and also a father who spent most of his time drunk, Garrett never had this kind of family growing up, and sadly, thanks to the path he'd chosen, Chassidy hadn't had it either.

Garrett bent toward Angie and kissed her cheek. "Happy birthday, hon. Thanks for letting me be here."

Her expression went soft. "Thanks for wanting to be here."

"Let's get this cake cut, shall we?" Roseanne, Angie's

mother, smiled at him. "Here, Garrett, you do it." She handed him a cake knife. "Serve our girl the first piece, please?"

Angie's eyes went wide. "But Dad usually cuts the cake for us."

"And when it's time, someone else takes that job over." Her father, Joe, smiled. "But I get the second slice." The man chuckled. "Happy birthday, sweet girl."

"Thanks, Dad." She glanced at her sister-in-law, Maiya and her sister, Cyn. "I still can't believe I'm twenty-ten."

"It's all downhill from here. Next thing you know, it'll be babies and no sleep." Cyn laughed.

Garrett's body went stiff at Cyn's comment, but he did his best to hide it. What would Angie say?

"Not quite yet!" Maiya waved her hand at Cyn. "Angie, you got a little more time to party still."

"Not much time left. Better hurry. The clock starts ticking pretty hard around thirty." Steph took the plate of candles Roseanne had cleared off the cake. "Ohmygod, totally gonna lick every bit of icing off of these."

"God, you guys suck!" Angie laughed. "Bum me out more, why don't you." Angie glanced up at Garrett. Catching her eyes, he raised both brows. Angie shot him a wink before focusing back on her sister-in-law. "Wow, Steph, go easy with the candles, huh? Looks like those pesky baby hormones are already swamping your system."

Okay, then. Apparently, Angie wasn't going to respond to the comments about babies or her biological clock, but likely she didn't have to. Her family knew her better, were privy to more than he was where she was concerned—especially her sisters.

"Ugh, I know! It's terrible. But I can't help it." Stephanie sucked on the end of the first candle. "Mmm! *Sooosoo* good, Roseanne!"

Roseanne laughed. "I think it might taste even better without the wax mixed in."

"Should I be worried?" Joey shifted Madi on his hip.

"About what?" Steph licked another candle clean.

"You wanting to eat wax." Joey laughed.

"I'm not eating wax, you goof. I'm eating frosting."

Garrett shook his head, laughing again as he cut into the homemade strawberry shortcake triple-decker cake. He slid the first piece, with a giant strawberry on it, onto a plate and moved it in front of Angie. "For you, birthday girl."

"Why, thank you, Mr. James." Angie clapped her hands, her eyes dancing as she grabbed the fork.

With a smile and a nod, he cut into the next piece, got it on the plate and handed it to her father. "Joe. All yours."

"Perfect size." Her father grinned and dove right into the piece of cake.

Garrett finished doling out the cake, and then settled against the wall and enjoyed a piece, too. "Delicious cake, Roseanne."

Roseanne smiled. "Thank you. It's Angie's favorite."

"Definitely, Mom. Thank you, I'll never get tired of this." Angie shoved another piece into her mouth.

"So, Garrett, I hear you have a daughter. How old is she?" Mary set her cake plate down.

Garrett swallowed his mouthful. "I do, yes. Chassidy. She'll be twenty-eight next month."

Mary's eyes went wide. "Twenty-eight? Wow, how old were you when you had her, sixteen?"

This was the grilling he suspected he might get. There was no way at least one person in Angie's family wasn't going to have an issue with their age gap. He couldn't blame them. He wouldn't exactly be okay if Chassidy started dating a guy seventeen years her senior. Garrett nodded at Mary. "Very sweet of you to think so. But, no, not sixteen. I was nineteen."

"Huh. Well, I guess that answers that." Mary sipped her coffee.

"Answers what exactly, Mary Claire?" Katie glared at her

sister. "I was nineteen when I had Sara. Is there some sort of problem you have with people having babies at a young age?"

Mary leaned forward and glared right back. "No, Katherine Marie, more like answers exactly how much older Garrett is than Angie. Not everything is about you and your *perfect* life, you know!"

Angie stood, the chair screeching on the hardwood floor. "Good God. Mary, whatever your issue is, it's yours. No one else needs to suffer for it. Do us a favor and keep it to your damn self."

"That's enough! Angie, sit. Now. Finish your cake." Roseanne gave Angie a stern look, and without arguing, Angie did as her mother told her. Then Roseanne's eyes were back on Mary. "Mary Claire, in the kitchen, now."

Angie gave Garrett a look filled with sadness and regret. Her emotion so palpable it hit him like a punch in the gut. She was being apologetic for something, which, first off, wasn't her fault and, second, was totally valid.

He *was* too old for her. Nothing would change that. Garrett shook his head, urging her to let it go for now. They could talk about it later.

Mary stood and stormed out of the dining room. Roseanne followed, but not two seconds later, Katie got up and moved in their direction. Oh, shit, things were about to get interesting.

Garrett blew out a breath and set his plate down on the table.

Angie's father grabbed Katie's arm, stopping her as she was about to pass him. "Katie, you can park your butt right back in that seat. Your *Mother* did not ask for your attendance nor your help."

Katie's eyes went wide. "Daddy, I..." She stared at him, waiting for him to change his mind, Garrett assumed. But then gave in to his instruction. "Fine." She turned and did as she was told.

Joe turned to Garrett. "Excuse my daughters. I apologize on their behalf. It's no one's business how old you are. I'm more interested in whether or not Angie is happy. Same goes for all my kids."

"Thank you, Dad." Angie stood, came over and wrapped her arms around her father.

"I wasn't worried about Garrett's age. So, no need to include me in that." Katie leaned back in her seat and crossed her arms.

Joe looked over the top of Angie's head at his eldest daughter. "Maybe not worried, but curious, I'm sure, 'Mother Katie.' So yes, it does include you."

"Ooh, burn. He's got you there, Katie." Joe Jr. shoved another piece of cake in his mouth.

"Shut it, Joey." Katie rolled her eyes, but the corners of her mouth twitched with a grin.

"Gotta love it when the Donnelly siblings fight." Shane shook his head, leaning back in his seat. "Never a dull moment over here."

Angie moved from her father to Garrett, wrapping her arms around his middle. Garrett nodded at Joe Sr. and then turned his attention to Shane. "A rite of passage?"

"Consider yourself inducted." Joey grinned.

"Aren't you all going out tonight?" Joe Sr. frowned at the group of them. "If so, I'm not sure why you're all still sitting here."

"Yes, we're going soon. Well, some of us, anyway. And you and Mom are babysitting, right? Please say you're still going to do that?" An innocent expression came over Angie's face.

Her father raised his finger and pointed it at Angie. "Fair warning, kid: that innocent look of yours expired when you turned thirty. But, yes, we're still babysitting."

Angie laughed, her hold on Garrett tightening. "Well, damn. I guess Christmas is ruined now."

Garrett tried to suppress a laugh. But Angie continued to

shake with laughter against him as the rest of the room erupted, too. Garrett didn't want to disrespect her father, but the man was also laughing, so Garrett let it go, laughing along with all of them.

Yup, this was a normal, far from perfect, family. Garrett was glad he'd been able to see most of them in action. He had a feeling Shane was right, too. There was never a dull moment with the Donnellys.

CHAPTER THIRTY-FOUR

GARRETT SPOTTED HIS PHONE WHEN THE TEXT ALERT WENT off. He bent to it and glanced at the screen. The message was from Angie. Smiling, he stepped away, grabbed four bottles of flavored Smirnoff from the back and lined them up behind the bar.

There was a ton to catch up on since he'd spent the weekend away with her in L.A. He'd hit her back up once he got inventory sorted. Garrett smiled as the memories of the weekend played behind his eyes.

He hadn't expected it, but they'd had a spectacular weekend together. Seeing her world was good, better than good, actually. As a result, even though he'd been trying to keep things in check, they'd gotten closer. He hadn't expected that either.

A little while later, he was up in his office going through paperwork when the business phone on his desk rang. Not bothering to glance at the caller ID, he picked up the cordless receiver and placed it to his ear. "Copper Halo."

"Garrett?"

"Oh, hey, Ang. What's up, babe?" He leaned back in his

seat as happiness spilled through him at the sound of her voice.

"Oh, ya know. Not much, really. Except…I haven't heard from you all damn day!" Garrett sat straight up in his seat, the tone in her voice immediately setting the hairs on the back of his neck on fire. "No biggie, right? Sent you a couple texts, no reply to those, either. Hmm…let me think what else. Oh, yeah, that's right. I tried *calling* your cell, but had no luck with that avenue, either. But yeah, *obviously* you're not dead because you answered the bar line, right? So, how about you tell *me* what the hell is up, *babe*?"

The lightheartedness that had filled him a mere three seconds ago was washed away in a flash flood of agitation. Garrett got to his feet and paced away from his desk. "Wow. You're kidding me, right? Because I know you can't be serious talking to me like this."

"Serious as a damn heart attack. It's almost seven at night, and I haven't heard from you *at all*! That's not cool. Really not cool, Garrett. And like I said, obviously you're not dead or in the hospital, so yeah, totally fucking serious."

Seven? Garrett glanced at the clock on the wall.

Fuck me.

Six fifty-four p.m. When had it gotten that late? He glanced over the surface of his desk before patting his pockets, looking for his cell. Shit…he must've left it downstairs.

Fuck.

Fuuuck!

"Okay, listen. I get that you're pissed." He ran his hand over the top of his hair. "But I am not cool with you talking to me the way you are. I don't like it, Angie."

"Well, I'm not okay with you blowing me off like this. And for the record, it isn't the first time you've left me hanging, Garrett. Christ, you do this like it's no big deal."

He blew out a harsh breath. "Because it isn't a big deal. Don't make it one."

She got quiet, and Garrett wondered what she'd throw at him next. Taking a seat, he braced for more. She'd mentioned his inability to communicate more than a few times before, but he'd brushed it off. It wasn't a big deal to him, and it wasn't anything personal he was doing *to her*. He wasn't good at the whole "touch base via text a thousand times a day thing," and he'd warned her that this would become an issue for her once they were long distance. Well, here they were.

It'd been a little over six months together and five months of long distance, but this, whatever they were, would end now if she kept up these off-the-hook, bitchy temper tantrums. No way he'd tolerate them.

"What'm I supposed to think, Garrett? I mean, really?"

"You're supposed to know that I'm working, that I'm busy. Where does this come from?"

"Where does what come from?"

Her harsh tone was still in full effect, and he bristled again. "This! Your inability to wait for me to contact you? Seriously, I warned you about this before we started seeing each other long distance. You said you'd have to accept it. I'd think by now you know, especially after the time we've spent together, that obviously I'm thinking of you. But I have shit to get done, Angie."

"I should *know* that you're *obviously* thinking of me, huh?"

"Yeah. You should."

A bitter-sounding laugh came out of her. "How is that even fucking logical, Garrett? Are you even hearing yourself?"

"Because it is. Look, I'm sorry, okay? Time got away from me, and I left my phone on the bar downstairs. I was going to text you after I got stock done, but then I lost track of time when I came up to my office."

"I can't read you. I don't understand you." She blew out a harsh breath. "It's not fair."

Hoping she was done with her tirade, Garrett resumed his seat at his desk. "What's not fair?"

"I just…"

He ran his palm along the back of his neck and waited. The woman lived to argue. Nothing would convince him otherwise. "Still there?"

"Yes. Just…thinking."

Her tone was so soft Garrett pressed the phone closer to his ear. "About?"

"What I'm doing and what we're doing."

Shit. Now, it was his turn to blow out a breath. "What is it that you're expecting, Angie?"

"I don't know, Garrett. I guess normal would be what I expect."

"What the fuck does that even mean?"

"It means, like I said, I cannot fucking read you. One minute, you're all over me; the next, it's like I don't exist, like I'm invisible. It's so goddamn confusing!"

"Now you're being dramatic." He shook his head and frowned as an ache started behind his eyes. He did not need this shit. "Look, I was going to text you. I was probably going to call, too. I got busy. That's all. It's not personal."

"That's the thing, Garrett, it's *very* fucking personal to me. And screw you for saying I'm being dramatic. That falls into the unfair category, too."

"Okay, fine." Agitation pulsed through him, making his hands tingle and smothering what little patience he'd had left. "You want to argue? Go ahead. Get it all out of your system. When you're done, I can get back to work."

"Wow. Okay then. Let's skip it. I'll let you get back to work right now. Have a good night, Garrett."

The phone went dead before he had a chance to respond.

Jesus-fucking-Christ, she was a relentless pain in his ass! Garrett slammed the phone receiver down on the cradle. Anger raced through him, his heartbeat pounding in his head. Too much drama, too much bullshit hysterics. He didn't need it. Any of it.

No matter how good the sex was, or the connection between them, or how things had grown—nothing was worth this amount of shit.

Jesus, why was he doing this again? Why was he even bothering? Maybe now was the time to end it. Just part ways and be done. No way they could sustain this back-and-forth travel shit, anyway. Their ending was inevitable. It was just a matter of time.

The ache that had started behind Garrett's eyes migrated south to his chest. He cleared his throat and leaned back in his desk chair. Fucking hell, even though there was no true future for them, he cared about her more than he wanted to.

Nothing would change the fact that he had nothing to offer her long-term. She needed a man who, despite what she'd said, would give her a future and a family.

Bile rose in his throat, and Garrett got to his feet. The idea of Angie with someone else… Fuck. The thought of another man touching her had a film of red coating everything before his eyes. God, he was going to be sick.

Garrett headed downstairs, found his cell phone and exited the building. He needed time to think, to get his head on straight and figure out what to do next. Maybe he'd call her later after they'd both calmed down.

Bottom line, he needed to do the right thing for both of them. Calling her later wasn't the right thing unless he planned to tell her goodbye. Question was, was he ready to tell her goodbye? As he opened the door to his car, he knew the answer. No, he wasn't ready to tell Angie Donnelly goodbye.

An hour after hanging up on Garrett, Angie blew her nose for what felt like the millionth time. Technically, she hadn't really hung up on him. She'd said goodbye, but still. It was nearly the same.

Her heart ached with sadness, and a brick, made of pure frustration, weighed heavy in her stomach. As tears, which seemed in endless supply, ran down her cheeks, she'd picked up the phone at least ten times, contemplating a text to him.

But what else was there to say? She'd pretty much said it all during their argument. Sort of. She'd said a lot but hadn't covered all of it, not by a long shot. Grabbing the pile of tissues off the bed, she tossed them in the trash can in the bathroom.

What she didn't tell him was how much it hurt when he rarely reached out first, and worse, didn't answer her texts or calls, or when she'd leave him a message and he didn't call her back. Sometimes for hours. And how when she called him and nearly *always* got his voicemail rather than his actual voice, it made her want to scream.

And after the fantastic weekend she'd had with him, not hearing from him today had spoiled all the progress she thought they'd made. Everything she'd been ignoring, all the things that had been bugging her over the past months, had rushed to the surface, and it was as if she was a pressure cooker that finally blew.

Why didn't he get it? Why couldn't he see that he was an incredibly amazing man in her eyes? That when she looked at him, she saw the moon and the stars. This past weekend, he looked at her in the same way. At least, it's what she thought she'd witnessed. God, she'd felt it straight down to her toes.

Angie grabbed another tissue. In fact, up until this past weekend, the man had been like a locked box. But over her birthday weekend, she'd gotten a clear glimpse of those deeper parts of him he normally kept out of reach.

Of course, being who she was, Angie reached for those hidden parts. She wanted to hold them close to her and never let a single piece of them go.

And then he'd gone and dropped her right on her ass today.

Desperation rode her like a bad storm. With a need to sort her thoughts, Angie left her apartment to wander around the complex in the warm evening air. With her eyes trained on the sidewalk, she filtered through all the time she'd spent with and without him over the past several months.

The memories were filled with good and bad. A fuckton of frustration, too. But then…moments of pure bliss. Moments where Angie knew she was right where she was supposed to be. And she knew she wanted more…

But it seemed, too often, she was always wanting more and always waiting.

Yet still, she'd somehow fallen hard for him. Totally and completely. Angie had tripped and fallen into a big fucking pile of in love for Garrett James—a man who had walls built so thick around his heart that even with a jackhammer, she'd probably never get to the center of him.

A man who didn't know how to show his emotions. A man who rarely gave compliments. She could count on one hand the few times he'd complimented her.

Angie wasn't a woman who needed to hear she was beautiful, or pretty, that sort of thing constantly, but getting it more than three or four times in the past six months would be nice. Hell, it would be normal.

God…why was she doing this to herself? She needed normal. And nothing about this situation was normal.

She'd spent an entire year figuring out her life and how she wanted to live. And this was not it. She emerged from that moratorium *knowing* she wanted more, knowing she deserved better, and she had planned to go after all of it. Yet she hadn't done any of that.

Angie was miserable. She hadn't applied for a job with Rolling Stone. Hell, she didn't even know if they were hiring anymore.

Nothing was moving forward for her, but she was going to change that. And change it now. With a tummy full of emotionally fueled motivation, Angie got to her feet and moved to the small desk in her living room.

After sitting down, she opened her laptop and headed to Rolling Stone's career website. Angie took a deep breath and scrolled through the job postings.

Please, please, be hiring.

Her eyes scanned the screen, and…bingo!

Angie smiled, clicked on the open position, and then began filling out the online application.

CHAPTER THIRTY-FIVE

"WHAT TIME ARE YOU COMING OVER AGAIN?" GARRETT shifted the phone to his other ear and stepped into his closet.

"I'm shooting for seven."

"Chassidy, I thought you told me on Tuesday you were coming at five? I got the bird in the oven already, and now it will be done too soon."

"Dad, it's only two hours. Plus, we weren't going to eat until around seven anyway. So, it'll be fine. We can eat as soon as I get there."

"But what about the appetizers I made?"

"Oh my God, seriously? I'm not the only one coming. The guys are coming over, too. They'll eat them."

Garrett sat on the edge of his bed and frowned. "That's exactly my point, Chassidy. You won't get to enjoy any of them."

Chassidy blew out a harsh breath. "Look, I know this is important to you. But it's important to Grammy and Papa, too. So, work with me here? You'd think this holiday stuff would get easier after all these years. But no. It hasn't."

Guilt filled Garrett's stomach. He wasn't trying to be a pain in the ass or put pressure on Chassidy, but yeah, having her with him for the holidays was important to him. Chassidy might be the only family he kept in contact with, but she still had Amanda's parents. "Sorry, honey. I'll make it work."

"Aw, Dad, it's okay. It's fine. Tell you what, set some of the appetizers aside for me in Tupperware, and I'll take them home as leftovers, cool?"

"That works. All right, let me run. I got a couple more things to get ready before the guys get here."

Chassidy laughed. "You're like an old woman, I swear."

Garrett frowned. "Very funny."

"See you at seven, Dad."

"Happy Thanksgiving, Chassidy. Give my best to everyone there."

"Will do." She disconnected the call.

Garrett pulled the phone from his ear and scanned the screen. He had a text message he hadn't replied to. It was from Angie, and he knew he needed to respond, but he also had a lot of shit to get done. Pulling up the message, he read through it again.

> Angie: Happy Thanksgiving, baby. Missing you! Please call me when you get some time today.

He hadn't had time to call her. Though she'd say he hadn't made the time. But it was true. He had to get the table set, finish prepping all the appetizers and finish a couple of the backup side dishes. Guests were due to arrive in the next three hours. That didn't give him much time.

He could call her and talk with her on speaker while he got things together, but he was still upset about the last fight they'd had right after her birthday and needed a little space.

To make matters worse, Angie had wanted to spend turkey day together. She'd mentioned it a few times, and he'd told her he would think about it, and he had. But in the end, Garrett felt it was best that she spend it with her family.

His trip to L.A. had brought them much closer. Closer than he'd expected or planned. But then she had that blow-up right when he'd gotten back, and things just hadn't felt right since. She might've started the fight with him, but he was the one who was holding onto his anger.

Another wave of guilt filled his stomach, this time in regard to Angie. Garrett swallowed down the bad taste it left in his mouth. She wasn't wrong the night she'd gone off on him. Not one hundred percent, anyway—her delivery had sucked, sure. And because of that, he'd struggled ever since with how to get back to where they'd been.

A longing filled his chest. He missed her. But he was choosing not to do anything about that. Instead, he decided to keep himself busy. The busy made it easier to *not* do anything about the missing her part...or the relationship part.

God, he was such a shit. Yes, he was avoiding her, but the least he could do was text her back on Thanksgiving, for fuck's sake.

> Garrett: HTD to you too hon

After hitting send, Garrett plugged his phone into the charger and went downstairs to finish cooking. As he rounded the corner, the sound of the doorbell got his attention. When he approached the door, he saw his friend Sean standing in the sidelight, his nose pressed against the glass.

Garrett couldn't help but chuckle as he opened the door. "You're cleaning that glass now, asshole."

"Sure thing, boss. Take this. I got more stuff in the car." Sean grinned and shoved a large casserole dish toward Garrett.

Garrett took the dish. "You're early."

"I didn't have anything else to do, and I figured we could watch the game," Sean called over his shoulder as he made his way down the flagstone stairs to his car.

Garrett let out a sigh. Worked for him. As shitty as he was feeling, having Sean there early would make it easier to get through the afternoon.

"You've reached Garrett James, I'm unable to answer your call—"

Angie disconnected the call. She'd heard Garrett's recorded voicemail message in the last forty-eight hours, more than she'd heard his *actual* voice.

She'd gotten one text message from him in the early afternoon of Thanksgiving Day—if you could call "HTD to you too hon" a message.

She assumed HTD meant: happy turkey day, but for all she knew, it could mean "holy trinity display" or even "honest turkey dick." Despite the frustration boiling in her veins, Angie giggled at her creative acronyms and stared at her phone.

Garrett *had* called her later that night, she assumed, when he'd found time, but of course, it was the one time she was away from her phone. So, she'd missed the call.

She'd tried to call him back, but no answer. Technically, he'd done what she'd asked in calling her, but nothing more. And since then, two days had passed, and she'd sent four text messages and tried to contact him three more times.

No answer.

No response.

Nothing but tumbleweeds blowing between L.A. and Arizona.

She knew why he was being so distant. It was all a result of that fight they'd had where she lost her shit on him.

A mere two weeks ago, he'd spent the weekend with her for her birthday; now it felt like a lifetime ago. They'd had an unbelievable time. Great sex. Awesome laughter. Dinner and cake at her parents. He'd met a lot of her family, plus endured the Mary drama. They'd even gone out after and saw Angie's friend, Tarra Layne, sing.

Everything had been great, better than great.

But then she'd gone and made things a mess, spoiled everything because she couldn't keep it together. Hearing from him regularly had always been a problem, and why she lost it that day, she couldn't say.

She'd also apologized, and they'd talked and made up as best they could over the phone, at least she thought they had. But considering he refused to spend Thanksgiving together, it was obvious Garrett wasn't over it.

And now, with the radio silence? Things weren't looking good. Angie physically felt him pulling away, and an ache had taken up residence in her chest that she couldn't shake. And God, she missed him—more than she'd ever missed anyone in her life.

It was hell.

She was in hell.

Angie typed out a text message to him.

> Angie: Heading to hear my friend, Tarra Layne, sing tonight. Hope you're doing okay. I'm really freaked out that I haven't heard from you. Please call me?

She stared at the screen, her thumb hovering over the send button. Desperation rose, filling her limbs and making her skin tight with anxiety. In reaction, anger flooded her system, smothering her desperation, and Angie deleted the message instead of sending it.

Fuck it, fuck him.

Fuck everything!

HALF ASLEEP, Garrett blindly reached for the ringing phone on his nightstand. It was Angie, he knew, without even looking at the screen. He glanced at the alarm clock—did that say four a.m.? Too tired to ignore the call or be annoyed even, he swiped the screen of his phone. "Mmmhi, hon."

"*Don yhuu* hi hon *me*."

Shit. She was drunk. This was gonna be so much fun. Not. Garrett blew out a breath. "Did you wake me up to fight with me?"

"Yessss—ow. Shit."

He shook his head. "Watch out for the footboard."

"You shushhhh, Garrett James! You don't care if I fit the hoodboard! Yhou *doneeeven* call me."

"Babe—" He closed his eyes, knowing she would likely go on and on.

"You don 'ext me neither. Jerk! An' I miss yhou, baby, I *missyousoooooomuch*."

Garrett had no idea what to say. She wasn't wrong. He'd been busy—seriously busy. But also using the time to figure out what to do next, how to handle that fight they'd had and what to do with their relationship.

"*Helloooo?*"

"I'm here, Ang."

"Say somethinn."

He let out a heavy sigh. "What do you want me to say? Considering you're drunk and you clearly want to fight, there's no point in saying anything. You're going to talk over me anyway."

"Not true." She groaned. "Don' yhou *missme*, too?"

"I do miss you, babe. I've just been busy. There's been shows all weekend at the Halo. Thanksgiving weekend is always crazy busy. I told you that."

"*Nooo. Nonono yhou din not!*" She hiccupped. "You know how I know? *Cuz you don' call me nanymore!*"

Okay, hell no, there was *no way* he was doing this with her.

"Okay, look. Angie, I'm going to hang up the phone. I'll call you tomorrow."

"*Noooooo*, don't!"

Well, that certainly came out a lot clearer. Except…he sighed again, realizing she was crying. *Fuck…*

Jesus, he was the biggest piece of shit on the planet. She's drunk and upset, and he's ready to hang up on her. But Christ, she was too much to deal with when she was like this. Not the drunk part, the fighting part. "Angie, don't cry."

"I can helppp it. I'm *soooo lohnley*, Garrett. And heartkiss." She sniffled. "*Fuck*, I mean, sick. *I'mmm* heartsick."

He had to stifle a chuckle. Even pissed and drunk, she was still sincere, and also, even he had to admit, cute. "I do miss you."

She sniffled. "How?"

"What do you mean, how?" He heard rustling against the phone, and then she moaned or maybe groaned, he wasn't sure. He turned on his side. "You okay?"

"Yep. Sssorry. Neened water. How do yhou miss me?"

"Are you in bed now?"

"Mmhmm."

"Good. You should try to sleep. You're going to have a hangover in the morning."

"Who cares?"

"I care."

"No, yhou don't. Liar."

The woman was relentless. Garrett blew out a breath. "Will you call me when you wake up tomorrow?"

"*Suuuure*. You won't answer, though."

"I will."

"Promise?"

A small smile arched his lips. "Yes."

"Say it! Say, you rompiss…shit. Promise."

"You promise."

"Ugh." She giggled but caught herself. "Such a jerk."

"Maybe so, but I got you to smile. Even a little."

"Dusint matter."

He rose on an elbow. "Call me tomorrow. We'll talk, I promise."

"*Finnnnne.*"

"Night, Angie."

"Mmhmm."

Garrett listened until the call was gone.

He was shocked she hung up first. He kind of thought she wouldn't and that he'd have to hang up on her. Not literally, since he'd said goodnight, but still. He set the phone on the nightstand and settled back under the blankets.

He should've tried to call her earlier that day. Better yet, the day before.

Hell, he should've done a lot of things.

Their situation had progressed past casual, and he hadn't wanted that. Then the blow-up happened, and it'd fucked with his mind. Now, he was in over his head, and there was no way to end things cleanly.

Whenever he tried to imagine himself without Angie, his stomach felt hollow, and he couldn't draw in a deep breath as if a lead weight was on his chest. He thought about her constantly, but he just kept doing the next thing in front of him.

Before he knew it, the day had passed, and he was exhausted. Too exhausted to get into a conversation that would be more like an argument because she hadn't heard from him. On and on it went—a vicious cycle.

Garrett flipped his pillow over before rolling to his side. An ache started behind his eyes, and anxiety tickled the back of his neck. For fuck's sake, would he even be able to get back to sleep now? What a goddamn mess he'd made, and still, he had no clue how to get out of it.

CHAPTER THIRTY-SIX

Angie rolled over in bed and could barely open her eyes without feeling like she'd taken an ice pick to the back of the skull. Her head was pounding in time with her heart, and she was sure she was going to die.

Jeezus chrispies, how many shots of Jameson had she done last night? In addition to her head pounding like a drum solo by Lars Ulrich from Metallica, her mouth tasted like something had died in there. Shit, had she thrown up? No…not that she recalled anyway.

The last thing Angie remembered was stumbling out of the Lyft driver's car and up the stairs to her apartment. Cracking one eye, she spotted the water bottle on her nightstand. Drumming up all her courage to battle the pain, she raised her head off the pillow and grabbed the container filled with hydration salvation.

After drinking half the bottle down, she burped like the lady she had no chance of being that morning and scanned the night table for her phone. And then another memory surfaced—shit, she'd called Garrett last night.

Angie's head pounded harder, and she dropped back onto the pillow. Unfortunately, she hadn't simply *called* him. She *drunk* called him—way worse than drunk texting by a million miles.

God only knew what she said. Well, Garrett knew, but that wasn't the point. Though technically, it was. Raising her head again, she took another long swig of water and then set it back on the table.

With slow movements, to not make stars burst before her eyes, she lifted the blankets and sheets, searching for her cell phone. No luck, and really, why bother?

Angie rolled to her side and pulled one of the other pillows against her. Eventually, someone would text her, or she'd get a Facebook alert, and she'd find the damn thing.

Sadly, Angie wasn't surprised she'd called him drunk. She'd been missing him like crazy and feeling so out of sorts. And apparently, getting shit-faced had been her solution.

Yes, of course, because hate drinking always worked. Yeah, right.

But for the love of all things, she was sad, she was angry, she was confused, and…she was lonely. Loneliness had been an unexpected emotion in the mix. Angie had spent a year deliberately single and hadn't felt lonely even once during that time.

Garrett left her alone a lot, especially since she'd stupidly lost her shit on him, and although she had her family and friends to do things with, a feeling of abandonment had settled so deep inside Angie's bones that when she wasn't with Garrett or hadn't heard from him, she couldn't quite manage to feel like herself.

In other words, he *left* her lonely.

Which was *not* what anyone wanted to ever feel in a relationship. And to make matters worse, it felt like he was doing it on purpose. It was the reddest of the red flags he'd shown her to date.

And…still, she wanted him.

God, was she crazy?

Was she really this desperate?

Angie pressed the heels of her hands to her eyes. Yes. Yes, she was because through all of the ups and downs over the past six-plus months, and all the uncertainty and insecurity, Angie still wanted the man.

But want and need were two *very* different things.

What Angie *needed* to do was leave the man. Walk the hell away now before her heart got any deeper and—

Despair settled in her veins like ice water, and Angie shivered beneath the blankets. She knew what she needed to do, sure, but the idea of doing it, following through to end things, had tears welling in her eyes.

Walking away from Garrett felt impossible. But why?

Yes, in the beginning, he'd intrigued her, resisted her, and admittedly, she'd liked the chase, the challenge of it. But now, although he intrigued her no less, she knew better than to think it was merely the thrill of the chase.

She wanted Garrett more than she'd ever wanted a man before in her life.

The problem was, Angie didn't think he'd ever give himself to her the way she'd already given herself to him, especially now. And that was too heartbreaking to even fathom.

She was heartsick—oh, shit.

She'd said that to him last night. More like she remembered practically yelling it at him. Jeezus chrispies, she'd done it again. Angie sighed as resignation filled her heart. He was probably so pissed at her there was no way she'd hear from him today.

Angie buried her face in the pillow, and the tears she could no longer stop from falling soaked the cotton case.

Unrequited love wasn't glamorous the way movies or songs often made it out to be. Loving someone and not being loved back was among the top ten most fucked up things a human being could ever walk through. And although Angie never would've thought it would happen to her, she was now experiencing it firsthand.

And it fucking sucked.

GARRETT HEARD his phone ringing again. This time, when he opened his eyes, it was not the middle of the night, but it was still way too early. How on earth could the woman be calling him at—he glanced at the clock—seven a.m.?

She'd been beyond plastered last night and should still be sleeping it off.

Without checking the caller ID, Garrett swiped the screen and put it to his ear. "How are you up this early?"

"I know, right? But I figured this was the only way I'd actually get you on the phone."

Fucking really? "What the fuck do you want, Chase?"

"Go easy, brother. I just want to talk."

Talk? Yeah right. Garrett rolled over and sat up. "About what now?"

"The interview. Us. The band."

This wasn't a conversation Garrett wanted to be having, especially with his lack of sleep and subsequent mood he was in. Seven in the morning was not the time to discuss this again. "Look, I said I'd think about it, and I am, but let's get something straight right now: there is no us. And there is no band."

"Don't be so dramatic. You know, you could've been a lead singer with all your theatrics." Chase laughed. "I mean that with all the love I have in my heart for you, Garrett."

"All the times I covered your ass when you couldn't sing? I guess, yeah, that could be true."

"Aw, c'mon. Maybe you covered once or twice. But let's be real, as fucked up as you were all the time, too? No way you could've truly held the crowd in your hands like I did. That's just facts, brother."

Agitation pulsed in Garrett's veins. His former friend was pushing his buttons hard, and Garrett was running on negative patience. "Look, as much fun as it is to throw jabs at each other, I have things to do. So, either say what you gotta say or keep it to yourself. You got about five seconds to decide."

"Okay, okay, look. I get you. A lot of bad shit went down, and you walked away. But this is a big opportunity for all of us. Not just me. I talked to Derrick and Jake, and they're both on board. We need you, man. Plus, my agent and publicist got together, and they want to plan a reunion show, maybe even a tour. Probably a tour. But yeah, either way, I think it's a shot we shouldn't pass up. Hell, we could even start the tour at your venue. End it there, too." Chase drew in an audible breath, then blew it out. "So, yeah, that's my pitch. That's all I got. What do you say? Do this with me? Do it with us?"

Garrett sat on the edge of his bed, dumbstruck. After all the bad shit that happened, all the drugs, and the painful spiral as a result. The fighting—God, the fighting within the band had been unbearable. How the fuck could Chase *ever* think this was a good idea?

Garrett signed through his nose and stood. "No."

"No?"

"That's what I said." Garrett walked to the bathroom.

"You're not even willing to think about it more or discuss it? Just…no?"

"No is a complete sentence, Chase." He reached in and turned the shower on. "Anything else?"

Chase laughed, but there wasn't any humor behind it. "Dude, come on, really? At least think about it some more."

"No." A pang of guilt slid through Garrett as he dropped his pajama bottoms. He had no reason to feel guilty, though. He didn't owe Chase Reynolds or Copper Seven, shit. Yet that hideous emotion was there anyway, loud and proud, making his skin crawl.

Garrett shoved the feelings aside as hard as he could. "Hanging up now, Chase. Good luck, *brother*."

He dropped the phone on the bathroom counter with a clatter and stepped beneath the spray in the shower. Annoyance spilled over his skin along with the water.

Christ, he'd been expecting to hear Angie's groggy, hungover voice, and although he wasn't looking forward to that emotional conversation, he sure as hell wasn't prepared to deal with Chase asking not only about the interview but to get the band back together, too.

Garrett poured shampoo into his palm and lathered his long hair and his beard. How the fuck? This was…no way. He didn't even want to think about it. But like his memory cared what he wanted?

As Garrett closed his eyes, flashbacks assaulted him. The exhaustion of performing, the constant hangovers. The staying up for days partying, drinking, puking, and the excessive amounts of drugs all in the mix. Finding Chase so out of it, they had to call the paramedics. The same happening to Garrett. Amanda OD'ing and dying, and Garrett finding out about it when he was halfway around the world.

Chassidy crying for him to come home…

Fuck!

He was not doing this again—any of it.

He hadn't yet dealt with the situation with Angie—

He'd been dragging it out, sure, but the last thing he needed was this shit with the band, too. He had a business to run. He had a life to live. He was busy living it.

Things weren't perfect, far from it, but that didn't mean shit. It wasn't supposed to be perfect. That was how life worked. It was complicated. He sure as hell didn't need to complicate it more.

Leaning back, he rinsed his hair, then turned and did the

same with his beard. After adding conditioner to both, he grabbed the body wash, lathered up a washcloth, ran it over his body, and then rinsed off.

He needed to call Angie like he promised he would last night…or at least text her. God, he didn't want to do either. The agitation already pulsing inside Garrett overflowed like a tidal wave, so much so, he was drowning in it.

If he reached out to her in the state of mind he was in, he'd likely end things between them. It was what he needed to do anyway, so he should just fucking get on with it.

Garrett cursed and got out of the shower. He hadn't felt this agitated in years; his skin was crawling with it. Considering the kind of alcoholic/addict he was, feeling the way he did right then was never a good thing. Definitely not safe.

Jesus, he needed to get out of the house. Maybe go for a hike. Something to calm his mind. Except, no, he had no energy for that either. Maybe a drive? He knew he should do something.

Fuck, anything would be better than being alone with his thoughts and now these sudden cravings because damn—

A drink would taste really great right about now.

CHAPTER THIRTY-SEVEN

ANGIE HIT SEND ON THE TEXT BEFORE SHOVING HER PHONE IN her purse. She hefted her computer bag on her shoulder and walked up the outdoor jetway to board her flight.

It'd taken another week past Thanksgiving to mostly resolve the communication constipation between her and Garrett. He'd been pretty tight-lipped regarding whatever it was she'd said to him during her drunk call, but then again, he'd been tight-lipped about everything lately.

The day after her drunk call, he'd finally called her and said he needed more time. She'd asked for what exactly, but he wasn't offering her more than just "to think."

Well, fine, she had shit to think about, too. She'd been thinking plenty before he called her, and she was still thinking now. Considering she was boarding a plane, things had eventually smoothed out over the past two weeks, or it seemed they had.

Garrett always knew the right things to say to her. Always knew exactly how to reel her back in. Not that it took much with her when it came to him. This time, it had been as simple as him finally saying, "I miss you, baby." Which likely translated to "I'm horny," but so was she, so whatever, right?

That said, she spent more time miserable than happy as of late. But still, hope was coupled tightly to the age-old recording of "What if…" playing on a loop in her brain.

So instead of staying home and giving them the space they maybe both still needed, Angie was boarding one of the flights she'd booked weeks ago and heading back to Phoenix to see him. They needed the time together, not apart. At least, that's what she kept telling herself.

It'd been nearly a month since they'd seen each other. Between not spending Thanksgiving together—which would've been a regularly scheduled weekend in Arizona—plus fighting for the entire week after, Angie missed Garrett in a way words could not describe.

And at the same time, she was ready to kill the man.

Love and hate were such powerful emotions, and so closely related, people often confused them. Well, Angie felt them both. Not that she could understand it. How was it even possible to love and hate someone at the very same time?

Caught so deeply in thought, Angie had boarded her flight, picked her seat, and the plane was taking off—all without her noticing.

Wow…what the hell? As if she was coming out of some sort of coma, she gazed out the small airplane window, the twinkling lights on the ground getting smaller—

The plane listed hard to the right.

Angie's eyes went wide, and she grabbed the armrest.

Oh my God!

With her head pressed firmly to the back of her seat, she watched out the window as the wing dipped farther to the right, and then abruptly, as if the pilot was attempting to correct, the plane banked hard to the left…

As instant fear blasted through her, and Angie sucked in a harsh breath.

"Oh, God! No nonono!" a woman behind her cried out.

In the next millisecond, they tipped hard right again. Holy! Fucking! Shit! This was not happening!

But then, they leveled out, the aircraft under control again, and all appeared to be fine as they continued the climb in altitude…like nothing fucking happened.

But, God—Angie shuddered as fear still had her in its grip. Throat gone dry, she tried to swallow. Jeez, they hadn't even made it to the ten-thousand-foot height where the pilot would sound off the audible ding for the flight attendants, and universally, all passengers knew they could recline their seats or put down the stupid plastic tray table.

Angie's hands were sweating like faucets, but no way was she about to let go of the armrests yet. With her heart pounding in her ears, Angie looked over at the passenger across the aisle. Their eyes were wide open, death grip on the armrests, too.

The whole ordeal lasted less than ten seconds. But without a doubt, if the pilot hadn't gotten the plane under control, Angie was damn sure they'd have hit the ground in no more than another ten to twenty seconds tops.

Crazy thing was, there was no announcement letting them know what had just happened. The pilot and the attendants said nothing.

The reality of what could've happened, and knowing her heart and mind were filled with a million doubts and "what ifs," hit hard.

What. The. Fuck.

Daddy: got busy at the bar. Chassidy is going 2 pick u up. she's on her way already. see u soon

THE MESSAGE CHIMED about two minutes after Angie had turned her phone back on. Thankfully, the rest of the flight had been uneventful, but that didn't mean she wasn't still shaken up.

Her limbs still buzzed with adrenaline, and all she wanted was to see Garrett, feel his arms around her and bury her face in his chest.

But he wasn't coming to get her.

God, how apropos.

As she stared at the message, a feeling of despair filled her stomach and chest. God, she wanted to scream. Angie took a deep breath and typed her reply.

> Angie: Kk.

She hit send. What else was there to say? She supposed, "No asshole, I want you to come get me," wasn't the best response. "Don't you know I need you right now?" would go over better, but she wasn't going to send that either.

After Angie gathered her things and deplaned, she headed straight to baggage claim. As she pulled her suitcase off the turnstile, her phone rang. Setting down her bag, she swiped the screen and put it to her ear. "Hey, Chassidy."

"Wow, you okay?"

"Yep. All good."

"You sure? You don't sound 'all good'."

"No worries. Are you close?"

"Yeah, just wasn't sure if I should pull into the cell phone lot or not."

"No, I got my bag already. Meet you on the south side? All the way at the end. Cool?"

"You got it. See you in a minute."

"Thanks." Angie disconnected, shoved the phone in her purse and headed in the direction of the exit.

Right as she emerged from the terminal, Chassidy pulled

up in her Volkswagen CC. Since the thing had four doors, it was both sporty and practical, kind of like Angie's Beemer. Funny part was both cars were red Germans. Not the only thing Chassidy and Angie had in common.

The trunk lid popped, and Chassidy hopped out of the car. "Hey, sweetie. Let me help you."

"Nah, I got it. I'm used to this." Angie forced a smile, and Chassidy hugged her.

Pushing back her tears, Angie hefted her suitcase into the trunk. Chassidy closed the deck, and they both got into the car.

Garrett's daughter pulled away from the curb and then out into the flow of airport traffic. "How was the flight?"

Angie cleared her throat. "It was…eventful."

"Eventful? That doesn't sound good. What happened? Bitchy flight attendant? Drunk passenger?"

"Shoot, I wish. I thought I was going to die on takeoff. All the passengers did. Pilot, or something, had the plane going all squirrelly, but then things got back under control, thank God."

"Holy shit!" Chassidy reached over and grabbed Angie's hand. "Honey, no wonder you sounded like you did on the phone, and why you look like you do. You poor thing!"

"How do I look?" Angie pulled the visor down and slid open the mirror.

"No. Sorry. I said that wrong. You *look* fine. But I could tell by the expression on your face that something was wrong, is all." She squeezed Angie's hand. "I wish I could hug you again."

A lump formed in Angie's throat for an entirely different reason. She swallowed it down. "You're sweet, Chassidy. Thank you."

Angie desperately wanted that tender care from Garrett, not Chassidy, but a person didn't always get what they wanted. God knew Angie didn't feel like she was getting anything close to what she wanted, but she kept coming back to the well anyway…and finding it empty.

But in her moment of emotional mess, she ended up getting what she *needed*, just not from the person she'd wanted it from.

There was that whole want versus need thing again. *Damn.*

Chassidy exited the freeway and headed for the Halo. Angie had work, so she planned to hang out in Garrett's office while he took care of whatever event was happening downstairs. Once they parked, Angie grabbed her computer bag, and Chassidy hefted her suitcase from the trunk.

"I could've gotten that, honey." Angie reached for the handle.

Chassidy smiled. "I know, but I got it for you. Come on, let's go."

"Wait, aren't you heading home?"

"Nope, I got some stuff I need to catch up on in my office." Chassidy moved past Angie, pulling Angie's suitcase behind her.

Angie caught up. "I have a few reviews to write. You mind if I camp out in your office with you?"

"Of course, you can." Chassidy's smile was as bright as the sun. "I figured you'd want to hang out with Dad, but I'd love to have the company. We're due for some girl time anyway."

Relief spilled through Angie. She hadn't realized how much she was dreading sitting in Garrett's office alone. "Perfect. Thanks again, Chassidy."

They entered through the staff entrance, and Angie parked her suitcase in the usual spot beside the back stairs. Even though they were buffered from the loud music in this back area, it was still loud. Angie leaned close to Chassidy. "I'm gonna go say a quick hi to your dad, then I'll be right up. You want me to bring anything?"

"Nope. I got the Keurig up there. Coffee and tea for days.

Hot chocolate, too." She winked. "Let me take your computer and purse up there for you."

"Thanks." She handed her things to Chassidy.

"Stop saying thanks. It's all good, sweetie. Now go, see Dad." She kissed Angie's cheek and climbed the stairs.

Angie couldn't help but smile, feeling a whole lot lighter than she had fifteen minutes earlier. Right as she turned to go find Garrett, he came around the corner.

Angie's smile got bigger, and she practically ran to him and into his arms.

GARRETT WRAPPED his arms around Angie. Something was wrong because she had a death grip on his waist and her face buried in his neck. He pressed his nose to her hair at the top of her head. "You okay?"

She tilted her head back. "I am now."

Tucking a lock of her hair behind her ear, he let his gaze roam over her features. "What's wrong, hon?"

"I'll tell you later. I'm just happy to see you."

"It's good to be seen." Despite his grumpy mood, he cracked a smile as he tossed one of her lines back at her. "Sorry, I couldn't come get you. Too much going on tonight. You gonna stay down here with me?"

"No, I've got some work, so I'm going to hang out with Chassidy in her office."

"Chassidy stayed?"

"Yeah, she took my computer and purse upstairs already. I wanted to say hi to you first."

"Glad you did." Garrett bent and touched his lips to hers.

God, he'd missed her. Not that he'd let himself think about it much. Out of sight, out of mind did wonders for the heart. But as soon as he laid eyes on her, feelings came rushing to the surface so fast he could barely process them—which was something he didn't want to do anyway.

Garrett wanted things to be easy. But nothing with Angie was easy anymore. She was relentless with nearly everything between them as of late. Nagging, getting annoyed with him, and most recently, yelling.

He had a hard enough time dealing with the fact that he'd continued with the relationship; he sure as hell didn't need to be fighting with her constantly, too. But he knew this would happen, knew the stress of long distance was going to be too much for her.

When she was sweet—as in not bitching at him for something he did or didn't do—he loved being around her. Like right now, she was being all nice and soft, and he wanted to kiss her again. So, he did.

Garrett ran his palms up Angie's back, threaded his fingers in her thick hair and pressed his lips to hers. She opened for him, and he swept his tongue inside. Her taste exploded through him, and all parts of Garrett caught fire.

Walking her backward, he brought her up against the wall. She moaned, arching into him as she twisted his shirt in her hands.

Garrett broke the kiss and pressed his lips to her ear. "Need inside you."

Yeah, he'd missed her. Dammit.

STILL BREATHLESS FROM the impromptu make-out session downstairs, Angie made her way to Chassidy's small office. If Garrett hadn't had a band on stage and another queued up to go, she had no doubt they would've been up in his office. He would've been naked, and she would've been on her knees.

Regardless, she was grateful he'd given her the amount of attention he had. It made her feel wanted and, in a weird way, appreciated, too. She was also frustrated because, hello, libido! Work be damned, his and hers. But especially his. Angie hated that when it came to Garrett and his business, work would *always* come before her.

Always.

Once more, rival emotions swirled through her system. Never a dull moment where he was concerned.

Knocking on Chassidy's door, she listened for a second before poking her head in. "All clear?"

"Of course." Chassidy peeked up from her laptop with a smile. "Come on in."

It was hard to believe Chassidy had ever been rude to Angie so long ago, but then again, if Angie had walked in on her father with a woman on his—okay, no. Not going there. Too weird. Angie went for her computer bag. "Thanks for letting me hang out with you."

"Absolutely. Sorry, I don't have a comfy couch like Dad has."

"No worries. I can sit at the little table here." Angie pulled her laptop from the bag. Opening it, she hit the power button. "I have three reviews to write, and I'll be good for the weekend."

"How long are you staying? Will you be here Monday night for his birthday dinner?"

Shock, then disappointment filled Angie's heart, making it so heavy there may as well be an anvil on it. Why would he not tell her there was a dinner planned? "There's a dinner? I didn't—I mean, I know his birthday is Monday, but I'm supposed to fly home Sunday night. I figured we'd celebrate his birthday this weekend."

"Shit. Sweetie, the look on your face right now…it's pure hurt."

Before Angie could stop them, tears rolled down her face. "Well, what the hell, Chassidy? Why does he leave me out of this stuff? I don't get it."

"Aw, sweetie, I don't get it either."

Angie swiped at her wet cheeks. "He alienates me from his life. He doesn't call, he doesn't text. He wouldn't let me come for Thanksgiving, then I barely heard from him for days after. Days." Chassidy handed her a tissue, which she took, wiping her nose. "I don't understand him. Or me. I don't understand how I can love someone like him and hate him at the same time." Angie sucked back a sob. Oh, God, she needed to shut up and get a grip on herself. She should not be talking like this to Chassidy. There was no way it was appropriate or comfortable for Garrett's daughter. "I'm sorry, Chassidy. I shouldn't be laying all this on you."

"Pshaw. No need to be sorry. When we talk like this, I try to forget he's my father and focus on being your friend. But just know, it does piss me off that he would treat any woman this way, but now that I know you, it pisses me off even more."

"But he's your dad. It's not your job to counsel his girlfriend." Angie let out a bitter laugh. "I don't think he even considers me his girlfriend."

"Angie, you are most definitely his girlfriend. He's an idiot if he doesn't think so. Listen, this might seem random, but have you ever considered going to Al-Anon?"

"What's that?"

"It's kind of like Alcoholics Anonymous, but it's for family and friends. I'm sure you know what AA is. Anyway, I think it would help you. Give it some thought, and if you want, we can go to a meeting on Sunday."

"You go?"

Chassidy nodded. "Since I was nineteen."

"But your dad doesn't drink anymore, so why do you go?" Angie blew her nose.

Chassidy handed her another tissue. "Well, let's just say, having the parents I had, both drunk or high, one around but not present. The other never around. Then, one dies from a drug overdose? Yeah, all that didn't set me up for picking the best kinds of guys to date.

"Plus, growing up like the way I did, with that kind of craziness happening, it's become about healing that past damage. But also, I'm not sure if you noticed, but my father doesn't practice any 12-step program, so he can be hard to deal with. He may not drink or do drugs anymore, but technically, he's not really in recovery. He's never done any work on himself to clean up his past issues, his mistakes, etcetera." Chassidy shrugged one shoulder.

"You know, he's mentioned something about that to me before, but I don't think I really understood what he meant. There's a lot more to it than just not drinking or using drugs, huh?" Angie tossed a tissue in the trash can nearby and then grabbed another.

"Oh yeah, a ton more. Think about it. He doesn't go to meetings. Doesn't have a sponsor and never worked the 12 steps. That makes him a dry drunk, and let me tell you, dry drunks can be the worst to deal with. Plus, I can only imagine how hard it is for him. To stop all that destructive self-medicating but then have nothing to take its place must be hell. Kind of like scuba diving without an oxygen tank. Just hold your breath and hope for the best." Chassidy shook her head and let out a sigh. "Yeah, Al-Anon works for me, and because of that, I keep going."

"And you think this will help me understand him better?"

"Well, yeah, sure. It's helped me understand him better. But more, it'll give you tools so that *you* can feel better."

Angie pushed her hair from her face. "I think if he started acting normal, I'd feel better."

"I know what you mean, but at the same time, what's normal anyway?" Chassidy leaned back in her seat. "Give it some thought and let me know. I'm happy to take you."

"Okay." Angie blew her nose again. "Jeezus chrispies, if I

don't get myself under control, I'll never get these reviews written."

"I'll make us some tea. You write, and I'll work, and before we know it, we'll be done."

"Sounds like a plan. Thanks, Chassidy. I mean it."

"I know." Chassidy smiled as she got up.

Angie drew in a deep breath and tried to clear her head. She was a hot-mess of emotion and suddenly exhausted. Focusing on her computer screen, she pulled up a fresh Word doc and began her first review. Two cups of herbal tea later, she was done with all the reviews she needed to write and had emailed them to her editor.

She was at a complete loss for what to do about Garrett. Or what to do about herself.

Angie just knew she had to do something, and soon.

CHAPTER THIRTY-EIGHT

"Oh...oh my God...yes!" On her knees, Angie had a death grip on the headboard, and Garrett had a death grip on her ass cheeks.

He was rocking his pelvis in a way that caused the head of his dick to rub over her G-spot each time he thrust into her. Little tingles echoed, getting stronger with each stroke and building her orgasm.

SLAP!

Angie let out a low, animalistic groan as the sting and subsequent heat from his palm connecting with one butt cheek spread to her clit.

"Fucking missed this big ass." He gripped one buttock hard, spreading it apart from the other. Then slapped one side again. "Love to watch it bounce and jiggle when I spank it and when I fuck you."

"More!" She arched, taking his cock deeper as her clit pulsed. "I want you to fuck my ass, Garrett. Please?"

"Goddamn, Angie." With one hand on her hip, he pulled out, and in the next moment, she felt him slide his thumb between her labia and into her cunt.

Angie squirmed and moaned as he fucked into her with

his thumb. "Baby—" She lost his thumb, and then his cock was back inside her. "Oh, God!"

Garrett slid the thoroughly lubricated thumb between her butt cheeks, finding her tight hole. "You know I want inside your perfect ass." He pressed the pad of his thumb against the opening, then pushed it inside her. "Want to fuck it. Want to feel how tight it is, squeezing my cock. Want to come deep inside your ass, too."

"Mmm baby…yes, please?" Angie pressed back against him, wanting more of his prick, his thumb—more of anything he wanted to give her. Her clit throbbed with the impending orgasm he was building, making her skin tingle.

With each drag of his hard shaft inside her core and across her G-spot, the pressure of his thumb moving in and out of her ass…and every fucking dirty thing he was saying to her, Angie's need to climax grew more urgent.

God, she loved him.

God, she wanted him.

She'd never get enough of him.

"Want to come inside you and all over you, Angie." He slammed into her. "*Goddamn*, your ass. My undoing every damn time."

She smiled, reveling in this moment. Knowing that, at least right now, she had all of him. She had every part of Garrett James and likely even his heart. Everything inside Angie became amplified.

Letting go of the headboard with one hand, she moved it between her legs, finding her swollen clit. "I'm yours, Garrett."

He grunted, increasing his pace. "Yes."

"Say it. I need to hear it. Tell me, Daddy."

"*Fuuuuck*!" Angie felt his dick pulse inside her. "You're mine, Angie. My bad girl. My good girl. Mine!"

He thrust harder, and Angie's climax hit. She threw her head back. "Yes, Daddy! *Yessss!*"

"Oh, God, Angie!" Garrett moaned and buried his cock to the hilt.

As the waves of her orgasm rolled through Angie, her cunt clenched over and over again on his cock, milking him. She could feel the little pulses from his shaft, knowing he was spurting inside her, filling her with his seed.

With a loud grunt, Garrett pulled free, and then she felt the hot lashes of his orgasm spurting over her ass and up her back. Endless lashes coated her skin, and he moaned, panting with each one.

When he was finally spent, Angie let herself fall flat on the mattress. Garrett leaned over the side of the bed and found his T-shirt. "Here, babe." He handed her the shirt. "Use that while I go get a wet rag."

Angie shifted and slid the cotton fabric beneath her and pressed it between her legs. Garrett returned a few minutes later and wiped down her back and then her ass.

"Thank you, honey." With a small smile, Angie rolled over, handed him the T-shirt and then got under the covers.

Through tired eyes, she watched as he put his pajama bottoms on and climbed into the bed next to her. Once he was situated on his back, Angie moved closer and laid her head on his chest. That orgasm was exactly what she'd needed.

Still the best sex of her life—even with all their issues, it was only getting better.

Garrett lay with Angie half-draped over his chest. Sprawled was more like it, but either way was fine by him. Even though it'd barely been a month, it felt like forever since they'd seen each other. Which also meant they hadn't had sex in all that time either.

Needless to say, Garrett hadn't lasted very long, but keeping in sync with how things had been between them sexually, he'd been right back in business nearly immediately. Embarrassing for some guys, but not Garrett. No need for all that injured male pride crap when he knew he was still in the game.

Angie snuggled closer. "I missed this…you. Us."

Garrett ran his fingers through her hair, sifting through the soft strands and reveling in the satin feel of them. "How do you keep your hair so soft?"

She let out a sated but tired-sounding sigh and shrugged. "Dunno, same as anyone, I guess."

"Chassidy's is soft, but it's thicker than yours, so it's different."

"I don't know. I've never touched it, so I'll take your word for it." She giggled.

He chuckled and gave her a squeeze. "You know what I mean. Brat."

She raised her head and rested her chin on his chest to look at him. "It's because she has so much natural curl in hers, makes it thicker and courser. Better, Daddy?"

Lust spiked in his system, and his cock twitched awake. Garrett stifled a groan. He both loved and hated when she called him Daddy. He still couldn't help but feel it was a level of kink he *should not* be turned on by, but with Angie, it hit all his buttons—especially the ones he didn't know he had.

He raised his head and pressed a kiss to her lips. "Much. But you should probably get a spanking for being so fresh."

She raised her brows. "Fresh?"

"Yes, fresh. It's an old term. Probably one you've never heard. Means misbehaving." He chuckled even though it was yet another reminder of their age disparity.

"If it means I get a spanking, I'm all good with it. Just sayin'."

"It's not a punishment if you enjoy it, Angela." Garrett smirked and smoothed his palm down her back to the curve of her full, perfect ass.

"This is true." She shrugged, grinning from ear to ear, then laid her head back on his chest. "But the way I see it, we both get something out of it, right? And that's the whole point."

"Agreed." Garrett trailed his fingertips up her spine. He'd never shied away from spanking, but with her, it'd become an obsession. Watching her fine ass jiggle and grow pink with his palm prints was damn near as earth-shattering for him. Garrett yawned. "Tired."

"Me too." Angie shifted from his chest to her pillow but snuggled close to him. Tilting her head back, she pressed a kiss to his cheek. "Night, honey."

"Night." Garrett let out a breath and settled into the mattress, and the feel of her lying beside him again.

He'd missed having her in his bed. On the off weeks, she wasn't there with him, he'd always wake himself reaching for her at night. It wasn't a big deal, and he'd never given it much thought.

But this past month, since they hadn't been together, his habit seemed to escalate. When Garrett reached for her in his sleep and didn't find her, he'd wake, confused, disoriented and immediately, sadness would well up in his gut.

"Garrett?"

"Yeah, hon?"

"Can I stay longer and be here for your birthday dinner?" She placed her hand on his chest. "Chassidy asked me if I was going, but I told her I hadn't heard anything about it."

Garrett let out an exasperated sigh. Damn, Chassidy, for telling Angie. "Can we talk about this in the morning?"

"Yeah, I guess. It's just…babe, your birthday is important, and I don't know why you didn't tell me about the dinner, but I really want to be here for it."

Annoyance sped through Garrett like a bullet, piercing the calm and happy bubble he'd been basking in not thirty seconds before. It wasn't like he'd been keeping it a secret. Angie wouldn't be in town anyway, so why mention it?

Plus, Garrett hadn't been sure he wanted her here for it. Which was selfish and fucked up of him, he knew, but true regardless.

He glanced at her. "Why are you doing this right before we're going to sleep? Can it not sit until tomorrow?" Garrett cringed at his harsh tone. He'd tried to keep from sounding so annoyed, but it was a waste of time. He was one hundred and fifty percent annoyed.

"Jeezus chrispies, Garrett. I'm sorry. I guess it's because I have you here in front of me, and there's no distractions. Ugh, fine. I shouldn't have even asked." Rolling over, she turned her back on him.

What the flying fuck, really?

She starts an issue, and then *she* turns her back?

Fine. Whatever. Goddammit!

"Ya know, Angie. I didn't say no. I said, let's talk about it tomorrow. You let me know if you want to do that or not."

Silence.

For fuck's sake, now she was going to give him the silent treatment? Such bullshit. Garrett yanked the covers up and turned over, giving her his back, too. He knew it was a stupid, childish move, but he couldn't help himself.

Except...wait, did she just say jeezus chrispies?

The desire to ask her to say it again rose inside him, chasing away all his feelings of annoyance and anger. Oh, for fuck's sake, this woman! One of these days, she was going to make him lose his damn mind.

ANGIE ROLLED over in bed as she heard the bedroom door click shut. Normally, she was a really heavy sleeper...except when it came to sleeping next to Garrett. It was almost as if she sensed his lack of presence beside her.

Whenever he got up before her, which was every time she slept at his house, she woke up when he did or shortly thereafter. She'd catch a sleepy glimpse of him getting in the shower or turn over right after he'd set a cup of coffee on the nightstand for her and was exiting the room, closing the door behind him.

Angie looked over to the nightstand. No coffee this morning. She frowned and rubbed her eyes. Waking up after a fight, one where they hadn't made up before going to sleep, really freaking sucked. Big time.

And she guessed the lack of coffee was his way of saying he was still pissed.

Which was fine because she sort of was, too. But she didn't want to be. She missed him and was looking forward to spending time together. Angie desperately wanted to have a good weekend together.

And although the topic of her staying in town a day longer to be with him on his birthday was far from over, she was willing to shelf the subject. For now.

Besides, it wasn't like he could stop her from changing her flight and as long as Angie could afford the difference in fare, it was a no-brainer. And also, none of his business. It was her money, after all, and she could do what she wanted with it. Hmm…Angie reached for her phone. Maybe she should just check the cost of the flight change now. That was one way to solve the matter.

Angie sat up, propped the pillows behind her, and pulled up the airline app on her phone. She went through the necessary steps to check prices and change the flight. And…*Ding, ding, ding!* Only a hundred bucks to fly one day later. Sold! Angie clicked on the "complete change" button; her return flight now set for Tuesday morning.

Feeling damn satisfied with herself, she set her phone back

on the table and lay down again. There was no need to discuss what she'd done with him right now. She'd tell him on Sunday. That way, it wouldn't ruin the weekend.

Too excited to go back to sleep, she got up and headed for the shower. Once ready, she'd head downstairs and smooth things over. Or maybe she'd get lucky, and he'd come back in the bedroom and then join her in the shower for some outstanding make-up sex.

Turning on the water to get hot, she gathered some of her necessities and set them in the stall, then brushed her teeth. Just in case… Not wanting to waste more water, she stepped under the spray and began the wash-down routine.

After a few minutes, and as she washed the shampoo from her hair, Garrett walked into the bathroom. He must've heard the water running from downstairs. She opened the glass door. "I'd really like it if you joined me."

On his way to the closet, he stopped and stared at her. His eyes went from her face down to her breasts and then further to her bare pubic area. Vulnerability crept down Angie's spine, and she felt like she should cover herself, his gaze making her feel embarrassed by her brazen invitation.

Angie had never been one to be embarrassed or ashamed or self-conscious, but at that moment, she felt all three. And she didn't like it at all. With an internal shake, she looked away and started to close the door, but was met with physical resistance. Startled, she looked back.

Garrett had moved to the shower and was now pulling the door back open. "Did you change your mind?"

Angie stepped backward. "No. Of course not. I thought…"

He slid his pajama bottoms off and then moved into the shower, closing the glass door behind him. "You thought what?"

"That maybe you weren't interested."

Garrett pulled her into his arms and kissed her forehead. "Of course I'm interested. Why wouldn't I be?"

"Because we fought last night, so you're probably still upset at me." Hesitating at first, Angie gave in, wrapped her arms around his waist and pressed her cheek to his warm chest.

"Yeah, but that doesn't mean I don't care about you." He ran his hands up her back and then into her hair. Garrett moved them backward until the spray was trickling down her back. "I hate fighting. I don't want to fight with you, Angie."

Thankful they were in the shower, and he wouldn't see she was crying, Angie brushed a tear from her cheek. "I don't want to fight either, babe."

"If you want to be here for my birthday, that's fine. I figured you had work and stuff, plus it's not that big of a deal."

Relief blasted through Angie, and she pressed her lips to his chest. She hoped that he really *was* okay with her staying, but if he wasn't, then she'd have to deal with that later.

Angie gazed up at him. "Thank you, baby. It may not be a big deal to you, but it is to me."

With a slight smile curling the edges of his mouth, Garrett cupped her chin in his hand and nodded. "I gathered as much."

Angie pressed a soft kiss on his lips, and then, remembering, she pulled back. "I forgot to tell you. I finally submitted an application to Rolling Stone, and the recruiter responded to me! I have an interview set up for next week." She smiled, excitement spilling through her. "Isn't that awesome?"

Garrett's body stiffened, and something Angie couldn't decipher flashed in his eyes, but then he relaxed, and his expression changed. What on earth… Angie frowned. She wasn't sure what was going on or what he was thinking, but her gut was picking up on something. Hmm.

"Wow!" He pressed a quick kiss to her lips. "That's awesome, hon. Congratulations, I knew you could do it!"

Okay, maybe she was imagining things and making something out of nothing? Angie swallowed and pushed all the noise in her head away.

"Thanks, baby." She shrugged. "Though, technically, I haven't done anything yet. Let's get through the interview first."

Garrett slid his hands down her sides and then around her waist, pulling her tighter against him. "They'd be crazy not to hire you."

He bent and pressed his lips to her neck, and Angie let her head fall back. "That feels good."

"Mmm. So do you." Garrett moved a hand down to her ass, then around to her leg, lifting her knee to his hip.

Angie slid a hand down between them, took his hard length in her palm, and stroked him, once, twice—Garrett's breath caught in his throat.

Positioning him at her entrance, Angie slid the bulbous head through her wet folds. It was time to put this behind them, and the best way she'd found to do that with him was to reconnect…sexually. Garrett pressed inside her, and Angie bit down on his shoulder.

They were going to be okay. They had to be. Angie knew deep down they belonged together. And come hell or high water, she was going to hold on.

Hopefully, someday, he'd let his walls down, and they'd be able to connect in other ways, but for now, the sex worked. Not perfect, but no relationship was.

CHAPTER THIRTY-NINE

Garrett pulled the Jag up to the valet. An attendant opened his door, and another opened Angie's. Chassidy had driven herself and was already there. Knowing his daughter, she'd also set up birthday decorations, too many of them.

He came around the front of the car and reached his hand out for Angie.

She glanced up, her small purse in her hand. "How do I look?"

Garrett clasped her hand. "You look nice. Come on."

Angie's face fell, presumably at Garrett's sad excuse of a compliment, but he ignored it and walked them to the resort entrance.

God, he was a shit. Why did he always do that to her? She looked more than nice; she looked downright beautiful.

Angie and his daughter had gone shopping yesterday for something both ladies deemed suitable for Angie to wear for his birthday dinner. Angie had picked a cream-colored, long-sleeved sweater dress. The skirt was fitted and then flared at the knee, and she wore a pair of brown suede, high-heeled ankle boots. The kind of boots he felt in his dick.

No, she wasn't just beautiful, she was sexy as hell, too.

Yet, Garrett wasn't going to share that observation or physical reaction with her. Whether that was his ego or plain old self-preservation, he didn't know. Her application at Rolling Stone was fucking with his head. It was stupid. There was no reason to think she might try to use him for her benefit, but he couldn't get the idea out of his head.

Things were definitely on rocky ground for them, or for him at least, and as a result, Garrett was holding back…more than usual.

It was obvious his lack of compliments and praise affected her, but more so tonight. The sad expression in her eyes had been like a slap in his face. She'd spent a long time getting ready, the least he could do was compliment the poor girl.

To add insult to injury, Angie had made no secret about how excited she was to finally meet his friends. Garrett wasn't excited in the slightest. Instead, he was irritable and annoyed, the furthest thing from excited a person could be.

He really would've rather done nothing for his birthday, but that would never have flown with Chassidy. She'd been throwing birthday parties for him since she was old enough to learn how to swipe his credit card from his wallet and schedule an event.

So, here they were, heading to a private party room at the Arizona Biltmore.

Angie was about to meet his two closest friends, or as close as anyone could be to Garrett, anyway. He didn't spend much time away from work, which didn't leave much time for anything else, and with Angie in the mix, aside from a couple times this past year and, of course, Thanksgiving, he hadn't seen his buddies much.

That said, he hadn't really talked about Angie to them, either. He'd only mentioned her to Freddie in passing early on when Garrett had first met her and then again on Thanksgiving because Freddie had asked. But he hadn't mentioned her to Sean at all.

To say the night was about to get awkward was an understatement.

In his defense, she wasn't supposed to be in town, so why bring her up? Why worry about it? He hadn't, and now he needed to. God, yeah, he was *such* a shit.

They walked through the double doors into the small room, and there everyone was. Garrett drew in a deep breath and braced for—

"HAPPY BIRTHDAY!" everyone yelled in unison as Chassidy threw some confetti in the air, a beaming smile on her face.

Balloons and streamers were everywhere. Yep, his daughter had gone overboard again. He loved her for it, though. Angie cheered along with the group, and he dropped her hand and took a single step forward.

As everyone clapped, Garrett forced a smile and let his gaze roam through the faces of the small group in attendance: Marlene and Cody, his head staff from the club, plus a few of his more long-term full-time staff were there, and then, of course, Freddie and Sean.

Chassidy moved to Garrett first, wrapping her arms around him. "Happy birthday, Dad." She kissed his cheek.

"Thanks, honey."

She stepped away and took Angie by the hand. "Come on, let's get a drink."

"Sure." Angie smiled at him, then walked to the bar with his daughter.

Garrett looked away in time to be greeted by Freddie and Sean. Both men pulled him into hugs, complete with back slaps. Garrett returned their embraces and then stepped back. "Glad you guys could make it."

Sean tipped his chin up. "We never miss this. It's the after 'Turkey Day, before Christmas' tradition we've had for what? A hundred years now?"

Garrett laughed and shook his head. "Forty-seven is a long way from one hundred, but who's counting, right?"

"I am." Freddie chuckled and bent toward Garrett and Sean, his voice low so only they could hear. "I'll remind you both I turned fifty this year, so I'm the one who's got the grim reaper knocking on my door, not either of you young fuckers."

"Now I feel better." Garrett grinned.

"Me too." Sean laughed. "I'm going to grab another drink. Garrett, water or soda tonight?"

Vodka soda— What the fuck? Where did that come from? Garrett cleared his throat. "Water's good, thanks."

When Sean stepped away, Freddie leaned close. "So, is that?

"Yeah. That's Angie."

"Damn, Garrett. She's gorgeous. And you said she was young, but I didn't think sh—"

"Don't fucking say it." Garrett shook his head. He didn't want to hear any shit about her age or their age difference or any of it. Christ.

Freddie raised both hands in a surrender gesture, chuckling the whole time. "All right, go easy, birthday boy."

Garrett watched as Angie chatted with Marlene and Cody, a glass of white wine in her hand. "She's everything I said she was and more."

"And you've been keeping her all to yourself."

"You know how it goes." Garrett shrugged. "Just been busy, is all."

Freddie blurted a laugh. "Yeah, aren't we all? That's a shit excuse."

Garrett frowned, a reply on the tip of his tongue, right as Sean returned, beer in one hand, water in the other. He handed the water to Garrett.

"Happy birthday, brother." Sean bent his beer bottle to Garrett's glass. They clinked, and after Sean took a swig, he cleared his throat. "So, been holding out on us, I see? Who's the hot and very young brunette you walked in with?"

Freddie blurted out another laugh. "I'm gonna go socialize and grab another drink."

Garrett glared after his friend and then focused on Sean. "Just someone I've been seeing for a few months."

Sean's brows hit his hairline. "How many are a few months?"

Garrett cleared his throat. "Almost seven."

"You've been dating that woman for almost seven months, and I'm just now finding out about it?" Sean shook his head. "Damn, my friend. You take private to a whole new level."

"Ah, come on. It's not that big a deal. She lives in L.A. We're just casual, seeing how it goes. You'd have met her eventually. I've just been busy."

Sean chuckled and glanced at Angie, then gave a low whistle. "Yeah, by the looks of her, I'd be busy, too. Damn."

A sliver of jealousy speared into Garrett's stomach. He knew his friend was just flipping him shit, but still, he didn't like how Sean was looking at Angie. Worse, Garrett didn't like that he was jealous of his friend, either. He shouldn't be. There was nothing to be jealous of. What a fucked up dichotomy of feelings. But still… Not cool. "Go easy, Romeo."

Sean looked at Garrett, both brows raised again. "Ooh, look at that. You like her. A lot."

Garrett just rolled his eyes. "Whatever. I'm going to go say hi to everyone else."

"All right then. You do that." Sean smiled and tipped his beer back.

Garrett stepped away, an ache starting behind his eyes. Fuck's sake, so far, things were going great. Just fucking spectacular.

"Thank you." Angie smiled up at the server as they took her dirty plate away.

They'd finished a wonderful dinner, and then the staff brought out an absolutely adorable cake. It had a stage and little plastic figurines set up like a rock band, complete with instruments, on the top.

Two of Garrett's personal friends were in attendance, and when Garrett had introduced them, he hadn't identified her as anything other than Angie.

She hadn't yet gotten to talk to either of them since they'd been introduced right before they sat to eat. It was probably for the best she didn't get to chat longer. Garrett didn't want to label things, certainly not label her as his girlfriend, but him not introducing her at the very least as someone he was dating had hurt her feelings. Too much. And honestly, it would've been hard to talk with the lump that'd formed in her throat at the time.

With every fiber of her being, Angie had forced herself to let it go, to just be present in the moment and choose to have a good time. And though she wouldn't have thought it possible, it'd worked. She'd *actually* been having a great time.

All through dinner and cake, Sean and Freddie were hilarious, constantly razzing Garrett about one thing or another. She'd had a great time talking with Marlene and Cody, who had been sitting next to her at the table. And, of course, Chassidy, too.

After she and Garrett's daughter had gone shopping on Sunday, Chassidy had taken Angie to that Al-Anon meeting she'd mentioned to Angie a few days ago. Angie wasn't sure if she'd go back to another meeting or not, but it was where she got the idea to *choose* to have a good time instead of letting Garrett's behavior upset her.

A guy in the meeting had read something in the beginning about "choosing to be happy," and lo and behold, it'd worked.

So yeah, maybe she would look up some meetings once she got home to L.A.

"Mind if I sit?"

Angie looked up and smiled. "Please do."

Freddie slid into Marlene's empty chair, coffee cup and saucer in hand. "Did you get a piece of cake?"

"I did, thank you." Angie smiled. "I'm really glad I got to be here for this."

Freddie smiled. "Me too. After all these months, I didn't think I'd ever get to meet you."

Angie's eyes went wide. "He's talked about me to you? I mean, it's okay, I just…"

"Of course, he's talked about you. Not a lot, but yeah." Freddie frowned. "Why do you look so shocked?"

"Because…" Angie shrugged one shoulder. "Well, because I honestly didn't think he talked about me to anyone. I mean, aside from some of the staff at the bar and Chassidy, I don't imagine people know I'm in his life. I've never met you guys. It kind of makes a girl wonder if the man she's hooked her star to is ashamed of her or something—" Angie shook her head and stared down into her coffee as the heat of embarrassment spread up her neck to her face. "And there I go oversharing. I'm so sorry. Please forget I said any of that. I swear to God, I talk too much. And one of these days, I'm gonna learn how to zip it."

Freddie chuckled and gave her arm a gentle squeeze. "You're good, Angie. Really. Don't worry about it." He leaned closer. "Look, I know Garrett can be a bit…well, closed off, but try and hang in there. He'll figure it out."

Angie just stared at him, unsure of what to say. Here was one of Garrett's closest friends telling her to hang in there. She cleared her throat. "What if I can't?"

"Then I guess it's his loss." Freddie shrugged.

"Can I join this private party?"

Freddie looked past her. "Sean, my friend. Come have coffee with me and Garrett's girlfriend."

Angie's eyes went wide. "Oh, shit, Freddie."

"Thought you'd never ask." Sean laughed and sat in what had been Garrett's seat. "Garrett's been keeping you all to himself, and I, for one, can't wait to get to know you."

Even with a knot of nervous tension in her throat, Angie smiled. "Well, for starters, I'm pretty sure I haven't earned the title girlfriend, so we might want to steer away from that one."

"Well damn, if that's the case, it'll be his loss and—" Sean shot her a sexy smile and a wink. "I really can't wait to get to know you."

Well, damn, was right.

Sean was an exceedingly good-looking man. Tall with a slender build, like Garrett, though Sean's slender was a bit thicker than Garrett's. Brown hair with a slight amount of gray threaded through it. Striking ice-blue eyes. And he had those smile lines around his eyes and mouth that she'd found so attractive on Garrett.

He was likely closer to Garrett's age than to hers. And although he was *very* easy on the eyes and definitely sexy, she wasn't interested in anything more than appreciating the view. Garrett was it for her, for sure.

Although she was sure Sean wasn't seriously flirting with her, Angie had no reason not to enjoy the attention. She was practically starving for it. And would Garrett even notice and get jealous? Likely not. But God, wouldn't it be nice if he were at least a little jealous? A giggle bubbled out of her. Yep, she was losing it.

Angie smiled. "Ask me whatever you want."

CHAPTER FORTY

"I really want to spend Christmas together, will you come here? Please?" Angie sat on her couch with her phone pressed to her ear, her favorite fleece blanket over her lap.

"I don't know, Ang. I mean, Chassidy and I spend it together, or at least most of it before she goes to see her grandparents."

Angie's heart fell. She'd brought the subject up a few times since she'd been there last weekend for his birthday, and he'd been pretty noncommittal, kind of like he always was with this sort of stuff. Christmas was next week, and they were running out of runway to plan. "But couldn't she come with you? We could maybe make a whole week out of it? We could spend New Year's here, too."

"Can't do New Year's, hon. Big show that night. Authority Zero plays, and about four other opening bands. Chassidy and I will be working."

Angie's heart fell further, crash-landing in her stomach like a solid block of steel. "Oh." Desperate to find a way to make this work, she shifted and took a sip of her coffee. "What if you come here for Christmas, and I go there for New Year's?"

"As I said, I'm working."

"You're working on Christmas, too?"

"No. Wait…what?"

Angie shook her head, trying to clear her jumble of thoughts. "I was saying, at least Christmas here with me, and we do New Year's with you. You said you were working. Did you mean both holidays?"

"Oh. No, I'm not working Christmas, but I'm working New Year's."

She frowned, frustration making her head hurt. "Why do I feel like this conversation just went in a circle?"

Garrett sighed. "I don't know."

"Okay, let me try this again. Do you want to spend Christmas together here? And then, since technically New Year's is a scheduled Arizona weekend anyway, being there for that works."

"Okay, listen—" He sighed. "—you know you're welcome here anytime, and I always enjoy seeing you. But I think… maybe it's best if we don't spend the holidays together."

"What?" Shock blasted through Angie so hard that if she were standing, she'd have fallen on her ass. He didn't want her there. Wow. A lump filled Angie's throat. "Any of them?"

"Look, I don't have the energy to fight with you tonight. I can already tell by how you sound that's what's going to happen. So maybe we should just talk tomorrow."

Angie stood, the blanket tumbling to the floor. "Are you fucking kidding me? Garrett, it's been seven months. We've been dating for seven months, and you don't want to spend holidays together?"

"Here we go. Why does everything have to be a fight with you?"

"No! Garrett James, you do not get to do that! Let me guess, this is way past your 'casual' line, right?"

"Sure, let's go with that. It's past my 'casual' line. Are you happy? If this is how things are always going to be, then yeah, casual is better for me. I *do not* want the stress that comes with this. I can't handle it. I don't want to handle it. I want things to be easy and casual. Low expectations."

Halfway down the hall to her bedroom, Angie stopped dead in her tracks. "Is that really what you think we've been doing for the past seven months, Garrett? Just casually dating?"

He let out a sigh. "No. We've been playing house."

"Holy shit! Are you kidding me with this?"

"Fuck, okay, listen. I'm sorry I said that. But you're not hearing me. If you want to come here on New Year's, then fine, come here. But I'll be working all day and night, and probably the day and night before, too, so it's not like I can spend time with you. You may as well be where you can have some fun."

Tears ran down her cheeks, but she'd be damned if she'd give him the satisfaction of knowing how emotionally torn up she was. After grabbing a tissue, she wiped her cheeks and did her best to wipe her nose without making any sound.

Angie was so devastatingly hurt, all she could do was let the anger boiling inside her, as a result of the immense heartache, explode at him. "You *don't fucking* get it, Garrett! *You aren't* hearing *me*! And no matter how much I try and show you, or explain. Or beg. Or be patient. Or go with the motherfucking flow… *You! Still! Don't! Get! It!*"

"Not doing this with you. Maybe we can talk tomorrow."

"Garrett don't you ha—" Angie pulled the phone away from her ear, and yep, the sonofabitch hung up on her. White-hot rage spilled into her stomach and spread to her limbs like some sort of volcanic overflow of madness.

Angie looked up at the ceiling and screamed…at the top of her lungs.

GARRETT SAT BACK in his office chair and pushed his long hair away from his face. He was done with this shit with Angie. The woman was making him nuts! She was fucking relentless.

Always pushing.

Always fighting.

Wanting more and more…and then more, and he was utterly convinced that if he gave her even an inch, she'd end up taking a fucking mile. Nothing would ever be good enough.

He blew out a breath and stared at the top of his desk. Memories of the last time he'd bent Angie over it, or even her merely sitting across from him, laptop on her lap, came rushing back to him.

Jesus, would he ever be able to be anywhere, his office, his home…fuck, his bed, without the memory of her stamped all over it? "Fucking hell!"

This was his own doing. Garrett stood, grabbed his jacket, and walked down the back stairs, out of the building, and to the staff parking lot.

Getting behind the wheel of his Jag, he started the car and headed for home. He needed to think, to sort this out. Angie wanted too much from him. More than he was able to give. He'd been telling her this, in one form or another, for pretty much the entire time she'd been in his life.

Garrett's cell vibrated in his pocket. The caller ID appeared on his nav screen, telling him it was Angie. He ignored it and let it go to voicemail. Enough for one night.

Before he made it home, his cell rang again. Caller ID: Chase Reynolds.

Rage boiled in Garrett's veins. That motherfucker wasn't gonna give up either. Garrett gave the nav screen the middle finger as if the guy could see him. "Fuck you, Chase. You and your interview and reunion bullshit."

Garrett drove up his driveway and into the garage. Closing himself in, he cut the engine, then sat in the car a minute and closed his eyes. He was in misery, full of anger and regret.

Goddammit, eighteen years of being drug and alcohol-free, working hard for a better life, and this was where he landed anyway?

He didn't want or need any of this added stress. Running the bar was hard enough. It took a considerable amount of his time and energy. As far as the band thing went, the risk of using or drinking again was too high, especially now.

Cravings to pick up a drink or drug were plaguing Garrett on and off, and for the first time in years, he was struggling. Add in how complicated things with Angie had become, and he was skating on thin ice.

Garrett didn't want things to end with her completely; he cared about her, but she needed to stop pushing him. If she wanted them to work it out, she needed to take what he could give, which right now was nothing more than casual.

He was monogamous to her anyway; he didn't want anyone else, so why she couldn't just respect that boundary and be satisfied with it was beyond him. Garrett didn't have the capacity to give her more—end of story.

She was young, and it was only natural she'd want to move forward. He understood that. Unfortunately, he would never want their situation to move forward. If she could be good with that, then they could continue for as long as she wanted.

She needed to walk away if she couldn't live with those terms. Leaving his ass in the dust would be the best thing she could do for herself, anyway.

CHAPTER FORTY-ONE

Garrett had already dealt with at least a dozen issues ranging from missing bar stock to insufficient security and everything in between, and it was barely ten p.m. That being said, he anticipated a lot more shit would need to be handled as it got closer to midnight and the start of a new year.

Gotta love the holidays and New Year's Eve especially. The drunks were out in full force and ready to play. Garrett shook his head and stared across the crowd. At least he was making money.

Christmas had come and gone, and as he'd insisted, Angie had stayed home. After their argument over not spending the holidays together, she'd been beyond angry at him, and it'd taken her several days to talk to him again.

When they finally did talk, it was four days before Christmas, and he'd laid things out for her as gently as he could. She said she needed time to think, her response a threadbare whisper he'd barely been able to hear.

Her faint voice hit him like a stab in the heart, and guilt had filled his veins. He'd left her alone, giving her the space she asked for until she finally reached out right before Christmas Eve.

Things had settled down again, but she'd been different since. Different and distant. They'd been talking less and less, and the last couple of days, there'd been only text messages between them.

Maybe she was moving on…he didn't know for sure. Garrett couldn't blame her if she were. Honestly, he didn't want to question it, figured it was best to just let it go.

Let her go.

It was time, but damn, he missed her. Missed her voice on the phone, missed her sense of humor and how she made him laugh, missed her in his bed. Just…missed her.

A blanket of sadness wrapped around him, and Garrett pulled his phone from his pocket and typed out a message to her.

> Garrett: Hope ur somewhere having fun with friends. if I don't get to talk to u tonight HNY.

He hit send and shoved his phone back in his pocket. This was it—time to move on for both of them.

Authority Zero was about ready to get on stage, and then he'd have to be sure all hands were on deck, security-wise. Especially for when the mosh pits got started.

Hopefully, the rest of the night would go smoothly.

AN HOUR LATER, Authority Zero was kicking ass. Like always, Jason DeVore, the lead singer, had the crowd in the palm of his hand. For the first time that night, Garrett let out a sigh and went to refill his coffee.

The pot behind the bar was empty, and his staff was too busy to brew another for him. Well, damn. Garrett headed toward the side hallway. Chassidy had gotten him a Keurig for Christmas for his office. Now was as good a time as any to break the thing in.

Garrett passed the public restrooms and then headed up the stairs and down the hall to his office. He opened the door and stopped short.

"Happy New Year!"

Garrett's mouth dropped open, everything in his body going tight as he drank in the sight of Angie.

Shit, she looked really good. Her dark hair was down and pin straight—fresh purple chunks in it. Her makeup was perfect, just enough eyeliner to accentuate her mesmerizing eyes. Her full lips were painted a shade of red that made him swallow hard. She wore a silver, off-the-shoulder top, black skin-tight pants accentuating her long legs, and knee-high, spiked-heel boots.

She smiled. "Surprised?"

"Very." He stepped inside and shut the door. "What are you doing here?"

Her smile faded. "It's New Year's Eve, and I wanted to see you."

"But, Angie, I told you. I'm working. I thought you understood."

"I know you're working. I know." She twisted her hands in front of her. "But Garrett, I miss you. And I hav—"

"I miss you, too. But I don't have time for this tonight." He shook his head. God, why was she doing this?

"So that's it? I was really hoping that you'd be happy to see me. That we could—"

"That we could what, Angie?" Agitation flowed through him. Jesus, all he wanted to do was kiss her until that lipstick was gone, then strip her out of those clothes and bend her over his desk—which was precisely why he was recoiling from her like a hot fucking flame.

Sex, especially right now, would only complicate things more.

"Garrett, look. I know you're busy, but I have stuff to tell you and…stuff to ask you, too. And I know you didn't want me to come, but I…never mind, I said that already…" She looked down and shook her head.

Fucking hell, this was killing him. Garrett blew out a breath and pulled her to him, wrapping her in his arms. "I'm sorry, okay?" He pressed a kiss to the top of her head.

They stayed that way, holding each other for what felt like an hour, but was probably no more than five or so minutes. Garrett smoothed his palm down her long hair and back. "As much as I want to stay up here with you, I need to get back, hon. What do you have to tell me?"

With her arms still around his waist, she tipped her head back. "I got the job."

He frowned. "The job?"

"With Rolling Stone!" Her excited expression was a thing of beauty.

"Wow, you got it?" He smiled. "That's awesome. I told you."

"You did, I know." She nodded. "They have me starting off doing reviews again. I have to work my way up to staff writer. I can do it, of course, but I was thinking, did you—"

"Did I what?" The hairs on the back of Garrett's neck stood on end, and he let go of Angie and took a step back from her.

She frowned and then wrapped her arms around her middle. "You haven't mentioned it again since telling me, but did you ever do that interview for Copper Seven?"

Garrett went stone still as bile rose up his throat. What the fuck was she saying, asking… Was she? "No, I'm not doing the interview."

Her face fell. "Oh. Okay, I was gonna…well, never mind. It doesn't matter."

"You were gonna what?" Anger surged inside Garrett, filling his mind. He knew he sounded furious, his tone so hard that Angie flinched. "*Gonna what?*"

Angie jumped and took a step back. "I…" She swallowed. "I was going to ask if you would help me. That maybe if I did the interview—"

"There it is." He shook his head. "I fucking knew it. All this time, right?"

"What? You knew what?"

He shook his head and stalked past her to the door. He couldn't even look at her. God, he was fucking stupid. How could he be so blind?

"All this fucking time, that's all I was to you, huh? Get your big job, then use me to help prove yourself? What better way to accomplish all that than jumping in my bed, right?"

"Garrett, is that what you think of me? You think I'd use you like that? Jesus, that doesn't even make any sense. You know I didn't even know who you were when we met. Hell, I hadn't even applied for the job yet when we met!"

She came up behind him and placed her hand on his shoulder.

He jerked his arm away from her. "Don't fucking touch me." He let out a harsh laugh. "All that may be true, but it doesn't change the fact that you want to use me now, does it?"

"Jesus Christ, how could you think that!"

He turned and faced her then. Her mouth was drawn into a straight line, her eyes wide and filled with anger. Fine, she could be as angry as she wanted. He was fucking angry, too.

Garrett shrugged and then crossed his arms. "If the shoe fits."

***

Despair spilled into Angie's limbs, and she felt her legs go weak with the sheer weight of sadness inside her. "I would never, Garrett."

"But you did, Angie. You fucking did."

Tears filled Angie's eyes, and she tried to blink them back but failed. One, then two, ran down her cheeks. She shook her head. "I love you."

She'd spoken the words so softly she wasn't sure he'd heard her. He wasn't even looking at her. But then his head snapped up, and his eyes were filled with anger. Angie flinched and looked away.

How was this happening? For him to think this of her… the man really had no idea who Angie was inside or how much he meant to her. He couldn't possibly because if he did, he'd know that she'd never, ever use him.

"Okay." She blew out a shaky breath and swiped away her tears. "What now, Garrett?"

He tipped his head to the side and drew in a breath. "You should move on. I think it's the best thing for you. Walk away from me, Angie. You deserve better."

She almost laughed out loud. If this wasn't so tragic, she would have. Yeah, he was right, she did deserve better. Someone who would love her back because it was obvious to her Garrett didn't love her. He never had.

And he was really going to force her to end it? How typical for him to take the chicken-shit way out. How was this her life?

Not anymore.

She couldn't do this one more fucking second. Anger climbed up Angie's throat, burning like sour bile. At least it was better than the tears. "You're a fucking coward, Garrett."

"Yep. Which is exactly why you deserve better." He turned and opened the office door, she assumed for her to leave.

God, what a fucking shit show. Fine. She'd give him what he wanted and make it super easy on him, too.

With his hands on his hips, Garrett stared at the wall to his right, drew in a long breath, let it out, and then looked back at her. "Angie, look, I can honestly say I'm sorry things didn't work out." He held his arms out to his sides, then let them drop as if he were the one feeling defeated. "I know better than to get involved. I shouldn't have let myself trust you, but I did, and worse, I let my guard down. That's on me, not you. Regardless, I wish things had been different."

Angie stared at him, unable to process the words coming out of his mouth. It was all her fault, yet it wasn't? Like he was doing her some sort of favor by taking it on himself? What the hell?

His eyes were hard as stone. Emotionless. Cold. Her hand tingled to slap some sense into him. To wake him up. Any sort of reaction from him would be better than the cold, brick wall he was giving her.

To stop herself from doing something so inappropriate as hitting him, she clenched her hand into a fist. Where the fuck had he gone in his head? The man standing before her was not the man she knew he was deep inside.

Angie shook her head and swallowed the tears that threatened to fall again. She was done crying in front of him.

Her heart was splintering into a million pieces right before him, and he was tossing bullshit lines at her. This whole situation was fucked. "Everything could have been different if you wanted it to be. So don't tell me how you wish it could be. You never wanted it to be, Garrett!"

"*You use*—"

"Don't." She gritted her teeth and shook her head. "Don't say another word. I'm done. Goodbye, Garrett."

Unable to look at him another second, Angie stormed out of the office and down the hall. She couldn't stop. Couldn't listen to another word. If she didn't keep going, she might collapse right there in front of him because he'd thoroughly gutted her and torn her to shreds.

The pain in her chest was paralyzing, but she couldn't let it stop her. Angie ran down the stairs and then out the club's back door until she reached the edge of the parking lot.

Her chest constricted, and she wrapped her arms around

her middle and bent forward. Unable to hold it in any longer, loud, guttural sobs erupted from her, echoing around her.

It was over. Garrett had just ripped her heart clean out of her chest. There was no coming back from that.

CHAPTER FORTY-TWO

Angie hit the snooze button on her alarm for the third time and then turned over, burrowing deeper under the sheet and comforter. The alarm had been set for eight a.m., like always. Now it was nine, and she'd really be behind if she didn't get moving.

But exhaustion—aka getting over a broken heart—had her yearning to stay in bed again. It wasn't like she had to call in sick or anything; she didn't work a nine-to-five. She worked when she had something to write.

Pushing the covers off her head, she rolled to her back and rubbed her eyes. God, she was a mess. She'd gone to bed at ten-thirty last night, so it wasn't as if she hadn't gotten enough sleep. More than ten hours was plenty, too much probably.

But apparently, healing a broken heart required more sleep than any normal human needed. Besides, staying in bed and sleeping made it easier to ignore the massive canyon in her chest.

Except, staying in bed didn't pay the bills. Translation: It was time to get up and work. Then later, it would be time to go to Maiya and Ryan's for dinner—at their insistence because her family knew she was in this fucked up mourning phase, and they refused to let her be. God help her.

After that, she'd come home and do some laundry because she was out of clean socks, clean underwear, and pretty much all her jeans had been worn at least three times.

So yeah, life.

It went on.

Dammit.

It wasn't like life had no reason not to keep on, keepin' on. The obligations Angie had, like car payments and rent, didn't care if she had a broken heart. Shit still needed to get done. Paid for. Washed. Call it the universe's screwed-up way of keeping a person moving forward, regardless of their feelings.

Angie didn't want to move forward, though. She just wanted to sleep…even if only for a few more minutes. She closed her eyes, and as always, there he was.

Garrett Allen James.

The love of her life.

The source of her pain.

In fucking Technicolor.

Thirty-two days, seven hours, and some stupid number of minutes—not that she was keeping track—had passed since she'd walked away from him. And she hadn't seen or heard from him since.

At first, having no contact with Garrett was like a thousand tiny cuts. Every part of her heart, body and soul was raw, as though she'd willingly peeled her skin off with a cheese grater.

She ended up turning down the job at Rolling Stone. There was no way she could've been on the ball starting there while walking through the hell she was in. Maybe once she got past all of this, she'd apply again. Maybe not.

It was only in the past week that Angie started to feel some relief—a few moments here and there where she didn't think of him. Miss him. Or wonder how he was. But still, every morning, he was her first thought. And, of course, she fell asleep with him on her mind each night, too.

The nights were the worst. When all was quiet and she was alone in her apartment, the rawness persisted. The thoughts, the memories, and the ache, too. With every part of her being, Angie dreaded the sun going down because with it came Garrett.

Tears pricked her eyes. Jesus, she was living in her very own Amy Winehouse song. *Ugh, so pathetic!* Angie tossed an arm over her face, swallowed past the lump in her throat, and willed the tears to stop. She was determined not to cry this morning. Earning the Drama Queen Award of the Year wasn't on her to-do list either.

Fucking hell, none of this mess had been on her to-do list. "Okay, enough."

With an exasperated huff, she kicked off the covers and rolled out of bed. In some sort of zombie haze, she made her way to the bathroom and managed to turn on the shower. While the water got hot, she pulled her knot of hair from the top of her head.

No point in looking in the mirror. Why bother? She knew her face was puffy from her daily crying jags. Hot-mess mode in full effect, Captain! Angie stepped beneath the hot spray and let the water run over her face, then her hair and down her body.

Today was going to be the day. She would wipe the slate of her soul clean as she washed her body, face and hair. She was going to clean Garrett from her heart...somehow.

Wasn't there a song from some musical before she was even born about washing a man out of a girl's hair? She could swear she remembered her mother joking and singing it.

Anyway, it didn't matter. She had to do it. It was time. Thirty days was enough misery and mourning. Angie wasn't foolish enough to think she could snap her fingers and poof, all would be healed in her heart, but she could at least stop living like she was dead.

Today was the day. This morning's shower was the place. Her heart would beat again. And it would start now…

Right after she got done with this last crying jag.

GARRETT SLAMMED the storage closet door so hard it rattled. Stupid door. With the inventory clipboard in his hand and a scowl on his face, he stomped down the back hall and out to the bar area.

Jerking open the heavy door of the walk-in cooler behind the beer taps, he slammed the clipboard down on top of a case of beer and counted kegs. Then, he counted the cases of beer.

When the cooler door opened, Garrett glanced over. Marlene stuck her head in. "Hey, Garrett. Delivery truck is here."

"'Bout fucking time those assholes got here. Fuckers were supposed to be here three hours ago." As annoyance bolted down his spine, he stormed past Marlene.

"Wow, okay…uh, how about I finish up in here for you?"

Garrett stopped short, turned, and shoved the clipboard at her. "Good. Make yourself useful for once."

With raised brows and wide eyes, she clutched the clipboard to her chest. But then she frowned. The hurt expression in her eyes hit Garrett right in the throat with a full shot of guilt and remorse.

But screw that mess. He kicked the unnecessary feelings aside. Unnecessary because everyone needed to pull their weight around there, and Marlene was no different.

That was the best bullshit excuse he could come up with as he turned his back and walked away from her. Truth was, Marlene *always* did a good job and pulled her weight. That said, too bad. She could go elsewhere for a paycheck if she didn't like it.

When he got out back, Cody was talking to the driver. Blazing hot rage filled Garrett's brain and spilled through his chest. He stepped in front of the driver and got right in the dude's face. "What the fuck with you people being late all the damn time! I'm trying to run a business here!"

The driver put his hands up as he took a step back. "Sorry, Mr. James. We—"

"Whoa, Garrett. Come on, boss. Go easy." Cody touched Garrett's sleeve.

Garrett jerked his arm away from Cody. "Do not fucking touch me, and don't you *ever* fucking tell me what to do! Not sure who the hell you think you are all of a sudden, but what you should be doing right now, what I pay you to be doing—" Garrett jerked his head toward the loading dock. "— Unloading this truck and putting inventory away!"

Cody paled and then shook his head. "Wow, Garrett. Whatever you say, man." The kid turned away, grabbed the loading dolly and then stepped into the back of the box truck.

Once again, Garrett focused on the driver and pointed his finger at him. "Tell your boss, next time you assholes are late, I'm going with your competitor. I don't need this shit."

Without another word, Garrett stormed away and bolted up the back stairs. Fury ran through his veins like hot lava, and his heart pounded in his ears.

It'd been so long since he'd felt this much anger—so long he couldn't even recall when the last time was. In some ways, it felt good, empowering, almost like a high. But when that high wore off, he felt like complete and total shit.

With his hands shaking, he opened his office door and slammed it behind himself as he stalked into the space. Flopping down in his chair, a single thread of guilt sped through him, piercing his haze of anger, and he pressed the heels of his palms to his eyes.

Dammit. He was being an asshole to everyone around him, treating them like shit, doing damage by taking his frustration and anger out on them, just like the selfish prick he'd always been.

He couldn't help it. The anger was the only solution he had. Fury the only thing keeping him up and mobile, and he knew that wouldn't last much longer. Eventually, he'd run out of steam, and when that happened, the longing and the heartache would plague him.

Garrett glanced at the couch across from him, then at his desk, and wanted to scream.

Everywhere he looked, everywhere he went, there she was. The memory of Angie assaulted him at every turn. He couldn't escape her. God dammit! It'd been a month, and he refused to deal with the void she left.

Garrett blew out a breath, laid his head down on his desk and closed his eyes.

WHAT FELT like only a few minutes later, Garrett jerked awake to the sound of his cell ringing. The caller ID said it was his friend, Sean. He sent the call to voicemail and glanced at the time.

Shit, he'd been asleep on his desk for over an hour. He tilted his head side to side and cracked his neck. Jesus, what the fuck was he doing? Grabbing his keys, Garrett went downstairs. Based on the lack of lights on, it was clear Marlene and Cody had left, and Garrett was alone in the building.

It was quiet as a church inside the big open area, and as he walked across the concrete floor, heading toward the bar, his footsteps echoed around him.

Loneliness crept down his spine, and his skin got tight. Garrett stopped behind the metal bar top and took in the bottles arranged atop the glass shelves on display against the mirrored back wall. The hollow void in his chest screamed for Angie, making every part of his body ache.

Garrett grabbed a bottle of Grey Goose and a rocks glass. He poured two fingers of the vodka into the glass and stared at the clear liquid.

Picking up the glass, he swirled the vodka, then smelled it. As he put the edge of the glass to his lips, his cell rang again.

With his heart pounding in his ears, panic filled his mind, and he put the glass down and backed away like it was filled with liquid death—because death was exactly what would be waiting for him if he drank even one drop of it.

Garrett closed his eyes and drew in a shaky breath. With the phone still ringing, he pulled the cell from his pocket. He swiped the screen, then put the phone to his ear.

"Chase…please..." Garrett grabbed the edge of the bar and hung his head forward. "Help me."

CHAPTER FORTY-THREE

"We doing shots?" Angie leaned toward her friend, Tarra, while they waited for the bartender to come their way.

"Girl, please. My first night off in two weeks? It's a Friday, and I'm *not* performing somewhere—which some might think is sucky, but I happen to think is freaking awesome because, like I said, I haven't had a night off in three damn weeks—hell, yes, we're doing shots!"

"Yee-haw!" Angie laughed. "Yes, this born and raised Cali girl did just go a little country. Figured you'd appreciate it." She winked at her friend as she raised her arm in the air and tried to flag the bartender down.

Tarra laughed and nudged Angie's shoulder with her own. "I'm really glad to see that you're getting back to your old self."

"I know. It hasn't been easy. I'm trying, you know? It's been nearly four months, and I gotta say, I'm real tired of soaking in my own sadness. I'm pickled." Angie held her hands out, palms up. "My fingers are wrinkly, for God's sake."

Tarra laughed. "You'll make it." Her friend's eyes darted over Angie's head. "Ohh, my my my."

Angie turned back to see the—oh, my, was right—hot as hell bartender. How had she not seen him when they came in?

"Ladies." He smiled. "What can I get you?"

"If I answer you honestly, I might get in trouble." With a sweet smile on her face, Angie batted her lashes. "How about two shots of Jameson and two Cali' Creamin's on tap, instead?"

"Coming right up." He smirked. "Just to say, though, getting into trouble with someone like you might be the best kind of trouble to be in." With a jerk of his chin to Angie, the guy stepped away and pulled the bottle of Jameson off the shelf.

"That is one *fine* piece of male specimen."

"I have to agree. Nice forearms, too."

Tarra leaned on the bar. "And ass, and chest, and…yeah, nice everything, is what I'm thinking."

"Yep, and I bet he's had half the chicks in this place, too." Angie laughed.

The bartender returned and set the two shots of whiskey and beers down on the bar. Angie handed him her credit card. He looked down at it, then back to her. "Angela…pretty name for a pretty girl. You want me to leave it open?"

"Thank you." Angie smiled. "Yes, please."

He smirked again. "I'll need your ID, too."

Tarra reached for one of the shot glasses, and as she did, she leaned close to Angie's ear and whispered, "Definitely all the chicks. But I'm pretty sure he wants you, too."

Angie suppressed her giggle and focused on the bartender. "My ID? When did that become a thing here?"

He pursed his full lips and crossed his muscular, tattooed arms. "Since about three months ago."

He was so full of it. Playing along a little longer, Angie rested her elbows on the bar and leaned toward him. "But then you'll know where I live. We can't have that now, can we?"

His smile got a little bigger, revealing dimples on both cheeks. The guy leaned down, mimicking Angie's pose, and licked his lips. "I assure you, you'll have no trouble from me… unless, of course, you change your mind and you want some of the trouble I can offer."

Jeezus chrispies! This guy was hot enough to light a pair of panties on fire. Practically the perfect guy to help her along on the "heal her broken heart" journey, too. After all, that particular road was a lonely one.

Angie took him in. Tall, at least six-one. Short-cropped, brown hair, straight nose, full lips. Light brown eyes. Very built —as in about as big and muscular as her brother-in-law, Shane. And lots of ink. So many tats, Angie knew she'd spend hours exploring them…probably with her tongue.

With her gaze still locked with his, Angie picked up her shot glass, and as if on cue, Tarra clinked her glass with Angie's. She heard Tarra say, "Sláinte," and then they both tapped the bottom of their glasses on the bar top.

Angie tossed the golden liquid back and swallowed. The familiar burn hit as she set the glass upside down on the bar. She did all of this with him watching her—in fact, he never took his eyes off her.

And yeah, it felt *awesome* to have a man focus so intently on her.

"Sweet Jesus, gal." He straightened, shaking his head. "Hottest thing I've seen in a long ass time."

"What's your name?" Angie smiled as Tarra hip-bumped her.

"Luke. Pleasure to meet you, Angela." He took her hand and kissed her knuckles.

Giddiness at his chivalrous gesture made Angie's tummy tingle—then again, the tingle could be the whiskey. Angie tipped her head to the side, appraising him. He looked to be around her age, give or take a year or two. Assuming he was single, he'd be a great distraction.

As tempting as the guy was, Angie wasn't in the business of taking a rebound hostage. Her conscience would get the better of her. "Well, Luke, forgive me, but I find that hard to believe in your chosen profession. I'm sure you see sexy things all the time."

"Didn't say that. I said 'in a long time'. Plus, if you don't mind me saying, you're beautiful—*and* you down whiskey like a badass. So, yeah, *that* is damn sexy in my book. Rare, too. So yeah, my statement stands." He crossed his arms.

And what nice arms they were.

Damn, even if she brought him home for a one-night stand—and God, she was tempted—that was not the person Angie was anymore. The year moratorium and the whole falling in love thing had taken care of that old habit.

But maybe a date would be good? Easy. No commitment or pressure. Just casual—Angie cringed at her reference to "casual".

She drew in a deep breath to cleanse that reminder of Garrett and then refocused on the man in front of her rather than the one from her past. "Tell you what, Luke. I'll give you my number, and *if* you call, I'll let you take me out to dinner. We'll see if you're half as charming outside your element."

"Done." He smiled, turned, grabbed a pen and paper from beside the register, and set them in front of her. "Tomorrow night work for you?"

"We'll see." Angie smiled and wrote down her cell number. She slid the paper toward him and grabbed her beer. "Bye, Luke."

She turned and walked away. Tarra was right beside her, and they linked arms. "You rocked that dude's world, Ang. He's *totally* going to call tomorrow. Shit, I bet he calls you tonight."

"Like I said, we'll see." Angie shrugged, and as they reached a table beside the dance floor, she sat down and sipped her beer.

There was a knot in her stomach, but she ignored it. She was doing this—unless he didn't call, of course. But if he didn't, that'd be okay, too. At least she was putting herself out there.

Dinner would be good. Dinner was easy. Dinner was harmless.

She needed to go on a simple date; a date meant she was moving forward. And that needed to happen. She was long overdue for healing.

Come hell or high water, Angie needed to get on with her life.

GARRETT HELD the pencil between his finger and thumb, tapping the edge of the clipboard resting on his thigh as he stared at the many cases of beer stacked in the walk-in cooler.

What's she doing right now?

God, he missed her…so much more than he ever realized he would. More than he'd ever missed anyone in his life. He went to sleep aching for her and woke needing her warmth.

Shaking off the thoughts, he stepped out and closed the cooler door behind him before heading down the hall and into the stockroom. Garrett moved to the long shelving along the back wall and reviewed the various liquor bottles. Five, six, seven…he made a note on the inventory checklist.

Was she seeing anyone?

Garrett blew out a breath and let his head fall forward. Bile rose in his throat, and he cringed at the thought of another man touching her. Once more, he forced the thoughts from his mind.

It wasn't his business. Nothing regarding Angie was his business. *He* made damn sure of that. Garrett's chest ached, and he rubbed the spot. The pain wasn't there because of any bullshit story he'd tried to convince himself of. No, his chest ached because the truth was, he'd taken plenty from her, but he hadn't really *given her* anything at all.

He'd tried, though, but no matter how much he gave, it wasn't enough. Never enough—

No, that was bullshit, too.

Angie hadn't used him. At the root of it all, Garrett had been terrified of her and himself, more specifically, of letting her in and allowing himself to feel something.

Christ, he'd almost drank trying to convince himself she was out to betray him when really, he'd been in deep denial of what he truly felt for her—almost thrown away eighteen years of being alcohol and drug-free because he was being a blind, selfish asshole, dragging a woman who did nothing but care about him, through his shit.

The night he'd almost drank, Chase had called, essentially saving Garrett's life. If Garrett had drank that night, it wouldn't have been long before he lost everything he'd worked for: his bar, his daughter, and likely his life, too.

After that, with Chase's encouragement, Garrett started attending AA meetings and got a sponsor within a few days. Thank God he'd done that because, for the first time in forever, Garrett felt…different. Better. Content.

His only struggle now was with Angie. He sighed and thought about what his new sponsor, Howard, had said he should do, which was to pray.

Since Garrett was willing to do whatever Howard told him to do, he sent up a quick prayer to his Higher Power and then cleared his mind from Angie and how he'd fucked up, and went back to taking inventory.

His reprieve lasted about three minutes before she was back in his thoughts. Fucking hell, self-will was a bitch to contend with.

Sadly, there was no way he could've made her happy in the long term. The fun and excitement would've eventually worn off, things would've settled down between them, and

Angie would want marriage, babies, picket fences—regardless of what she'd claimed. He'd be a fool to believe otherwise.

Truthfully, she deserved all those things and more. Garrett had convinced himself that he never wanted to get married again, but if he thought about it—strictly from the hypothetical, of course—the only woman he *could* see himself wearing a ring for would be Angie.

As far as babies went, that ship had sailed long ago. Having a baby now, at age forty-seven, was too much to even imagine.

Setting the clipboard down, he took a seat on the stool beside the little worktable in the center of the stockroom. Except, the thought of Angie carrying his baby made his chest fill with joy, but then…constrict with fear, aching in a way he couldn't handle. He rubbed his sternum, trying to soothe the pain.

This was the root of the issue for him, where all their problems stemmed from. Fear. He blew out a breath.

Since going into AA and working with a sponsor, he was finally able to understand why he'd done what he'd done to her. The risk of going all in, being a partner…a husband, starting a family, only to lose it all again, was too great.

Garrett let out a resigned sigh. Being apart was for the best, and Angie was better off without him. It didn't matter if letting her go and watching her walk out his door had turned out to be the latest addition to an already too-long list of worst nights of his life.

No, letting Angie go *had* been the right thing to do. He knew that. Still, every inch of his gut, heart, and soul was at odds with his decision because, unfortunately, Garrett now knew what he'd denied for so long…

He was in love with her.

Christ, he'd fucked this one up. Here he was, four months later, and Garrett *could not* stop thinking about her. Couldn't stop fantasizing about her either.

No other woman from his past had forced him out of his comfort zone sexually the way Angie had. She'd woken a side of him he'd always suspected was there but never dared to look too closely at. Garrett couldn't imagine being that free with another woman—

"We still on for tonight?"

Yanked from the fantasy just beginning to play in his mind, Garrett looked up to find his friend standing in the doorway. "What's up, Sean?" Garrett stood and moved to his buddy. "Yeah, I was pretty much done in here, anyway."

"You okay?"

"Nope, but I'll live." Garrett clapped his friend on the back. "Let me toss the clipboard in my office and lock up. I'll meet you out back, cool?"

"Sure thing, man."

Garrett watched as Sean headed down the hall. Thank God for his friends. Thank God for his sponsor and AA, too. He'd hit bottom again, hard, but at least now he was on his way back up.

Emotionally, spiritually and physically sober for the first time in eighteen years.

Garrett was on his knees, morning and night, praying like his sponsor wanted him to be. In addition, he was working the twelve steps with his sponsor. Whatever it took, Garrett was willing to do it.

He was doing the best he could to get on with his life. He just hoped Angie was doing okay and getting on with hers, too.

CHAPTER FORTY-FOUR

As Angie waved to Chassidy, she crossed the street and then made her way up the sidewalk to the French bistro where they were meeting.

Chassidy gave Angie a tight hug. "It's so good to see you!"

Angie patted Garrett's daughter on the back and gave another squeeze before pulling away, her lips arched into an appreciative smile. "It's good to see you, too. You look fantastic!"

"Thank you. So do you." Returning Angie's smile, Chassidy opened the door to the restaurant. "Are those blue highlights in your hair?"

"Sure are. A change from the purple." Angie moved to the hostess station. "Hi, two?" She turned back to Chassidy, a single brow raised. "At the time I did it, I figured my hair could match my heart."

Chassidy frowned. "Well, shoot, Angie. That's really…sad."

"Relax. I'm kidding. Sort of." Angie linked arms with Chassidy, nudging her playfully as they followed the hostess to a small table on the back patio. After they were both seated, napkins in their laps, Angie went on. She pointed to her hair.

"Honestly, I just needed a change. Probably time to switch it up again."

Chassidy drew in a breath, reached across the table, and clasped Angie's palm in her own. "Kidding or not, I can't say enough how sorry I am that things turned out like they did."

"There's nothing for you to be sorry for. You sure can't be sorry on behalf of him. It didn't work out. That's all." Angie shrugged and forced the lump filled with emotion back down her throat. Dammit, would this ever go away?

"I'm not apologizing for him. I'm just apologizing in general. I know how much you love my dad. He's an idiot for letting you go."

Angie pulled her hand away and opened the menu. "Maybe so, but nothing I can do about that. Over four months and counting. I've moved on." She let out a little chuckle. "I will say that Carley Pearce's song 'Day One' has become my new theme song."

The server took their drink order, and then someone else filled their water glasses.

"I'll have to look it up." Chassidy grinned and then took a sip of her water. "I'm glad you're moving on. I mean…let me be clear: I don't want you to move on because I want to see you two together, but this isn't about me. Moving on is exactly what you should do."

"It hasn't been easy. In fact, it's been the hardest thing I've ever walked through. I think I spent the first month in bed, and really, I should've bought stock in Puffs Plus tissues." Angie smirked as she adjusted her silverware. "I even turned the job down at Rolling Stone."

Chassidy put her glass down. "Oh my God, are you serious?"

Angie shrugged a shoulder. "Like I said, I couldn't get out of bed, let alone start a new job. Especially there. It was better I didn't take it. Would've been horrible if I had and then fucked up and got fired. This way, maybe I'll try again someday."

Chassidy frowned. "I get it. I hate it, but I get it."

"By the end of month two, I'd just…I'd had enough, you know? Totally sick of myself. Definitely sick of crying. And I mean, I finally knew, or accepted, I guess, that he wasn't going to call, or show up, or anything." She shrugged and swallowed that persistent lump back down. "So, I decided to let go."

Chassidy's frown deepened, a small crease forming between her brows. "I should've come to see you sooner."

"Girl, I was a hot-mess, and it might've made me worse. You're him." Angie shook her head. "Not *him*, but you know what I mean."

"Yeah, I get it. I hadn't thought about it like that before. Does it bother you now? The last thing I want to do is——"

Angie raised a hand. "No, no. Sweetie, it's fine. It's all good. Besides, I've missed you. And I adore you. And I don't want to lose contact because things didn't work out between me and your dad."

"Same." Chassidy smiled, her light green eyes filled with unshed tears.

"God, he's *such* a dumbass."

Angie laughed. "You said it, not me."

"Yes, I most certainly did." Chassidy looked over the menu. "Ooh, this place is fancy. Maybe I should've taken French when I was in school." She laughed.

"Right?" Angie looked over the menu and figured out what she wanted.

The server came back, and they ordered their meals—a salad for Chassidy and a sandwich for Angie.

So far, although some emotions had surfaced, Angie was handling the unexpected visit pretty damn well. Go her! Waiting for their food, they chit-chatted a little more, this time about work and hair and Chassidy's dating life. Or lack of one. Which Angie found interesting because since she'd decided to let go of Garrett and move forward, Angie's dance card had been completely full.

Their food arrived, and Angie dug into her French ham and gruyere cheese sandwich. After she'd gotten a few bites in, she picked the dating topic back up. "So…this may be a surprise, but I've been dating."

Chassidy was mid-sip of her drink and almost choked.

"Careful." Angie smiled.

She set the glass down, cleared her throat and wiped her mouth. "Holy shit, really?"

"Yeah. If I'm gonna move on, I gotta put myself out there again."

"Ugh, I so don't want you to be dating." Chassidy shook her head, another frown on her pretty face. "But you're right." She took a bite of her salad and spoke as she chewed. "Okay, lay it on me. I'm all ears. How's it going?"

"It's been about two weeks. And I've gone on ten dates, I think? Yeah, ten."

Chassidy's eyes went wide. "Holy shit, really?"

"Second time you've said that today." Angie laughed.

"Crap. You're right. But wow, ten? Maybe I need to start spending weekends out here with you. Some of your dating mojo can rub off on me." Chassidy laughed. "So, did all ten suck?"

"No, actually. Six of them have been with this one guy, Luke."

Chassidy's eyes went wider than saucers, if that were possible. "Holy shit—okay, let me stop right there. Six with the same guy?"

It was obvious Chassidy was having a hard time because Angie was actually moving on. She hated upsetting her in this way, but at the same time, Garrett's daughter would understand. She had to.

This time, it was Angie's turn to reach for Chassidy. She clasped her palm over Chassidy's. "Are you sure you want to hear about this? You look like…well, like it's upsetting you. I don't want to do that."

"It's totally upsetting me. How could it not? My dad is an asshat. I'm still so pissed at him. Even more so now. But at the same time, of course, I want to hear all about it. I need to. Because you deserve to be happy." Chassidy squeezed Angie's hand. "Tell me about Luke. And also, you think I might like any of the other guys?" She laughed.

"Maybe!" Angie laughed, too, and then settled back in her seat. "Let's see…Luke. He's thirty-two. He runs a bar. Go figure, right?" Angie rolled her eyes. "And he's really…*really* hot. As in the muscled, tattooed hot…*with* personality and brains. A rare find."

"Oh, damn. The total package, huh?"

"No joke. He's like fitness or romance book cover model hot. I don't even know what he's thinking, wanting to date me." Angie bit into her sandwich.

"What the hell do you mean by that? You're totally fucking hot, that's why he wants to date you."

Angie groaned and rolled her eyes. "Thank you. But still. He runs this bar in Hollywood, and of course, he also bartends there. Friday nights. And the women? Holy God. They're hitting on him all night. It's a little too much for me to handle, so I doubt it's going to last long. But it's like he doesn't even see them." She shook her head. "I don't get it."

"Don't get what?" Chassidy took a bite of her salad.

"Why he's interested in me. I mean, when I met him, I didn't even flirt. Well, not really, flirt. Not like I did with your dad or anything." Angie groaned. God, she should not have said that out loud. Poor Chassidy. "Sorry, that was weird."

"Angie, listen—" Chassidy leaned forward. "You're a total catch, and what makes that better is you don't even know it. You're gorgeous. You're independent. You're a fully self-supporting woman. You take care of yourself. And you're smart. Did I mention you're also gorgeous? Yeah, smart and gorgeous. Deadly combo right there. I know being with my father did a number on your self-confidence, but don't believe any of that crap your head is telling you. You are a catch, Angie. An amazing one. And it sounds like this guy Luke knows it."

Angie shrugged. Chassidy was at least right about not listening to the negative crap her mind kept playing on repeat. Moving on wasn't easy, but Angie was determined to make her way through it.

Chassidy took a sip of her drink and then leveled her gaze on Angie. "Now, I gotta ask, even though I shouldn't. But… good in bed?"

"Oh my God." Not expecting that question, Angie laughed as she wiped her mouth with her napkin and then shrugged. "Well, I honestly don't know. I haven't had sex with him. Hell, we haven't gotten past kissing." She laughed again and took a sip of her iced tea. "Kissing started to turn into a little make-out session the last date we were on, but I cut it off." She picked a piece of cheese off the side of her French roll. "Like I said, he's drop-dead gorgeous, with a body to die for, but no…no sex yet."

"I can't believe I'm saying this, but you should go for it. Just…do it! I bet it'll be awesome."

"Maybe." Angie shrugged one shoulder. "I'm not even sure I'm going to keep seeing him. I might be moving on, but I haven't fully moved on, and I don't want to hurt anyone, you know?"

Chassidy leaned her chin on her fist. "Yeah, I get that, too. No hostages."

"Exactly." Focusing on her sandwich, Angie contemplated things progressing forward with Luke, but also sex with him. She wasn't sure she could do it. She was attracted to him, sure, but in more of the generic way she'd always been attracted to guys—nothing like how she was attracted to Garrett. And when Luke had kissed her, it'd been a regular kiss.

No sparks.

No chemistry.

Just…a kiss.

Angie did like the guy. He was fun, easy to talk to. And attentive. So maybe…maybe she'd *become* more attracted to him over time? She hoped. Heaviness settled in her heart, the same heaviness she'd gotten used to being there for the past four-plus months.

Luke was a good guy, and she needed to give him a chance. But she needed to give herself a chance, too— At least to fully heal.

CHAPTER FORTY-FIVE

"Dad, you got a minute?"

Garrett looked up to see Chassidy's head peeking around the doorway to his office. He stood. "Hey! You're home. Of course, honey."

"Thanks." She moved into his office, gave him a quick hug and then plopped down on the couch.

Garrett resumed his spot in the office chair. "I thought you weren't going to be back from L.A. until later tonight."

"Well, I got done early, so I changed my flight." She smiled.

Garrett stared at his daughter, the question he wanted to ask nipping at his heels like an annoying, Miniature Doberman Pincer. He ignored it as long as he could, but when the silence got to be too much to bear, Garrett finally broke it. He rubbed the back of his neck. "So, did you see her?"

He barely got the words out without choking on them. Part of him didn't want to know; it was easier not knowing. But the other part felt like he'd die if he didn't ask.

"I did, yes. And that's what I want to talk to you about."

He nodded and swallowed past the knot in his throat, wishing he hadn't asked. Chassidy had been furious with him for how things went down with Angie. "Is she okay?" He drew in a deep breath and braced himself for her answer.

Chassidy crossed one leg over the other and linked her hands over her knee. "She's...well, to put it frankly, Dad, she's dating."

"I'm sorry, what did you say?" Heat filled Garrett's body, and he started to sweat. There was a high pitch ring in his ears, and the office suddenly felt really goddamn small.

Was some guy holding her hand? Touching her body? Kissing her?

Garrett struggled to draw in a breath, and his vision narrowed. He was either going to pass out or fly into some insane and highly inappropriate jealous rage. *What the hell...* He shook his head, trying to clear his mind. Angie had found someon—fuck, he couldn't even finish the thought.

"She's dating. She met a guy, older than her but younger than you. And she likes him, but I can tell she doesn't *like him*, like him. Not like she liked you. Or loved you, rather."

Loved...

Past tense. Garrett looked away from his daughter and did his best to catch his breath. Jesus Christ, it was hot in his office, and his skin felt tight all over.

Chassidy stood. "I figured you should know." She stepped closer to the desk and touched the top with her pointer finger. "Dad, this is it. If you love her, you better do something now because you're about to lose her. For good."

Garrett smoothed his palm over his face and looked up at his daughter. "Sounds like I already did."

Chassidy bent forward so she was eye level with him. "I love you. But *you are* a fucking moron."

"Come on, Chassidy!"

"What?" She threw a hand out to the side. "Don't fool yourself. That woman? She's the best thing that's ever happened to you. And yeah, that even includes my mother. You and Mom had your time; maybe it was love, but maybe it wasn't. Not that it matters because it ended in a fiery blaze, and then she died. But Angie? Dad, if you think you're going to find with someone else what you had with her, you won't. Fat chance in hell you'll ever find it again. A woman as incredible as she is, who loves you as much as she does, despite all the shit you put her through? And you're going to let that go? That's stupid! If you want to live the rest of your life with yet *another* regret, go for it. Knock it out of the damn park."

"That was harsh, Chassidy." Garrett frowned and rubbed his sternum as he stared at his daughter and the dead serious expression on her face.

"Yeah, well, you've earned yourself a little harshness. Oh, here's a little more. She turned down the job at Rolling Stone, so that's on you, too." She straightened and propped her hands on her hips. "Look, I get that you're going to do what you want, and nothing I say will sway that. But at least now you know the deal, in case you want to fix it. And I hope you do fix it. I really do, Dad." She shook her head. "It would suck to watch you miss out on something great in your life because you were being stubborn or caught in some useless web of fear."

"It's more complicated than that, Chassidy." That was all he could come up with, and it sounded weak to his own ears. Garrett let out a resigned sigh. He wanted to tell her how wrong she was and to mind her own business. But he couldn't. Chassidy wasn't wrong, and she'd hit about eight million nerves with her little intervention speech.

"It's only as complicated as you want to make it." She shook her head. "Like I said, you do what you want. I know you will anyway, but you needed to know." She turned and moved to the door.

Garrett slumped in his chair, all strength gone from his body. He had no fight left in him. "I love you, Chassidy."

She glanced back as she opened the door. "I love you, too."

Garrett sat for a long time behind his desk, feeling deflated and weak as chaos rang out in his mind. It was one thing to wonder, another to know for sure. Knowing Angie was with another man had all of his emotions on a rollercoaster ride.

Christ, he was better off not knowing. But that ship had sailed, and now he was going to go out of his fucking mind with all the knowing. For fuck's sake, she was Garrett's—in every way possible. No amount of distance was going to change that.

Plus, she didn't take the job? For fucks' sake, it was her dream, and she'd given it up for what?

God, he'd done that. He took that from her.

With his heart pounding in his ears, he focused on trying to slow his breathing. Garrett needed to calm down. He needed to think. He needed to figure out what he was going to do. He knew if he didn't get his brain to settle, he'd end up doing something rash or doing nothing at all. Neither was an option.

He closed his eyes, sank to his knees, and prayed, asking his Higher Power to carry him, to wrap him in his love and grace, and to show him where He wanted Garrett to be, what He wanted Garrett to do. Garrett prayed for the right thought or action.

When he was done, he shot a text off to Chase and then called his sponsor. Garrett couldn't do this alone, and the good news was he didn't have to.

AFTER GARRETT GOT off the phone with his sponsor, he pulled his leather duffel bag out of his closet. As he tugged shirts and jeans from the hangers, his cell rang.

Garrett glanced at the screen and then put the cell to his ear. "Chase. Thanks for calling, man."

"You doing okay, brother?"

Garrett paused in the packing and sat on the edge of the

bed. "Yeah, I'm good. Actually, I'm better than good. I know what I need to do."

"This sounds serious, should I sit down?" Chase chuckled.

"I know we're doing that interview, but I have an idea, a special request, and I can't do it without your help."

"I am at your disposal. Hit me."

Garrett grinned. "You still sleeping with your publicist?"

Chase barked a laugh.

"I'll take that as a yes. Listen, I need you to conference her in. Can you do that?"

That got Chase's attention, and he got his laughter under control. "I can do that, but you want to fill me in first?"

Garrett got to his feet, went into his bathroom, and started packing his shaving bag. "Sure, but I don't have a lot of time. Figured I could just fill you both in at the same time. I have to catch a plane to Burbank in an hour."

"About time, man. Hang on, I'll conference her in."

While Garrett waited on hold, he finished packing.

CHAPTER FORTY-SIX

Garrett got off the plane in Burbank and walked into the narrow terminal. He'd barely made the last flight out of Phoenix. It was almost ten p.m., and he had no idea where Angie could be. He was going straight to her apartment, though, and if she wasn't there, he would sit in front of her door and wait for her.

He probably should've called or texted…but he didn't want to risk her not answering or, worse, telling him to get fucked. Which, technically, he deserved. Regardless, he wanted his shot to talk to her face-to-face, and if she told him to take a long walk off a short pier after that, he guessed that was how it was supposed to be.

Garrett was following his gut and not his fear, which meant he was going with what he felt his Higher Power's will was rather than his self-will. Now it was time to simply do the footwork and then trust his Higher Power to take it from there.

His HP would either block or bless this relationship with Angie, as well as the plan he'd just set in motion with Chase and Chase's publicist. That said, Garrett was still human and couldn't help but hope that she'd get another shot at Rolling

Stone even if Angie didn't take him back. This time as a staff writer. He could at least give her that.

He pulled up the Lyft app on his phone and requested his ride. Boom. A car was four minutes away. Old dogs *could* learn new tricks, after all. Garrett followed the sidewalk to the rideshare spot across from Terminal Two and waited for his ride to show.

Once inside the car and on his way to her apartment, he sat back and prayed again.

He'd never done the things he'd been taught in rehab eighteen years ago, like praying. Never went to meetings during all those years either, and as a result, he'd managed to fuck up damn near all of his relationships. Plus, he'd almost drank again.

Garrett was done playing with fire.

The driver pulled into the parking lot of Angie's complex. Garrett thanked him, got out, grabbed his bag from the trunk, and then headed up the stairs to her apartment. He glanced at his watch: ten forty-five pm.

Nervous energy pulsed in his veins, and he drew in a deep breath as he neared her door. Reaching the threshold, Garrett paused before knocking.

Shit, what if she had that guy she was dating in there?

Fast as lightning, jealous fury rose inside his gut, and he pushed it down as quickly as it'd reared its ugly head. There was no place in this moment for that kind of reaction. Plus, he had no right. Even if his heart and head thought he did. Garrett knew better.

After setting his bag down, he dropped to his knees, closed his eyes, and prayed again. *Please guide my words. Please help me to listen and give me the courage to make the amends needed to clean the slate with her. You're in charge.*

Opening his eyes, Garrett stood, drew in another deep breath, and then knocked. For a second, he thought he heard voices. The television, maybe? He listened, but now it was quiet. He knocked again.

That's when he heard the faint "what the fuck," mumbled from the other side of the door. Good girl, she'd checked the peephole, which was exactly what she should do because it was goddamn late.

But the downside was, now she knew it was him, and maybe she wasn't going to open the—

The door swung open, and Garrett's breath caught in his throat.

A shiver zipped down his spine as he took her in. Fuzzy, purple socks covered her feet, but her long legs were bare— God help him—and led up to a pair of men's boxers, rolled low at the waist. A thin white tank top with no bra covered her torso and breasts. Her hair was piled in a messy bun on top of her head, and she had no makeup on.

She looked more beautiful than he'd ever seen her look. Or maybe he hadn't been paying close enough attention before.

Angie crossed her arms and leaned a hip against the door-frame. "What are you doing here, Garrett?"

"I needed to talk to you."

"So, you flew here? Why not just call or text? Oh, wait, never mind. I forgot you suck at that."

Direct hit!

Okay, yeah. He'd earned that one. "Can I come in?"

Angie stared at the man in front of her in utter disbelief. Garrett—broke-her-heart-into-a-thousand-pieces—James stood in living color outside her open apartment door, looking all sorts of beautiful.

Angie wanted to scream. She wanted to cry. She wanted to

fall into his arms. And she wanted to slap his goddamn gorgeous face.

Nearly five months had passed. Five months! And nothing, not one text, call, or message in a friggin' bottle…and suddenly he shows up at her door? *Oh, hell no!*

Chassidy must've kicked him in the ass when she got home and maybe even told him about Luke. But God, would she do that? No, she wouldn't.

But…

Well…maybe?

Yeah, probably.

Shit!

Angie frowned. Wait, what was she thinking? Even if Chassidy *had* told Garrett about Luke, it didn't matter. Angie wasn't doing anything wrong by dating Luke or half of Los Angeles if she wanted to, for that matter.

And if Garrett didn't like that she was seeing someone else, too bad. He should've done right by her when he had the chance. Shoring up her resolve, Angie stepped aside and waved him in. May as well let him say what he needs to say, so she could escort him right back out the door. "Fine."

"Thanks."

When Garrett passed her, she caught the scent of his cologne and wanted to drop dead. Just lie down, right there on the tile entryway of her apartment, and fucking die.

Panic, fueled by self-preservation, filled her stomach. She had to make sure this didn't take long. Angie couldn't trust herself to be alone with him. She might hate his guts, but that didn't mean she wasn't still insanely attracted to him.

With another deep breath, she moved into the kitchen. "Can I get you anything? There's fresh coffee."

"Coffee'd be great, thanks."

Angie glanced over her shoulder and caught him setting down his overnight duffel bag. The one she hadn't noticed when he walked in. What the fuck? Did he think he was staying? Jeezus chrispies, this was not happening.

Seriously.

Was.

Not.

Happening!

Annoyance mixed with anxiety crawled along Angie's skin as she pulled down two mugs and set them on the counter. Before she'd finished filling both, Garrett had come into the small kitchen, opened the refrigerator and taken out the coffee creamer for her.

He moved beside her. "Which one's yours?"

Angie swallowed down the scream that threatened to erupt out of her. In addition to the scent of his cologne, this polite, tend-to-her-needs bullshit was going to be the death of her. "I got it."

Without looking at him, she took the cream from his hand, opened the carton, and poured it into her coffee. He drank his black, so she slid Garrett's coffee his way, then put the creamer away in the fridge.

"Thanks."

"Welcome," she mumbled as she moved past him, careful not to brush against his body in the tight space, and returned to the couch. Sitting, she tucked her legs under her and then grabbed the remote, pointed it at the TV and hit the mute button.

Garrett came out and took a seat in the chair instead of on the couch, thank God.

Raising her mug to just below her lips, she blew on the hot liquid before taking a sip. Angie swallowed, still managing to avoid meeting his eyes. "You wanted to talk, so talk."

"Okay…right." Garrett set his coffee on the end table and rubbed his palms on his long thighs. "Let me start with the fact that I owe you an enormous apology."

With her coffee still poised below her lips, she held the

mug with both hands and did her damnedest to look everywhere but at him. "For?"

This was beyond painful. Giving in to the urge, Angie looked at him.

Garrett leaned forward, pressed his palms together, and sighed. "For so many things. For failing you over and over. For breaking your heart in little ways, too many times. I know I pushed you past your limit with my inconsistent and frankly unfair behavior, and after I accused you of trying to use me, I left you no choice but to walk away from me. I don't blame you for that..."

Was he really saying all of this to her?

Angie shook her head and blinked a few times, clearing away the tears that were trying for all they were worth to fill her eyes. Another sip of coffee, as he continued, helped her swallow down the lump that had lodged in her throat.

"...I was wrong, Angie. So wrong. I'm the one who fucked things up for us, not you." He ran his palm over the back of his neck. "Babe, you gotta know that an hour hasn't passed where I haven't thought of you. You—" He blew out a harsh breath. "—You're everything, Angie. You're a kind heart with good intentions. You're smart, beautiful, fun, and...well, I'm better for knowing you. You call me on my shit, and I need that. I do..." He caught her eyes then, and it felt like he was looking right into her soul. "I need you, Angie. I don't know why it was so hard for me to show you how I felt, to tell you, too." He shook his head and then cleared his throat. "No, that's not true. I do know why."

Angie set her coffee down. Her hands were shaking, and she didn't want to spill or, worse, drop the damn thing. A strange sensation coated her skin, making her limbs feel like they weighed a ton. At the same time, she felt like she was floating. God, she was losing it. "Why?"

"I was afraid."

She shifted her legs from beneath her and raised her

knees, cradling her arms around them. Trying to hold herself together. "Of what?"

"So many things." He closed his eyes. "Of not being enough. Not being able to give you what I know you would eventually need—"

"Garrett, again with the what I needed bullshit? You don't have a crystal ball, you know! Why do you think you can tell me what I will or won't want? God…" Annoyance from hearing him use his typical line regarding what she "needed or would need" blazed through her brain, and she slammed her fists down on the couch beside her legs.

"Babe, I know, and I was wrong for that."

Babe…

Ugh, that was the second time he called her that!

The endearment was like an arrow straight to the heart! Angie flinched from the direct hit and somehow managed to stifle the gasp that rose in her throat. She took a few deep breaths, and when she was ready, she tried again. "You were wrong. So what? What do you want from me now?"

"I want your forgiveness."

Angie stared at him. Was that it? God, for a minute there, she thought he might want… "Why? What does it matter if I forgive you?

He looked at her, the expression in his eyes a mix of sadness and regret. "It matters. You matter."

It mattered? She mattered? What the fuck!

Anger spiked, hot and fast, mingling with her heartache. "You make no sense, Garrett!" She flung her arm out to her side. "What is it you want from me? And so help me…you better fucking answer me."

He stood, fury and frustration evident in his expression. "I want you. All of you. Don't you understand? I want to get married. I want to give you babies. You deserve all of that, but more, you deserve someone who isn't so terrified of losing it that he won't give it to you at all. Fuck!" Garrett turned his back as if he couldn't face her, and his head fell forward. After what felt like forever, with his back still to her, he spoke again. "It's why you're better off with someone else. God, baby, you deserve so much better than me."

The last was spoken in such a low tone she almost couldn't hear him. But she did. She heard all of it…and Angie couldn't breathe.

Angie got to her feet. Did he want her or not? "You… Wait, I'm confused."

Garrett turned to face her. "You and me both."

"You and me both?" Angie frowned and then shook her head. "That's your response? Garrett, oh my God, you *suck* at communication."

"I know…I know, babe." He raised his hands as if in surrender, but the corner of his mouth twitched. "And you suck at reading minds."

"Are you kidding me? You're trying to be funny and cute? At a time like this?" Angie drove her fingers into her hair, pulled tight at the top of her head, and tugged at the strands. "I swear to God, you're insane. And you're trying to make me insane with you." She pointed her finger at him and frowned harder. "I'm going to tell you right now, Garrett James, you can forget it. It's not going to happen."

He crossed his arms, and a small grin spread across his lips. "Now you're the one being cute."

"*Uggghhhhh!* No, I'm not!" Angie stormed past him. "And I'm not doing this either." Garrett grabbed her arm, and Angie yanked from his hold as she whipped around. "Don't! You just told me you wanted to marry me and give me babies, and then proceeded to tell me I was better off with someone else, deserved someone better than you! And now you're going to stop me from walking away? What the fuck, Garrett?"

"Swear to God, Angela, I don't think I can watch you walk away from me a second time."

Angie felt his words from the top of her head to the tips of her toes. But it didn't matter. An unbearable ache filled her chest, and she pressed her palm to her sternum as tears filled her eyes and then ran down her cheeks.

He didn't want to give her anything, but the man wouldn't let her go? Did he have no conscience?

Christ, Angie had no clue how to navigate this. She swiped the wet from her cheeks. God dammit! She didn't want to cry in front of him. "Why are you doing this, fucking with my head like this?"

"I'm not, I swear to you. I'm not trying to. I just…" He blew out a breath. "I'm scared. Angie, I'm fucking terrified."

She wrapped her arms around her middle. "Of what?"

"I've been alone for a long time. After Chassidy's mother and I split, and then she OD'd and died, my heart was decimated. I was so deep into my alcoholism and addiction I didn't let the pain in. I never mourned her." He rubbed the back of his neck. "After that, everything got worse. The drugs, the booze—" He shook his head. "I practically abandoned Chassidy to her grandparents. I definitely abandoned the band. I destroyed everyone and everything close to me."

"But then you got cleaned up and made a life for you and Chassidy. You saved her and yourself. How can you not see how wonderful that is?"

"I'll never fully understand how you see me so differently than I see myself." His lips curved into a small, gentle smile, and Angie had to stop herself from reaching for him. "Here's the thing, I don't get an award for doing the right thing. Look, I loved my wife, and it was my fault we broke up. It was my fault she became an addict, too. Thus, my fault she died. Living with that was hard enough. There was no way I was going to open my heart to another woman. It wasn't worth it. The risk was just too great. Then I met you."

Angie sniffled and dropped her gaze to the floor. "Yes, you met me. And nothing changed."

"Not true. Everything changed."

"Not from where I'm standing, Garrett."

Garrett placed his hands on her upper arms. "You changed everything, baby."

God, he was killing her. The warmth from his palms was like a brand. She wanted to move into him, press her nose against his neck, and breathe him in. But she held herself still. "Please don't say things you don't mean. I can't take it. Please…"

"Fuck, I know I suck at communication, but I'm trying." He cupped her face in his palms. "Listen to me, please? I'm in love with you, Angie. I want to marry you. I want to have babies with you. And, yes, it scares the fucking shit out of me that I could lose you someday, that you could wake up and realize I'm not it for you, but I'd rather take the risk than live another day without you. I want you, all of you. I want to be the man you want and need me to be."

Confusion pulsed through Angie's brain. "Why would you do that? You told me yourself you didn't want to get married or have kids. You'd be miserable. I don't want you to be miserable, Garrett."

"Jesus, you're amazing." His eyes went soft, and he wiped a tear from her cheek. "Babe, if I close my eyes and picture myself married again with babies, it's only you I see standing beside me."

Panic rose inside her chest.

Was he…

He couldn't be, could he? "Are you…wait, Garrett, are you proposing to me?

CHAPTER FORTY-SEVEN

With a soft smile arching his lips, Garrett tucked a lock of her hair behind her ear. God, she was beautiful. "Well, no, not technically. Not yet, but yeah, you're it for me, Angie. If you'll have me."

She gazed into Garrett's eyes and appeared to be at a loss for words. A rare thing, but happening regardless. Garrett almost laughed, but he wasn't trying to get his head chopped off. What he'd said had thrown her, though that hadn't been his intention at all.

She pulled from his hold. "I'm sorry. I...I need a minute to process all this."

"Okay." Garrett dropped his hands to his sides. "I understand."

Angie resumed her spot on the couch and scrubbed her palms over her face.

A tense silence settled around them, blanketing her small living room. He watched as several different emotions played over her features, and it was all he could do not to go to her, to pull her into his arms and show her everything he felt.

Just when Garrett was about to give in and break the silence, she spoke up.

Angie looked at him, her eyes bright with tears. "I love you, Garrett. I think I have from the very beginning, and there were times where you… God, you just took advantage of that love, and other times you simply ignored it." She blew out a breath and sat back. "So much hurt. You caused so much hurt."

"I know, babe." Every word she spoke hit him in the throat. Garrett resumed his seat in the chair beside the sofa. "That's exactly what I was saying. That was all about my fear. But I'm working on that, working on healing."

"Stop!" She snatched a tissue and pressed it to her tear-filled eyes. "Seriously, Garrett, you cast more bait than a damn fishing expedition, and now you're casting the biggest bait on the planet? I mean, good Lord, how can I trust that?"

"Bait?" He shook his head. "Angie, I'm not casting bait. I'm serious."

Angie blew her nose on the tissue she was holding. "You always cast bait. And I bite—hook, line, and sinker—every damn time. And here I go again. Fine, tell me, how is it that you're working on it?"

Garrett drew in a deep breath. He knew this wouldn't be easy, and she was really pushing him like she always did, but he could handle it. No way he wasn't giving up now. "I'm going to AA now. I have a sponsor and I'm working steps with him. It's not easy, but I feel better than I have, well, ever. I know that doesn't just fix all the damage I did to us, but I hope it's a start." He shrugged. "Babe, I'm prepared to do whatever's necessary to show you things will be different. I'll earn your trust. I know there's a lot of issues to overcome, but I know we can get through this."

Angie blinked, and tears ran down both cheeks. "I'm the one who's terrified now."

Garrett moved and sat beside her on the couch. "I know, baby girl." He took her hands in his. "Me too. But I love you,

Angie. Totally and completely. I swear to you, you have all of me."

Crying, Angie threw her arms around him and buried her face in his neck.

Garrett wrapped his arms around her, pulling her tight to him, and then he threaded his fingers through her hair. God, she was killing him. He hated that he'd hurt her so much. "I got you, baby." Rocking them side to side, he held her tight in his arms. "I've got you."

After her tears finally subsided, she pulled back and looked into his eyes. Cupping his face in her palms, she stroked her thumbs over his cheekbones and then along his chin. "So beautiful."

He sighed. "I see myself different in your eyes."

She tilted her head to the side. "What do you see?"

"I guess I see the man my Higher Power wants me to be instead of the broken man I thought I was. You gave me that."

"I love you, Garrett James." Angie's face went soft, and his heart melted in his chest.

Relief filled every cell in his body. Thank God she'd stuck by him. "I love you, too, Angie Donnelly."

ANGIE PRESSED a soft kiss to his lips before pulling back again to gaze at him. Then she smiled. "Can we just date or…live together for a little while first? I mean, I don't want to rush into anything, you know? You are pretty hard to handle. Oh! I should probably start going to those Al-Anon meetings, so I don't kill you, huh? Yeah, that'd be a goo—"

Garrett burst out laughing…and the sound of it, the most glorious sound of it, rippled over her skin and landed right in the center of her chest. It was the best sound in the world.

Angie kept going, wanting to hear him laugh again. "Plus,

if we do live together, obviously, it'll be in Arizona, so I'll have to figure out work. Though maybe my indie press will let me stay on, and I can review bands there. There's plenty to do between the Copper Halo and all the other venues local bands play at."

Garrett's face got serious. "Yeah, about that. No more Rolling Stone?"

"No." Angie frowned and drew in a slow breath. "I couldn't have handled it…"

He tipped his head to the side and grinned. "I had an idea."

Angie looked up. "Should I be nervous?"

"Definitely." Garrett laughed and then kissed her.

EPILOGUE

ONE MONTH LATER...

LOS ANGELES

Nervous energy ricocheted around Angie's stomach as she stared down at the notebook in her lap, and then the small digital recorder squeezed tight in her palm. If she wasn't careful, she'd break the damn thing.

Angie set the device down on top of the notebook. Her sweaty hands couldn't be good for it anyway. She had one leg crossed over the other, the foot of the crossed leg bouncing as if it were being pulled up and down on a puppet string.

She really needed to calm down.

Breathe…

The door opened, and there he was, one of the more senior staff writers at Rolling Stone. Angie scrambled with the notebook and recorder and got to her feet. Amazingly, without dropping either item.

"Hey, you must be Angela. I'm Andy." He walked to her, his hand outstretched in front of him.

With a smile, Angie shook his hand. "It's great to meet you."

"Please sit." He motioned to the chair she'd been sitting in, and then he took the one beside it. "You ready for this?"

"I am, yes. Thank you so much for letting me do this."

Angie drew in a deep breath, praying she sounded calmer than she felt.

"Yeah, all good. When Julia proposed the idea of you conducting the interview with me, I looked up your stuff and was impressed. When I took your info to the bosses, they remembered you from when you interviewed a few months ago. They took a deeper look at your reviews, and yeah, they all agreed with me. You've got a strong base, which means great opportunity to grow, so why not see what you can do in action, right?" He shrugged a shoulder, and then pulled his courier bag over his head and got out a notebook and a Go-Pro.

Okay, maybe her mini digital recorder wasn't as adequate as she thought it would be. Damn, she should've brought a Go-Pro, except she didn't have one. And she didn't even think of it. Shit. Angie swallowed. "I guess maybe it worked in my favor that I didn't take the job back then, huh?"

He laughed. "Looks that way, yeah. But seriously, Julia may have called in a favor, but it's your work in the industry that got you back in the door." He smiled, the expression in his brown eyes genuine. "Doesn't happen often, so take advantage of it."

Wow, that was…

"I will." She smiled. The man probably had no idea how much knowing that meant to her. Garrett hadn't wanted to do this interview from the start, but when he finally decided he was ready, his only stipulation was that Angie perform the interview. And that was before he and Angie had gotten back together. He'd done this for her because he loved her, with no guarantees that she'd take him back.

The fact that he'd done this was a huge deal for her; it meant the world to her, but she had to admit that not earning it on her merit had concerned her. Finding out that it was actually her work that got her in the door made it all the better.

"Angie? You look a little nervous. You want a water or anything?"

And fabulous, she sounded calm but looked nervous. Oh, God. "Um, no, I mean, yes…wait, I'm not. Shit—" Her eyes went wide, and then slapped her palm over her mouth.

Andy barked a laugh. "Want to try that again?"

Thanks to Andy's laughter, Angie relaxed a little. She could do this. "Sorry." She let out a low laugh, shaking her head. "Let me try that again. No, I'm not nervous about the band. I've already gotten to meet all those guys, and they're hilarious. But *I am* nervous about you, this." She shrugged. "And yes, I'd love a water."

"Bah, don't be nervous about me. Follow my lead, it'll be all good. As I said, I've seen your reviews. You've got talent, so I'm sure you're a shoo-in." He paused and set his stuff down on the small table between them and moved to the mini fridge in the corner of the room. As he returned, he handed her a bottle of water and took his seat again. "I gotta say, I'm the one who's a little nervous. Copper Seven was an awesome band. Could be again, actually. The guys are legends, and I've been waiting to do this exposé on them for mont—"

The door opened, and Julia Martin, Chase Reynolds' publicist, walked in and following right behind her, practically up against her was Chase, the lead singer, and then behind him were Derrick Holmes, Jake Gould and then…her Garrett.

She and Andy stood, and he said, "Showtime."

Angie stayed where she was as everyone filed in and picked spots where they wanted to sit on the large U-shaped couch across from her and Andy. To be honest, they all looked a little…tense. Were they all nervous?

Julia came over and shook Andy's hand first, and then focused on Angie. "Nice to see you again, Angie."

"Same to you, Julia." As Angie started to turn away, a hand clasped around her arm.

She turned back to find Garrett before her. She barely got

out a "Hi" before he pulled her close and pressed a soft kiss to her lips. After he drew back from her mouth, he tapped her nose with his fingertip and then stepped away to take his spot on the couch.

All Angie could do was smile…

Andy clapped his hands together, breaking her spell. "Welcome, guys. Whadya say we get started?"

"Fuck yeah, let's do this," Chase said.

Andy took his seat, and Angie followed suit.

Andy hit the button on the GoPro. "All right, gentleman, let's start at the beginning. How was Copper Seven born?"

Chase and Garrett looked at each other, then back to Andy and Angie. Garrett leaned forward, elbows on his knees, but it was Chase who answered, gesturing with his thumb toward Garrett. "This asshole over here and I met—"

"Takes one to know one." Garrett shook his head, chuckling.

Jake and Derrick busted up laughing, and Chase had a grin on his face, a devilish glint in his eye. Apparently, that was the icebreaker they needed.

Oh, yeah. This was going to be fun.

TWO MONTHS LATER…

LOS ANGELES

"Everyone, raise 'em up! To Angela, Rolling Stone's newest staff writer!" Garrett raised his glass. Everyone around the table joined in.

There were a bunch of hoots and hollers from the group and one "Yassss!" from Angie's sister-in-law, Maiya, and then everyone clinked their glasses and drank.

Angie smiled at him, her expression filled with pure joy and excitement. Garrett felt every bit of that in his chest, too. He wanted her to have the world, and Rolling Stone was just the beginning.

With his glass of water still in hand, he leaned to her ear and whispered, "Love you, babe."

With a soft sigh, Angie pulled back, but only enough to press her forehead to his. She snaked her hand around his neck and threaded her fingers into his hair. "Love you, too, Daddy."

Garrett grinned and then pressed a soft kiss to her sweet mouth before pulling away and righting himself in his seat. He opened the menu in front of him. "Let's get some appetizers going."

"God, yes, I'm starving," Chassidy said as she opened her menu.

"Me too." Angie bent close to him, peeking at his menu. "Definitely, let's get a couple Caprese salads, ooh, and calamari."

"How about the spinach dip and chips?" Angie's sister Cyn turned her menu over and then back again.

"Get whatever you want, Cyn. Seriously." Garrett nodded at her, then glanced across the table to Angie's brother Ryan and then to her parents, Joe and Roseanne. "Any appetizers catching your eye over there?"

"Garrett, if you're buying, I'm getting oysters." Joe Sr. laughed, and Roseanne slapped his shoulder.

Garrett burst out laughing. "Get whatever you want, Joe."

Joe laughed again but then focused on his wife, both brows raised. "You love when I have oysters."

"Joe!" Roseanne laughed, shaking her head before looking around the table, her face flushed from embarrassment. "Dear God, I swear the older he gets, the more ornery he becomes!"

"Uh, huh. Like I said, you'll thank me later." The man winked and then pulled Roseanne close and gave her a full kiss.

"Ooohkay, can you two stop, please? I'm getting grossed out." Cyn scrunched up her face.

"Tell me about it." Liza took a gulp of wine. "Freaking hippies."

The looks on the rest of Angie's family's faces in attendance were priceless. Garrett couldn't help but laugh. Beside him, Chassidy was laughing, too.

Roseanne dropped her forehead into her palm and shook her head. That's when Joe Sr. drove it home. "Hippie is a compliment. I know all you kids think we only had sex ten times, but believe it or not, your mother and I have always had a very active and healthy se—"

"Joseph!" Laughing, Roseanne put her hand over her husband's mouth. "Stop!"

A series of "Oh, God, Dad!" and "Please no! Quick, get the brain bleach!" and "Make it stop!" comments were called out from around the table, all with laughter threaded through them.

Joe's eyes danced with laughter, but then they went soft, his gaze locked on his wife's face. He circled Roseanne's wrist in his fingers, pulled his wife's hand from his mouth, and kissed her palm. She smiled, shaking her head, but smiling nonetheless.

They loved each other. That was plain to see.

"God, they're cute." Garrett felt Angie's hand on his thigh, then her head on his shoulder.

"Yeah, they are." He pressed a kiss to the top of her head. "Have they always been like this?"

"Yep." She sighed.

"Nice. Hashtag relationship goals?" Garrett laughed again.

Angie laughed and patted his chest as she straightened. "No pressure, honey."

"Don't you worry." He smoothed his hand down her thigh and gave it a quick squeeze. "I got this."

That got a giggle out of her, and she smiled, her love for him shining clear in her eyes.

It was true, he did have it. They were good, their relationship solid. Angie was moving to Arizona and in with him. She had her job with Rolling Stone, and for him, things were happening for the band again.

His whole world had changed, actually, both of their worlds, and life was good. Better than good, and still, the best was yet to come…

EIGHT MONTHS LATER...

TEMPE, ARIZONA

Angie shifted beneath him, still coming down from her climax. She stroked the back of Garrett's neck with her fingertips. "Love you."

"Love you, too." After another minute or two passed, Garrett slipped from her tight channel. He reached for the tissues and handed a couple to her, then took some for himself. "Gonna spank your ass when we're home later tonight. Really hard, too."

She giggled as she cleaned up. "What for?"

"Not warning me that you'd be dressed like this tonight." He grinned. Seriously, what the hell did she expect? She'd walked into the venue in that short schoolgirl skirt, thigh-high socks and spiked-heel booties. For fuck's sake, his dick had gone steel hard the minute he spotted her.

Angie laughed again. "Not my fault your dick has a mind of its own."

"It seems your pussy does, too. You were wet before I even touched you." He stepped back and buttoned up his jeans.

"Pfft, that?" With a shrug of one shoulder, she got to her feet and put her panties back on, and then straightened her skirt. "That's because the whole way over here, I knew you'd be fucking me as soon as you saw me. Besides the panties, I didn't even have to take anything off." She winked. "So, what time do you go on again?"

"Such a tease." He shook his head and glanced at the clock. "In thirty minutes."

"Tease? Garrett James, did you just have an orgasm?"

He grinned. "I did."

"Then you are wrong, sir." She propped her hands on her hips. "No teasing happened. I delivered." Stepping closer, she pressed her sexy body against him and took his mouth in a kiss.

Stroking over her tongue with his own, Garrett smoothed his hands from her tiny waist down to her gorgeous ass. As he squeezed the plump flesh like he had a few minutes before, she groaned and rubbed against him. Garrett broke the kiss but kept her close. "Oh, yeah. Definitely, spanking you later." He gave the willing flesh another squeeze. "Maybe I'll fuck this hot ass tonight, too."

"Oh! *Now*, who's the tease?"

"Guess you'll have to wait and see." Garrett bent and gave her another quick kiss, and then nipped her bottom lip as he pulled away.

"Mmhmm. I'll believe it when it happens. So, hurry up and go perform in your damn reunion show so we can go home, and *you* can make good on your threat." She licked her lips and winked.

"Bossy, I see?"

"My insurance policy." Angie giggled and strolled out of his office.

Damn, the woman was completely adorable and beyond sexy. Garrett couldn't imagine his life without her.

Before Angie had arrived at the Halo, he'd been a nervous wreck. Now, he was feeling nothing but relaxed.

Of course, she'd have known he'd be nervous and overthinking the hell out of what he was about to do. Leave it to his woman to find the fastest solution.

He'd figured on coming upstairs and hitting his knees before the performance, and he still intended to do that, but the orgasm had been an added bonus. With the support of a loving Higher Power, a loving woman, *and* an orgasm? Garrett felt like he could do anything.

Drawing in a deep, calming breath, he got down on his knees and did what his sponsor, Howard and AA had taught him to do: he prayed.

Garrett asked for support, love and guidance. Then he thanked his HP for giving him this opportunity to make right another wrong in his life. Direct amends paved the way to serenity in his heart and soul.

After another few moments of quiet contemplation, Garrett rose, left his office and walked downstairs to the back-stage area.

It was showtime!

"Hey!" Angie found her family and friends in the VIP section in the main area of Copper Halo. Her friend, Tarra, was there, too. She must've just returned from the backstage area. She'd performed as one of the opening acts, which was fucking awesome.

Angie hugged Tarra, then made the rounds to her family and then Sean and Freddie, as well as Garrett's sponsor, Howard. "So excited for this!"

Howard put his hand on Angie's shoulder. "How's he doing?"

Of course, she wasn't about to tell the man she'd just screwed Garrett's brains out in his office, so instead, she smiled and decided to keep it short and sweet. "He's good. Perfect, actually."

Authority Zero had finished their set when she'd been upstairs with Garrett, and now the stage crew was rapidly setting up for Copper Seven to come out and play. A waitress came over and delivered a round of water and a drink for her and the others who were imbibing alcohol.

The Halo was packed to the gills with fans—from the stage back to damn near in front of the bar. A sharp zing of nerves shot down Angie's spine. Garrett was good; she knew that. He'd kick ass for sure. But now it was her turn to be nervous.

It'd been a long time since her man had been on the stage, and she couldn't help but battle some butterflies on his behalf over it. Instead of freaking out, Angie did a shot of Jameson with Tarra and Celia and then took a seat, waiting the last few minutes for the band to start.

"You look nervous." Tarra sat beside her.

Celia sat on Angie's other side. "Yep, you do."

"I'm not gonna lie. I'm totally freaking nervous."

Tarra grabbed Angie's hand. "You know he's gonna kick ass."

Celia leaned forward to look across Angie. "Speaking of kicking ass, you did, too, Tarra!"

"Thanks! This is a great venue. I'd love to play here again."

"You'll definitely play here again!" Angie smiled.

The lights dimmed, and Angie snapped her attention to the stage. Then, the sound of an electric guitar rang out.

One spotlight came on and focused on the lead singer, Chase Reynolds. "Hey Phoenix, you ready for this?"

The crowd went nuts, and Angie jumped to her feet.

Another spotlight illuminated a band member as Chase continued. "On drums, we have Jake Gould, kicking ass like always. Lead guitar…y'all remember the awesome Derrick Holmes, right?" Another spotlight illuminated Derrick, and the crowd got louder. "Now, I know you all know this guy.

How could you not? Your hometown boy and our badass mother fucking bassist, *Garrett Jaaaaaaames*!" The final spotlight was lit, and there was her man.

Angie sucked in her breath as he nodded to the crowd and shot a grin at Chase. Garrett bent to his mic. "Let's get this reunion going, shall we?"

The crowd went insane, and the band kicked off their first song of the many they planned to play. Angie hollered, clapped, and sang along, and not once did she take her eyes off of Garrett.

Pride filled her heart, the same heart that was already filled to the brim with love for him.

Once again, Angie was in awe of him. Yes, getting to this point had been hard. But Garrett was worth it. Even with all the heartache and pain they'd gone through, Angie wouldn't change a second of it.

All of it had led them to the place they were now, to the beauty they had between them. Angie closed her eyes and let the moment and the music wrap around her.

Like she'd always known, she was right where she was supposed to be.

ABOUT THE AUTHOR

Dorothy F. Shaw lives in Arizona, where the weather is hot, and the sunsets are always beautiful. She's a self-proclaimed sex scene snob and is proud of it. When she's not writing, she's thinking about writing.

With her ever-open heart, bright red hair, and many colorful tattoos, she truly lives and loves in Technicolor!

ALSO BY DOROTHY F. SHAW

Head to my site to find all links to my available backlist:

www.DorothyFShaw.com

Start at the beginning of
The Donnellys series with:
Unworthy Heart

The Donnellys Book 1
© 2019 Dorothy F. Shaw

Opposites not only attract, sometimes they spontaneously combust.

Ryan Donnelly's past relationship may have failed, but he's determined to make single fatherhood and his career a resounding success. He's got his eye on the top of the ladder at an L.A. marketing firm when his gaze snags on co-worker Maiya Rossini.

She's a feisty, witty, tattooed redhead who's nowhere near his type, but she pushes every one of his hot buttons.

Maiya clawed her way out of her dysfunctional, trailer-park childhood to earn a college degree and establish a promising career. Her future dreams are big, bright and packed with full-throttle fun, but when it comes to matters of the heart and men—especially stuffy corporate types like Ryan—her past slams on the emotional brakes.

In the office and in the bedroom, Maiya and Ryan rub each other in all the *right* ways. Though Maiya is everything Ryan didn't know he wanted, he's got his work cut out for him convincing her she's worthy of love—or the bright light she's brought to his life could slip through his fingers.

Defensive Heart

The Donnellys Book 2
© 2019 Dorothy F. Shaw

*Uptown girl, tattooed bad boy. Think you know which
one is wild? You'd be wrong.*

Greenwich Village is home to successful artist Jimmy
Donnelly, and the world is his playground. A broken heart in
college left him with zero interest in being tied down. But
when he meets a sexy, quick-witted Manhattan attorney, he
reconsiders his bad boy ways.

Sonja Martin's life is filled with work, an ex-husband who
refuses to stay gone, and a teenage daughter who won't follow
the rules. Jimmy, with his myriad of tattoos and piercings,
looks more like one of her clients than a potential lover. But
when every argument between them feels more like foreplay,
she can't seem to stay out of his bed.

The heat burns through whatever defenses Sonja thought
she had. And Jimmy finds his every fantasy fulfilled—and

exceeded—by a woman whose fire burns as bright as her fiercely guarded vulnerability.

But his case for breaking her out of her self-imposed mold might just be dismissed. And he'll lose the best thing he's ever found.

426

The Donnellys Book 3
© *2019 Dorothy F. Shaw*

A crush is just a fantasy. The real thing packs some serious heat.

When Cynthia Donnelly lays eyes on her high school crush at her brother's wedding rehearsal, she regrets her self-imposed, one-year moratorium on dating. If possible, he's even hotter now than when they were teens.

Back in school, Shane made a point to ignore his best friend's cute, sassy little sister. Now that she's grown into an incredibly sexy woman full of Irish spunk, resisting her is out of the question. Besides, in his book, all "hands-off" rules have expired.

One sizzling night together should have been enough. Instead, the heat rises, tempting Cyn to take a chance on a long-distance relationship and making Shane consider pulling up stakes and moving back to L.A.

Cyn's recently dumped ex, however, has other ideas. His quest to get her back escalates into violence, shattering Cyn's faith in herself, and in anyone else of the male persuasion, and leaving Shane with his work cut out for him to repair the damage—or lose his shot at a once-in-a-lifetime love.

428

Stripped Bounty

© 2016 Dorothy F. Shaw

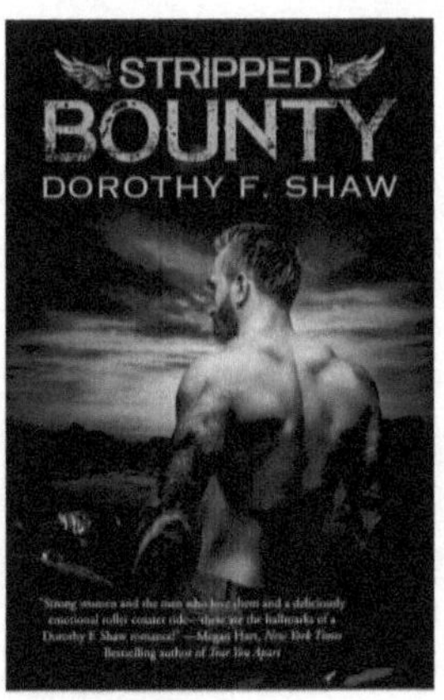

Protecting her isn't an option.
It's a requirement.

Badger finally got Rosie in his bed, but in order to keep her there, he has to figure out how to save her life.

After her drug-running husband gets himself killed, Rosie Santini figures Phoenix is a fine place to get a fresh start. Deuce's strip club isn't too fresh, but the money's easy. As she works the pole, the only gaze she can't ignore belongs to the club's head bouncer, Badger Baxter. But Rosie's seen her fair share of tall, dark, and dangerous, and no way is she heading down that road. Not even for a hot hunk of muscle like Badger.

When he's not bounty hunting, Badger runs security at Deuce's. Rosie should be just another piece of fresh meat in the club's stable of pole jockeys, but all her sexy parts add up to a ride Badger would like to test drive. Trouble is, Badger likes his women submissive, but not broken. She's definitely got baggage he wants no part of. But when her husband's killer shows up looking for stolen cash, she fits naturally under his protection—and it isn't long before she's hooked deep into his heart.

So deep, losing her now would make him bleed in more ways than one.

Turn the page for a sneak peek…

Stripped Bounty

PROLOGUE

The sound of the phone ringing split the silence of the dark bedroom, startling Rosie awake. She rolled beneath the covers and slapped at the nightstand in search of the cordless receiver on its base, missing it a couple of times.

"Fuck…really?" Finally getting a hold of the now torture device and flopping back onto the mattress, Rosie hit "Talk" on the handset and raised it to her ear. "Someone better be dead!"

"Rosie!"

She bolted upright in bed at the urgency in her husband's tone. "Joey? What's wrong?"

"Nuthin'." He coughed. "All good. Listen careful, baby girl." His voice was low and out of breath. "You listenin'?"

Christ, he was always doing that to her—scaring the crap out of her for no damn reason. And he accused her of towing the drama line. Whatever. Rosie swallowed down the panic-induced lump that had risen in her throat and looked at the digital clock on her nightstand. It was after three in the morning. Joey should've been home by then. What the hell had he gotten himself into now? "For the love of… Just get to the point. I'm listening!"

"I took something and hid it. If I don't come home, you need to get it and then, no matter what, you get the fuck out of town."

"What do you mean if you don't come home?" Rosie pushed her hair over her shoulder. "Are you getting arrested again?"

"No. Why do you always assume that? Fuck's sake." He grunted and then coughed again.

Why did she…was he serious? Rosie rolled her eyes. "Do you really want me to answer that question?"

"Whatever. Just listen. Go to the ladies' room at the train station. Under the sink, behind the pipes, you'll find a locker key taped to the wall. Grab it, and go to the self-storage lockers."

"Train station? Which fucking train station? What the hell did you take?" With a shove of the covers, she threw her legs over the side of the bed.

"I took our future, baby."

Good God, she could practically hear the smile behind his words. Rosie looked up at the ceiling, knowing this was going to lead nowhere good. The only place that damn ego of his ever led him was back to jail. Unless… *Oh fuck no.* Cold dread slipped down Rosie's spine, and she shivered. "You rolled the dealer, didn't you? Jesus-fucking-Christ! Are you trying to get us both killed?"

Joey let out a harsh sigh. "Keep your drama ass in check, Rosie! For real. I got this. That small-town fuck has no clue what he's doing. His crew is no better. Trust me, it's gonna be fine. Just take a damn breath for once and do what I say, got it?"

"Do *not* yell at me, *Joey*!" She got to her feet and paced in the small space between their bed and dresser. "You go do something insane, and you expect me to be calm?"

"Yeah, that's exactly what I expect."

Rosie ran her fingers through her hair. She wanted no part of the world of drug trafficking he'd gotten himself into. And she'd made that *very* clear. Not that he ever respected what she wanted or needed. Too busy screwing up to bother. Regardless, Rosie had managed to stay far away from the people he'd been associating with.

What he'd gotten himself into was a one-way ticket to jail or the morgue. Joey had already been to prison one too many times. Jesus, he hadn't even been out more than six months from the last stint. At the rate he was going, it wouldn't be long before he was back behind bars. Or dead.

God, Joey had done a lot of stupid things, made a fuckton more stupid choices, but Rosie never thought he'd do something *this* stupid.

She should've known, though.

Always so goddamn greedy and always wanting more. Joey Santini thought he was a big-time hustler—big enough to pull something this insane off. But he wasn't. He was small-time. Small-town—small fucking potatoes. Especially in the drug world. He was nothing but a runner. A peon. And he'd just put both their lives at risk. She blew out a harsh breath. "Which station, dammit! Where are you?"

"Bridgeport."

Holy shit. That was nearly forty minutes away. The gravity of the situation hit her in the gut like a hard punch. She had no idea what to do. A tear dripped down Rosie's cheek, and she brushed it away. "Are you coming home?"

"I hope so."

CHAPTER ONE

Three months later...

"No Colors or Weapons Allowed."

Rosie Santini read the sign mounted on the brick exterior wall of the establishment. Shaking her head, she opened the solid wood front door and stepped out of the Phoenix hundred-and-four-degree heat and into the dimly lit, air-conditioned strip club.

Back in the day, "colors" meant a biker's patches—as in motorcycle club patches. Commonly found on the back of a leather or denim vest. Considering there was a pack of Harleys parked on the sidewalk out front, Rosie figured in Arizona, that's exactly what the sign referred to. Plus, as she'd learned pretty quickly after arriving in town, barring having a criminal record, people could carry a gun in AZ right out in the open for all to see.

She took a moment as her eyes adjusted, no longer sure if this was such a good idea, and looked around. Type O Negative's "Christian Woman" blared from the speakers as Rosie walked forward on the old green and white—or gray, rather—linoleum-tiled floor. A small birdcage-style stage sat empty off to her left. To her right, the mahogany bar with its large, mirrored backsplash and various bottles of booze stretched along the wall. In the center of the large space sat a collection of small round tables, a tealight candle atop each one, with two pleather chairs arched around them. Doing a quick count, around twenty or so customers occupied the bar. Not uncommon for the middle of the day in a strip club.

Ahead of the tables was the main stage in the shape of an upside-down T. Mirrors lined the back wall with red curtains draped theatre-style at their edges. White rope lights ran along the edges of the narrow stage, leading down to the wide part, which held a pole on each end. There was also a spinning wheel mounted on the ceiling near center stage; she hadn't seen one of those in years. And, finally, another pole near the mirrors along the back wall.

Two girls had the big stage, clad only in their G-strings and stripper heels. One circling a pole, the other on her hands and knees as a patron stood behind her, dollar bill at the ready. Rosie shook her head. Dancers these days barely danced— hardly did anything to put on an actual show or striptease. That was the whole point, wasn't it? At least back in her heyday, it was.

She drew in a deep breath and blew it out. Deuce's Cabaret wasn't seedy…necessarily. But it wasn't plush, either. More that it needed a face-lift. Desperately. Not her first or even eighth choice for employment. But it'd do. At least the music was good.

Rosie circled in place, scanning the corners of the club, looking for cameras. And there wasn't a single one to be found. Anywhere. Hopefully, they had good bouncers. She'd spotted at least two of those throughout the space.

Hiking her big pocketbook a little higher on her shoulder, Rosie blew out a breath and stepped to the bartender. "Hi there."

The big man, clad in a black T-shirt, turned from the cash register and faced her. Rosie lost her breath when she caught sight of his face, but managed to get a grip on herself as he walked toward her. He dipped his chin, cocking his head to the side, as he wiped the bar top directly in front of her with a white bar rag. "You lost?"

Rosie swallowed past the layer of glue that'd suddenly appeared on her tongue. Jesus, he was breathtaking…speech-taking, too. Perfect nose, full lips, the bottom one a tad fuller. Incredible bone structure. Freaking guy could be a model. He was huge, too—muscular and at least six-one, maybe taller. She blinked a few rapid blinks and glanced away from his piercing light-brown gaze.

In an attempt to gain some control of her thoughts, Rosie plopped her pocketbook down on the closest barstool and, after a breath, looked back to him. "No. Not lost. Are you, by chance, hiring?"

He crossed his muscled arms, his biceps bulging, testing the limits of his T-shirt sleeves. "Bar or stage?"

"Bar." She managed a smile.

"Nope." His stare didn't waver and Rosie took in the small lines around his eyes, but also his strong jaw, partly hidden by a goatee and way-more-than-five o'clock shadow. Yeah, definitely a good-looking man.

"What about waitress?"

"Nope." He dropped his arms and turned his back.

Wow! Had he really just dismissed her like that? *What the hell?* Rosie faced the stage and the dancers again. The Pretty

Reckless's "Make Me Wanna Die" played now. She hadn't been onstage in about two years, and it was the last place she wanted to be again. But she was broke. Getting across the country from Connecticut to Arizona had cost Rosie more than she'd thought. She hadn't anticipated the freaking car dying. Twice. She hadn't anticipated her husband dying, either. *Jerk.* Rosie would never forgive him for putting her in this position.

Biting the edge of her barely existent thumbnail, she turned back around and faced the bartender. Desperate times called for desperate measures. "Okay, fine. Stage?"

With his back still to her, he glanced up from the bottle he was wiping down and caught her gaze through the reflection in the mirror. "You sure about that?"

Was she sure? Rosie'd already been to six other bars that day and three the day before. No, she wasn't fucking sure, but she needed a goddamn job. "Absolutely."

He turned, stepped to the bar top and rested both his hands on the edge. Did a muscle in his jaw just tick? Again he dipped his chin and cocked his head to the side—almost as if he was sizing her up and judging her abilities right there on the spot.

A beat of nervous energy rolled through her. Talk about feeling like a bug under a microscope. Jesus, she was uncomfortable. Rosie crossed her arms and jutted out her chin. The guy might be hotter than hell, but the last thing Rosie needed was bullshit from some stranger right now. "What?"

He pursed his lips, his firm gaze steady on her for another few moments before rubbing his palm along the side of his whiskered jaw and letting out a sigh. "Far side of the stage. Follow the hall to the back. Evie'll help you out."

"Oh." She cleared her throat. "Okay then." Rosie shouldered her bag, feeling a bit like she'd disappointed him. Which was pretty weird, considering she didn't even know him. "Thanks."

Turning on her heel, she stepped away from the bar. He was still staring at her. She knew it. Rosie could feel his gaze like a physical touch, skittering down her spine and over her skin as she made her way across the club in the direction he'd sent her. The screwed-up thing was, rather than creepy, the feel of his eyes on her was titillating.

Considering she'd only lost her husband three months ago, her body's reaction made her feel even more uncomfortable than she'd felt standing in front of him. Shrugging all of it off, Rosie walked through the narrow doorway in the far corner of the bar and down the empty, almost sterile hall.

And back into a world she hadn't wanted to ever visit again.

***

Badger shook his head as he watched the tall, slender brunette with the sad, dark-brown eyes walk toward the back hall. "Shame."

"What's that, Badge?" Deuce came up to the bar.

Badger glanced over to him. "Fresh meat."

The owner took a seat in his spot at the end of the bar. "Fresh meat's always good in my book. Nothing shameful about that."

Badger grunted and reached for a fresh glass. "You want something?"

"Eh, just a seltzer water. Evie's been nagging me about soda." Deuce clasped his hands together on the bar top and looked toward the stage.

Badger filled the glass with the clear carbonated fluid. "Hate to break it to you, boss. But this is soda."

"Like hell it is. It's water with bubbles in it. Smart ass. Now, grab me a lemon."

Badger chuckled and placed a lemon wedge on the edge of the glass. "We're fresh out of umbrellas."

"Kiss my ass." Deuce chuckled and sipped the drink.

"Maybe later." Badger grabbed the clipboard from the side of the register and went back to taking inventory.

Didn't matter what the boss said. Pretty girl like that one ending up being another stripper was a damn fucking shame. No two ways about it.

For a minute, since she'd asked about tending bar or waitressing, Badger thought, or maybe hoped, she might not be another pole jockey. So much for that. She had to have been on stage before. Sadly, you could take the girl out of the strip club, but you couldn't take the stripper out of the girl. Eventually, they came back. Especially if they still had some looks and a body. This one had both…in spades. Her eyes had gotten to him, though.

Badger looked up from the beer cooler to see her walking back across the bar toward the exit. She glanced over at him but quickly looked away before stepping out into the bright Arizona sun. Yeah, eyes were always a weakness or a warning for him. Hers were sad, like she'd seen some hurt in her days. But they were skittish, too. The skittish smacked of more than hurt in her past.

Regardless, he didn't mess with the strippers anymore. Those days were long gone. But even if she hadn't turned out to be a dancer, Badger would've steered clear anyway. There was enough "more" behind those sad and skittish eyes of hers for Badger to keep his distance. He didn't need the drama or the headache that came along with that amount of luggage.

The front door opened again, and the weekday bartender, Wendy, walked in. "Hey, Badger." She waved as she passed by him on her way to the office as if she wasn't over thirty minutes late for her shift.

"You're late, and I got shit to do besides cover your ass behind the bar."

She spun around, facing him, and shrugged, arms out at

her sides. "Sorry. I had a flat." She continued walking backward before turning again and disappearing down the hall.

Badger grunted before staring down at the clipboard in his hands again. Damn bar staff were just as bad as the dancers. It wouldn't matter so much if he wasn't always the one on point to cover until they brought their asses in. He was supposed to just run security, not the bar staff, too, but the lines tended to blur. Mostly because Badger had a tendency to blur them.

Not that he'd admit that to Deuce if his life depended on it.

"You got some bounty hunter work to attend to?"

He glanced over at Deuce and nodded. "Yeah. Got a lead this morning on a skip I've been tracking."

His boss looked at his watch. "Good luck. See you back here 'round eight?"

"'Course." He set the clipboard down and jerked his chin at Deuce as he stepped out from behind the bar. "Earlier if I can. Order's ready to go. Don't wait up, honey."

"But, darling, we haven't had any quality time together."

"Yeah, yeah." With a wave over his shoulder, Badger chuckled and headed for the same hall he'd sent the brunette down. As he passed the dressing room, he gave a nod to Evie, Deuce's old lady. After a quick stop in the office to grab his gun, he stepped out into the daylight, lit a cigarette, and made his way to his pickup.

It was time to give his other career a little attention.

Want more?
Head to my site to find all links to my available backlist:
www.DorothyFShaw.com

Available from all major e-sellers in digital and print.

This book is a work of fiction. Names, characters, places, and incidents are the product of the author's imagination or are used fictitiously. Any resemblance to actual events, locales, or persons, living or dead, is coincidental.

Dorothy F. Shaw
Phoenix, Arizona
JADED HEART
Copyright © 2022 by Dorothy F. Shaw
ISBN-10: 0-9978310-4-9
ISBN-13: 978-0-9978310-4-7
Draft2Digital ISBN: 978-1-0054585-5-3
Edited by Tera Cuskaden
Cover by Kanaxa

Red Queen Publications electronic and print publication: August 2022

Publishing History
Digital/Print 1.0 edition / July 2022

Red Queen
Publications